Mr. January

by

Jules Hahn

Mr. January

Cover Art by *Lisa Dawn MacDonald*

The Wild Rose Press, Inc.
PO Box 708
Adams Basin, NY 14410-0708
Visit us at www.thewildrosepress.com

Publishing History
First Edition, 2022
Trade Paperback ISBN 978-1-5092-4322-8
Digital ISBN 978-1-5092-4323-5

Published in the United States of America

"All women make things too easy for you."

His hands clutched her waist, and his thumbs made lazy circles along her back. "Not all."

She arched a brow. "Oh? Really? Name one."

Leaning down, he brushed his lips over hers. "You."

Through his damp shirt, she could feel the beat of his heart and feel the heat of his flesh. "We're all just a convenience to you."

His eyes darkened, and the vein in his neck pulsed. "Ah, Sugar, don't you know?" He wound fingers through her hair and lowered his head. His lips grazed hers, softly for just a moment, then firmer and more determined. "You've never been convenient."

His words came out so soft and so husky, she closed her eyes and sighed. He trailed lazy kisses down her neck, scorching her flesh with the heat of his touch. She clung to him as if her life depended on it, and at this moment, she wasn't so very certain it didn't. Desire swelled, a rolling burn needing to be quenched.

With each caress of his lips and stroke of his fingers, she could feel her resolve weaken. Closing her eyes, she dug deep inside for all the reasons why she couldn't let his words sway her. He only wanted sex. He'd burned her once before. He'd do so again. And yet, her biggest fear loomed, the very one she couldn't chance happening. She dug fingers into his hair and pressed her body against his. A little ache settled in her heart. "Dax, we can't. We're friends."

Dedication

To my mother-in-law, who was always one of my biggest champions.

Chapter 1

Ellen followed the line of taillights weaving through the bends in the road leading from the town of Aberdeen and toward the town's pride and joy—Pleasant Lake. Trees, cloaked in glistening white fluffs, whizzed past. Dusk slowly descended, blanketing the area in patches of gray. Tapping fingers on the steering wheel, she considered the night she was about to endure.

Of course, her brother, Ben, with his wife, Lily, would be there. After all, the celebration was for him becoming the town's mayor. Her mother, Claire, would be there too, all beaming and proud at her eldest's grand achievement. Most of the residents would attend as well because everyone loved and worshipped Ben.

An aching bubble settled in the pit of her stomach.

Would Dax, her childhood friend and the man she worked so hard to forget these past years, be there?

The bubble burst, and a sour taste filled her mouth.

Of course. He was practically a third child in their family and Ben's best friend. Could she spend time with him again and not relive that one night? She chewed her lip. What choice did she have?

Up ahead along the dark, country road, brakes lights flashed red. Cars slowed. At the sight of The Lake House, Ellen's heart pounded. The familiar white cottage loomed ahead. A wide, wooden deck led from the back of the restaurant over the lake. Lights, sparkling like glistening diamonds, draped along the deck's railing. Their dazzling splendor broke through the pitch-black darkness and reflected off the lake's smooth surface. More lights glowed from the restaurant's windows. Easing out a breath, she pulled into the lot. "Just paste a smile on your face and avoid him. Worked at the wedding."

Of course, at Ben and Lily's wedding, Dax had enough women circling him, he hadn't the time to notice her. Not that she wanted him to. The last time they hung out together, really hung out together like friends, he'd walked away the victor, and she was left with the spoils—which FYI, the spoils had hurt. Skimming the area, she spotted the reserved parking sign stating *E. Jordan,* right next to a far-too-familiar truck.

Seriously?

Was it too late to turn around and head right back to Albany? She peered into the rearview mirror, toward the restaurant, where even now, her brother celebrated his mayoral win. She slumped her shoulders and sighed.

Yeah, she couldn't hurt Ben, but seriously, why did the universe hate her? First, her now ex-boyfriend, Grant, received Ellen's dream promotion. Then, she became unemployed. And now she was stuck parking next to Dax.

Slamming the car into Park, she shoved open the door and stepped out. Bitter wind whipped off Pleasant Lake, snagging a few loose tendrils of hair and thrusting them in her face. Shoving them aside, she glared at the massive truck. If she didn't know better, she'd think Dax overcompensated for low self-esteem.

However, the one thing she knew with certainty was Dax didn't lack in the confidence department. She suspected the reason for his over-inflated ego had more to do with him being a firefighter and less to do with the vehicle.

As she eyed the restaurant, Ellen felt all quivery and jumpy. Inside, was Dax, mingling with people, flirting with women who fell easily for his far-too-charming lines.

She stiffened. Wait a minute. *She* was one of those women. She gripped her clutch. *Was*, she qualified—but not anymore. Only, with each step she took, a teeny, tiny part of Ellen worried she just might fall again.

Stepping inside the lobby, Ellen was greeted by welcoming warmth. Through the closed banquet doors, laughter competed with the soft strains of chamber music. Forcing a smile, she walked toward the coat check while nodding to familiar faces.

Jimmy Mason, a high school honor roll student, stood behind the counter and stared down at his phone. The black tuxedo he wore looked awkward and far too large on his gangly body. Glancing up from his phone, he smiled. "Hello, Miss Jordan."

Ellen slipped off her coat. "Evening, Jimmy." She glanced toward the banquet room. "Sounds like a lot of people."

"For sure." Jimmy bobbed his head. "I think everyone in town has shown up at some point."

Smoothing a hand down the front of her dress, Ellen took a deep breath. "I guess I should go in and see my brother."

Jimmy handed her a ticket. "He'll be happy you made it."

Digging fingers into the soft, copper, satin fabric purse, Ellen stepped into the large banquet room.

A crush of people filled the room, sipping champagne and chatting.

Everyone appeared happy and content. Of course, they would. *They* lived the life they wanted. She, on the other hand, had yet to figure out why the great guru in the sky made her life a puzzle. Sighing, she ran her gaze over the area in search of her brother. Only, blast her eyes, she spied the back of Dax's head.

Her stomach did another weird tumble. A head taller than most people in the room, he was by far the easiest man to spot. By the number of women surrounding him, he was the best looking too.

Freaking Dax.

She yanked away her gaze and spied a blond-haired server holding a tray loaded with tall, crystal champagne glasses filled with bubbly drinks. *Bingo.* Just what she needed to calm the nerves. She caught his eye.

He strolled her way.

Selecting a glass and napkin from the tray, she wigged her brows. "Just what the doctor ordered."

His brow creased, and his gaze skimmed the room.

Great. Now he thinks I'm nuts.

Yeah, well, if *he* knew what awaited her, he wouldn't give her one drink, but the whole damn tray. Sipping the sparkling wine, she spied her bother standing in the opposite direction of Dax.

Perfect.

Moving through the crowds, she carefully kept her gaze fixed on the man Aberdeen proclaimed as their future, and not on the sexy, blond-haired man from her past.

Ben stood with an arm draped over Lily's shoulder.

Claire stood beside them, beaming at her son's achievement.

The knot in Ellen's stomach tightened. Dang it. She spent so much time focusing on seeing Dax, she hadn't considered what to tell her mother about the recent developments in her life. She quickly added to the plan—avoid disappointing her mother.

Pasting a smile on her face, she fisted a hand and slugged Ben's arm, wincing. Jeez, was the punch the normal sisterly kind, or had she put more effort into the act than necessary?

He turned, and grinning, he gave her a bear hug. "Hey, Sis. So happy you're here."

The familiar scent of spicy cologne enveloped her. She burrowed her face into the safety of his chest. For so long, Ben had been her rock, the man who'd stepped up when their father died. "Me, too." Pulling back, she brushed a fleck of lint off his shirt. "Proud of you. Knew you could do it."

Releasing his grip, he shot a wink toward Lily. "Some people had some doubts."

Lily nudged his side. "Not doubts. Just didn't want to ruin things for you."

"Sweetheart, you could never ruin anything." He ran a hand down Lily's back. "You only enhance things."

Pink crested Lily's cheeks. She pressed a palm against his chest and stared into his eyes.

Ellen kept her face impassive. Inside, she rolled her eyes. *Ah. Newlyweds—gag.* Realizing how mean her thought was, she immediately smiled. After all, Ben and Lily were perfect together, and truly, she was happy for them. They each found their perfect soul mate, and someday, she would, too.

But jeez. Seriously, when would the stupid man show up anyway? She was twenty-eight, for heaven's sake. She couldn't be expected to wait forever.

Ben pressed a kiss against her cheek. "I hate to leave you right away, but I've got to meet with Lyle Pickler."

Ellen fanned the hand holding the drink. "Sure. I understand."

He squeezed her shoulder. "Thanks for coming. We'll circle back in a bit." Clutching Lily's hand, he navigated them through the crowd.

Finished speaking with Mrs. Peabody, Claire turned her gaze in Ellen's direction.

At her mother's hawk-like stare, Ellen fought to keep her smile from wavering. Surreptitiously, she glanced downward, wondering if she spilled a tiny amount of drink on her dress. The way her luck ran, she wouldn't be surprised if she had or if her mother spotted it.

Finally, Claire smiled. "You look amazing." She pressed a kiss to Ellen's cheek. "That color really makes your eyes glow."

A relieved sigh ripped from Ellen. "Thanks, Mom." Sipping her champagne, she peered around the room. "So, looks like the whole town's—"

Suddenly, Dax turned.

Their gazes locked.

Dang it. Why did she have to be so dang tall? Just once, she wished she'd received the short stature genes like Maybelline and was not blessed with the tall-as-a-tree genes.

Within seconds, she noted every little thing about him—from the dark suit that fit his muscular form to the crisp, white button-down with the top button undone to the strong, firm jawline, and finally to blue eyes crinkling upward. He didn't just look incredible. He looked downright amazing—and not alone. A beautiful brunette stood beside him, clinging to his arm.

The woman stared at Dax's profile with a bright smile on her raspberry-pink lips.

Ellen's heart plunged to her stomach. Of course, he brought a date. Did she even remember a time when Dax didn't have a date?

"Are you okay?"

The once sweet, bubbly wine turned bitter and flat against her tongue. She swallowed past the lump, and clearing her throat, she turned back and faced her mother. "Um. Sure." She took another sip, hoping to cover her surprise. "I see Dax has a date."

"Oh, Angel." Tapping a nail against the crystal stem, Claire studied the couple. "He should really consider getting married."

Dax was in love? A fierce pain pricked her heart. She ripped her gaze from Dax and his date. Since when did the player of the year want to get married? The Dax Ellen knew disappeared at even the slightest hint of fidelity. "Are you kidding me? Dax won't settle down."

"Don't be ridiculous. He just doesn't realize it yet, but trust me, I know him. He's just a little boy fearful he'll be like his father. Of course, nothing could be further from the truth. Dax is so much better than Thomas ever could be."

Seriously? He wants to get married? The stabbing

in Ellen's heart suddenly became an aching pierce.

Claire frowned. "Is everything okay?"

Nothing was okay. Ben was married. Her mother believed Dax was on the hunt for a wife, and here she was, without a job and no boyfriend in sight. Jeez, when had her life gone off the rails? Swiveling her gaze, she spotted her cousin across the room. *Perfect excuse for an escape.* "Oh, Maybelline's here." She squeezed her mother's arm. "You mind?"

"Of course not." Claire pressed a kiss to Ellen's cheek. "I need to speak with Mitch anyway." She buzzed away.

Ellen strode toward Maybelline.

Holy cow…

Maybelline was known to dress a little left of conservative. But tonight, her outfit reached epic portions. If the menagerie of leather patchwork resembling something off the pages of a biker magazine wasn't bad enough, the spiked leather boots and towering beehive hairdo certainly put her appearance far beyond conservative and somewhere close to outrageous. "Wow. You look…" Ellen licked her lips, searching for a compliment that wasn't an outright lie. "Bold."

Patting her mile-high hair, Maybelline fluttered her lashes. "Why, thank you. I thought tonight deserved something audacious." She smoothed a hand down the front. "Can't get much more daring than this dress."

Ellen tilted her glass in salute. "No argument there."

Alexis, garbed in a shimmery gold satin dress, strolled over.

Unlike most of the people, Alexis looked like she

belonged at a high-brow cocktail party—from the perfect cut of her blonde hair to the large diamond pendant shining from a thin gold chain. Of course, her elegant appearance was expected. After all, this was Alexis Armstrong—former super-model, actress, and ex-wife of the world-renown plastic surgeon Ted Armstrong.

"So, ladies, what are we discussing?"

Curiosity got the best of Ellen. Turning to Alexis and Maybelline, she feigned a nonchalant attitude and tilted her head toward Dax. "What's this about Dax and Angel?"

Maybelline scowled. "Ah, you've heard."

Ellen's stomach tumbled. So, her mother was right? She slid her gaze toward Dax and his date, watching as the brunette smiled at something he said. They certainly seemed like a happy, loving couple. She swallowed. "So, he's actually going to do it?"

Alexis frowned. "Do what?"

Ellen worked hard to keep her voice calm, and more importantly, her face neutral. "Marry Angel."

"What?" Gasping, Maybelline shot a glance across the room and glared. "That bit—"

"Easy there." Rolling her eyes, Alexis turned to Ellen. "Really? Who said?"

Ellen shrugged. "Mom. She just mentioned Dax getting married. I just figured she meant those two."

Pressing a fisted hand against her chest, Maybelline exhaled. "Jiminy crickets, Ellen, monitor your words, would you? You nearly had me in a panic."

For a moment, Ellen thought her cousin was ready to start a riot and all because Dax was the bachelor every girl hoped to nab. "My mistake. So?"

Alexis tapped a nail against the stem of the glass while studying the two. Finally, she turned back. "I don't think Dax is interested in her."

A little zing of relief ripped through Ellen. "Exactly. I mean, hello—we're talking about Dax." She sipped her wine. "He's not one who searches for commitment."

"Oh, I don't know." Alexis shrugged. "With Ben married, who knows? Maybe his plans have changed."

Wait—what was this? Was her mother right? Dax was on the hunt? Great…now one day, she'd come home and meet Mrs. Moore? Ellen froze, knowing the thought was possible and hating it. She needed a minute to regroup. "I'll be right back." Smiling tightly, she held up her purse. "Just need to drop this off at Mom's table." She scooted away before either could stop her.

Grabbing another drink from a passing waiter, she darted across the room toward her mother's table. Spotting a row of potted palms and Ficus trees dripping with lights, she ducked behind and took a moment to collect her thoughts.

Dax wanted to get married? The idea was more than a bit baffling. Dax was a playboy. He had spent his adult years carefully creating a carefree, serial dater attitude. He didn't settle down with one woman for longer than a date, let alone a lifetime. Yet, his best friend just got married. He was thirty with a stable job. The next natural step would be to get married and have children.

So then, why was she bothered?

Was it because he had found his perfect Miss Right and she still searched for Mr. Right? Or was it more? A teeny, tiny thought popped into her head. She was jealous.

She stiffened. *Ridiculous.* Suddenly, the air changed, becoming more electrified and the energy more tense. Slowly, she turned and froze.

Dax stepped into the secluded area without the beautiful, sexy Angel. With a cocky smile on his face, he strolled over. "Ellen."

The clean smell of sun and surf surrounded her. A little thrill tickled her flesh. "Dax…" Her words came out soft and feathery.

"I've been hoping to catch you alone."

Her heart pounded. Absolutely *everything* about him exuded sexiness—from his long, muscular limbs, to his strong, square jawline, to his sparkling blue eyes. Ellen didn't know one woman immune to his charms, including herself. However, she refused to allow him to see how he affected her. Swiveling her gaze, she searched the room. "What happened to your date?"

Dax furrowed his brow. "Date?"

She rolled her eyes. "Have you already forgotten Angel?"

"Oh, her…" He flicked a glance over his shoulder before turning back. His lips twitched. "She's just a friend."

Oh please. How many times had she heard the very same line coming from him? "Right." Tucking her purse under her arm, she smiled. "I'd hate for you to keep your *friend* waiting." She pivoted.

He reached out and caught her hand. "I've missed you."

His words came out soft and husky. Warmth spread through Ellen's veins, like little pulses of fire burning her. She didn't see his thumb caressing her wrist.

Instead, the memory of six years ago flashed through her thoughts.

A naïve twenty-two-year-old woman. An experienced twenty-four-year-old man. Too much alcohol. Too few boundaries. The offer of brunch. The sting of rejection.

Knowing his motives, she refused to buy into his plan. She peered across the room to the cluster of women shooting glances his way. "Really? Hard to believe since you've kept yourself busy dating."

The minute the words slipped from her lips, she regretted them. *Great.* Now he probably thought she kept track of his love life. She had, but still, he didn't need that information.

He brushed a strand of hair off her shoulder. "Jealous?"

His fingers scorched her skin. Blood pounded through her veins, and every sense in her body came alive at his touch and his words. She licked her lips and forced herself to step back. "Don't be ridiculous."

Leaning closer, he locked gazes. "I think you're lying."

She was, but darn him for recognizing the truth. The mocking laughter lurking in his gaze only increased her fury. Without thinking, she thrust out her arm. Cream-colored fizz shot from her glass, splashing his face and wetting his shirt. "You know what, Dax?"

He widened his eyes for just a moment before composing his features. A second later, he swiped a hand over his face, then shook off the droplets of wine.

"Unlike some women…" She jammed the purse under her arm. "I actually learn from my mistakes." Pivoting, she started away. A hand reached out and caught her arm. His eyes darkened to a dangerous blue.

He ran a thumb over the inside of her wrist. "So did I."

"Great. We're both in agreement." Breaking free, she stormed from the building. Stepping outside, she closed her eyes and fisted her hands. Dammit. She should have just stayed in Albany.

****

Dax watched Ellen stride away. He scrubbed a hand over his eyes. He hadn't planned on the evening turning out this way. The one woman he wanted to speak with avoided him, and the one he wanted to avoid refused to take the hint.

Hell. When had his life become so complicated?

Like tunnel vision, the one night that changed everything roared through his thoughts. Adrenaline pumped through him. He stared at the door Ellen just dashed through. She might have regrets, but not him—not one. Correct that. Maybe one, but he refused to allow that fact to stop him.

A soft touch drew his attention. He turned to see Angel dressed in a slinky white dress. Her brilliant green eyes were sharp and observant, and her perfume, cloying and harsh, hung heavy in the air. The muscles in his shoulders tensed. He flexed his fingers.

What the hell had he ever seen in her other than sex?

Once, he'd been satisfied with such a mutual agreement. Now, though, her hair wasn't the right shade of chestnut with thin strands of shimmering gold, and her eyes didn't dance with laughter at something he said. A tightness settled in his chest.

"What happened to you?" With a white napkin, she

patted his chest.

His skin crawled. Shoving away her offer, he glanced toward the banquet door. "Just an accident." Smoothing a hand down his damp shirt, he turned back. "I'm heading home."

Catching his hand, she threaded fingers through his. "I'll come with you."

He slid his gaze over her. The expected burn of desire escaped him, just as the feeling had for longer than he cared to admit. He pulled free his hand. "No."

Stepping back, she furrowed her brow. "But—"

He put up a hand. "Listen. I need to be alone." He didn't wait for the argument he knew would come. During their brief relationship, Angel proved beyond relentless—as determined as Peri, Lily's sister, and his past mistake. "I'll see you."

Striding toward the door, he fanned a hand toward Ben, saying goodbye to familiar faces he passed before shoving open the door and stepping into the night. Jamming a hand into his pocket, he yanked out the truck key and trotted down the steps. A sharp gust of wind caught the opening of his coat. Bitter cold slashed against his damp shirt. His flesh pebbled but did nothing to remove the heat burning inside.

The crunch of gravel drowned out the soothing sounds of waves lapping along the rocky shoreline. He unlocked the truck door and climbed inside. Heaviness weighted his arms, and tightness filled his chest.

The memory of one night, too many years past, floated through his thoughts. What started as a drunken adventure turned his once perfectly crafted life into a hollow shell of existence. Since then, he'd desperately strived to move on, move past the moment, and for the most part he had—until Ben's wedding and everything he'd worked to avoid came back in a flash.

Gritting his teeth, he thrust the key into the ignition. Shifting the gears, he peeled out of the lot. Normally, his drive through town would fill him with a sense of contentment. He loved Aberdeen, even with all its faults. But tonight, no peace filled him.

Angel.

He drove fingers through his hair. He wasn't on a mission. A harsh laugh ripped from him. Hadn't he made his sole purpose in life to bed as many women as possible? Hadn't he succeeded? In the past, he wore the title of hometown heartthrob like a badge of honor. Now, the name stung.

Rolling down the truck window, he inhaled. The pungent scent of pine teased his nose, and the slight chill of air tickled his flesh, reminding him winter lurked. Twinkling lights broke through the black velvet sky, blanketing the night in mystery. He slowed his vehicle and turned onto Timber Road—a slight detour, but he couldn't stop himself. Easing his foot off the gas, he stared at the window of Ellen's childhood room.

Soft yellow light glowed behind the sheer white curtain. He imagined Ellen just behind the thin film. Was she pacing in that perfect copper dress that made her hair shimmer and her eyes glow, or had she changed into her favorite flannel pjs? His stomach tightened, and a low heat flared, reminding him of one blazing night.

Pressing his foot against the pedal, Dax pulled away. Somehow, he needed to repair the damage of the past.

Chapter 2

Ellen slowly opened her eyes. With the memories of last night still fresh in her thoughts, she stuck one hand beneath her head and stared upward at the play of light and shadows against the ceiling. She felt out of sorts and disjointed—no doubt from lack of sleep. Or rather, from dreams filled with Dax and his mocking smile.

Dang.

Why couldn't the man just have stuck to his side of the room? Turning onto her side, she peered out the window. Fluffy white clouds floated across a sky, as brilliant blue as Dax's eyes. Sighing, she shifted her gaze. On her nightstand sat a familiar picture of her and Dax in front of the placid lake with its blue-green waters and pebbled shore. Pine trees, like pointed steeples against the brilliant blue summer sky, edged the far banks.

A piercing ache settled in her chest. Carefully, she grabbed the frame. Staring down at the scene, she remembered the day with fresh clarity. At fifteen, she'd been quite a tomboy, as exhibited by the tangled mass of dark curls swirling around her head and the thick, black smudge streaking across her cheek. In one hand, she held a fishing pole. In the other, she gripped a line. On the end hung a large lake trout. She hadn't stared at the camera but instead turned slightly and smiled upward toward Dax. With one arm draped over her shoulders, and the other pointing toward the fish, he, too, had avoided the camera and stared down at her.

The ache in her chest intensified. How come she'd never noticed before? Of course, for years, they'd been best friends, and she couldn't remember a time when a romantic thought about him filled her. Instead, he was the boy who taunted her when she was a child and the athlete who had tormented her as a teenager. Now, he was the man who used her as an adult.

Softly, she returned the picture and flopped back on the bed. The past was gone. Nothing she could do to change things but move forward.

Besides, she had bigger issues than her ruined friendship with Dax. Namely, dropping the bombshell on her mother. She couldn't lie. First off, she was a terrible liar, but more importantly, her mother was an excellent lie detector, which meant Ellen had one choice—she'd have to tell her mother the horrible turn her career path had taken.

Stupid Grant. Stupid Mr. Jorgensen. Both really threw a wrench in her life.

Groaning, she kicked aside the blankets and climbed from the bed. She grabbed her robe and marched into the bathroom. Twenty minutes later, Ellen headed downstairs. Over the back of the brown recliner peeked Great-Uncle Burt's bald head. The loud infomercial salesman's voice selling age-erasing cream boomed from the television. Fearful Burt would catch her movement, she tiptoed across the room. The last thing she wanted was to engage in some long conversation discussing his favorite topic—namely, her lack of direction, especially now, considering the truth of his assumption. Quietly, she pressed open the pass-through door and stepped into the kitchen.

Her stomach knotted. Hoping to exude an air of nonchalance, she strode toward the counter. Casually, she shot a glance toward her mother. Claire looked as tired and worn out as herself. Great-Aunt Kitty was nowhere in sight. At least, she caught one break. Licking her lips, she opened a cupboard and grabbed a cup. "Rough night?"

Claire looked up from the paper and shoved away the mug of steaming coffee. "Just tired." She stifled a yawn. "Your Uncle Burt and Aunt Kitty will be the death of me."

"Hey, they're *your* uncle and aunt." After picking up the coffee carafe, she filled the mug. The deep, rich smell of coffee surrounded her, giving her a momentary reprieve from questions sure to come. She was a firm believer in putting off the inevitable, especially when the inevitable involved disappointing her mother. "What did they do now?"

A loud sigh rumbled from Claire. "For starters, they tried to sneak out all the leftover food."

Ellen stifled a chuckle.

Claire frowned. "Now, Kitty has it in her mind to start a neighborhood watch."

Returning the pot to the warmer, Ellen laughed. "Here?" Extracting a bottle of cream from the fridge, she poured a dollop into her mug. "In the safest town in America?"

Shaking her head, Claire fanned a hand. "Don't ask." She leaned in and smiled. "So, *tell me*, when do you start your new position?"

Ellen's stomach knotted. The moment of truth.

Dropping into the chair across from her mother, she pushed aside her cup and stared down at the maroon placemat with yellow roses. "I didn't get it."

"What? How is that possible?"

Ellen wondered the very same thing. Five years with the same company, spending endless hours working her way up the ladder, giving up weeknights and weekends...only to lose the position to Grant, all because he had television advertising experience. She fisted a hand. Life was so unfair. "Mr. Jorgensen decided to go in a different direction. He chose someone he believed would diversify the company."

"That's ridiculous." Frowning, Claire picked up her cup. "Who could possibly be better than you?"

Ellen pasted a smile on her face. "Actually, he chose Grant."

Claire furrowed her brow. "Your boyfriend, Grant?"

Oh boy—looked like today was a day of total truth. Ellen traced a thumb around the rim of her cup. "Actually, ex-boyfriend."

"Ex?" Placing her cup on the table, Claire leaned back. "Don't tell me, because he got the promotion, he decided he was too important and so he broke up with you?" She shook her head. "What a scoundrel."

Whoa. Wait a minute. Who said anything about Grant breaking up with her? "Why do you say he was the one to initiate the breakup?" Ellen sipped her coffee.

"Oh, for heaven's sake, Ellen." Claire fisted her hand. "Now what the heck was wrong with him?"

The brew tasted bitter on her tongue. Okay, maybe she should have let Grant take the hit. After all, she hadn't exactly been stellar on keeping relationships either. Swallowing, she lifted one shoulder. "Nothing was *wrong*, per se."

Claire arched a brow.

Ellen put up a hand. "Wrong word choice." She licked her lips. "I just didn't feel a connection."

"Oh, for goodness' sake." Claire frowned. "Every time you break up with a guy, I hear that excuse. When will you settle down with one man? You're almost thirty!"

"I'm twenty-eight." Ellen gripped the mug. "And Ben was thirty when he got married."

Claire rolled her eyes. "A man shouldn't marry young. You, my dear, are a woman. You should be married and have two kids by now."

What the heck? Was her mother living in the fifties? "I believe, Mrs. Cleaver, it's time for you to enter the twenty-first century."

A red flush crept up Claire's neck. "Oh, you know what I mean." She tapped fingers on the table. "I just want you to be happy."

"Of course, the only way I can be is with a husband and children?"

Claire sighed. "Of course not."

Ellen picked up her mug. Steam curled upward, and the heady smell of coffee surrounded her. "I'm twenty-eight, which is nowhere close to being considered an old maid." She took a sip and licked her lips. "Besides, can you really say you liked Grant?"

Claire threw up a hand. "How should I know? You hardly ever brought him home."

"Which is just another example of how things weren't right between us." Moving aside her cup, Ellen reached out and grabbed Claire's hands. "Mom, I know you want me to be married and have children. I promise you, one day I will be, but I just haven't found Mr. Right. But once I do, I'll let you know."

"Honey, no Mr. Right exists." Claire heaved a sigh. "They're just men. You have to accept the good with the bad."

Maybe, but Ellen wanted more. She didn't want to be one of those sappy girls who believed in fairytales and knights in shining armor…but dang it, she wanted fairytales and knights in shining armor. She straightened, thrusting back her shoulders. "Perhaps, but I think I should at least feel *something* for the guy other than just ho-hum."

Claire fixed her gaze on Ellen. "So now what? Will you work for him?"

Oops. Looks like she wasn't done with her disappointment. Ellen fingered the edge of her sleeve. "Actually, I quit my job."

Claire snapped up her chin. "Excuse me?"

Taking a deep breath, Ellen debated the best way to explain. Finally, she just went with the easier answer and the not-painful part. "Considering our history, I didn't think it would be ethical for Grant to be my supervisor."

Claire sighed. "I suppose you're right." She ran a thumb over the rim of her cup. "So, what's your plan?"

Ah…the plan. The one commandment her mother and father drilled into her and Ben since they were children. Always have a backup plan. Only now, she didn't have any plan at all.

She supposed finding another job was possible. Only, how many creative director jobs were available?

21

Not enough, for sure. She supposed accepting a position in a less-prestigious role was an option, but the idea of starting over, of spending the next half decade working up the ladder just to reach the place she had vacated, seemed like a lot of time, plus, once she had children, she'd want to stay home and raise them.

Whoa. Wait just a second. Who said anything about children? Heck, she didn't even have a fiancé, let alone a husband. *Kind of putting the cart before the horse, don't you think?* She pasted a smile on her face. "I'll just find—"

Suddenly, the door swung open.

Kitty stepped inside.

Never had Ellen been so happy to see her aunt arrive. "Morning, Aunt Kitty."

Kitty shuffled over and thrust a booklet in Ellen's face. "Woo-wee, Ellen. Check out this picture."

Shifting her gaze, Ellen stared down at a picture of Dax stretched across the front with a tiny portion of a polar bear rug covering his mid-section.

Holy cow...

Suddenly, the six years melted away like butter on a hot griddle. She ran her gaze over Dax's incredible body with sculpted muscles and tanned flesh. He looked good. Actually, he looked better than good. He looked like the best kind of sin, just like she remembered, only better, harder, and more incredible.

She stilled the urge to snatch the sheet from her aging, great-aunt's gnarled grip and trace a finger across the glossy pages, as if touching the image would be the same as caressing the flesh. What the heck was wrong with her? She acted like she hadn't ever seen him naked. Of course, the last time she'd seen him sans attire had been two thousand, two hundred, fifty days, and twelve hours ago—give or take, not that she had kept track…much.

Still, as impressive as he'd looked then, but damn if he didn't look even better now—from the rugged squared jaw, to the perfectly muscled pecs, to the bulging thighs just begging to be touched. Her mouth watered. Swallowing, she shook off the images. So much for eliminating Dax from her thoughts. Just seeing the image brought back one delicious memory she couldn't banish.

Grabbing the coffee mug, she took a huge gulp. Hot coffee burned her mouth. Pressing a palm against her stinging lips, she turned. "The Men of Aberdeen? What the heck is that?"

"Oh, right. You don't know. Aberdeen has its very own calendar." Leaning in just a bit, Claire stared down at the picture.

Ellen frowned at the soft smile that sliced across her mother's face.

Finally, Claire shook her head and sighed. "Dax is our very own Mr. January."

Of course. If any man was calendar worthy, Dax would be the one. Slowly, she ran her gaze over the image—shaggy blond hair, sharp blue eyes, and sensual lips twisted in a sultry smile. His tanned upper body was propped on an elbow, revealing powerful biceps, broad shoulders, and shredded abs. One leg was stretched out, the other bent at the knee. Thighs, roped with muscles and fine hair, tantalized the eyes and teased the mind. She remembered every inch of his body, every nuance, and every hard muscle. Her mouth dried.

Cover boy—oh yes, if any man belonged on the glossy pages, that man was Dax. A sour feeling settled in the pit of her stomach. "Just the ego stroke he needs."

"Don't be ridiculous." Claire waved a dismissive hand. "He's helping the hospital."

How could her mother be so naïve? He dangled a new date on his arm every weekend, if not every night. The man snagged women easily, quickly, and effortlessly, just like one of nature's best predators. This stint was just another calling card to draw more groupies.

"He sure is tasty looking, isn't he?"

No denial there, still, Kitty was approaching ninety and married. *Married.* She shouldn't be staring at Dax like…like…she hadn't eaten in a month.

"Oh, brother." Claire glared at Kitty. "Dax is old enough to be your great-grandson."

"But he's not, which means I'm entitled to look." Rubbing one finger across her ruby-painted lips, she turned to Claire. "You know what? He reminds me of Paul."

Glancing toward the calendar, Claire furrowed her brow. "Paul who?"

"Newman." Kitty shook her head. "Jeez, don't you know anything?"

Okay, again, Kitty was on some strange, memory lane journey. Ellen had heard so many stories during her lifetime, she couldn't keep them straight. She turned. "Mom, about Dax—"

"I actually met him." Kitty rubbed her palms together. A twinkle lit her eyes, and a wide smile split her lips. "Woo-wee, talk about exciting. I had just turned eighteen—this was 1951, and boy did I look amazing. Remembered the way the pinups looked?" She swiveled her gaze between Ellen and Claire. "I looked just like one of them stepping off a calendar. Anyway, I stopped at the corner of Hollywood and Vine, and who do you think bumped into me?" She nodded. "Yup, Paul Newman, and let me tell you—"

"Don't be ridiculous, Kitty. You didn't meet Paul Newman." Claire turned toward Ellen and pasted a smile on her face. "Now, what was it you wanted to ask?"

Ellen's pulse raced, and her mind whirled with questions. She pointed toward the calendar. "I just don't understand."

Claire reached over and picked up the calendar. "What's to understand? The hospital is raising money for the new children's wing, and Dax agreed to do the calendar. Not hard to wrap your brain around."

Was her mother kidding? Ellen thought her brain had exploded.

With a smile curling on her lips, Claire sighed. "Personally, I think Dax looks amazing." She cocked a brow. "Don't you?"

Ellen jerked back. First Kitty, now her mother? Had everyone lost their mind? "Mom, he's Ben's best friend. You practically raised him."

"So?" Leaning back, Claire crossed both arms over her chest. "I'm not allowed to think Dax is attractive?"

"No. You're not." Ellen gripped her cup. "The thought makes my stomach turn."

"Don't be ridiculous. He looks far better than the rest of the men." Claire held out the calendar. "Look and tell me I'm wrong."

Ellen shoved away the calendar. "Ah...no thank you." Only, no matter how hard she wanted to ignore his image, damned if her eyes didn't have other ideas. She jabbed a finger at the page. "He's lying on a polar bear rug, for heaven's sake. The whole thing is cliché."

"Wish I was on that rug with him." Kitty licked her lips.

Ellen groaned. *Holy cow, this cannot be happening.*

Dropping the calendar on the table, Claire tilted her head. "You sound jealous."

Ellen jerked back. Hurt? Yes. Humiliated? For certain. But jealous? No way. Yanking away her gaze, she placed the cup on the counter. "What I am, is disgusted."

Claire frowned. "Honestly, I don't know why you're so upset. You two are friends. He's like a brother."

"Yeah, well, I already have one." Ellen strolled to the rack and grabbed her coat. Too bad she hadn't remembered that little fact six years ago.

Chapter 3

Pushing Dax from her thoughts, Ellen left her mother's, and while walking to Maybelline's, she focused on her many issues—namely, the fact she was out of a job, did not have a prospect of a job, and thanks to the purchase of a new car, she faced an abysmally low savings account.

Hurrying past ancient oaks and massive maple trees, she spied Mrs. Tindrow's house nestled between stately Victorian homes painted in a rainbow of colors. She turned into the driveway and scooted around Maybelline's clunker. Stopping at the base of the stairs, she stretched her gaze up the long stairway tacked to the side of the peppermint-green home. Someone weaved orange ribbons through spindles the color of cotton candy. On each rung sat dusty, black-feathered crows with beady, orange eyes. They looked like they'd seen better days a half century ago.

Maybelline fancied herself as a decorator extraordinaire, but seriously, no matter how fabulous the decorations, keeping them up two weeks past Halloween seemed a bit excessive.

Grabbing the railing, Ellen pulled herself upward. Reaching the top platform, she stifled a shriek. Propped in the corner was the most horrific scarecrow she'd ever laid eyes on. A ragged, long-sleeved, black T-shirt imprinted with a white skull covered his torso. Zebra-striped leggings encased thick, bumpy legs and clunky, biker boots covered feet. A shriveled, hollowed-out pumpkin wearing a black, leather mask rested upon lumpy, straw-filled shoulders. The soulless eyes seemed to follow her every movement. Ellen rang the doorbell.

Seconds later, the door opened.

"Hey, what's up?"

Ellen pointed toward the scarecrow. "What *the hell* is that *thing*?"

"This guy is Gordon." Smiling, Maybelline stroked his head. "Great, isn't he?"

"He's chilling." Ellen gripped the leather strap of her purse. "Halloween was two weeks ago."

"I know." Maybelline shrugged. "But he makes me happy."

"I thought we'd go to lunch. You know—catch up."

"Sounds good. Gimme a second." Maybelline dashed inside, leaving the door open.

Skimming her gaze past rows of houses toward the center of town, Ellen spied the steeple of All Saints and the very top of the greenish-brown dome of city hall.

"Ready?"

Ellen turned to see Maybelline decked out in a green-and-yellow, faux tiger-print coat from the closet. Everything about Maybelline ran toward the extreme. "Yup." She pointed to one ragged bird. "Where did you get them?"

"From Mrs. Tindrow's attic. They were stuffed in this dusty, old trunk." Maybelline stopped, and leaning down, she petted a bird's head. "Hi, Harold."

Ellen grinned. Only her cousin… "You named him, too?"

Straightening, Maybelline smiled. "I named them all." She pointed to one with feathers out of whack and one eye missing. "I call this one Jenny."

Ellen shook her head. She couldn't really fault Maybelline for her dislike of the woman. After all, Maybelline had caught her boyfriend kissing Jenny. "You know, Jenny isn't the only one to blame."

Pivoting, Maybelline scowled. "Whose side are you on, anyway?"

Stepping onto the gravel, Ellen turned. "I'm just saying, John was part of the problem, too."

"Exactly." Maybelline nodded toward an upturned gargoyle tossed in a pile of muck. "You see how I punctured his heart with an arrow? Nice touch, right?"

Ellen thought her cousin had lost her mind. "More like disturbing," she grumbled, following Maybelline across the driveway.

Skidding to a halt, Maybelline turned. "Where's your car?"

Brushing a strand of hair from her face, Ellen strolled toward the sidewalk. "I walked."

"Walked?" Maybelline pinched her mouth downward. "If I had known, I would have stayed home."

Ellen waited for a car driving down the road to pass before crossing the street. "Come on, the fresh air and exercise will do us good."

"Ugh." Hurrying behind, Maybelline sniffed. "You know I hate both of those things."

Yeah, Ellen did know. She wasn't thrilled with the whole exercise/fresh air gig either. A soft breeze floated in the air, brushing her cheeks, and tangling in her hair. Shoving aside a strand, she walked toward town.

Maybelline chattered in an incessant stream of nothingness.

Ellen hardly paid attention. In her experience, her cousin was adept at one-sided conversations. Instead, she ran her gaze around the quaint town preparing for the winter holidays. Red velvet ribbon swirled around old-time light posts, and sparkling lights dangled from leafless trees filling the city park. Sliding her gaze past the city hall, she spied the fire station and searched the parking lot for the familiar white pickup without success.

Probably still entertaining Angel.

The muscles in her neck bunched, and her chest burned. She took a deep breath. The little voice in her head sounded just a touch jealous...which was quite ridiculous because she didn't get jealous. "So, where do you want to eat?"

Maybelline paused in her barrage of chatter. "Oh, right." She swiveled her gaze and waggled her brows. "Papa's."

Ellen ripped her gaze to the red brick building with the green-striped canopy. A banner hanging from the awning waved gently in the breeze. Scrawled across the front in bold black writing read *Proud Sponsor of Aberdeen Police and Fire.*

Her stomach knotted. What were the odds of Dax showing? A snapshot image of Angel trailing her finger down his chest flashed through her thoughts. Not a chance. Besides, if he was there with his "friend," she could prove he lied. She shot her cousin a tight smile. "Sounds perfect."

Pulling open the door of Papa's Pizzeria, she inhaled, then sighed. A warm blast of air, smelling of roasted garlic and yeasty dough, beckoned Ellen. She stepped inside. Like most Saturdays, Papa's was busy.

Men sipped beer at the bar while watching a college football game on the television screens perched upon the wall. People sat at tables, eating and conversing quietly. In the back, young women filled several tables.

Ellen skimmed her gaze across the room. No gorgeous blond head in sight. *Figures.* Just when she wanted to show she didn't care, he wasn't around. Fine with her. She slid into a booth next to the row of windows facing toward the street. Grabbing two plastic menus wedged between a stainless-steel napkin holder and salt and pepper shakers, she slid one to Maybelline and flipped open the other. She wasn't certain why she bothered, seeing the menu hadn't changed in twenty years.

"Hey, ladies." Lisa, Ellen's babysitter back in the day who now worked at Papa's, stood at the end of the booth. Pulling a pad and pen from her pocket, she smiled. "Glad to see you could make it. Got a lot going on today. What can I get you?"

Snapping open a white paper napkin and placing it on her lap, Maybelline turned to Lisa. "We'll go with two glasses of red wine."

"Two glasses. Got it." Lisa scribbled on the notepad. "Anything else?"

Ellen tapped fingers on the table. "You wanna split a pizza?"

"Excuse me?"

Maybelline's words came out with a sharp bark. Ellen yanked her gaze from the menu. "What?"

Maybelline scowled. "Are you sabotaging me?"

Sighing, Lisa tucked her notepad into her pocket. "I'll give you two a minute."

Ellen propped elbows on the table. "What are you talking about?"

Glaring, Maybelline tossed down her menu. "You know I can't eat pizza. I'm a no-carber."

Ellen furrowed her brow. "You're a what?"

A long, lengthy sigh rumbled from Maybelline. "I don't eat carbs."

This was news, considering at Ben's wedding, Maybelline had certainly enjoyed her share of cake. "Since when?"

"A few weeks now. I've lost ten pounds in the process." Maybelline frowned. "By the way, thanks for noticing."

"Sorry." Ellen wiggled in her seat. "You do realize wine has carbs, right?"

Maybelline lifted one shoulder. "I don't count alcohol carbs."

Okay, now she knew her cousin was off her rocker. "So, let me get this straight. You can drink your carbs but not eat them?"

"What can I say?" Maybelline picked up the menu and shrugged. "It's not a perfect world."

Right. Only Maybelline could justify her decision. Ellen shoved away her menu and sighed. "Fine. I'll skip Papa's Pick and go with wings."

"Hey, don't let me stop you." Maybelline's gaze bored into the menu. A muscle flexed in her cheek. "Have whatever you want."

Ellen swept her gaze over Maybelline's tight lips, straight back, and white knuckles gripping the menu's edges. She arched a brow. "You sure?"

"Of course." She slipped her gaze over Ellen. "I mean, you're tall and willowy and can eat whatever you want. I got the short, pudgy, slow genes." She shrugged. "I'm cool with it."

Lisa returned with their drinks. "So? You two decide yet"

Maybelline snapped shut the menu. "I'll have a regular salad with the house vinaigrette and a half-dozen wings."

Chewing the inside of her lip, Ellen debated whether to satisfy her cravings or support her cousin. She wanted to be there for Maybelline, but she really had envisioned a slice of ooey-gooey, cheesy, meat-filled pie, too. After tomorrow, who knew when she'd be back to get one. Licking her lips, she slid another glance toward Maybelline.

Maybelline scowled. "Oh, just get the dang pizza."

"Okay." Ellen turned to Lisa. "But just a small Papa's Pick." She pushed aside the menu. "Oh, and a small salad. Bleu cheese on the side." She smiled at Maybelline. At least she gave her cousin some support.

"Really?" Maybelline snapped. "If you're gonna order the best pizza in town, at least get your money's worth and order the medium."

"She's right," Lisa agreed, scribbling on her notepad. "The medium is a better deal.

Ellen picked up her glass. "Fine."

Lisa nodded. "I'll be back."

"So, tell me, what do I call you now?" Taking a sip of her wine, Maybelline wiggled her brow. "Madame Vice President?"

Even now, days later, the truth seemed surreal. After years of dedication, why did she get passed over?

33

Ellen still couldn't figure out the answer. "Actually, Mr. Jorgensen awarded the promotion to Grant."

Maybelline's eyes widened, and her chin dropped. "Your boyfriend?"

Shoot. Another person she hadn't told. She ran a finger along the stem of her fork. "My ex."

"Your ex?" The words fairly erupted from Maybelline.

Ellen glanced around the restaurant. Thankfully, no one paid them the least bit of attention. She turned and scowled. "Jeez, why don't you take out an ad with the *Aberdeen Times?* I don't think everyone heard you."

Maybelline's cheeks turned pink. "Sorry. I was surprised." Reaching across the table, she squeezed Ellen's hand. "So, what happened? Did he break up with you because he got the promotion?"

What the heck? Now Maybelline thought she'd gotten dumped? Did she have loser written across her forehead? Ellen yanked away her hand. "For your information, I broke up with him—*months ago,* before the job even came up."

"*Months ago?*" Maybelline flung out a hand. "You never said anything."

Ellen pinched her mouth into a frown. "*Again,* keep it down. I don't need the whole town to know."

Maybelline furrowed her brow. "I thought you two were serious."

Uncertain how to explain her reasons, Ellen pushed aside her wine and leaned forward. "Remember when I came home this past summer?"

Maybelline nodded.

"After church, I walked out and saw Ben with Lily. As I watched them, I noticed they shared this

34

chemistry—an almost palpable electricity." She traced a finger along the base of her drink. "Seeing them made me realize Grant and I had problems."

Maybelline arched a brow. "Really?"

Smoothing a hand across the table, Ellen thought back on her time with Grant. She wouldn't say they had a horrible relationship, but somewhere in the mix, they lacked an integral component—like two people who enjoyed each other on a personal level and not just professionally. She picked up her glass. "Do you realize, the whole time we were together, Grant and I never fought? Not once."

Maybelline frowned. "And you want to fight?"

"Of course not." Ellen sipped the sweet wine. How to explain? She set down the glass. "But, after a while, I felt…" She shrugged. "Nothing."

"Hmmm." Maybelline tapped fingers on the table. "Not what I'd call promising."

You think? Ellen shrugged. "Anyway, when I found out he would be my boss…well, ethically, I couldn't work with him considering our past history, so I quit."

Maybelline's eyes widened. "You quit?"

"Yup." Smiling, Ellen realized that saying the words didn't sting as much as before. *Go figure.*

"Oh man." Maybelline pinched together her brows. "What did your mom say?"

"About the job or breaking up with Grant?"

"Both?"

"Disappointed about the job. Depressed because I'm single again." Ellen scraped a thumb along the edge of the placemat. "She thinks I'm an old maid."

"Ha!" Maybelline snorted. "Good one."

Ellen frowned. "Hey, you're the same age and not married."

"Humph. I never thought about it." Scowling, Maybelline fisted a hand. "Great. Now, I'm an old maid just like you."

Ellen rolled her eyes. "We're not old maids. We're selective."

"Selective?" Maybelline ran a finger over her lip. "Sounds much better. So, now what will you do? Go back to Albany?"

"I suppose. I have my apartment." Curling the edge of the paper placemat, she glanced out the window. "Plus, I'll need to—"

Dax stood outside—no Angel in sight.

All train of thought departed. What the heck...what in heaven's name was he doing here?

A few seconds later, a group of men surrounded him on the sidewalk.

She knew every single one, and all were as familiar as the faces on the calendar. Slowly, Ellen scanned the restaurant. A long table with six chairs faced out toward the dining room. In front were more tables filled with women. A low thrum of excitement throbbed in the room. Lisa's words floated through her thoughts. The final peg dropped into place. Her stomach flip-flopped, and her chest tightened. She turned and frowned. "Did you know Dax would be here?"

Bright red rushed up Maybelline's neck and cheeks. She leaned back. "No. Why would you think such a thing?"

The guilt written all over Maybelline's face confirmed Ellen's suspicions. She jabbed a finger. "Spill the beans."

Maybelline huffed. "Okay, fine. The fire department is having a calendar signing." She snapped open her napkin. "Big deal. Dax is our friend. We should support him."

The soft memories of years past floated by. He *had* been her friend. Maybe her best friend. Why had they ruined things? "I suppose." With shaking hands, Ellen grabbed her wine glass and sipped.

The restaurant's door opened.

Dax stepped inside.

His gaze collided with hers. A soft smile flitted across his lips. Breaking away from the group, he strolled over with a swagger only the very confident or a fireman could muster. In Dax's case, both applied. She curled fingers into the napkin.

Nudging her side, he dropped into the seat.

Scowling at his presumption, she shoved back into the wall. Sharp wood bit her back, and still, she could feel the heat radiating off him. She glared. "Gee, Dax, would you like to sit?"

Laughter lit his eyes. "Don't mind if I do."

Lisa arrived, and placing the food on the table, she slid a glance toward Dax. "Need anything, Dax?"

Ellen stilled the urge to roll her eyes at the way Lisa batted her lashes. Even Lisa, a good ten years older than Dax, fell for his handsome looks and his honeyed charm.

Dax made a half wave. "I'm good."

"If you change your mind, you let me know." Pivoting, Lisa strolled away.

Ellen watched Lisa swing her hips. Shifting, she glanced toward Dax. If he noticed Lisa's overt action, he didn't give a sign. Instead, he kept his gaze fixed on her. She frowned. He was like a little kid who had so many toys that none interested him. *Pathetic.*

Sweeping his gaze over Ellen, Dax furrowed his brow. "Is something wrong? You're pressed against the wall like you can't stand my presence."

Did amusement lurk in his gaze, like he knew she wanted to avoid him? Like heck. She narrowed her eyes. Oh, she'd teach him. Pressing a hand against her chest, she feigned a cough. "Actually, I might be coming down with a cold. Wouldn't want to get you sick and ruin the possibility of a date."

Pausing in biting a chicken wing, Maybelline scowled. "Gee, thanks for being concerned for me."

Dax flicked a glance at Maybelline before returning to Ellen. A smile twitched on his lips. "Glad to see you're worried about my love life."

Ellen gritted her teeth. Figures, he put a positive spin on things. She flicked a glance toward the back. "Does Angel know your fan club is here?" She arched a brow. "Better be careful. You might experience a first and actually get dumped."

He cocked a brow. "So, I didn't get a chance to ask you about your boyfriend. Greg, is it?"

Picking up the fork, she stabbed a limp piece of lettuce. Figures he'd put her on the defensive. "Actually, his name is Grant, and he's busy."

Maybelline snapped up her head. "But you just said—"

Ellen narrowed her gaze at Maybelline before turning to Dax. "He's a vice president."

"So, too busy to hang out with the little people?" Leaning back, he stretched an arm across the top of the booth. "You're too good for him."

The lazy circles he made with his fingers on her shoulder drove her to distraction. Her stomach fluttered, and every muscle in her body turned to liquid silver. "Gee, thanks for the information." Oh, to hell with the salad. She placed the fork on the plate and grabbed a slice of pie instead. "But I don't think I need advice from a man who can't settle down with one woman longer than a few hours."

His gaze collided with hers, holding her in his mesmerizing blue trance. For a moment, Ellen wondered if his eyes were always this blue with chips of black and streaks of silver weaving through them—both magnetic and mysterious. A slow, soft smile creased his mouth.

"The only reason I haven't is because I'm waiting for the right one."

"They're women. Not miracle workers." She waved a finger toward the crowd of women eyeing him. "You have to give them more than two hours to discover if they're right or not."

"Nope." Dropping his hands to the table, he stood. "Two hours is all I need, baby girl."

Oh, how she detested the nickname. More importantly, Dax knew how she hated the label he and Ben gave her when she had been a little girl. "I am not a *baby* any longer."

Leaning down, he locked gazes. "Trust me, baby girl. I remember."

Heat pooled in her stomach, and a delicious, tingling feeling spread from her center outward, and a flash of memory tore through her—of calloused fingers and smooth flesh, of long limbs and hard muscles, of passionate kisses and tender touches. "Good to…ah…"

She licked her lips. "Know." Her words came out all breathy and soft.

He swept his gaze over her for just a moment before shoving away and strolling to the back where the other men waited.

"What the heck?"

Ellen turned to see Maybelline's furrowed brow and her fork poised mid-air. She rolled a hand outward. "What?"

Maybelline pointed her fork. "Is something going on between you two?"

Heat burned her face. She picked up the slice of pie. "Please. I'm not stupid." Only, for one moment, impossible dreams of the past had washed through her, scaring her more than she thought possible.

Chapter 4

Rolling over the next morning, Ellen scrubbed hands through her hair, wishing for just a few more minutes of sleep. Fogginess and fatigue clouded her thoughts. Of course, why wouldn't she be tired? One cannot function on two skimpy hours of sleep. With the continual replay of her encounter with Dax, she was lucky she slept at all.

She tapped fingers on the mattress, remembering how easily he stated Grant wasn't worthy of her. Oh, she knew his ulterior motive. Having witnessed his carefree lifestyle firsthand, she knew how easily he could charm the pants off a woman. Only now, the naïve girl who prayed for a miracle from a man who didn't know the meaning of love, faith, or commitment no longer existed.

A knock sounded.

"Come in." Her voice sounded as tired and out-of-sorts as her body.

The door cracked open.

Claire popped her head through the opening. "Oh good, you're awake."

Ellen shoved up on elbows. "What's up, Mom?"

"Just wanted to make certain you remembered church."

The urge to close her eyes and groan tugged. Of course, church—the sacred family tradition. When would she ever catch a break? Ellen forced a smile. "Right. Church."

Claire slid her blouse's frilly lace sleeve up her forearm, exposing a gold watch wrapped around a delicate wrist. She tapped the watch's face. "We're leaving in thirty minutes."

Ellen glanced at the clock. Eight a.m. A full hour before church started. Of course, her mother, with Kitty and Burt, loved to arrive early, providing them an additional opportunity to gossip. No doubt she'd be the focus of questions, too. *Nope.* No way would she deal with all the questions bound to come her way. She fanned a hand. "I'll meet you."

"Oh, I don't know..." A deep crease furrowed Claire's brow. "You know how Father Frank feels about tardiness."

Right. Father Frank—the second stickler for timeliness. The first being her mother. Ellen kicked off the sheets, and standing, she stretched arms over her head and yawned. "I won't be late."

One deep-brown eyebrow spiked upward.

Dropping arms, Ellen huffed. "I *promise*."

Claire eyed her once more. "Just make sure. I don't want another repeat of the last time you were late."

Oh sure, her mother would bring up *that* incident. "Mom, I was sixteen, and it was winter." Ellen strolled toward the closet. "Jeez, you'd think nothing else happened in this town in the past twelve years."

"Don't be ridiculous, dear." Claire fanned a hand. "But, if you had just ridden with me and your father, you wouldn't have knocked over Father Frank."

Ellen whipped around. "I didn't *knock* down Father Frank. I slipped on the wet, stone floor at the same time

Father stepped into the vestibule. Total accident." She frowned. "But, hey, thanks for your concern over my near-broken ankle."

"Don't be dramatic." Claire shook her head. "Your ankle was fine."

So much for motherly concern. Ellen snagged a dress out of the closet. "Don't worry. I'll arrive in plenty of time." She peered at the clock. "If *someone* will let me get ready."

Claire sighed. "I'll make certain Father knows you'll arrive on time."

Great. Now Mom is my timekeeper? Her life had reached an all-time low. Ellen gave her mother a tight smile. "Yes, please do." Once the door shut, she raced around the room. Like heck she'd allow the past to repeat itself.

The good news was she hadn't arrived late. At least, not by the dials on the clock. Unfortunately, she cut her arrival just a teensy, tiny bit close. Okay, maybe she cut her arrival too close—say minutes before Mass started.

Of course, she would have arrived on time, if *someone* hadn't decided to play a joke and remove her keys from the holder next to the door where they always hung and hid them in the stupid junk drawer where—FYI—things went to get lost and not found. But had anyone mentioned the new key arrangement plan? Of course not.

Peeling into the parking lot of All Saints Church, she spied one available parking spot. Unfortunately, the one spot just happened to be right next to Dax's truck. Little bubbles swirled in her stomach. *Just freaking great.*

43

Yesterday floated through her thoughts—the warmth of his body, the smell of his cologne, the familiarity of his friendship—all reminding her of things she wanted to forget. *Nope.* She wouldn't go there, because the last time she did, she got burned hard.

She whipped her car into the empty spot and parked. She snagged her purse off the seat, and shoving open the door, she stepped out and eyed the building. Inside sat Dax, no doubt wearing some outfit stretched across his incredible chest and strained over his muscular thighs. *Oh man.* Now, why did she have to go and imagine him? Shaking her head, she mentally scrubbed away the images. Nope. Still there. *Freaking past.*

Clutching the purse, she marched across the lot and straight up the church's steps. Maybe she was bothered, but she'd be darned if he'd *ever* know. Ripping open the wide, red, wooden door, she stepped inside.

The smell of beeswax and incense filled the room, and the low hum of the organ playing wafted through the closed door. Father Frank stood off to the side speaking with Peter Bench.

He turned slightly, and narrowing his gaze, he dug gnarled fingers into Peter's bony, age-spotted arm and scowled. "Oh no. Ellen's here."

Heat burned Ellen's cheeks. She swept her gaze across the black mat covering the floor. Not a speck of wet lined the surface. What the heck? Did he think she was such a klutz she'd slip on dry slate? She jangled her keys. "Sorry, Father. Couldn't find my keys."

Frank sighed. "Maybe in the future you should remember where you placed them."

Ellen didn't bother to mention she knew exactly *where* she placed them. She smiled tightly. "Yes, Father, I'll make sure I do." Stepping inside the nave, she was immediately struck by a blast of warm air and overpowering perfume.

Murky swirls of dust twisted through the colorful light shining from the stained-glass windows, and the crackle of paper competed with shuffling feet.

A few people turned and glanced her way.

Pasting a smile on her face, Ellen strode up the aisle. Nearing the family pew, she spied the back of Dax's blond head and broad shoulders. Her stomach wobbled. *So, the guy is gorgeous. No big deal.* She'd seen plenty of attractive guys in her life. Yes, they had sex, but did she spend six years fantasizing about the night?

Hot, steamy images filled her. Her breath caught, and her skin tingled. She clutched the end of the pew and prayed her knees didn't buckle. Okay, maybe she remembered more than she wanted—still didn't mean anything. Besides, the fact he had promptly dumped her meant the night meant nothing to *him*, which was just fine with her. Only, why did the truth still sting?

Suddenly, he pivoted.

His gaze locked with hers. A surge of warmth rushed through her. *Dang.* Why did the man have to be so attractive? Why couldn't he have plain brown eyes and ordinary brown hair—like her? Instead, he looked like a golden god with blue eyes that she swore could entrance a woman, and from the number of discarded women littering his past, she knew he had. She stiffened. *Wait. She* was one of those women. She shot him a hot scowl. A devilish and completely charming grin sliced across his lips.

Her mother turned. "What happened to you?" She lifted an arm and pointed toward her wristwatch. "I warned you about being late."

Ellen ripped her gaze from Dax. Had she known he would be attending, she would be a heck of a lot later…say like not at all. "I wouldn't have if *someone* told me where *she* hid my keys. By the way, since when did the junk drawer become the key repository?"

"Oh, that idea was your brother's." Claire stepped from the pew. "You know, with the window right next to the key rack anyone could break in."

Figures the move would be Mr. Protect-and-Serve's idea. She shot a glance toward Ben. He and Lily stared at each other in worshipful adoration. *Yuck.* She turned back. "Well, I wish someone would have shared the change with me."

Claire shrugged. "You can sit next to Kitty."

Ellen glanced down the aisle toward the seat her mother indicated which just happened to be next to the one man she *didn't* want to be near. She slipped her gaze over him, noting the blue button-down stretching across his mouth-watering torso and charcoal-gray slacks hugging dangerously sinful thighs. A low stirring tingled in her belly. Dax's gaze collided with hers.

He waggled his brows and mouthed the word *scared?*

Oh heck, yeah, she was. She dug nails into her purse. *Nope.* She didn't care about appearances, because the last time she noticed, she flopped into his bed only to get her heart broken. No, thank you. Not happening again.

She lifted her chin, letting him know without words

she wasn't even a tiniest bit scared. Casually brushing her damp palms along the coat sides, she inched her way into the pew, and dang if his gaze never left hers. She knew his intention. He wanted to bother her. Well, score. He did. Only, she would rather die than let him know the truth.

He winked.

Freaking Dax. Glaring, she dropped into the seat. His rock-hard thighs pressed against hers. A little buzz zipped through her veins, and warm heat singed her flesh. She tossed down her purse, forcing him to move his thigh. "Surprised to see you here."

He slid his arm across the back of the pew, and brushing his fingers against her shoulders, he leaned close. "Oh? Why?"

His warm breath brushed softly across the top of her hair, and the spicy scent sea and surf surrounded her. Little tingles zipped over her skin. What the heck? Where did the man purchase the dang stuff? At the hot and sexy store? "Well, considering it's Sunday, and you have your pick of fan club members—" She lifted one shoulder. "The math is pretty simple."

"Bothered, are you?"

Threading together her fingers, she stared straight ahead. "Don't be silly."

"Good to know."

His voice was deep and rich, like the best, aged whiskey, and held just a hint of laughter. She ripped her gaze upward. Did he know? Could he tell how his presence bothered her? She dismissed the odious thought. *Of course not.* But just to be safe, she vowed she wouldn't pay him any further attention.

The music piping from the organ increased in

volume, signaling the start of Mass.

Ellen exhaled. Now, at least, she had something to concentrate on instead of Dax.

The task became impossible. How the heck was she expected to focus on anything when she had sinful cologne tickling her senses bringing back hot memories?

Before she knew it, Mass had ended without her hearing a word of the sermon. She followed her mother down the aisle, far too aware Dax stood just scant inches beside her. Did the man have to cling like a vine on a house?

The path narrowed. The crowd tightened around them.

Suddenly, his hand pressed against her lower back, and *holy cow,* heat, like a nuclear bomb exploded inside her. All the thoughts she insisted on avoiding, in church no less, suddenly filled her. She arched her back, hoping to remove his touch. However, the man's hand was like a damn magnet, refusing to budge.

Sliding a glance toward her mother, she saw her in deep discussion with Betty. She leaned into Dax's side. "You know, I'm quite capable of making it on my own. You don't need to keep your hand on my back."

He met her halfway. "I know."

His blue eyes sparkled. Her stomach did a tumble. Didn't he understand she didn't *want* him to touch her in public? *No, wait.* She didn't want him to touch her any time. She yanked open the heavy wooden door and stepped outside.

Bright sunlight lit the area.

She spotted her mother at the base of the steps, keeping a keen eye on Kitty and Burt.

Betty moved off.

Ben and Lily slowly made their way over.

Ellen darted down the steps. Dax kept pace with her, his hand still resting on her lower back. She frowned.

He winked.

Shaking her head, she turned and caught her mother watching them. Ellen quickly stepped away. Jeez…wasn't it just her luck her mother would notice and jump to the wrong conclusion? She cleared her throat. "Dax was just helping me through the crowds."

"I see." Pursing her lips, Claire flicked a glance toward Dax for just a second, then back. "I have some exciting news."

Ellen slid the purse strap higher. "Oh?"

Claire nodded. "Betty has a job for you at the café."

Ellen ripped her gaze toward Dax.

He arched a brow.

Great. Just great. All her hard work yesterday destroyed by five little words blurted out by her mother. "Why would I work at the café?"

"Remind me…" Claire frowned. "Did you happen to acquire a job overnight?"

Oh, too cruel, Mom, too cruel. A searing warmth suffused her body. Crossing arms over her chest, Ellen lifted her chin. "No, but I'm sure I will."

Claire sighed. "Listen, I know you believe you'll get another job in advertising but think about the timing. With the holidays approaching, who will hire you?"

Her mother made a very valid point. However, did she really need to admit this embarrassing fact? "Did you ever consider I might have other reasons to go back?"

Claire thrust out a hand. "Well, it's certainly not because of a boyfriend."

Jeez, what did she have—a target on her back? Shoving hands to hips, Ellen swung her gaze past Ben and Lily and landed on Dax. "Just so everyone doesn't think I'm a complete loser, *I* quit my job." She glared at him. "And *I* broke up with Grant."

He cocked a brow.

Again, Ellen crossed arms over her chest. Although, in truth, working at the café would solve her temporary lack of income, but still… "Mom, don't you think I'm a bit over-qualified for Betty's?"

"Of course." Claire shrugged. "But the job is only temporary. Just through the holidays."

Through the holidays? A heavy weight pressed against her chest. Had her mother lost her mind? No way could Ellen remain with her mother for two whole months. Why, if Ben wasn't thrilled with keys hanging on hooks right next to the kitchen door, he for certain wouldn't be happy when one of them murdered the other. "Mother, I cannot stay with you."

Smoothing a hand down the front of her coat, Claire frowned. "Whyever not?"

Was she serious? Ellen clutched the purse strap. "Well, for one thing, the last time we lived together, we argued a *lot*."

A soft laugh sounded from Dax.

She glared.

"Teenage years." Claire fanned a hand. "Completely normal. I doubt we'd have those same problems now."

Figures her mother would come up with a reasonable solution. Ellen shoved both hands into her pockets. Heat burned her cheeks. Of all the places they could have this conversation—say at home—her mother had to pick the church's parking lot filled with half the town. A part of her wanted to refuse to answer. However, she couldn't be so dismissive of her mother. "Okay, fine. How about the fact I'm an adult who wants my own place?"

Claire narrowed her eyes. "Why? To entertain strange men?"

Okay, maybe this was her penance. Ellen froze and flicked a glance in Dax's direction. His deep blue eyes sparkled, and his lips twitched. She ripped her gaze back to her mother. "Why would you say such a thing?"

"I'm not so old that I don't remember having—" Claire's face turned crimson, and she dropped her gaze. "Urges."

Seriously, was this conversation *really* happening? Since when did her mother talk about urges? A shudder rolled down Ellen's spine. Why the heck had she returned home anyway? *Oh right.* Because of Ben's election celebration—and the fact she really *didn't* have a job.

Dang it. Now what? Should she reject the offer, knowing her account balance was abysmally low? Yet, returning to the house she grew up in seemed like she'd thrown in the towel and accepted being a complete failure. What other choices did she have, though? "I guess—"

Lily stepped closer and waved a hand. "I have an idea."

Ellen ripped her gaze to her sister-in-law.

"You could stay at my parents' house." Lily glanced toward Claire. "This way, she's close but has her own place."

Claire beamed. "Excellent plan."

Ellen jerked back. The Evanses' house—where she could clearly see the back of Dax's house and driveway from her backyard—not to mention his coming and goings? *No, thank you.* Warm, strong hands settled on her shoulders. A bubble formed in the pit of her stomach. She peered over her shoulder.

Smiling, Dax winked. "Don't worry, Claire. I'll keep my eye on her."

Claire patted Dax's shoulder. "You're such a good friend."

Ellen closed her eyes. Seriously…when would she catch a break?

Chapter 5

After church, Ellen went directly to her room. Plucking the copper dress off the back of the chair, she carefully hung the garment over the hanger before slipping the outfit inside the garment bag. She laid the bag beside the opened luggage. A million thoughts spun through her mind—of her staying in Aberdeen, of her living in the house next to her mother, of her working at a high school job *again*. But the most concerning was the proximity to Dax's house and the promise he made to her mother.

Smoothing a hand over the plastic bag, she imagined opening the door and finding him standing in front of her looking too gorgeous for any girl's peace of mind. Oh man...seeing Dax for one night was one thing. For two months...pure torture. Could she avoid him?

She considered the possibility. Aberdeen was small. Places to go and things to do were limited. The town had one bank, two churches, a few restaurants, a café, and two bars. In other words, Aberdeen was not a place where you could hide from people.

When local residents purchased groceries, they stopped at Stop 'n Shop. If they wanted pizza, they went to Papa's. When they desired coffee and gossip, they went to Betty's.

She could probably forgo grocery shopping,

because honestly, she and cooking did not mix. Resisting Papa's would be harder. Not only did she love their pizza, but they were also the *only* pizza joint in a twenty-mile radius. Sure, she could give up the delicious meal for two months, but did she really want to just to avoid seeing Dax? Besides, the point was moot, because in the end, he'd show up at Betty's—where she was now employed. Didn't it just figure?

The door clicked open.

Ellen peered over her shoulder.

"Just wanted to check about dinner tonight." Claire strolled into the room. "I can expect you, right?"

Ugh. The family dinner. The one meal her mother insisted everyone attend, including Dax. How the heck could she get out of this one? Reaching inside the closet, Ellen yanked out a green, satin blouse. "I can't."

"What?"

Focusing on the fabric, Ellen folded the blouse to prevent creases. "If I am staying for two months, I have to go back to my apartment to pick up some clothing."

"I suppose." Sighing, Claire propped a hip against the dresser. "Now, are you sure you want to stay at Lily's parents' house?"

Nestling the shirt inside the compartment, she turned to see Claire holding the silver frame. Ellen's heart slammed. Walking to the closet, she scooped up a pair of boots. "I've lived on my own for a while now."

"I suppose." Claire held out the picture. "This is yours."

Dropping her gaze, Ellen peered at the image of herself with Dax. Happiness wreathed their faces. Her stomach fluttered. "You keep it."

"Don't be silly." Claire smiled. "I have one, too."

She did? Ellen looked up. "Since when?"

"When I found this picture, I took it over to Copy Creations and had them make a duplicate." She held out the frame. "Nice, isn't it?"

Yeah, just precious. Yanking away her gaze, Ellen shrugged. "It's a long time ago."

Claire sighed. "You two were always the best of friends."

Running a thumb along the rough zipper, Ellen thought back to her youth. As a teenager, she had rebelled against all the accolades Ben received. Then, Dax had been her anchor and the one person who kept her centered. Now, though... Sighing, she set the boots inside the luggage. "Yeah, well, nothing remains the same."

"What is going on between you two?"

Ellen peered at her mother. Worry and concern filled Claire's eyes. Turning aside, she smoothed a hand over the soft leather boots. "What do you mean?"

"I'm not blind, you know. I can see something is off between you and Dax."

Great. Was she so obvious? She strolled to the bureau. "Nothing is going on." Peering into the mirror, she saw her mother watching her. She put a half smile on her face and turned. "We've just moved apart. Nothing more."

"Then this picture is even more important." Claire held out the frame. "It will remind you of your past."

If only her mother knew how much she wanted to forget that part of her past. She stared at the image in her mother's hand. No way could she get out of taking the blasted thing now. Sighing, she tossed the hairbrush into the luggage.

Claire pressed the frame into Ellen's chest.

Having no other choice, Ellen held the picture without glancing at the image. "Gee, thanks, Mom. Appreciate the thought."

"I knew you would." Claire strolled to the door. "Now, you'll drive safely, right? Or should I see if Dax can go? I'm sure he wouldn't mind."

Oh heck no. Ellen gave her mother a tight smile. "No need. I'd hate to ruin his day."

Claire pinched her lips into a frown. "I really think Dax should go along. If a storm strikes, I don't want you driving on ice-slick streets."

Ellen huffed. "Mom, I'm an adult. I think I can handle a little snow."

"I'm calling Dax."

She clenched her teeth. "*Mom...*"

"Just to check."

Ellen gritted her teeth. Like heck she wanted to be alone with Dax for three hours. What the heck would they talk about? Would he want to discuss their last time together? Yeah, like she wanted to relive such a horrifying moment. She clutched the frame against her chest. "Seriously, I don't—"

The door clicked shut.

Looking down at the frame, Ellen narrowed her gaze. She tossed the frame into the luggage and finished packing. If she had any luck, she'd be gone before her mother found Dax.

Pulling into the Evanses' driveway, Ellen peered across the backyard. Just across the shrubs, she spied Dax's empty parking spot. A rush of air ripped from her. Of course, he wasn't home. Knowing him, he probably had a date. A bitter taste settled on her tongue.

She parked the car and stared at the back of his house. What did she care if he had a date? In the next two months, she was bound to witness him on a date once or twice—or a couple dozen times. Her stomach twisted.

She tapped fingers on the steering wheel. If she put the car in Reverse, she could be in Albany in an hour. In no time she would be settled in her tiny, bland apartment and moving on with her life. Maybe even hanging out with her girlfriends and laughing over the disastrous turn of events in her life. Sure, her mother would be disappointed, but she'd eventually get over it, right?

Tightness crept up her back. Pressing her head against the headrest, she closed her eyes. No way could she hurt her mother again. She heaved a sigh. She'd have to stay, at least until she could figure out her next move.

A knock sounded on her window.

Yelping, she snapped open her eyes. Her heart leaped, and her breath caught.

Dax stared back.

A sparkle of laughter lit his eyes, and a sexy smile split his lips. A bit of wind ruffled his hair. She frowned. *What the heck?* How had he snuck across the yards? She yanked free the keys and shoved open the door, forcing him to step back. "You've got to be kidding." Just her luck, the one day she actually wanted Dax to be on a date. But could the universe answer her request? No, of course not. Frowning, she stepped from the car. The sharp gust of cold air sent shivers skittering over her flesh. "I'm surprised my mother found you."

"Yeah?" He smiled. "Why?"

She rolled her eyes. Yeah, like she'd feed his ego. She brushed past him. "You know, you don't need to worry. I'm a big girl now."

Waggling his brows, he dipped his gaze slightly. "No doubt about it."

This time she couldn't help herself. She rolled her eyes and stomped toward the trunk. "Seriously. I don't want you to keep your date waiting."

"Worried, are you?"

She spun about. "Not even a little."

He laughed. "Now. Now. You're sounding a bit defensive."

Snapping back her head, she glared. "I am *not* defensive." She pressed the button on the fob. The trunk popped open. "And I *don't* need a chaperone. Despite what my mother believes, I am *quite* capable of driving myself to Albany."

Dax propped one hip against the side of the vehicle and crossing arms over his chest, he sighed. "No one is saying you're not."

Ellen frowned. "Oh yeah? Mom doesn't think I'm capable." She reached inside the trunk. "She wouldn't have called and asked you to drive me to Albany, if she did."

Nudging aside her hand, Dax snagged the luggage handle. "Maybe she's worried." He hefted the bag with a low grunt. "Jeez, Ellen, what did you pack?"

"Just a few outfits."

Shifting the bag into his other hand, he closed the trunk. "You sure you have any clothes left in Albany?"

"Ha. Ha. Very funny." She marched up the porch steps and jammed the key into the lock. Shoving open the door, she glanced over her shoulder. "Maybe, my luggage isn't the problem."

He stepped inside the kitchen. "Oh yeah?"

Warmth surrounded her, which she was positive had nothing to do with the furnace and everything to do with the man standing far too close. However, she refused to let his presence affect her. "Maybe it's you." She tossed the keys in the air before snagging them again. "Maybe, you're weaker than you think."

A burst of laughter ripped from him, causing the muscles in his chest to flex against his shirt. "Yeah. Maybe that's the problem." He looked around the kitchen. "So, where do you want me to put this case?"

Excellent question. Seeing as she'd never been inside the Evanses' house, she really had no idea where she'd sleep. However, she refused to let Dax step inside *any* bedroom. She fanned a finger toward the table. "There." Gripping her purse, she stepped outside. The crisp air caused a shiver to slide down her spine. She hugged both arms over her chest. "I suppose I don't have a choice but to let you go. Even with the guilt trip, I don't want Mom to worry."

"Smart girl." Quietly shutting the door, Dax started across the yard.

Frowning, Ellen watched Dax walk toward his house. "I thought we'd take my car."

He stopped and looked toward her car before turning back. "No way. Your car is a death trap." He pushed through the shrubs.

Ellen hastily locked the door. She should just leave. That would show him. Only, an image of her mother's worried gaze flashed through her thoughts. Dropping her shoulders and fisting her hands, she marched after him. "I'll have you know my car is brand new and rated extremely safe on the road."

Dax stopped next to the passenger door of his large truck. A smile twitched on his lips. "Sugar, I don't care how the auto industry rates that vehicle. One ice patch and we'll spin out of control. My vehicle is much safer." He pulled open the truck door. "Climb in."

Ellen considered telling him to pound salt. After all, she *hadn't* wanted him to come in the first place, but remembering the image of her mother's anxious gaze, she sighed and climbed inside. "Fine. But just know, I don't *need* you."

Pressing his forearms against both sides of the open door and leaning in, he swept his gaze over her. "Baby girl, someday you just might believe that lie."

The smell of heat and man surrounded her. A little shiver slid down her spine—not so much from him calling her baby girl, but the way the words fairly dripped off his lips, like warm honey on a cold night— soft, sensual, and far too alluring.

She slammed the seatbelt into place. Dang it. She should have listened to the little voice inside her head insisting she go back to Albany. If she had, she wouldn't be stuck with Dax for the next three hours. She wove fingers together. Now what the heck would she do?

****

Rumbling down the mountainous road, Dax slid a sideways glance toward Ellen. Her back was ramrod straight, her fingers clutched tight in her lap, and her lips pinched into a frown. She looked completely unnerved and uncomfortable. He hated the wedge separating their once-close friendship. He tapped fingers onto the steering wheel, wondering what he could say to break the tension. "Listen, Ellen. You'll be in town for the next two months."

She stiffened and, turning slowly, she furrowed her brow. "Yeah. So?"

Why did she have to make things so difficult? He sighed. "Well, I just was thinking maybe we should at least try to keep up the pretense of friendship."

Ellen jerked back and narrowed her eyes. "Oh, so now you want to be friends?"

Her words stung. A part of him wanted to demand what she expected from a twenty-four-year-old whose home life had been cobbled together by a mother working two jobs and caring neighbors? But pride and pain held him back. He stared straight ahead. "I never wanted to lose your friendship."

The silence stretched between them.

Finally, a sigh rippled from her. "Fine. We'll pretend nothing happened. Worked for six years, right?"

He gritted his teeth. *Ouch.* "I just thought—"

"No, you're right." She sighed again. "I don't want Mom or Ben to be upset."

He understood her concern, but what about their friendship? Didn't she miss their closeness even a little? Right now, though, he'd take whatever she offered. "So, what about Betty's? How do you feel about working there?"

Reaching out, she flipped the button for the radio before settling on a channel. "It's not exactly brain science."

"Not everything has to be about solving the world's problems." He flicked a glance toward the radio. Some ridiculous pop tune blared from the speakers. "This song proves my point."

Her mouth dropped open, but a sparkle lit her eyes. "I'll have you know this song is very popular."

He arched a brow. "But not very interesting."

She laughed. "Yeah, you're right." She settled on some classic rock. "Better?"

"Much." He slid a sideways glance in her direction and saw she stared out the window. "What's wrong?"

Running fingers along the window's edge, she sighed. "I worked hard to move up in my career, and now, I can't help but think I've wasted my life."

Dax arched a brow. "You're twenty-eight. You've got a long life ahead."

She fanned a hand. "Oh, I know."

The sound of sadness in her words broke his heart. Dax tightened his grip on the steering wheel. He'd learned enough of the story from Ben to wonder what kind of man would steal a job from the woman he dated. Reaching down, he grabbed her hand and gave a little squeeze. Yes, he was greedy. He wanted her to remain in Aberdeen until he could convince her to see him in ways other than a guy who breaks hearts. However, he couldn't, *wouldn't*, hold her back from her dreams. "Just a minor detour."

For a moment, her fingers cupped his, and then, just as swiftly, she stiffened and snatched back her hand. "I don't know." She returned her gaze to the window. "Maybe I'm not cut out to be a vice president. Maybe Grant is the better choice."

How could she defend a guy who stole her job? He glared. "No, he's a loser."

She turned and frowned. "You don't even know him."

"Listen, I have no idea about advertising or what the business is like." He pulled his gaze from the snow-covered scenery. "But one thing I know is if a guy really loves a woman, he doesn't steal her job, and that, sugar, is fact."

Her lips thinned, and her eyes narrowed.

Did she still have feelings for Grant? The idea that she might really torqued him. Pressing his foot to the gas, Dax blew out a ragged breath. "If you don't want to be a barista, do something else." He fanned a hand. "Start your own ad agency."

"Yeah, right." She snorted. "Because Albany needs one more agency."

"Maybe not Albany." Dax tapped fingers on the steering wheel. "But Aberdeen sure could."

"Aberdeen?" She burst out laughing. "What would I market?"

"I could name a couple dozen places needing help." He stared at the skyline of Albany. Tall skyscrapers grazed the gray clouds. He hadn't even pulled into the city, but already he felt the muscles tightening in his neck and shoulders. He couldn't imagine preferring the busy, over-crowded, claustrophobic city to the relaxing, slow-paced, wide-sweeping area and fresh, pine air of the mountains. "But I'll give you one example—The Holiday Festival."

She rolled her eyes. "Seriously?"

"Take the name—Holiday Festival." He shot a quick glance in Ellen's direction. "We need something snappy, like—" He thought for a moment. "The North Pole."

She laughed. "Yeah, real original."

"Okay, I get your point." He chuckled. "Good thing I didn't go into advertising, right?"

She turned away and stared out the window.

Dax sighed. *Maybe driving her hadn't been a good idea.*

"Hometown Holidays."

Her words surprised him. Dax furrowed his brow. "What?"

"Hometown Holidays." She tapped fingers on her legs. "We could promote everything from Santa's arrival to the lighting of the Christmas tree and all the rest of the holiday hoopla."

He nodded. "See? The town needs you—Betty's, Sandy's Real Estate, and all the other little shops. They need a professional."

She chewed her lip.

Dax knew when not to push. He planted the seed. She'd need to make it grow. He turned into the parking lot marked by a sign reading *The Regency*—Ellen's apartment complex. For such a regal name, the building looked weathered and worn, especially compared to some of the newer, swankier communities surrounding the area. A row of moss-green buildings, three stories tall, lined the sidewalk. Snow-coated shrubs separated the sidewalk from the patios. In six years, little had changed.

Pulling into a vacant visitor space, Dax shut off the vehicle and yanked the keys from the ignition. He shoved open the door and stepped out.

Ellen stopped in the front of the vehicle and shot a quick glance toward the building before turning. "You remembered?"

Like he could forget. He met her wide-eyed stare

and smiled. "Baby girl, I remember plenty of things." He saw the way the pulse leapt in her throat. Smiling, he caught her hand and guided her along the walk and up the stairs.

She opened the apartment door. After tossing her purse and keys on the jet-black coffee table, she turned. "Be right back."

He wandered around the apartment, wondering how often Grant had spent the night. The muscles in his neck tensed. Of course, the man spent the night, but damn if the truth didn't irk. Everything in the place reminded him of Ellen—from the white painted walls to the ebony furniture. Even the row of vibrant red and glittering gold pillows covering the leather couch screamed Ellen.

A tiny glass table filled a space just off from the galley kitchen. A bouquet of silk flowers in blues, reds, and purples arranged in a speckled gold vase graced the surface. A three-shelf plant stand held pots filled with brown stalks. Poor things. They never stood a chance with Ellen's inept gardening skills.

He strolled into the living room and sat. Grabbing the remote, he flipped on the screen and scrolled through the channels. After two turns through the guide, he realized his choices were limited—either watch a cricket game or some ridiculous romance. He had no idea how she survived with such barbaric options. Disgusted, he tossed the remote on the tiny coffee table and stood.

The soft hum of her voice floated into the living room.

Strolling over, Dax peered inside her bedroom. The bed, now covered in a soft-cream comforter and filled

65

with fluffy pillows in colors ranging from soft pinks to cool blues to vibrant greens, held his attention.

The one night, six years ago, came back in a flash—the smell of her velvety flesh—all flowery and fresh, the touch of her hair—silky and smooth, the taste of her breath—minty with just a hint of beer, to the look she gave him the next morning—nervous and worried. His chest tightened.

Ellen, buried deep within her closet, turned. "I know. I know. I'm hurrying."

He shifted his gaze to the mile-high mound of clothing covering her bed. One tiny carry-on lay open on the bed. "Not sure how you plan to fit that pile into your luggage."

Tucking a strand of hair behind her ear, she flicked a glance toward the bed, then to him. "Oh, I'm not taking them."

He pulled one outfit out of the pile—a silky, black number with a deep vee down the front and a matching one down the back. An image of him slowly removing the gown from her body flashed through his thoughts. Heat filled him. Yeah, he liked the image. "Bring this." He held out the dress.

Glancing toward the garment, she shook her head. "That dress is for summer, not winter."

What the hell did she mean? A dress was a dress, wasn't it? Besides, didn't matter what season she wore the gown, given the opportunity, he'd have it off her in seconds. "I like it."

Laughing, she turned back to the row of clothing hanging on the wooden rod. "You would."

He didn't know what she meant by that comment, either. Smiling, he held out the dress, imagining her wearing it to the station's party. "It's the holidays. You'll need a dress to wear."

Ellen peered over her shoulder. "Working at the café doesn't require cocktail wear."

"Okay, maybe not, but you might attend other parties."

She studied him for a moment before shrugging. "Fine." She collected the dress and placed it in the luggage. "Though, to be honest, I'll look completely out of place in such a gown. It's more for hobnobbing with CEOs and business owners."

He could picture her in such a place too, mingling with the sleek and powerful all the while laughing and charming them. His stomach tightened. All the things she loved, and he hated. He leaned back against the wall and watched her finish packing, wondering what the heck he planned. They lived in two different worlds, and the bridge separating them was too far to cross.

Closing the luggage's lid, she slid her gaze around the room. "I should have everything."

Her words jerked him back. He eyed the bag and compared it to the mound of clothing covering the bed. "You sure?" He pushed away from the wall and walked over. Flipping open the top, he skimmed his gaze over the clothing—two pairs of jeans, a couple of shirts, the dress, and some leggings he knew she'd look great in, but surely not enough for two months. "You can't be serious. Those outfits won't last you a week."

She slapped away his hand. "I can do laundry."

Shaking his head, he strode toward the closet. He reached inside, and skimming fingers across the tops of metal hangers, he shifted through the outfits. He chose a mixture of blouses, sweaters, and tees, then added another couple pairs of jeans and dress slacks. Walking over, he dropped the selection next to the luggage. "Bring them."

She frowned. "How long do you think I'm staying?"

The word forever almost slipped out. Instead, he shrugged. "You never know, but I have a sister, and I know women like a lot of clothing."

Crossing arms over her chest, she nibbled her lip. Finally, she sighed. "I guess you're right." She walked over to the closet and stared upward at the luggage on the top shelf. On tippy-toes, she stretched an arm upward. Her fingers grazed the rim.

Reaching above her head, Dax extracted the bag and placed it on the bed. Remembering the overabundance of clothing, shoes, and jewelry his sister had always packed, he leaned against the bureau. "Better grab some shoes. Jewelry, too."

She snapped up her gaze and shot him a look.

He shrugged. "Just in case…" A look of confusion settled in her gaze, but she did as he suggested. While she finished packing, he strolled toward the window and peered out to the courtyard. In the distance, he could see the pool, draped in blue plastic and surrounded by a black iron fence. The once-lush landscape was cloaked in white.

"Okay. I should have enough."

Turning away, he skimmed his gaze over the contents. Inside, she'd tucked a pair of boots, another pair of flats, two pairs of sneakers looking suspiciously new, and one pair of black heels. Remembering a pair of sexy leopard print shoes, he walked to the closet and snagged them. He strolled to the bed and dropped them into the luggage.

"These?" She looked up and knitted her brow. "Where would I wear them?"

He pictured her dressing in nothing but them. Desire burst inside him. He let out a strangled cough. "Alexis is in town. I'm sure you'll find a reason"

She curled her lips and sighed. "Yeah, you're probably right."

Grabbing the luggage handles, he walked from the room and opened the door. Long shadows spilled across the ground and a sharp nip in the air bit his flesh. He turned to see her right behind him. "Ready to go?"

She looked around. "You think I'm doing the right thing?"

Noting the apprehension in her eyes and the white knuckles from clutching her purse, Dax debated the answer. Giving up one's dream had to be difficult. He couldn't imagine what he'd do if he suddenly found out he couldn't be a fireman any longer. His whole identity was wrapped in his career choice. Now, she was forced to take a job beneath her dreams just to make her mother happy. The choice was impossible. He supposed all he could do was reassure and hope he wasn't wrong. "Sugar, I believe everything will work out just fine."

A shudder ripped through her. "I sure hope so."

After he got her luggage settled in the back of his truck, he drove her to the Tin Tinker. The bar held fond memories. When Ben played ball, they'd come to the restaurant after the game.

"Aren't you going to Mom's for dinner?"

Eating Sunday dinner with the Jordans was the one family ritual he savored. Today, however, he thought to make an exception. Dax parked the truck. "She'll understand."

Ellen eyed him for a moment. "I don't want you getting any ideas."

Too late. He already had plenty of ideas. Too bad he couldn't share any of them with her. Chuckling, he pushed open the door. "Sugar, I wouldn't dream of it." Stepping inside the bar, Dax slid his gaze around the area. The scent of fried food and stale beer filled the area. The place was only moderately full. A half-dozen or so men sat at the bar eating chicken wings and sipping beer. Every few moments, they'd either cheer or curse, depending on their team's play on the overhead screens. A group of young college boys played pool while eyeing a tableful of young women. A middle-aged couple ate at another table. No one paid them any attention.

She glanced around. Clasping fingers together, she clutched her hands against her chest and shot Dax a wide grin. "I haven't been here in years."

Her announcement surprised him. He couldn't picture her inside the dingy place. He stopped at the bar and pulled out two stools. "Yeah? You've been here?"

She climbed onto one and dropped her purse on the counter. "In college with my girlfriends."

Settling himself in the vacant chair, he grabbed a menu and shot her another glance. "Slumming it, were you?"

"Sure. Why not?" Shrugging, she peered around the room. A soft smile split her face. "Great place to end the night."

He stilled, knowing only too well what her words meant. Many a night he finished in the place, and he never left alone either. An image of some guy picking her up and taking her home burned through him. He clenched the menu. "So, I'm assuming you never went home alone?"

She arched a brow, and a smile twitched on her lips. "Nope. I always left with someone."

How careless—reckless. Images, one after another flashed through his thoughts, and all of them were horrid and frightening. He couldn't believe she'd take such a chance. Tossing down the menu, he turned in the seat. His knees pressed against hers. Fisting a hand on the bar, he held her gaze. "You went home with a stranger?"

Her eyes sparkled. "You're acting like my brother."

Hell. He didn't know what insulted him more—the fact she'd just equated him to her brother, or her laughing off the risk. "Do you realize how much danger you put yourself in?"

"Dax, relax." She picked up the discarded menu. "I just meant I went home with my friends."

The burst of jealousy evaporated, replaced by a feeling of foolishness. He should have known by the sparkle in her eyes, she teased him. He held her gaze. "I don't like the thought of what could have happened."

"I was careful." The laughter in her eyes faded. She pressed together her lips for just a moment before dropping her gaze to the menu. "Besides, I've learned my lesson. One-night stands aren't my thing."

Her words were meant to sting. However, he couldn't dredge one ounce of regret. If the only thing he taught was safety, then so be it. He snatched the menu from her hands. "Good. You're worth more than a fling."

A flash lit her gaze. "Yeah?" She fisted a hand. "I seem to recall a time when that wasn't the case."

Ouch. Dax waved a hand to the bartender before facing her. "Yeah, well, I guess we all have regrets."

She stared for a moment before the bartender arrived.

Dax ordered a beer.

Ellen ordered a soda.

After the bartender left, he skimmed the menu. An unnecessary effort considering the place was known for one thing. "Burger?"

She fanned a hand. "Of course."

Dax turned his attention to the television over the bar. A college football game played over the screen. He leaned back, and picking up his drink, he pointed toward the game. "Sometimes, your dad and I would come here and watch the games."

Ellen widened her eyes. "Seriously?"

Taking a sip, Dax nodded. "Yup. When Ben was in season, we'd come here before the game."

"You and Dad?"

Placing his drink on a small, square paper napkin, Dax turned and stared. "You act surprised."

She swallowed her sip. "I just never knew. Whenever he came to see me, he was alone."

"I drove myself, seeing I'd be spending the night." He smiled. "But I always knew to meet Robert here."

"He liked being with you." Lifting her drink, she swirled the glass. Ice clinked against the side. "Thought of you like a son." Sipping liquid up the tiny straw, she shrugged. "Of course, he was probably like most fathers. Any time he could get to watch a game with you or Ben, he jumped at the chance."

He compared the man he thought of as his father to the man whose genes ran through him. The comparison was laughable. He didn't want to ruin Ellen's picture-perfect image of family, though. Dax picked up his drink. "Yeah." Taking a sip, he ignored the lump in his throat. "Maybe."

Chapter 6

The next morning, a persistent screech jolted Ellen upright. With her heart slamming, she smacked a hand against the snooze button. Blessed silence filled the room. Slipping deep beneath the blankets, she snuggled the pillow and let out a soft sigh before drifting back to sleep.

Nine minutes later, the alarm blared once more. Again, Ellen silenced the noise before dozing off. Three more times the alarm buzzed, and each time, she shut off the alarm and fell asleep. By the fifth, she had enough. Snapping open her eyes, she grabbed the freaking thing, and yanking the cord, she ripped the plug from the socket. The numerals turned dark. She hurled the blasted thing across the room.

The clock sailed through the air, missing the discarded stack of pillows tossed on the floor. The loud crash of glass shattering into a million sparkling pieces of regret broke the silence.

Jerking upright, Ellen stared at the gaping hole. The curtain fluttered softly in the sharp, cold breeze. Goose pebbles covered her flesh. Raking fingers through her hair, she closed her eyes and groaned. Her first night at the Evanses' house, and she'd already broken something. *Criminy...*

She kicked off the sheets and put on her slippers. Darting across the room, she carefully avoided any shards. Pushing aside the curtains, she stared out into the night. Twinkling stars glittered in the pitch-black sky.

She searched the shadows for the clock—nothing. Scooping her robe off the foot of the bed, she shoved her arms through the sleeves, all the while dreading explaining this debacle to Ben. No way would he understand. He *never* used an alarm clock and still woke up at the crack of dawn without fail. *Figures. He* got the auto-alarm gene while she was blessed with the sleep-in one.

Why the heck had she set the alarm anyway?

She stiffened. *Oh man.* She forgot about her newly acquired job. *Great. Just great.* She never caught any breaks. A sharp breeze whistled through the window, sending goosebumps across her flesh. Shivering, she hurried to the closet. Spying a raggedy blanket, she tugged it out and proceeded to cover the opening.

Thirty minutes later, with the window finally covered and a few of her outfits relocated to the downstairs bedroom—the only logical solution, considering the whole upstairs was freezing—Ellen finally stepped out of the house.

She immediately spied Dax's place through the gap in the trees. Her stomach fluttered. Dax had suggested they have a truce—at least for the next two months. Could she trust him? She chewed her lip. What choice did she have?

If she was honest, a teeny, tiny part wanted to move beyond that night. If they couldn't return to the friendship they once shared, maybe they could create something new—something safer and easier. Besides, after New Year's, she'd return to Albany, leaving behind Dax and the past.

She ignored the lump in her throat and climbed inside her car. After all, she had more important things occupying her thoughts—namely, starting her high school job. *Yay*.

The faint glow of sunrise softened the horizon's edge, cutting through the inky, purple-blue sky. Overhead, a silver crescent moon slunk behind thick, gray clouds. The glow of streetlights illuminated puddles dotting the empty roads.

Life in Aberdeen woke slowly.

Ellen drove down the familiar streets, and the tightness in her chest eased. Despite her escape years past, she'd missed the comfortable simplicity of a town she'd called home for eighteen years.

Turning onto Main Street, she skimmed her gaze around the deserted area and turned into the alley behind the café. A shiver slid down her spine. She hated the narrow, deserted passage with the dark shadows. Sure, crime was practically non-existent in Aberdeen, but the way she figured, if someone had nefarious intentions, this alley with its oversized dumpsters and recessed doorways provided the perfect hiding places. Pulling into the spot adjacent to the back of the café, Ellen slid her gaze around the area.

Litter and debris clung to the chain-link fence along the property line. On the opposite side of the fence, a few lights lit the back area of Manson's Mini-Mart. She looked down the length of the alley. Other than a stray piece of paper drifting along on a gust of wind, the area was deserted.

Ellen grabbed her purse and climbed from the car. Clutching the opening of her coat in one hand and her purse in the other, she raced down the lane. Bitter wind whipped her face and snagged her hair. Brushing aside the strands, she hurried to the front of the café and skidded to a stop. Not a scrap of light shone from the café's window. *What the heck?* Her mother had insisted she arrive promptly at five. A quick glance at her watch showed three minutes before.

She peered down the empty streets. Leaves mingling with snow flurries swirled across the road. An empty can clattered along the sidewalk. A few cars sat parked in front of Karla's Kitchen, and bright lights shone from the massive window of the police station, but otherwise, the town remained in deep sleep.

A flash of headlights turning onto Main Street drew Ellen's attention. She watched the car slow before disappearing down the alley. Seconds later, the car's engine shut off and the soft patter of rubber soles sounded on the concrete.

Betty stepped from the alley. "Didn't expect you this early."

"Mom said you're here by five."

Laughing, Betty slipped a key into the lock and opened the café's door. "Yeah. *I* am." She flipped on the lights. "I don't expect you for another half hour."

"Great." Raking fingers through her hair, Ellen stepped inside. "I broke Lily's window, thinking I was late."

Betty peered over her shoulder. "Seems a bit extreme, doesn't it?"

"You think?" Ellen clutched the strap of her purse. "Ben will kill me."

"Yup."

Ellen scowled. "Gee, don't sound so sad."

Shrugging, Betty made her way across the room. "Just a realist." She stopped behind a long, stainless-steel counter and tossed down the keys. "You ready for your big day?"

No. Ellen forced a smile. "Yup."

"Aw. Don't look so scared. You'll do fine." Reaching beneath the counter, Betty extracted a folded piece of red fabric which she handed to Ellen. "Come on. I'll show you how to open this place."

Slipping the apron over her head and tying the sash, Ellen followed Betty into the backroom. She noticed two things right off the bat—the strong smell of solvents in the air and sharp utensils on hooks tacked to the wall. Her stomach knotted. Everyone knew she wasn't a cook. Heck, the last time she tried the Suzy Homemaker routine, she blew her monthly food budget in one shopping trip and came darn close to burning down her apartment in the process. Her landlord suggested she stick to takeout. She heartily agreed.

Now, looking around the kitchen with its massive, industrial fridge, the large gas stove, and knives and appliances of every kind, she wondered if perhaps her mother hated her. Maybe her instinct yesterday was right—maybe returning to Aberdeen, even for two months, was a bad idea. First, with Dax, and now the death-trap job, surely, those had to be signs from heaven, right?

Betty leaned against a long stainless-steel counter. "What's wrong?"

Ellen cracked her knuckles. "I think clawing my way up the marketing ladder was easier."

"Yeah?" Betty arched a brow. "How did that work out?"

Too cruel, Betty... Ellen lifted her chin. "Just a temporary setback."

A short laugh rippled from Betty. "Well, I, for one, am glad." She shoved away from the counter and walked to the desk. "By the way, I'm looking for a manager."

"Oh yeah?" Ellen pulled her gaze from the rack of sharp knives. "I wouldn't think you'd need one."

"Well, I've been an early bird most of my life. Now, though, I find I'd rather sleep in." Betty peered over her shoulder. "So, I need someone to open in the morning. Someone who I can trust to run the place—my backup, so to speak. You think you might be interested?"

Stay and see Dax *every day?* Wasn't two months enough torture? *Nah uh. No way.* "I had planned to go back to Albany after the holidays."

Betty removed a piece of paper from the bulletin board. "You might change your mind."

Ellen couldn't imagine such a thing. After all, she wasn't supposed to be a barista. Wasn't her goal in life to be a high-powered ad exec?

"This guide will help you until things become familiar." Betty fanned a laminated sheet. "You won't need it today, but you might in the future."

Grateful to avoid answering, Ellen took the paper. At some point, Betty had created a step-by-step list of the whole day, from opening to closing. Little notes scratched in ballpoint pen littered the margins. Some were phone numbers. Others were added instructions.

"Leave it on the bulletin board." Betty waved a hand. "So, it's always available."

After tacking the paper onto the corkboard, Ellen

turned to see Betty by the stove. She strolled over. "What are you doing?"

Betty turned a knob. A second later, a blue flame sparked. Grabbing a large griddle, she placed it upon the burner. "Cooking bacon." She unwrapped a brown-paper-wrapped package exposing a slab of meat mottled with thick strips of white. She tilted her head toward the far counter. "You'll cut the bagels."

Ellen's stomach lurched. Weaving together fingers, she glanced at the boxes littering the space, all presumably filled with bagels. "Is Mom aware of these plans?"

Betty dumped the meat in the pan. "Of course."

Okay, now she knew her mother had foul intentions. Chewing her lip, she flipped open one box and peered inside. A dozen bagels stared back—all nice and neat without a drop of blood staining them. A queasy feeling settled in her belly. "And she knows I'll be using a knife?"

Betty whipped around, holding the tongs elevated in the air. "Heavens, no. She's not looking for your death."

Ellen heaved a sigh. "Oh, thank goodness. For a minute, I wasn't certain."

Chuckling, Betty set the tongs on the counter, then walked over and pulled out a metal stand. "You'll use this slicer." She selected a bagel, and dropping the roll into a slot, she flipped the handle.

Seconds later, a blade swooshed down, splitting the bagel into two perfect halves.

Betty grabbed out the two halves, waving them in the air. "See? No knife and all fingers remain intact."

Seemed easy enough. A half-hour later, as she

watched Betty wind gauze around her thumb, Ellen reconsidered her first thoughts.

Peering upward, Betty frowned. "Tell me again how you cut your thumb?"

Ellen tried her best to ignore the sting of pain and the burn of embarrassment. "I followed your directions to the T. I put the bagel in that guillotine-thingy and pressed the lever."

"Not possible." Betty tore off the tape with her teeth. "The guillotine-thingy has guards to prevent injury."

Chewing her lip, Ellen stared at her misshapen thumb. "The thing is dangerous."

Betty laughed.

Ellen glared "What? You don't believe me?"

"The bagel slicer isn't dangerous. You are." Dropping the roll into the metal compartment, Betty placed the kit on the shelf. She fanned a hand. "Let's see what damage you can do making coffee."

Happily, Ellen could say she didn't burn down the place. She did steam off a few fingerprints, though, which just added to her pathetic look. But, in the end, she figured out the whole coffee/latte-making business and only had to remake a dozen or so drinks in the process. Bonus, only one customer complained—Horace Miller—no surprise considering he was the grumpiest policeman patrolling the town. The rest took her mistakes in stride.

Mrs. Emerly declared the drink Ellen made was the tastiest she'd ever tried.

"Come and help me set up this table."

Betty's voice drew Ellen from staring at her sorry-looking hands. Sighing, she walked to where Betty stood with a table leaning against the wall. The morning rush had ended, and except for Mrs. Peabody, the café was empty. "Where do you want it?"

Scanning the room, Betty pointed to the far wall. "There. This way the crowd won't block the customers getting coffee."

Gingerly grabbing one end, Ellen assisted Betty with the table. "Got something special going on here?"

They stopped by the wall.

Ellen dropped her end.

Popping out one table leg, Betty looked up. "The guys are signing calendars today."

Ellen's stomach lurched. *What was that?* Swallowing past the lump in her throat, she fumbled pulling out the table leg. "All the guys or just some?"

Betty flipped the table. "Not sure."

Ellen wasn't fooled. She knew without a doubt no calendar signing would be complete without Mr. January. On a vacant table sat a small, white vase with a plastic daisy tucked inside. Grabbing the urn, she ran her thumb along the rough, plastic edges, imagining Dax walking in and spying her. Could she handle seeing him again? Did she have a choice?

"What are you doing?"

Ellen jerked up her gaze to see Betty smoothing a hand over a white cloth draped on the table's surface. Her cheeks burned. Quickly, she arranged the vase in the center of the table. "I just thought I'd make the area a little more attractive."

Betty snorted. "Trust me. In about ten minutes, it will be attractive enough."

Oh boy, wasn't that the truth. Ellen hurried to the counter and slipped a paper cup off the stack. Shoving the cup beneath the spigot, she flipped the lever. Her mind spun. Could she seriously endure working the rest of her shift with Dax in the same room, pretending she didn't notice him or the crowds of fawning women? Did she have a choice?

The bell over the door sounded.

Ellen turned. Dax strode into the café looking impossibly attractive wearing a brown-leather bomber coat and dark denims. A whole kaleidoscope of butterflies swirled in her stomach. *Dang it.* How had he worked his magic in just one afternoon, whittling away the entire wall she'd painstakingly built these past six years?

He glanced across the room.

His sapphire gaze collided with hers. In that moment, she realized all the disdain she had carefully reinforced over the years had disappeared somewhere between Albany and Aberdeen. She swallowed. Staying in Aberdeen wasn't just dangerous but wrought with landmines and broken hearts.

Chapter 7

The line of women standing out front of Betty's Café surprised Dax. He never understood the whole, sexy fireman vibe that attracted women. However, when he wanted a woman, he used any tool at his disposal to achieve his goal—including his role in the fire department.

Of course, attracting women had never been a problem. Only now, he didn't necessarily have to include dinner and a movie. He could just drive a woman to his house without a whisper of a complaint. Hell, half the time, the woman made the suggestion. He couldn't find a reason to argue against that happy occurrence.

Because he knew what was expected, he flashed the crowd of women a quick smile and a slow wink, before pulling open the door and stepping inside the café. More giggling, simpering women wearing ridiculously tight dresses and too much makeup stood inside. Any one of them would be more than willing to go home with him tonight. But none capture his attention like the one across the room.

Ellen stilled.

She looked as worn out as an overused pair of sneakers. Auburn tendrils had escaped the disheveled ponytail and now framed her face. A dark smudge, which he suspected belonged to the icing from one of the chocolate-covered pastries in the case, stained her right cheek. Faint shadows circled her eyes. He wondered if she had spent a sleepless night, just like himself.

Curling fingers into a fist, she tucked the hand behind her back.

But not before he caught the unmistakable strip of white gauze padding her thumb. He checked the smile sliding across his mouth. Had she injured herself here or last night after he dropped her off? He dropped his gaze to where she hid her hand, then back up. "Everything okay?"

Straightening, she lifted her chin. "Of course."

He cocked a brow. So, that's how she planned to play it—pretend everything was fine? *Okay*. He could be patient. He leaned in and smiled. "So, sugar, you have a good night's sleep?"

Pink rushed up her neck. She jerked back and narrowed her gaze. "Do you actually want something, or did you come just to remind me of all the reasons why I've stayed away?"

Pressing his palms against the cool, metal surface, he slowly drew his gaze downward. "Maybe both." And just because he so enjoyed seeing her flustered, he added, "*Sugar*."

She pinched her lips into a tight scowl. "Save the endearments for your fan club."

He chuckled. "Oh, baby girl, I know you'll always be my biggest fan."

Ellen gasped. "You wish." She stomped toward the espresso machine.

Despite enjoying the banter, he knew he couldn't continue. Even now, excited voices rose an octave, and the already charged air burgeoned on frenetic anticipation. Pushing away from the counter, he turned and spied Angel across the room. Dressed in an austere black suit with the innocent lace peeking out from the deep *V* of her silky blouse, she conjured images of teeth nips against velvety flesh and low moans and hard thrusts.

She caught his gaze before glancing past him for just a moment, then back. Her green eyes flashed, and her full lips pulled into a thin line.

She had painted her lips in dark red—a color he was certain she chose just to tantalize men. She'd been correct. Her lips had teased and tempted him. Now, they reminded him of all the things he wanted forgotten. Dismissing her, he strode toward the table covered in white linen. A white vase with a yellow, plastic daisy stuck inside decorated the surface. Moving aside the vase, he grabbed the black felt-tip marker.

Jakob Newsome took the seat beside him.

Angel stopped in front of him. "Who is she?"

Clenching the pen, Dax drew his gaze upward. "Excuse me?"

She yanked her gaze from Ellen to Dax. "That woman you were talking to."

Flicking his gaze across the room, Dax locked gazes with Ellen. Her gaze narrowed slightly before she turned aside and dismissed him. He shrugged. "Just a friend."

Jakob snorted.

Angel glanced at Jakob, then back to Dax. "That's it? Just a friend?"

The little bite in her tone was one of the many reasons he was tired of Angel. Her possessiveness, her bossiness, and her endless need to be the center of attention reminded him of all the things he disdained. He leaned back in his chair and shot her a hard look. "Not any of your business." Turning away, he forced a smile and waved to the young woman in line.

The woman rushed forward, forcing Angel to take a step back.

Ignoring Angel, Dax accepted the calendar. "Morning, darlin'." After that, he had little time to do anything but sign calendars and make pleasant small talk. One woman after another strolled past, each seeking an autograph while flirting. After an hour, his hand began to cramp, and his cheeks hurt from the forced smile.

By the time the event ended five hours later, his head throbbed, and his back ached.

Several women lingered in the café.

He searched their faces. None belong to Ellen. Of course, she'd left hours ago without sparing him another glance or goodbye. Tossing his pen on the table, he stood and glanced out the window. The sun had faded, bathing the passing cars in a soft, golden glow.

Angel hurried over and rested a hand on his forearm. "Sorry about earlier." She leaned in and trailed a finger over his bicep. "I just get a little—"

"I've got to go." Disentangling his arm, he reached for his coat.

Angel grabbed his arm again. "I thought we could go out for dinner."

He ground his teeth. For five hours, he signed one calendar after another, and not once during the whole event, had she asked how he did, whether he needed a break, or wanted a drink. Oh, he knew he was a commodity—no better nor worse than an animal—one who made her a lot of money and provided her plenty of pleasure. His needs and concerns were only relative to her own.

But, for her to even suggest he would want to spend another minute with her... He pulled on his coat, breaking the contact, and then dug keys from the coat pocket. "Sorry, darlin'. Not in the mood." He maneuvered around the table.

Her hand caught his arm.

He turned and frowned. "What?"

"What happened?" She peered upward. "I thought—"

The rejection filling her gaze caused his chest to tighten. He ran a thumb over the sharp edge of the key. He never intended to hurt her. However, he knew she wanted more than he could ever give. "Angel, from day one, I told you the deal. Nothing has changed. We're not a couple. We're a convenience. Don't get confused by the two."

Chapter 8

After watching the women-crazed spectacle for hours, Ellen couldn't wait to escape the café. Ducking into the backroom, she whipped off her apron.

Betty strolled inside. "Heading out?"

Pausing in hanging up her apron, Ellen peered over her shoulder. "You don't mind, do you?"

"Nah." Betty walked over to the desk. "Besides, Sissy just arrived."

Ellen dropped the apron on the hook. "I thought you didn't have employees."

"She's a high school student. Hired her just before you." Snatching the laminated paper off the bulletin board, Betty sighed. "She's a sweet one, but let's face it, she'll be just like all the rest of the women in the room. Too busy ogling Dax to focus on coffee."

Go figure a woman staring at Dax—an occurrence she'd seen far more often than she cared to recall. "She'll have stiff competition."

Chuckling, Betty pushed away from the table. "Trust me, there ain't no competition."

Ellen yanked the elastic band from her hair, then raked fingers through the strands. She let out a soft sigh—sweet freedom. "I think you've forgotten about the crowd out there."

"Oh, I haven't forgotten." Betty fanned a hand. "But, if any of those women think they have a chance at

Dax, they're in for a quick lesson. Angel will make certain they understand her intentions."

Wait. What was that? "You mean they really are dating?" Frowning, Ellen snagged her purse from the rack. "Dax told me they were just friends."

"Probably are, but if you ask me, Angel's working hard to keep him. She has her claws in deep." Betty strolled across the room. "And she doesn't look like the type to give up easily."

Ellen remembered the look of possession Angel had given her earlier. Stopping at the pass-through door, she peered back at Betty. "Bummer for her. Considering she is just one in a million." Shoving open the door, she gasped before jumping and facing Betty. *What the heck?* "Mom's here."

"Yeah?" Betty strolled over and peered out. "Oh look, she's getting Dax's autograph."

What the...? Peeking through the gap, Ellen stared past the silly women to the one person she never expected to see in the crowd.

Dax scratched something across the pages causing Claire to chuckle.

A nauseous feeling swirled in Ellen's stomach. She glared at Betty. "You have *got* to be kidding."

"Not sure why you're so upset." Betty turned. "She's not doing anything wrong."

Oh, heck yeah, she was. The whole idea was more than a little disturbing. "Dax is *like* a son." Ellen flung out a hand. "Why does no one remember this fact?"

Betty patted Ellen's shoulder. "Honey, she's not asking out Dax on a date. She's just getting his autograph."

"Doesn't make things better." Stepping back, Ellen

clutched her purse against her chest. No way would she stay and watch her mother acting all silly in front of Dax. She moved toward the back door. "I think I'll just go out this way."

Traumatized by the whole scene, Ellen made a quick stop at Burger, Burger, Burger. She figured she was totally justified—after all, she just witnessed firsthand, her mother as a groupie, and FYI—she wasn't thrilled. If the universe even had a little sympathy, she never would again experience such a hideous sight.

After ordering a greasy, cheesy double-double, an extra-large, super-crunchy, double-crispy order of fries, and a triple-thick, double-fudgy chocolicious milkshake, she drove home. Ripping the keys from the ignition, she grabbed her purse and bag of food. The bandage on her finger caught the edge of the bag. White-hot pain exploded up her arm. Wincing, she yanked back her hand. The lumpy mass of gauze fluttered onto the passenger side of the floor. Gritting her teeth, she scooped up the dressing, and ignoring the throbbing in her finger, she shoved open the door and stepped out.

Inside the kitchen, she dumped her purse and keys on the counter and deposited the bag of food on the table. She peered at the tip of her thumb. A droplet of blood oozed out. Sighing, she dug through the cupboards until she found a first aid kit. Go figure, the blasted thing was in the last one.

A half-dozen tries later, she finally had a strip of adhesive tacked against the wound—kind of. Okay, one corner of the bandage was stuck against itself, and a teeny, tiny bit of redness peeked out from the edge, but otherwise, the cut was covered, which in her opinion was all that mattered. Plus, by now, she practically shook from hunger, and forget rumbling stomachs— right now, she had a full-born hangry rage going on.

Taking a seat, she finally pulled the bag toward her. Every part of her body hurt—her feet throbbed, her head pounded, and her back ached. She leaned back and sighed. *Only forty days left.* Digging inside the bag, she pulled out the paper-wrapped burger followed by the carton of fries. Her thumb burned. Wincing, she looked down to see specks of salt covering the tip. *Great.* Another battle with wrestling a bandage on her thumb to look forward to. Ripping off the adhesive, she hurried to the sink and flipped on the faucet.

Footsteps pounded on the steps.

Ellen peered out the window. The sting disappeared replaced by an acute sense of frustration. Closing her eyes, she exhaled. *Double great. Mom.* She slammed an elbow against the lever, and pasting a smile on her face, she opened the door. "Mom, what a surprise."

"Oh, I know I am supposed to call you first, but I figured just this once you wouldn't mind." Claire stepped into the room and waved toward the outdoors. "Did you know there is a broken window upstairs?"

Seriously? Did her mother think she was blind? "Yes, Mom. I am aware, considering I broke it." Ellen shut the door.

"Oh, for heaven's sake." Claire shook her head. "Now why would you do that?"

Ellen shrugged. "Wasn't planned."

"So, what are you going to do?" Claire glanced around the room. "Maybe you should stay at my place?

You know…just until it's fixed."

Ellen saw the hopeful look in her mother's gaze. She hated to be the one to disappoint her, but no way would she leave here. "No need. I put a blanket over the window for now. I'm sure Ben will fix it." She nodded toward the door adjacent to the back door. "For now, I'll sleep in the guest bedroom."

Claire's shoulders dropped. "I see."

Ellen strolled toward the table. "So, what's up?"

"I stopped by the café to see you, but you'd already left."

Ellen sat. "My shift was over."

Dropping her gaze to the pile of food on the table, Claire shook her head and frowned. "Please, do not tell me you've forgotten what happened to Lily? She got food poisoning eating that stuff. The whole town thought she was pregnant."

Yes, yes, she did remember. Still, if she had to pick her favorite fast-food place, Burger, Burger, Burger made the top of her list. "I haven't had a chance to go grocery shopping yet, and I promise…" She made a cross over her chest. "I'll make certain no one thinks I'm pregnant."

Claire shook her head. "Honey, you really need to take care of yourself. You're not getting any younger." She smoothed a hand over Ellen's cheek. "Greasy junk food has a way of catching up and stealing that youthful glow, not to mention the weight gain. Then, you'll really have a hard time finding a guy."

Just what every woman shy of thirty wants to hear—she was old and fat. "Thanks, Mom." Ellen unwrapped the burger. Grease and melty cheese dripped down the sides. She slid a finger over the mess and licked off the juices. "Always a pleasure to learn such valuable information." *Or not*...Grabbing a french fry, she shot her mother a smile. "Did you come by for a reason?"

Sighing, Claire strolled over. Whipping out her arm from behind her back, she waved a pamphlet. "Ta-da!"

Ellen stopped chewing. The once-delicious fry now tasted like cardboard. Setting on the table, like the worst gift ever, was *the* calendar—the very one she wished never to see again. Picking up the milkshake, she took a deep gulp, hoping to swallow the fry without choking. She set down the cup and turned to her mother. "What's this?"

"For you." Grinning, Claire flipped open to the first page. "And look. I had him autograph it."

Ellen stared at the page with the all-too-familiar scrawl. *Forever yours, baby girl. Dax.* The cardboard french fry weighed heavy in her stomach—much like a cement block. "Oh gee, Mom, you shouldn't have."

Pushing the calendar closer, Claire pointed. "And look, he even used your childhood nickname. What a dear."

Ellen's appetite disappeared. "Yup. Just the best." Re-wrapping the burger, she dumped the uneaten sandwich into the bag. "Listen, Mom—"

"Oh, I know. I'm sure you're tired, so I won't stay." Claire walked to the door. "I just wanted to drop off the calendar and see how your first day went."

"Just perfect." Ellen curled the fingers on her cut and burned hand. No need to show her mother her ineptitude. With her free hand, she rolled the base of the shake cup back and forth "By the way, you really didn't need to ask Dax to drive me to Albany yesterday. I *am* capable, you know."

"Dax?" Claire fanned a hand. "Oh, I meant to call him, but I forgot."

Ellen stilled. "But…" She flicked a glance toward the window. "He showed up."

"See what I mean? He's such a dear." Opening the door, Claire turned and smiled. "You are so lucky to have him as a friend." She gave Ellen a half wave before shutting the door.

Grabbing the discarded food, Ellen marched across the room and tossed out the bag. "Just the luckiest," she grumbled to the empty room. Staring out the window, she narrowed her eyes, wondering just what the heck was Dax's game.

****

Ellen woke, disoriented, buried beneath a thick, orange-and-brown, crocheted afghan. Propping herself up on elbows, she glanced toward the television. Some silly romance playing across the screen. With bleary eyes, she glanced at her cell phone. Nine at night. *What the heck?* Since when did she fall asleep on the couch?

Never, unless she was required to wake at some ungodly hour in the morning—which apparently was her new life. *Ugh.*

Scrubbing fingers through sleep-tangled hair, she kicked off the afghan. Pain shot up her leg—courtesy of the sharp jab from a branch when she collected the clock. She swiped at the thin stream of blood dripping down her shin. *Stupid clock.*

Of all the places for the thing to land, it had to choose the center of the fat, thorny shrub. For what seemed like eternity, she had wrestled with the leafless branches, getting poked, pricked, and scratched, until finally, she nabbed the dang thing. Of course, this was *after* she ripped open the wound on her thumb, broke a blister on her hand, and almost lost an eye, thanks to the branch slipping from her grip and snapping her in the face.

Less than twenty-four hours in her *new* life, and she had more scars, cuts, and bruises than she'd received in ten years in Albany. By the end of her stint in Aberdeen, she figured she'd be a bloody mess.

A knock sounded.

Frowning, she stared at the kitchen pass-through door. *What the heck?* Who would possibly show up at night? Certainly not her mother. At nine, the time was far too late for a "surprise" visit, which FYI—Ellen didn't really think the visit from earlier was a mistake—more like the first of many. Not Ben either, especially since she hadn't gotten around to calling him. Dax, then?

She immediately dismissed the notion. If he wasn't with Angel, then certainly another woman had agreed to his offer for the night. Either way, he'd be too busy to come by and torment her, which…whew…at least she had something to be thankful for, right?

The knocking continued—persistent and demanding.

She ran through a list of possible names, discarding them all. They were either married, had young children, worked tomorrow, or all three. Either way, they wouldn't stop by now. A sliver of fear sliced down her spine. Of all the rotten luck. She was about to die—right here—in the middle of the safest town in America.

Pressing a hand against the pass-through door, Ellen peeked inside the kitchen toward the back door and spotted a far-too-familiar face. *What the heck?* He was supposed to be on a date. She slammed a hand against the wooden door panel.

The pass-through door crashed against the kitchen wall.

She marched across the room and ripped open the back door.

Dax stood, with hands bracing each side of the door.

In Ellen's opinion, he looked far too tantalizing in his Aberdeen Fire shirt. *Dang it.* Just once, could the man *not* look impossibly sexy? She scowled. "What the heck are you doing scaring me like this?"

Chuckling, Dax snuck past her and into the kitchen. "Someone is cranky."

Heck yeah, she was cranky. No one knocked on people's doors in the dead of night unless they had nefarious intentions. Yes, okay, no one would ever consider nine the dead of night, but it also wasn't social hour either.

She started to inform him of this very fact, only the way his gaze skimmed over her made her stomach flutter in ways she really wished it wouldn't. *Freaking man.* Figures, he had perfected the look to make women's knees shake and their blood race. "Did you need something?"

Leaning back against the counter, he wiggled his brows. "What happened to the upstairs window?"

Just freaking great. The man had to have the eyes of an eagle. She wasn't all that impressed with the amusement she saw in his gaze either. Crossing arms over her chest, she bit back a wince at the soft fabric of her shirt brushing against the open wound. "Just a little accident." *If* you could call throwing a clock out the window an accident.

A smile twitched on his lips. "Let me guess, you're still not a fan of early morning waking."

Hello? Who is? "Just so you know, four is not early morning." She flung out a hand. "It's late night."

Dax caught her wrist. "You're bleeding."

A zip of electricity shot up her arm. Distant memories of calloused palms scraping over heated flesh assailed her. Suddenly, she was very aware of the kitchen's small confines. Slowly, she drew her gaze upward. Sharp, blue eyes held hers. A little flutter of excitement swirled through her stomach. Most people wouldn't put danger and Dax in the same sentence. She was not one of those people. She pulled back ever so slightly, hoping to break free. "It's nothing."

He tightened his grip and drew her hand closer. "It's dirty." He looked around the room. "Come on. I'll clean it."

Yeah, right. Like she wanted him hovering over her and tempting her with his very nearness? Talk about sheer torture. "I'm fine, really. And, despite Mom's opinion, I really am capable of taking care of myself." She waved her thumb. "Which includes doctoring minor wounds like this one."

"Oh yeah?" He arched a brow. "Well make sure you tell Dr. Carlson I said hi."

Ellen frowned. She liked Dr. Carlson, and given the size of Aberdeen, she figured she'd probably see him once or twice while here, but still, Dax mentioning his name was odd. "Why would I see Dr. Carlson?"

"For the nasty infection you've got brewing." Dax nodded toward her hand. "Hope he doesn't have to drain the abscess."

Ellen's stomach lurched. Abscess? Draining? Seriously? Was this a ploy of Dax's, or did he speak the truth? Chewing her lip, she debated her odds. The throbbing in her thumb increased. She really liked Dr. Carlson. When she was younger, he'd been both kind and gentle. But, even knowing how patient he could be, she still didn't want to be on the receiving end of him ripping off her torn skin and probing her reddened flesh. *Ah, no thank you.* She scowled. "Fine. You can clean the wound." She wagged a finger. "But nothing else."

He leaned in. "I won't do anything you don't want." Making a sign of the cross, he waggled his brows. "Promise."

With that little glimmer of mischief in his gaze, she had some serious doubts. Vivid images, too…of her doing all sorts of wonderfully delicious and completely off-limits things with him—activities she vowed would *never* happen again. She gazed at her thumb. Did she actually need ten fingers? "You know what?" Snapping up her gaze, she caught the bottom of his chin with her head. She ignored the sting and curled fingers into a fist. "I think I'll take my chances."

"Oh, come on." He leaned back. "Don't be a baby."

A knowing smile split his lips. She gasped. Heat, not even close to what she felt moments before curled upward from the pit of her stomach. "I am *not* a baby."

For just a moment, Dax gazed at her lips. "No, darlin', you sure aren't."

The flutter in her stomach returned, and all she could wonder is whether his kiss would be as spectacular as she remembered. *Oh man.* What the heck was wrong with her? *Everything*, a little voice inside her head warned. Stepping aside, she strolled to the sink. "Well? Are you taking care of this cut? I don't have all night."

Chuckling, Dax turned on the faucet and began to soap his hands. "Sure."

She stared at his strong, tanned fingers. She was in hell—delicious, torturous, tempting hell. She snuck a peek upward. He didn't even spare her a glance. So, only she was affected by his nearness? *Figures.*

He rinsed his hands in the water. "So, what happened?"

She debated not telling him, but the way gossip ran through town, she was surprised he hadn't already heard. "Betty has this bagel slicer. I'm not sure what happened. I dropped the bagel into the slot. The blade shot down. The next thing I know, I'm bleeding all over the bagels." She scowled. "Frankly, I think the thing is defective."

He laughed. "Sugar, the slicer isn't dangerous. *You* are."

She opened her mouth to protest, only he caught her hand, surprising her. "What are you doing?"

Shooting her a quick glance, he flipped on the tap. "Washing the dirt from the cut."

She stared at the stream rushing downward and imagined the sharp prickles stinging the wound. *Oh, heck no.* She pulled against his grip.

Dax tightened his hold. "Back to being a baby?"

She glared. "Why don't I slice off the tip of your finger, then blast water over the cut and see how *you* react."

"Don't be so dramatic." Dax reached for the bar of soap. "Now hold still."

She bit her lip, and closing her eyes, she let out a big sigh. "Okay. I'm ready."

A chuckle rumbled.

She snapped open her gaze to see him grinning.

"I remember when you were little, you acted the same way. If Ben and I came near you, you'd run off crying."

Ellen stiffened. "Maybe if you hadn't held something disgusting like worms or spiders, I wouldn't have run."

"And deny me such pleasure?"

He gave one of those heart-breaking, knees-quaking smiles. The butterflies in her stomach swirled. She cursed silently, hating her weakness. Pressure on the tip of her finger drew her attention. She looked down to see him carefully cleansing the wound. Water washed away the suds pooling on her flesh. "I didn't even realize you cleaned my cut."

"Distraction is the key." He shut off the faucet, then grabbed a paper towel. Gently, he patted the wound. "Where's your first aid kit?"

"Over there." She nodded toward the farthest cupboard.

"Have a seat." He fanned a hand toward the table before grabbing the kit.

She ran her gaze over his broad back, reveling in the flex of his muscles. A little sigh settled in the back of her throat. But dang, the man was too sexy for any woman's peace of mind.

He turned.

His gaze locked with hers. Ellen jerked back,

hating the way her cheeks burned. *Great. Just great.* The man caught her checking him out. Glowering, she tapped her uninjured fingers on her knees. "How did you know I was awake?"

Setting the kit on the table, he flipped open the lid. "I just arrived home. Saw the kitchen light on." He peered upward. "I know how you hate the dark, so I thought I'd come and check on you."

"I don't hate the dark." *Much.* Ellen watched him draw out a pair of blue latex gloves, tape, gauze, small nippers, and a whole assortment of other items deemed necessary for first aid. She eyed the scissors. They looked a bit too sharp for her painful thumb. "No way you're using those scissors on my thumb."

"I would if skin needed removing." Dax slipped on the gloves. "You took care of that problem, though."

Ellen winced. "Gee thanks."

He placed a roll of gauze on the table. Removing the cap from the antibiotic, he knelt in front of her and took her hand. "It's a clean cut so the wound will heal better."

"Wait a minute." Ellen stared at the top of his head. "You told me I'd get an infection."

Squirting a thin glob of ointment on the top of her thumb, he winked. "Let's just say I hedged my bets."

Ellen narrowed her gaze. "What you really mean is that you lied?"

"Nah." Wrapping the gauze around her thumb, he looked over. "Just like taking care of you."

Again, her gaze connected with his. She held her breath. If she moved just an inch closer, she could brush her mouth against his. A little tingle warmed her, reminding her of one delicious night filled with heady kisses and sensuous touches. Would the kiss be the same? Or better? Was such a thing even possible?

Suddenly, she realized pretending friendship wasn't the most difficult part of returning to Aberdeen. Ignoring her attraction to Dax—now that was a different issue. Ellen's stomach tumbled. *Dang it.* She never should have agreed to her mother's plan. *Now what the heck would she do?*

Chapter 9

Ellen woke the next morning groggy, disoriented, and more than a little disturbed. After all, she *wasn't* supposed to dream of Dax, let alone kiss him in said dream. And she most definitely wasn't supposed to *want* to kiss him, for heaven's sake. And yet, here she was, not more than seven hours later, having done all three.

What the heck? How could she have forgotten her never-to-contemplate list? She didn't have to remember a ton of items—just the usual ten commandants—which she mostly followed, plus two more—do not kiss Dax and *never ever* consider sleeping with him. Now, in one fell swoop, she came far too close to repeating the first, and she definitely failed the second.

Shoving hair out of her eyes, she climbed from the bed and dragged herself into the bathroom. Perhaps after a nice cold shower, she'd forget about the completely absurd dreams.

By the time the shower was over, she realized the whole theory of ice-cold showers removing thoughts of sex was a damn lie. Ripping aside the shower curtain, Ellen yanked the towel from the rack. A sharp sting pierced her thumb. She looked down. Bright red blood intermingled with raw, pink flesh. She glanced at the bottom of the tub. Only a tiny scrap of adhesive stuck to the drain. The gauze was M.I.A. *Just freaking great.*

Cursing Betty, Dax, and life in general, she wrapped a wad of tissues around the open wound, then stormed into the bedroom. With excessive care toward her thumb, she quickly dressed. Stepping into the kitchen, she spied the first aid kit on the counter where Dax had left it. Walking over, she reached for the box. A flash of glossy blue caught her attention. Moving aside the kit, she stared down.

Perfectly blue eyes and a seductive smile she knew only too well stared right back, and with it came the far-too-vivid memory of last night. *Seriously?* Could her morning get any worse? Yanking away her gaze, she flipped the kit's latch and forced herself to focus on her thumb.

Ten minutes later, two tiny adhesive strips covered the wound—kind of. One corner was stuck to an edge and along the side, a tiny gap exposed raw flesh, but most of the wound was hidden which was enough for her.

Of course, if the dang calendar hadn't distracted her, she might have done a better job. Even turning over the blasted thing hadn't helped because a tinier image of Dax stared back. *Freaking man...*

She glanced at the clock. Eight minutes to get to work. Grabbing the calendar, she ripped open the drawer and dropped the packet inside. "That's the last time you'll distract me."

Rushing inside the café, Ellen ripped off her coat and hung it on the rack. "Sorry."

"Everything okay?"

"Yeah. I just..."

Grabbing a cup from the stack, Betty arched a brow. "You what?"

Yeah, right, like she'd admit Dax's picture distracted her, not to mention last night's near kiss, and definitely not the sexy dreams where a lot more, never-to-be-discussed thoughts occurred. Boy, wouldn't Betty just love to share those tidbits with Claire. *Ah, no, thank you.* Sighing, Ellen brushed a wayward strand of hair from her eyes. "Had to bandage my thumb."

Chuckling, Betty grabbed a cup. "Sounds like you had a rough morning."

Morning, night, evening—*all* were rough. Tucking her purse beneath the counter, she shrugged. "Just not used to waking up early."

"I agree. It takes some getting used to." Placing a cup beneath the coffeemaker spigot, Betty flipped the handle. "But, before you know it, you'll be an early bird."

Ellen couldn't image any morning where she willingly woke before the sun rose. "Can't see it happening."

"Yeah? I said the same thing." Betty slid the cup to Ellen. "This will help."

"Thanks." Reaching toward a silver container, she spied a stack of calendars placed next to the register. Now how the heck was she expected to work if Dax's face kept distracting her? Snatching a sugar packet from the holder, Ellen ripped one corner and poured the sweetener into the drink. "What's up with the calendars?"

Betty poured another coffee. "Angel thought we should keep some to sell." Setting down the cup, she snagged the top calendar and studied the image. "Lucky us. Now we get to sneak a peek every now and again."

Wait. What was this? Betty wanted to look at Dax,

too? *Since when?* Ellen grabbed a stirrer from the bin. "You're gay."

"So?" Betty replaced the calendar. "Doesn't mean I can't appreciate great art." Sipping her coffee, she winked. "And let's face it, even the great masters couldn't replicate Dax's perfection."

Considering Ellen spent most of two college semesters studying the masters, she could hardly argue. Still, Betty was the same age as Ellen's very own mother—the same age as Dax's mother. Had all the women in town lost their minds? The whole thought was beyond disturbing, especially since her own very bizarre reaction to Dax. Swirling the stirrer through her drink, she leaned against the counter, purposely keeping the calendars and all thoughts of Dax behind her. "Okay, so what's the plan for today?"

Betty handed Ellen a pair of plastic gloves. "How about today, we try and keep you alive."

Ellen figured the comment was a little uncalled for, considering she only did minor damage yesterday. Plucking the gloves from Betty's hands and ignoring the sting of her wound, she scowled. "I think I'll be just fine."

Grinning, Betty grabbed a pair of metal tongs off the counter. "Yeah, well, we'll see." She clicked them twice.

A sharp metal twang sounded.

"Now, these don't cut or slice, so you should be fine."

Too cruel, Betty. Ripping the tongs from Betty, she narrowed her gaze. "Ha ha."

Betty patted Ellen's shoulder. "I kid. Anyway, go ahead and put these pastries in the case." She started toward the backroom. "I'll start on the bacon and bagels."

Considering the barb Betty just shot, Ellen wanted to insist on helping. Only, could she really afford the possibility of losing a digit, or worse, having Dax administering first aid again? *Oh, heck no.* A girl can only handle so much temptation before she caves, right? And considering caving was as high on her list as not kissing him, she figured she'd be better off staying out front. Still, guilt warred with self-preservation. "You sure…?"

"Yeah. Besides, I've got some other things to take care of while I'm back here. Once you have the front mastered, we'll discuss the back." Betty walked to the backroom door. "Now listen, just make the drinks like they request, and you'll do fine." She shoved open the door. "Call me if you need me."

Turning to the boxes of pastries, Ellen flipped the lid. Nestled inside were row upon row of deliciously sugary confections. She took her time removing each one, arranging them in neat rows on the metal tray.

A few people trickled in.

Ellen decided to tackle making the drinks on her own. Thankfully, the orders were simple—just a couple basic lattes and plenty plain old cups of joe. Not once did she have any issue, and bonus, her thumb only caused her a minor inconvenience. A little zip of happiness ran through her.

Okay, in the grand scheme of life, having an error-free day of coffee making wasn't a huge deal, but after the humiliation of losing her job, then the ordeal of yesterday—yeah, she'd take any win she could get. Smiling, Ellen grabbed a fresh towel and wiped up crumbs and coffee dribbles.

The bell over the café door rang.

"Good mor—" Ellen glanced up. The smile slipped from her lips. Digging fingers into the soft cloth, she slowly dragged her gaze over Dax's broad chest covered in a blue Aberdeen Fire jacket, past his lips curling upward just slightly, to his straight nose, and finally to sparkling blue eyes. Her mouth dried, and her stomach churned. *Oh man...*

Of all the freaking people, *he* had to stop by today of all days, when last night's near reckless kiss and the subsequent dreams were still far too fresh? *Didn't it just figure...*

"Morning, sugar." Strolling inside, Dax blew on his hands for just a moment.

His words jerked her out of her stupor. Ellen snapped down her brows. "I am *not* your sugar."

Waggling his brows, his mouth spread into a wide grin. "Well, you don't like baby girl."

"You know what I like, Dax?" Scrubbing the counter, she hoped she gave off an air of nonchalance, when in truth, she was all jittery and flustered. "I like to be called Ellen."

He wrinkled his nose. "Now what kind of endearment is Ellen?"

She rolled her eyes. Did he really think she'd play his game? The man had a lot to learn. "It's not any kind, which is why I prefer my name."

Laughing, he leaned against the counter and crossed both arms over his chest. "Someone's grumpy."

Ellen narrowed her gaze. *Well, duh.* She almost *kissed* him. Who wouldn't be irritated over that knowledge? Tossing down the cloth, she sighed. "Are you here to get coffee or annoy me?"

He leaned in just a bit.

The smell of his cologne surrounded her. She tightened her grip on the towel. *Oh boy...*

"Maybe I just wanted to see you."

His blue gaze met hers. A warm, tingly, feeling crept outward through every inch of Ellen's body, reminding her of how close to falling off the precipice she came last night and doing the dastardly deed—with him of all people. Only one way she could stave off doing something beyond calamitous. She shot a quick glance at the backroom. "Oh gee. I think Betty needs me." Pivoting, she inched past him, careful to keep her body from touching his, and darted toward the door. "Nice seeing you, Dax. Have fun at work."

A soft chuckle sounded followed by heavy footsteps. She peered over her shoulder. *What the heck?* He followed? Talk about persistent. She stopped and glared. "Dax, I told you—I need to help Betty."

A smile twitched on his lips. "I know."

Was the man being purposely obtuse? She narrowed her gaze. "What are you doing? You're not allowed behind the counter."

"I think I'll be fine."

His smile deepened. She scowled. Just because he could make most women do his bidding didn't mean he could just go wherever he pleased. She flung out a hand toward the door leading into the backroom. A small, black placard was stuck to the front. "See that sign? It says *Employees Only*." She glared. "Last time I checked you weren't an employee."

Reaching over her head, Dax pressed a palm against the door. "For today, we'll consider otherwise."

The door opened.

Swiveling in the chair, Betty frowned. "What's going on?"

Marching toward the desk, she pointed to Dax. "I told him he couldn't come in the backroom, but he wouldn't listen."

Dropping the pen on the stack of paper, Betty stood. "Dax is one of the few who are allowed."

She should have known Betty would be a pushover for Dax's flirting ways. She glared in his direction.

He burst out laughing. "Won't be long, Betty." He walked over to a row of shelves and removed a small white box. "Just checking her thumb."

"My thumb is just fine. See?" Holding up her injured hand, she wiggled her fingers before turning to Betty. "Tell him I'm fine."

"Oh no. You're not dragging me into this mess." Betty pushed back the chair and stood. "I'll leave you two to fight out this one."

Wait. What? Betty intended to abandon her? What kind of person ditched a friend? "I just want you to tell him—"

The door swung shut behind Betty.

Dax turned aside, placing the box on the desk.

Pivoting, Ellen glared at his back. "Do you see what you just did?"

Peering over his shoulder, Dax pulled out a chair and waved a hand for her to sit. "What did I do?"

Was the man really playing dumb? Dropping into the seat, she glared upward. "You've got Betty thinking something is going on."

"Something is going on." Dax tugged on a pair of latex gloves. "I'm checking your thumb."

She fisted her hand. A burst of fresh pain shot up her arm. She ignored it. Like heck she'd let him administer first aid. "I told you my thumb is fine."

Crouching low, he grabbed her injured hand. When he snapped up his gaze, a furrow creased his brow. "What happened to the gauze?"

The strength of his grip, the smell of his cologne, and the intensity of his gaze made her forget all her arguments. She stared at his strong fingers moving her thumb left and right, presumably to get a better view. "Not sure. I noticed its disappearance after my shower."

His fingers stilled for just a moment, and his gaze dipped to her lips. "Yeah?"

His words came out all rough and gravelly. She peeled her gaze from his hands to his face. *Oops. Bad call.* His eyes had darkened to a deep sapphire. The muscles worked in his neck, and his fingers fumbled over the tape.

He shook his head and cleared his throat. "These bandages aren't much protection."

The adhesives were the least of her worries. However, the widening crack in the wall she'd built was a real concern. She licked her lower lip. "It's all I had."

Their gazes locked. The air seemed to crackle with a super-charged energy.

Ellen's breath caught, and dang if she couldn't pull away her gaze.

The soft sound of some customer's laughter floated into backroom, breaking the moment.

Dax jerked back and finished wrapping the wound. After clipping the gauze, he dropped the roll into the kit. "So, did you have a rough night sleeping?"

Stiffening, Ellen snapped up her gaze. Did he know about the near-kiss and her dream-filled night? Or did he just assume with enough time, she'd fall under the sexy spell he cast? An icy chill slid down her spine, and a heavy weight settled in her stomach. Of course, he did. What woman didn't? He just figured she'd be like the rest—like she had six years ago. What other reason accounted for his constant attention? "I knew it." She ripped back her hand. The white gauze dangled from the tip of her thumb. "You expect me to sleep with you."

Grabbing her hand, he jammed a piece of tape onto the ends. "What are you talking about?"

Blind fury and bitter disappointment filled her. How foolish for her to think—to actually believe...He didn't want her friendship. He just wanted sex. "This..." Jumping from the chair, she waved her injured thumb in the air. "Your sudden concern for me last night, and then this morning. And what about driving me to Albany, which FYI—I asked Mom why she called you, and guess what? She never did, but then, you knew that didn't you? So don't act all innocent."

"Let me get this straight..." Dax crossed arms over his chest. "You're upset because I didn't want you to get hurt?"

"Oh please." Did he think she was stupid? Ellen glared. "You forget, Dax. I *know* you. I know what you're about. You think with enough charm, I'll be in your bed. Well, forget it. I'm not so easily duped these days."

"You forget. *I* know you, too." He fisted hands to his hips. "I knew if you thought I made the offer, you'd

113

refuse. But, if you think I would allow you to drive such a long distance alone on slick roads, then you don't know me at all."

Ellen stiffened. *Oh heck no.* Stepping close enough that their toes touched, she tilted back her head and narrowed her eyes. "Who are you to *allow* me to do anything?" A sudden darkness surrounded Dax, like an ominous black cloud just waiting to ravage everything in sight. In all her years, she'd only seen Dax angry a handful of times, and even then, his response remained contained and controlled. But right now, he looked darn close to exploding.

"I'll tell you who I am…" He ground his teeth, forcing the muscles to flex in his cheeks and his nostrils to flare. "I'm the man who didn't want to pull your inert body out of tangled wreckage."

Heat, fierce and red, surged through her veins. She glared. Why the heck was he so upset? "Oh please." She jabbed a finger into his chest. "You weren't even working that day. Remember?"

"And that changes things?" He imprisoned her palm against his chest. "The thought of you—" His Adam's apple bobbed, and the vein in his neck pulsed. "Just—" He shook his head. "No."

Ellen stared, watching the emotions play across his face. He looked genuinely concerned. But surely only because of her family—nothing more. *Right?* She shook her head. Of course. She wasn't stupid. A whoosh of air ripped from her. "Fine. But remember—" She wagged a finger. "No thinking we'll have sex."

His gaze searched her face. Finally, he cupped her chin and drew her closer. "Sugar, last night, I promised I wouldn't do anything you didn't want. I haven't changed my mind, but, if you're asking me not to think about us having sex—" He brushed a thumb across her lower lip. "You ask the impossible."

His breath was warm and sweet, and his words were soft and thick—like warm honey on a cold morning. Was it her, or did the room suddenly feel about a thousand times hotter? A second later, his mouth captured hers in one incredibly hot, totally arousing kiss.

Fire zipped through Ellen's stomach. Rough stubble and calloused fingers caressed her chin, and languid warmth licked every inch of her body. She clung to his shoulders, hating herself for succumbing to his touch and praying the moment would never end. A low moan ripped from her lips.

Suddenly, sounds of voices broke through the magic Dax created. She jerked back, breaking the kiss.

His gaze held hers for a moment before he dropped his hands and stood. "See you later, sugar."

Pressing fingers against her mouth, Ellen watched him leave. In that moment, she had two epiphanies— one, as impossible as it sounded, his kisses *had* gotten better, and two, her day *could* get worse.

She closed her eyes and groaned. *Now what was she to do?*

Chapter 10

The rest of Ellen's week didn't get any better. First off, no matter how hard she tried, she couldn't rid her memory of the thoroughly scorching, entirely captivating kiss from one totally hot, completely off-limits-by-her-own-choice fireman. *Criminy*...

They weren't supposed to kiss. Hadn't she explicitly stated that very rule on Friday night? Okay, maybe stating was a rather strong word, but jeez, did she actually have to say—gee, Dax, after you so painfully dumped me the last time we kissed, don't expect another go? Of course not, because even the most ignorant man should get the hint, right? Dax was anything but ignorant—especially in the ways of romance and wooing women.

Still, she had insisted on Tuesday, he couldn't think about them having sex. But could he even follow that simple dictate? Nope. He just had to go and kiss her. What the heck did he think would happen after such a kiss? For three straight days, *all* she thought about was Dax, the damn kiss, and now sex. *Freaking Dax*...

One week home, and already, she could feel her willpower fading. *Ugh.* Here she thought informing Ben of the broken window would be the worst part of her week. News flash—being chewed out by her brother didn't even come close to the top of her list.

If only *he* had kept to his side of the yard... If only *she* had kept the kitchen door shut... Maybe then she wouldn't wonder how they'd gone from feigning friendship to kissing.

Ellen stared past the few couples sitting at tables toward the large front window. Snow drifted downward, just a light dusting, but enough to remind her the holidays lurked. Across the street, city workers strung strands of lights from leafless branches and draped gold ribbon from the park's newly built gazebo. She shifted her gaze past the large, gray building housing city hall, where her brother was probably diligently working, to the red brick fire station just beyond.

What happened to Dax?

For the past three days, she expected him to stop by and taunt her, if for no other reason than to remind her he could have any woman he wanted, *including* her. Only he'd vanished like a thin mist on a hot day. She tapped fingers on the counter.

Had the kiss meant so little?

She scowled. Of course, it did. The man was the town's version of Casanova. By now, he'd probably moved onto the next woman. A flame she chose not to identify licked her stomach. What the heck? Why did she care? Plopping on a stool next to the cash register, she propped her chin on her hand. A stack of calendars with Dax's glorious image stared back. Her stomach wobbled.

For four days, his face occupied a space in her thoughts, and not just in the teeny-tiny-part-of-her-wanted-to-kiss-him-again way either. But, in an oh-man-I'm-in-trouble kind of way. She sighed.

What did he have that made women go gaga—that made *her* forget the second most painful event in her life? After all, he was built like every other man—a head with all the expected features: arms and legs, fingers and toes, shoulders and a torso. All perfectly normal…if perfectly normal meant sparkling blue eyes lighting with mischief, or an exquisitely formed nose above firm, sensual lips, and the scruffy five o'clock shadow he had perfected.

And his body…

Inching her way downward, she took in the broad shoulders, the toned arms, the cut pecs, the shredded abs, and the brawny thighs. The memory of his body wrapped around hers—pressed against her—caused her stomach to flutter. A warm, tingly feeling followed quickly by a deep, aching memory of the one night rushed through her.

The bell over the door sounded.

Jumping, Ellen knocked into the forgotten cup of coffee.

Tepid liquid spread across the counter, inching ever closer to the stack.

Maybelline strolled toward the counter. "What's wrong?"

Scooping up a pile of napkins, Ellen quickly sopped up the mess before the coffee ruined the calendars. "You mean besides your outfit."

Maybelline huffed. "I'll have you know, by Christmas every woman will want this coat."

Ellen didn't see how that was even remotely possible. Who in their right mind would wear a pink-and-white, nylon camouflage parka with a neon-pink faux fur collar besides her cousin? She crumpled the napkins and tossed them in the trash. "So, what's up?"

Shrugging, Maybelline dropped a purple, fuzzy purse resembling a ginormous pom-pom on the counter. "Thought I'd stop by on my way to work and get my morning brew." She glanced at the large overhead blackboard. "Today, I think I'll have a pecan praline non-fat latte. Extra syrup, please."

Ellen walked to the espresso machine. "I thought you were off the carbs."

"Your point?"

Pumping the flavoring into the cup, Ellen peered over her shoulder. "You do realize how much sugar is in this syrup, right?" She placed the cup under the spigot and pressed a button.

Thick, black liquid slowly dripped into the cup.

"Of course." Maybelline smoothed a hand across her purse. "I'm not stupid. However, Sara explained how carbs in the syrup don't count."

"Sara Fischer?" Ellen poured milk into a canister. "The very girl who wondered why they named a drink tequila sunrise when it was made with vodka?"

"She's the one."

Placing the canister beneath the long wand, Ellen swiveled the knob. A sharp hiss and a burst of steam rose upward. Glancing at Maybelline, she arched a brow. "She's your authority?"

Maybelline nodded. "See, she explained how the heat from the coffee burns off the carbs." She pulled at a piece of fuzz on the front of her purse. "So, in theory, I can have all the syrup I want."

Ellen decided it was official—Maybelline *and* Sara were nuts. "I think Sara is confused."

"Don't be crazy." Shooting a glare in Ellen's

direction, Maybelline flicked the fuzz onto the floor. "She came very close to receiving a degree in nutrition."

Ellen swirled the cup beneath the wand. Fluffy foam crested the top. "Close?"

Maybelline scraped her palms together. "Well, you know, she had to do a research paper comparing fast-food with home-cooked meals. She decided for effective research she needed to eat both for each meal. Let's just say, by the time the semester ended, she had gained ten pounds and discovered fast-food tasted better than what she cooked."

Ellen couldn't really argue the point. A decade later, and she was still in the process of losing her freshman fifteen. Turning off the steam, she poured the foamy liquid into the cup. "If I were you, I'd be careful." She pushed the cup across the counter. "You wouldn't want to wake up one morning and find out you've been lied to."

"I'm not worried." Maybelline handed Ellen a five-dollar-bill. "Hey, you wanna go out tonight?"

Ellen stilled for just a moment. Did she want to? Not really. Only, the idea of sitting home *didn't* appeal either, especially knowing the whole time she'd relive Monday night's near-kiss and Tuesday morning's actual kiss. A whole kaleidoscope of butterflies swirled through her stomach. *Oh man.* She had it bad. Only one thing to do to get herself back on track. Dropping the cash into the register, she pulled out two quarters and placed the coins in Maybelline's hand. "What time?"

"How about eight?" Maybelline slid the purse strap on her shoulder. "I'll pick you up."

"Sure."

"How awesome will this be?" Scooping up her drink, Maybelline waggled her brows. "A bar full of men picking up women. I guarantee we will have us a *most* excellent time."

Ellen stilled. Even if she wanted to say something, she couldn't. Her mind was too busy processing Maybelline's words. Men...picking up women? Would Dax be one of the men? A sickening feeling settled in her stomach. Who did she kid? Friday night at Martinis? Of course, he'd show, and she just knew he'd be the first to leave with a hot woman, too. The knot tightened, and a burning sensation spread through her chest.

Slamming shut the cash register drawer, she dropped onto the stool. Was it too much to hope for her to be struck by lightning? She looked out the window. The snow had stopped falling, and the clouds had disappeared to reveal blue skies.

Figures. Like she could expect a miracle.

****

Dax skimmed the hotel's banquet room with the deep maroon carpet and the gold paneled walls. Women dressed in skimpy gowns snaked around the perimeter, casting hopeful glances toward him. He made certain to flash a smile and say a flattering word or two to each woman who requested an autograph, but his heart wasn't really into it.

Hell, he was in Albany, and Ellen still crowded his thoughts. Or maybe he couldn't remove her *because* he was here—in the town she'd called home for nearly ten years and the one place where their friendship had shifted and changed irrevocably?

He went through the motions of signing calendars

121

and making small talk, but all the while, thoughts of Ellen filled him. Did she miss him? Did she hope he'd stop by? Or had the kiss that brought back so many bittersweet memories for him only reaffirm her dislike?

How many times had he wanted to stop by her place and pick up where they left off at the café? Ten? Twenty? A hundred? He hadn't, though, using work and these blasted signings for staying away. But in truth, her reaction to his arrival was what stopped him. Would she accuse him of taking advantage of the situation or pretend nothing happened?

He couldn't blame her if she believed the first. After all, he *had* taken advantage of the moment, not that he had an ounce of regret. Given the opportunity, he'd do so again. But her ignoring what they had shared? *No way.*

Not because his ego couldn't handle it, but because he knew the truth, even if she refused to acknowledge it. The way she had clung and sunk into the kiss—she might not want to own her actions, but she couldn't deny the facts. She wanted him as much as he desired her—which explained why she insisted he not think about them having sex.

A genuine smile split his face. For longer than he cared to recall, sex with Ellen had been his *only* thought. Of course, he completely understood why she would rebel at the idea. Hadn't he done the very same thing six years ago?

Tightening his grip on the pen, he scanned the room. Only a few women remained, eagerly awaiting their chance at one of the firemen. He couldn't wait for the event to end. After two days of covetous looks and inappropriate innuendos, he needed a break.

He never had a problem with eager, willing women. Hell, he considered himself liberal-minded, welcoming their uninhibited, carefree seduction. Now, though, he found their propositions just a bit annoying, like he was a coveted trophy. Yes, he got the irony. But just because he understood their motivation didn't make the whole situation better.

After today, though, he wouldn't have to attend another signing for a few days. Other than working tomorrow, he could pursue what really interested him. Or, rather, who...

An image of Claire and Robert flashed through his thoughts. Theirs was the first marriage he'd witnessed without a knot forming in his stomach or bruised feelings in his heart. He wasn't under any illusion he could ever aspire to what Claire and Robert had, and more than likely, Lily and Ben. But he was loving and caring, and besides, he wasn't asking Ellen for forever, but to just return to the space they once shared.

He knew his plans involved risks, but right now, he didn't care. More importantly, he had to figure out how to get Ellen to throw caution to the wind and recognize how perfect they were together. His job wouldn't be easy. Stubborn didn't even begin to describe the Jordans.

Ben and Claire might be headstrong, but Ellen wasn't a slouch in the area either. Not to mention, she *would* overlay all her other concerns like his friendship with Ben and her mother's disappointment, which in the end would make her difficult.

He wasn't worried. He knew how to woo a woman. Ellen might be harder to charm, but he had no doubt he would be successful. A tall woman with strawberry-blonde hair and bright blue eyes slid a calendar in his direction.

"So, darlin'…" Leaning in, she curled her lips into a seductive smile. "If you want to do something, I'm available tonight."

Deep cleavage and enhanced breasts crossed his line of sight. Yanking away his gaze, he turned his attention to signing the calendar, knowing her words were just code for *let's skip dinner and head right to my place*. In the past. he would have jumped at the chance. Tonight, though, he had other plans, none of which involved some easy woman who held little interest other than a few hours of fun. "Thanks, love, but I can't." He handed back the calendar. "Company policy." The lie slipped easily off his lips, not that he cared. After all, a canned response was better than a bruised ego.

The woman made a slight moue. "Your loss." Snatching the packet, she pivoted. Long, shimmering hair swirled outward. She turned and peered over her shoulder. "Unlike the rest of these women, I guarantee fun." She stomped away.

A nudge clipped him in the side.

He turned.

Arching copper brows, Jakob grunted. "Dude, what the hell is wrong with you?"

Dax frowned. "What are you talking about?"

Jakob tilted his head toward the door. "She wanted you, and you let her go."

Swiveling, Dax watched the woman walk out the door. In the past, she'd be exactly his type, but not now. He turned back.

A young woman stood in front of the table.

The smile she gave him was both coy and seductive. He knew his role and what women expected. Pasting on a smile destined to melt a woman's heart, he winked. "Now why would I settle for her when an even more beautiful woman is in front of me?" Those words got him the reaction he expected.

A blush crept up the woman's cheeks. "Aren't you just adorable?"

Bending his head, Dax scratched his name across the front of his image—something cheesy and suggestive—just like women desired, and Angel demanded. Returning the calendar, he waggled his brows. "I try, darlin'."

Giggling, she clutched the calendar and hurried off.

"Dude, you're killing me." Shaking his head, Jakob picked up a water bottle and took a drink before swiping a hand across his mouth. "A hundred women want to sleep with you, and you say no. Doesn't sound very Dax-like."

Dax skimmed his gaze down the table. The line had stalled. Austin Bender, Mr. March, appeared engaged in a lively conversation with a petite blonde. Kyle and Ian, Mr. April and Mr. May, signed calendars for the last two women. James Lefton, Mr. June, stood in the corner, chatting up an ebony-haired woman. He eased out a breath. *Not much longer now.* He turned back to Jakob. "Not sure what to tell you. Not interested."

"Oh wait…" Jakob waved a finger. "It's Angel, isn't it? You two are an item now, right?"

What was this? Had Angel told people they were a couple? Since when? Gripping the pen, Dax peered across the room and caught a glimpse of her pacing along the far wall with a phone pressed against her ear. He scowled. She never missed a signing. She said she attended to make sure everything ran smoothly, but he wouldn't put it past her to appear just to keep eyes on him.

Today, she was dressed in a tight-fitting, green, slinky number that skimmed the top of her knees and showcased her considerable assets. She embodied both sensuality and curve-appeal. Controlling, bossy, sexy, and sinful, she had the innate ability to make a man love and hate her at the same time. Dax had experienced both emotions. Now, he couldn't even summon an ounce of desire.

The line started moving again.

Picking up his pen, he signed another calendar. "If you're asking whether we're exclusive, we're not."

"You sure?" Jakob winked at the women in front of him. "She seems to think otherwise."

"Not sure why." Dax's fingers ached, his eyes hurt, and all he wanted was to climb into his truck and head back to Aberdeen. He waited for Jakob to finish the next attendee. "Angel knows where we stand." Which was true. He'd been upfront with her from the first day. Nothing had changed, at least not in that regard. Besides, he couldn't worry about Angel's ideas. He had a bigger wall to climb—one he had helped build six years ago.

The last woman stepped forward.

Dax used every ounce of willpower he possessed to greet the woman. In his mind, though, he was back in Aberdeen, surprising Ellen with his presence. He scratched his name on the last calendar, thanked the young women, then tossed down his pen. Standing, he snagged his coat from the back of his chair and slipped his arms into the sleeves. A hand caught the back of his jacket. He turned to see Jakob drop his pen and stand.

Austin came up and stood next to Jakob.

"Hey, you and Ben used to hit the clubs in Albany, right?" Jakob dragged a hand through his hair.

Dax mentally rolled his eyes. In all the years he'd known Jakob, he was forever primping—making certain each strand of hair was in place, that his shirt was wrinkle free, or his face was blemish free. He had never met a man who took such care with his appearance. "Yeah." He zipped shut his coat. "Why?"

Jakob nodded toward Austin. "We're curious which bar has the best action."

A hundred different clubs flew through Dax's thoughts, all with available chicks, but only one held a bittersweet memory—the Tin Tinker. A part of him, though, refused to share the memory, even abstractly, with either man. Fishing keys from his pocket, he considered other establishments. One came to mind filled with plenty of party-girls. "Head to Madison and hit Posh Pit. You won't have a complaint." He winked before walking around the table.

"You wanna join us?"

Dax turned.

Jakob arched a brow. "I mean, if you and Angel aren't a couple, don't see why you'd want to rush back to Aberdeen. Nothing going on there but Martinis, and we all know what that place is like on a Friday night." He nudged Austin in the side. "And it's not like we haven't done most of the local ladies."

"Besides—" Austin grinned. "With all the rich city guys in town with their deep wallets, none of the women will look our way."

Dax didn't know what irked more—Jakob being such a cocky jerk or the lumping of Ellen in that group. Either way, he knew a dozen men would seek the attention of a woman as classy and sexy as Ellen. Every muscle in his body tensed. He fisted a hand and gritted his teeth. He'd be damned before he'd allow such a thing to happen. "Nope. Got plans."

Pivoting, he strolled out of the hall, suddenly more than a little eager to get back to Aberdeen. Whether anyone knew it or not, Ellen Jordan belonged to him.

Chapter 11

By the time Dax whizzed past the *Welcome to Aberdeen* sign, he had calmed his fears. After all, just because Friday night was prime pick-up night didn't mean Ellen would be out. *Right?*

Approaching Martinis, he spied the line of people waiting to enter. Loud music wafted from the building. Quickly, he scanned the faces. None were Ellen.

Relief and disappointment swelled inside him. He wasn't certain which situation boded better for him—the unexpected meet-up at Martinis or a surprise visit to her house. Driving on, he noted the high-end sports cars occupying most of the spots along the sidewalk. Most were out-of-towners on vacation, bragging about their high-powered jobs while they tossed around endless wads of cash. The irony of the whole situation was the town needed them *and* their money.

A rush of breath ripped from him. He didn't worry about holding his own against some rich guy. He just hated the idea of Ellen being seduced by one of those city schmucks who just wanted a quick fling. Approaching Betty's Café, he spied a very familiar, brown clunker wedged between a luxury sedan and a flashy sports car.

Slowing the vehicle, he stared at Maybelline's car before shooting a quick glance at the bar. A heavy feeling settled in the pit of his stomach. Not because he knew Maybelline was inside, but because he knew she hadn't gone alone.

He spied an empty spot and whipped his truck into the space. Pocketing his keys, he strolled toward the bar, more than a little aware of the women's gazes landing on him. He gave them his most seductive smile, but the whole time, all he could imagine was some city guy hitting on Ellen. *Like hell...*

Garrett, one of the bouncers Martinis retained, stood at the entrance. He thrust out a hand. "Hello, pretty boy."

Dax grinned. The term irritated a few of the men who had participated in the charity, but not him. A little razzing was a minor inconvenience compared to the benefit the children's hospital would receive in return. Grasping Garrett's hand, he tilted his head toward the street. "Looks like a lot of people up from the city."

"Just the usual weekend visitors."

The pinched look on Garrett's face said it all. He didn't appreciate the influx of out-of-towners any more than Dax did. "Noticed Maybelline's car parked down the street." Dax nodded toward the entrance. "Is she alone?"

"Nah." Garrett pulled open the door. "From the looks of things, she dragged along Ellen."

Bingo. Dax peered into the dark room. From this vantage point, he couldn't see much but a crowd of well-dressed men standing at the bar. But just because he couldn't see Ellen didn't mean some joker wasn't already making his moves. "Anything Ben needs to worry about."

Garrett glanced at his watch. "Still early. But you know Maybelline. Anything is possible at any time."

Dax laughed. Yeah, he did know Maybelline. He also knew Ellen. Together they equaled one thing—trouble. "Then, I guess I arrived at the perfect time." He winked. "Hate for a blemish to mar Ben's first week as mayor."

He stepped inside the dimly lit room. The stench of stale beer mingled with the aroma of fried food, and loud voices competed with the band on stage. On a weekend night, Martinis was guaranteed to draw a crowd. Tonight was no exception. Clusters of people filled the narrow space between the bar and tables. He recognized most, but plenty of out-of-towners filled the space.

Nodding to friends, Dax worked his way toward the bar. A space opened near the back corner. Wiggling into the spot, he rested one arm on the wooden surface and surveyed the room. A throng of women surrounded the stage, swaying and dancing to the band's loud music. Several slick dressed men circled the area, no doubt choosing their next prey.

Dax scanned the tables filled with people drinking and laughing. In the far corner, he spotted a familiar brunette head. Bottles and empty glasses crowded the table.

Some man leaned in and said something.

Ellen pulled back and sipped her drink.

Watching the stranger with his suave attitude and the smooth moves, Dax scowled. Some New York City hotshot out to impress Ellen. He had no idea how long the man had been hitting on Ellen, but had he been in the guy's shoes, the deal would be sealed by now. He waved a hand toward the bartender.

Charlie walked over and swiped at the bar with a

damp towel. "What can I get you, Dax?"

"I'll take a beer." Dax peered at Ellen before turning back. "And a vodka and soda with a twist of lime."

Charlie rapped his knuckles on top of the counter. "Coming up."

Turning, Dax watched the man catch Ellen's hand and tug.

She shook her head.

The man continued to pull.

Jeez, didn't he get the hint? She wasn't interested. Pinching his lips into a thin line, he dug his wallet from his back pocket.

"Dax…"

Swiveling, Dax spotted Charity Hanson, a pretty redhead recently moved to town. This past summer, he'd considered pursuing her. Now, though, he couldn't imagine what about her he found attractive. Flipping open his wallet, he thumbed through the bills. "Evening, Charity."

"You wanna dance?" She stepped closer and swayed her hips. "It's my favorite song."

With each move, her breasts brushed against his arm. He flicked his gaze across the room.

Ellen remained in the same seat, nursing her drink.

The man, still persistent, had released her hand but now occupied the vacant chair beside hers, leaning far too close in Dax's opinion. "Sorry, darlin'." Pulling out a twenty, he slapped the bill on the counter. "Not in the mood."

Charlie slid the drinks across the bar.

"Thanks." Dax turned back to Charity. "Have fun, darlin'." Stepping aside, he left her standing alone in the empty spot. He weaved his way through the crowd until he reached Ellen's table.

Lifting her drink, Ellen turned and froze, staring upward. The rim of her forgotten glass rested against her lower lip.

Dax noted the glimmer of relief in her gaze.

Swiveling, the man eyed Dax and scowled. "Beat it, buddy. We're busy."

Noting the man's perfectly highlighted brown hair, the expensive silk shirt, and the glass no doubt filled with high-end, premium whiskey, Dax snorted. He knew the type—overly confident, threw around his importance as often as his money, and expected women to fall for him and men to envy him. Dax was unimpressed. He immediately shoved him into one category...*Fancypants.* Fixing the man with an unflinching glare, he nodded toward the chair the man occupied. "You're in my seat."

Looking away, the stranger flexed his fingers around the tumbler before turning back. "I don't think so."

Dax cocked a brow. "You calling me a liar?" The words held just enough of a threat to get the man's attention.

Mr. Fancypants straightened. "If this chair belongs to you, how come you haven't been around all night?"

"Not your business. Now—" Dax leaned down, close enough that he could see the pulse leap in the man's throat. "I suggest you leave."

Mr. Fancypants's Adam's apple wobbled. Bolting upward, he kicked aside the chair and shot a glare in Ellen's direction. "Last time I buy you a drink."

Dax stepped in front of him. "If you ever touch her

again, you won't have to worry about buying drinks." Watching the man slink away, he smiled.

Problem solved.

****

Grasping the glass, Ellen stared upward. For a moment, she forgot to breathe, forgot about the drink pressed against her lips, forgot about everything but the sight of Dax standing above her like an avenging god. A soft sigh slipped from her lips. Wow—*just wow.*

Having never directly experienced a man's bravado, seeing Dax with his hands curled into fists and the steely look in his blue eyes, Ellen understood the appeal. Not to mention, Dax looked nice.

Check that—dressed in the brown bomber jacket, the scruffy stubble lining his chin, and his disheveled hair, he looked a little *too* freaking attractive for her peace of mind.

Yanking away her gaze, she studied Brandon Eric Michelson, III, as he repeatedly reminded her during their far-too-long conversation and decided either his ego was larger than she first thought, or he was incredibly stupid. *That* thought was quickly followed by two more—the first being whether his highly prestigious position in the extremely exclusive brokerage firm paying him millions upon millions each year—again per his long-winded ad nauseam dissertation—included decent insurance, and the second was whether Ben would blame her for Dax's arrest.

Thankfully, she needn't have worried. Brandon had the good sense to realize not only did Dax tower over him by an easy four inches but outmuscled him, too.

After a swift kick to the chair and a hard glare in Ellen's direction, he slunk away.

Dax continued staring at Brandon's departing back before turning.

Ellen watched the steel fade from his eyes, replaced by a smile so warm and inviting that for a nanosecond, she had an insane urge to pat her hair. Her do-not-contemplate list popped into her thoughts. The first item had only one name—Dax Moore. Okay, technically two, but together they amounted to one thing—trouble, and she'd be smart to remember that fact, too. Dropping her hand, she curled fingers into a fist.

Dang Dax. They shared one stupid, incredible, inappropriate, and totally captivating kiss, and she had completely forgotten he was public enemy number one. She picked up her drink. What she needed was a buffer—a voice of reason, so to speak.

Had Alexis been around, she'd remind Ellen of all the reasons why men were dangerous—like the fact they tended to cheat, had hearts made of stone, and didn't appreciate a woman. Of course, Alexis was in the middle of a bitter divorce after ten long, painful years of marriage, so maybe not the most objective opinion. Still, she wouldn't hesitate to remind Ellen not to trust any man—as if Ellen needed that little nugget of wisdom. The larger problem was with Alexis in California signing the docs closing the chapter with her no-good cheating ex—Alexis's words, not Ellen's—she had limited options.

Chewing her lip, Ellen glanced at the clock on her cell. Early evening in Malibu. Should she call Alexis, just for a quick pep talk? If she did, what would she say—Dax kissed her on Tuesday, and now she couldn't remove the memory—and oh, by the way, six years ago, they had sex, too…so…?

Oh boy…wouldn't Dax just *love* to hear that conversation. Why, talk about inflating his ego. She scowled. No thank you—which meant she had only one person to rely on—Maybelline—who in no way could be considered an ideal choice, *but* she would keep Ellen in line. Scanning the room, she searched for her cousin.

Go figure, of all the women wearing normal, Friday-night-out-to-find-a-date attire, she couldn't find the one person dressed in dominatrix-meets-retro-sixties, not-so-chic attire with a towering beehive hairdo. *What were the odds?* Ellen frowned. The one time she needed her cousin, and Maybelline had gone M.I.A. Now what was she to do?

A tiny voice whispered not to worry. One of the scantily clad women would catch Dax's attention soon enough, and just like that, he would be gone. Only, instead of leaving, he dropped into the recently vacant chair. *Whoa. Wait.* He wasn't supposed to stay, and he certainly wasn't supposed to sit. The soft smell of surf and spice surrounded her. Her thoughts fled, and her knees weakened.

His cologne? Again…? What the heck? Did he purposely torture her? "What are you doing?" Her voice came out sharp and squeaky. She took a quick sip of her tepid drink and somehow kept her face from wincing.

Dax laughed. "Sitting."

Oh, didn't he just think he was *so* funny. She swept her gaze over him and took in his dress shirt tight across his muscular chest. Heat simmered low in her belly, mingling with the swirl of butterflies. Suddenly, she found she desperately needed something—anything wet and distracting. She glanced at her drink. *Dang.*

Empty. Clearing her throat, she waved the glass. "Dressed kind of fancy for Martinis, aren't you?"

Chuckling, Dax glanced out to the dance floor. "Had a calendar signing in Albany today."

Ellen's stomach squeezed. *Figures.* Twisting about, she skimmed her gaze around the room before turning back. "And Angel let you leave without her?"

Ripping back his gaze, Dax scowled. "Angel knows the deal." Stretching out his long legs, he slid a beverage toward her while sipping his drink. He set down his bottle and fanned a hand. "Thought you could use a new drink."

His fingers brushed against hers, briefly, but long enough for a sizzle to zip across her nerves. Her breath caught. *Nope.* She refused to go there. Clasping the cool glass, she sipped. Sparkly bubbles broke the clear surface to tickle her nose, and the sharp taste of lime and the crisp bite of soda danced on her tongue. She shot a look to Dax. "Vodka and soda? You remembered?"

"We've been friends forever." Smiling, Dax shrugged. "Did you think I'd forget?"

The way his gaze skimmed over her caused a thousand ideas to scroll through her thoughts, and every single one of them took her right back to Tuesday.

Dang it. Why did he have the ability to make her forget her best intentions?

She looked around the room, wondering where the heck her cousin had disappeared to. Gulping her drink, she considered making some lame pretense, like needing to use the restroom and leaving, only she refused to act like a coward and run away. She slid a sideways glance toward Dax and frowned. How come *he* didn't look bothered?

Of course, why would he? Friday night at Martinis guaranteed him a date. She pushed back in her chair and clenched a fist in her lap. *What the heck? Why hadn't the kiss affected him?* She dug fingers into her palm. He probably figured she'd just chalk up the whole incident as a little flirtatious fun—like he shared amazing, earth-shattering, knees-quaking, breath-stealing kisses with every woman. *Unless...*

She stilled. *Oh jeez.* Maybe *only* she experienced that sensation? Maybe for him the kiss had been run-of-the-mill— Her stomach squeezed. Turning, she studied his long, powerful fingers, his full, sensuous lips, his strong jawline...

Oh, who did she kid? He was the expert at determining good, better, and best, and knowing her luck, she probably ranked somewhere between vanilla and humdrum. An uncomfortable warmth crawled up her neck. *Just great—the man hated vanilla anything.*

She took a deep breath and regrouped, reminding herself ho-hum was what she wanted, because they couldn't be anything else, right? Which should have been fine, only she didn't feel fine. In fact, the idea made her feel quite prickly. That thought really annoyed her, which was beyond ridiculous because she didn't want to be annoyed, and that annoyed her even more. Clutching the glass, she nodded toward the women eyeing him like tonight's dessert. "Looks like tonight you've got your choice of women."

"What if I said..." Setting his bottle on the table, he picked at a corner of the silver label and turned. "I just want to hang out with my friend tonight?"

At his slow, sexy smile, her stomach quivered.

Licking her lips, she remembered past times—of her at eight years old, choosing the perfect Christmas gift, knowing he'd be lucky if he received any gift from his parents, of taking his mind off the state championship game in his senior year because he'd been banned for doing what was right, and then watching him graduate from high school, and finally the fire academy, knowing the only family he had was her own. All were juxtaposed against images of him championing her during school, of easing her loneliness in college, and of holding her when her father died. He wasn't just Ben's best friend, but hers, too.

As if he too remembered, his blue gaze collided with hers.

In that moment, she realized she had a problem—a big, brawny, blond-haired, blue-eyed problem. *And dang it.* This very moment was why she needed a voice of reason, because right now, she couldn't seem to find any rational thought at all.

Chapter 12

The next morning, Ellen woke to a hammering in her head—like a dozen large, glass marbles slamming into each other inside her brain. A stabbing pain, similar to a pick crashing into a sheet of ice, pierced not one, but both eyes, and oddly enough, a sharp cramp spasmed in one calf. For the moment, she couldn't do anything about the riot occurring behind her eyes or in her skull, but she could work on the knot in her leg.

She flexed her foot. As the tightness eased, she groaned softly. Sighing, she rolled over, and pulling the sheets against her face, she snuggled deeper into the soft pillow. The silky fabric brushed against her cheeks, and the distinct smell of sun, surf, and oh-so-sexy surrounded her. She stilled, and her heart plunged straight down to her stomach. The throbbing pain in every part of her body disappeared. *What the heck...*

Either she was in the middle of a most vivid dream, or—

The soft sound of falling water filled the room.

Her breath caught. So, *not* a dream. Snapping open her eyes, she ripped her gaze to the master bathroom door. A thin stream of light shone from beneath the crack. Her stomach lurched. She turned back to the sheets and scowled. *Black? How cliché.*

Pinching the sheets between two fingers, she peered beneath. *Uh oh. So not good.* Scrambling upright, she ran her gaze to the sable-colored curtains framing the windows. Weak sunlight peeked from the fabric edges. Mounds of clothing formed a trail of guilt from doorway to bed. Chewing the inside of her cheek, Ellen peered over the side of the bed. The heel of one dress boot jutted out from beneath another pair of discarded jeans. The other leaned against the front of the bureau.

A rush of air ripped from her. Pressing a shaking hand against her forehead, she closed her eyes. Memories of last night floated through her thoughts, reminding her of the little thrill at his request to hang out with his friend, of them sitting side by side, sipping drinks, and talking companionably, of his fingers playing over the soft flesh of her shoulder, and her leaning into his side, of loose limbs and easy laughter, of her pulling him onto the dance floor for a fast dance, and him keeping her there for a slow one. They had stood so close a card couldn't be wedged between them.

And then later…

Maybelline disappeared, and Dax drove her home. Had she been drunk?

Gripping the sheet, she recognized the truth. Not drunk, but tipsy enough that she had tripped in the ankle-deep snow and fallen straight into Dax's outstretched arms.

She remembered how his arms wrapped around her, protecting her from tumbling to the ground, and the decadent, delicious feeling of his body's heat and strength against hers—like the best forbidden fruit waiting to be tasted. The dark whiskers edging his chin had tempted her, making her wonder if the stubble would tickle her fingertips. Moments later, she gave into the insane urge and brushed fingers against his chin.

His gaze had held hers, and the fear she'd experienced in the bar returned. Was she less palatable than vanilla? For the second time in a week, Dax had dipped his head, sharing with her the most sinfully, lusciously, exquisitely perfect kiss.

She groaned. So that explained the aching leg *and* how she arrived in Dax's bed...naked. *Just freaking great.* Suddenly, she realized the shower had shut off.

She jerked her attention to the door.

Metal scraping against metal broke the quiet.

The noise was enough to get her moving. Kicking aside the sheets, she bolted out of bed. She grabbed her pants from the floor, all the while searching the room for her shirt and bra. No such luck. *What the heck?* Giving up, she yanked on the jeans. Her hands shook so much she could hardly zip them.

A sharp clatter against the counter reverberated just seconds before more rushing water.

Hurrying across the room, she ripped open Dax's closet. The provocative scent of his cologne surrounded her. Feeling her knees weaken, she gripped the doorknob. *Jeez.*

Shaking off the arousing memories, she reached inside and grabbed a shirt off a hanger. She slipped the soft cotton over her head, gritting her teeth and forcing herself to ignore the heady fragrance. Retrieving the boots, she plopped on the bed. While staring at the bathroom, she opened the boot flap, ready to slip a foot inside.

The faucet shut off.

Her stomach lurched. *Skip it.* She needed to escape

now. Clutching boots in one hand, she darted from the room and down the stairs. In the living room, she spied her white lacy bra draped over the back of the couch. Her shirt lay discarded on the coffee table.

Footsteps sounded overhead.

Her pulse raced. Snatching both the bra and the shirt, she bolted into the kitchen and ripped open the back door.

Soft flakes drifted down from the milk-white sky.

She shut the door, then rushed down the steps. The harsh air stung her lungs, and the crusty snow bit her feet. Gripping the boots and clothing against her chest, she dashed past Dax's truck and hurried toward the shrubs. Shoving aside the branches, she lunged through the thicket. Leafless twigs struck her face and tangled in her hair.

Wincing, she pulled one branch free and broke through to the other side. She peered across the yard to her mother's house. No light shone from within. She eased out a breath. *Finally, a break.*

Racing toward her house, she peered over her shoulder. No sign of Dax—not that she expected him to follow. No doubt he was thankful she had left—made life easier for him. At least now, he didn't need to make uncomfortable conversation with her while ushering her toward the door.

How freaking annoying. Just like the first time they'd slept together. Only, then, she was the one who made uncomfortable conversation, hoping to return things to normal, *and* he was the one who made the escape. Either way, he got what he wanted in the end.

She hurried up the porch steps, while digging through first one pocket, then the other. No silk ribbon tickled her finger, and no sharp edges bit her flesh. Pressing her head against the door jamb, she closed her eyes. "Now what?" Shoving away, she peered down at the rough doormat. A whoosh of air ripped from her. *Right.*

Dropping to both knees, she flipped the mat. Silver flashed in the sunlight. Right now, she didn't care if her brother knew she hid the key under the mat. "Oh, thank goodness for Maybelline and her crazy ideas."

Ellen grabbed the red string and stood. Juggling the boots and clothing in one hand, she slipped the key into the lock and shoved open the door. She shot one quick glance toward Dax's before darting inside. Shutting the door, she pressed her back against the hard wood and cold glass. She knew Dax's angle now. Last night, his words about hanging out with his friend had only been a line—one she had fallen for before.

Flinging the clothing onto the table, she closed her eyes and pressed a shaky hand against her forehead. What the heck was wrong with her?

****

While rinsing off the razor, Dax rubbed a hand across his jaw. Perfectly smooth without a nick in sight. He smiled. *Would Ellen be disappointed at the lack of stubble?* He turned off the tap and placed the razor on the shelf just below the mirror. If last night was any indication—maybe.

A deep, satisfied laugh rumbled from him. *Go figure.* He knew plenty of ways to woo a woman into his bed. But a five o'clock shadow? Had to be a first. Not that he complained. Ellen was the trophy he had wanted for a long time.

He rolled his shoulders, enjoying the loose, limber

feeling in his muscles. His thoughts were easy and peaceful, too. His smile broadened, knowing both were a result of last night. Yup, things had gone better than he had planned.

Glancing toward the bathroom door, he pictured Ellen lying on his bed. Black satin draped over her trim, golden form, hinting at all the perfectly, wonderful curves he knew lurked beneath the sheets. Her dark hair, so rich and deep, like a perfect cup of black coffee, spilling over the pillow in tangles and waves. A soft contented smile creasing her full, luscious lips and thick lashes resting against rosy cheeks. His scent would now mingle with the flowery perfume she wore that tortured him at every turn. Bursts of electricity shot through him. Yeah, he liked those images—a lot.

His mind tormented him further by adding visions of placing soft kisses along the column of her neck until little moans rumbled from her. Heat curled in the pit of his stomach. He liked that idea, too.

Sighing, he scooped the fresh Aberdeen Fire shirt from the door hook and tugged the fabric over his head. For the first time ever, he regretted the constraints of his job. He'd never been envious of those who had nine-to-five, Monday through Friday careers. Today, though, he'd give anything to skip work and spend some quality playtime with Ellen.

Unfortunately, with all the time he had spent recently promoting the calendar, he really needed to be a presence at work—if for no other reason than to feel like he was a part of something bigger than just a pretty face. Besides, he couldn't ask his co-workers for more favors.

And really, knowing Ellen, she'd probably sleep

half the day—especially, after a week of rising early. Despite his desire to indulge himself in her very nearness, he wasn't *that* selfish. He knew she needed her rest. Sighing, he tucked the shirt ends into his pants. He'd just have to wait until tomorrow for them to spend the day together.

Grinning, he pulled open the door and immediately glanced toward the bed with the empty pillows to the rumpled silk sheets tossed aside. The smile slipped from his face, and his chest constricted. *What the hell?*

He shifted, noting only one pair of discarded pants—his—on the floor before moving his attention to the wide-open wooden door. Red heat—fiery and raw—slowly spread from his core outward. He gritted teeth and fisted hands. She left? Without saying goodbye? *Like hell.* Rounding the bed, he marched across the room and yanked open the bedroom door.

A soft knock echoed upward.

Grabbing the railing, Dax hurried down the stairs. Stepping into the kitchen, he glanced out the window and skidded to a stop. The flashy red coat, the ebony hair, and the sharp, cold smile caused his chest to tighten and his muscles to tense. He strode across the room and opened the door.

Tugging off her red leather gloves, Angel smiled. "Morning, sexy." Reaching up on tiptoes, she pressed a hand against his jaw and leaned in.

Dax stiffened and turned his head. Her kiss landed on his cheek.

Frowning, she brushed fingers against his flesh. "Everything okay?"

Nothing was. Only she wasn't the one he needed to deal with. He grabbed her hand, removing her touch.

"What are you doing here?"

She studied him for just a moment before wiggling past him and stepping into the kitchen. "You left yesterday before I could catch you." Tossing the gloves on the counter, Angel opened one cupboard while facing him. "I stopped by, but you weren't here."

Dax shut the door. "I went to Martinis."

Drawing out a mug, she peeked over her shoulder and wrinkled her nose. "That place is disgusting."

Dax planted wide his feet and crossed both arms over his chest. He had little care whether she liked Martinis or not. "Don't recall inviting you."

She made a soft moue with her mouth and skimmed her gaze over him. "I thought we'd go out."

Leaning against the table, Dax curled fingers over the edge. "Had plans."

Angel stared for just a moment before turning away. Her head snapped backward. When she turned back, two bright spots covered her cheeks, and a flash of green fire lit her eyes. She held out a hand. "Plans?"

Dropping his gaze to the brown purse dangling from two hooked fingers, he shrugged. "I never made any commitment to you." He fanned a hand. "From the beginning, the only thing we had in common was a mutual physical need."

Angel threw the purse. "You think?"

Reaching out, he snagged the bag, tossing it on the table. "I do."

"Yeah?" She snatched her gloves from the counter and sauntered over. "So, just like that, you're ending what we have?"

Dax sighed. Her reaction was the reason why he never entertained a second date—too much assumption on the women's part. "Darlin', you know whatever we shared ended a while ago." He pulled open the door. A gush of cold air ripped through the opening, matching the bite filling Angel's gaze.

She lifted a hand and traced a nail down his cheek. "You'll change your mind. I promise you."

He caught her hand, stopping the action.

Ripping free from his grip, she yanked on one glove, then the other. She stepped onto the stoop and pivoted. The wind caught her hair, flinging the strands in her face. Red gloved fingers shoved aside the errant wisps. "I don't lose, Dax. Remember that."

The sharp click of her heels on the steps broke the silence of the morning. He watched her stroll toward the car with her head held high, and her back ramrod straight. For the first time in his life, a woman had left angry. Shifting, he skimmed his gaze across the yards toward Ellen's house. Okay, maybe for the second time.

Then, he remembered Ellen sneaking out, leaving without a goodbye kiss. Grabbing her purse off the table, he slammed shut the door, and fixing his gaze onto her house, he trotted down the steps. "Like hell."

Chapter 13

Hooking a finger into the white, cotton curtain, Ellen peered out the window. No sign of Dax coming to demand answers. His absence didn't surprise her. In fact, her escape probably gave him plenty of relief, knowing he wouldn't have to deal with another ugly situation.

Ellen shoved away from the door and paced the kitchen. Last night certainly turned into a surprise—and not a welcome one, either. Jeez, of all the stupid things she could have done, falling into his bed topped the list. Check that. Falling prey to his easy line wasn't the stupidest thing she could have done. Having sex with him— She raked fingers through her hair. *Criminy.*

Never again would she take up Maybelline on any offer. If only she had stayed home. Okay, sure, maybe she would have spent the night wondering about Dax, but she certainly wouldn't have spent the night doing— well, *him.* She closed her eyes. Vivid images, hot and urgent, of calloused palms caressing heated flesh, of warm breath tickling slick skin, of erotic words stoking uncontrollable fires, washed over her, causing her knees to weaken, and her mouth to water. *Jeez.*

Why hadn't he just followed her plan? If he had just stayed true to course, he wouldn't have even stopped at her table, because he'd be too busy seducing one of the silly, giggling, fawning women just waiting for his attention. Instead, she ended up being the one seduced by his charming smile and easy ways. *Disgusting.*

Stopping in front of the sink, she propped elbows on the counter and stared out the window. She pressed her lips into a thin line. Oh, he was good. So very, *very* good. The rat-a-tat-tat of her nail against the counter broke the silence. Was Tuesday's kiss part of his plans or a test to see if she would fall, again? She stopped tapping and fisted her hand.

Of course. Didn't she know him? Know his every move? Hadn't she experienced them firsthand? She groaned. Each word and every action were all a part of his seduction. The drinks, the line about hanging out with his friends—all guaranteed to ensnare her in his trap, and she had fallen easily, swiftly, and completely.

Closing her eyes, she scrubbed fingers through tangled waves. Witnessing his proverbial revolving door was enough torture, but to be a part of it—twice? *Ugh.*

At least the first time, she could blame the error on youth and naïveté. Neither reason filled her with pride, but she had clung to them like a life-preserver. What excuse did she have now? *Absolutely none.*

She blew out a breath. Why had he zeroed in on her when he had dozens of women all eager for a shot at Mr. January? Was it the challenge of nabbing her again? Or proving her wrong about wanting him? Either way, of all people, he shouldn't have let his ego get in the way of his relationship with her mother or his friendship with Ben. Why jeopardize either for sex? And what about their past?

Through the years, he'd been like an older,

annoying brother, one whom she loved and hated at the same time. Had he forgotten that part, or the fact he had attended every holiday with her family and shared countless Jordan-Sheffield family reunions? And what about when her father had passed? He certainly had showed the same amount of pain and misery she and Ben had endured. Heck, even at the funeral, he had been there, with an arm draping over her shoulders and his fingers gripping her flesh.

Did the fact that he was a part of her family escape him—just like she'd forgotten? She groaned again. *Okay, fine.* Maybe they had made a mistake. Everyone knew too much alcohol had a way of making people drop their inhibitions. So, they slipped up again. Just because they had didn't mean Ben or her mother needed to know. And, if they never had sex again, all the better, right?

A tightness settled in her chest. She ignored the sensation. Right now, she would just remind him of their complicated relationship—force him to understand her family was involved, and deception wasn't possible. Surely, he'd see the truth and realize she was right.

Pushing away from the counter, she started across the room and, pausing for a moment, she glanced out the backdoor window. An unfamiliar white car filled the vacant space in his driveway. A sharp chill raced down her spine. She ripped her gaze to his house.

Angel stood on his doorstep like she owned the place. A gust of wind sent her jet-black hair cascading across the back of her cardinal red jacket. One hand reached up and brushed aside the strands, while the other knocked.

Ellen swallowed past the lump in her throat. A

punch in the gut would have felt better than seeing the woman he supposedly had no interest in stopping at Dax's. Worse was the fact she was no better than any other fling he had in town. To him, she was just a cheap, easy thrill. *Fine.* If he could dismiss her so easily, so could she.

Only a tiny voice inside her mind called her a liar.

****

A sharp gust of bitter air lashed at Dax's face and ruffled his hair. He glanced upward. The thick, gray clouds hung heavy in the morning sky, and a cascade of snowflakes floated to the ground. The sharp yelp of a lone dog sounded in the near distance. Puffs of smoke billowed from the back of Mr. Avery's beat-up old truck rumbling down the empty street.

Dax maneuvered past his pickup. Shivers coursed down his spine, and goosebumps pebbled his flesh. The low fury burning in his belly kept him warm, though. Damn Ellen for leaving without saying a word. Damn Angel for arriving without an invitation.

With one hand, he dug fingers into the soft leather purse. With the other, he jammed a hand against the sharp branches and shoved them aside. Forcing his way through the tangle, he ignored the sting and tug of spikes against his skin and shirt. He marched across the lawn and up her porch steps, heedless of whether neighbors watched and wondered.

Every muscle in his body tensed, and his head throbbed. He pounded a fist against the door. No sounds emanated. He flexed his fingers and waited. Nothing. He pounded again. This time louder.

Seconds later, the door swung open.

Dax jerked back and dropped his hand. Ellen stood

in the doorway wearing nothing but an impossibly fluffy white robe. Her long hair draped over her shoulders in thick coils of damp brunette. A floral scent teased his nostrils, and damn if he didn't find the smell arousing. The memory of last night and what hid beneath the robe slithered through his thoughts. His mouth dried, and his stomach clenched.

Golden chips in deep brown eyes flashed angrily. Two rosy spots covered her cheeks. No gloss or tint covered her full lips and not a speck of makeup distracted the eye. He stilled the urge to wrap her in his embrace.

"Gee, Dax. Didn't expect to see you."

Ignoring the sneer in her voice, he shoved his way past her. Like hell she had any reason to be angry. *He* wasn't the one who snuck out. Tossing her purse on the table, he leaned against the counter and glared. "Why did you leave?"

"I would think you'd be relieved." Crossing her arms over her chest, Ellen lifted her chin. "Wouldn't want to get caught in a difficult situation, now, would you?"

He fisted both hands and glared. "What the hell are you talking about?"

"Oh please! I'm not stupid." She ran her gaze over him and snorted. "At least, not anymore."

Closing his eyes, he prayed for patience. "I have no idea what you mean."

She shook her head. "Tell me, Dax, when did you make your plan? On Tuesday after you kissed me, or did the idea come to you last night when you spotted me in the bar?"

Her words stung. He clenched his teeth. Did she

really think so little of him? "Nice, Ellen." Sarcasm dripped from his words. Shoving away from the counter, he strode across the room. Within two strides, he closed the gap. Grabbing the lapels of the robe, he drew her closer. Heat filled him, but whether from anger or desire, he wasn't certain. He stared down at her full lips, remembering their taste against his. Warmth flooded him. "When did you become so cynical?"

She jammed fists against his chest. "How about when you stated you wanted to be friends only to seduce me?"

Her chest heaved. The gap in her robe widened. Dax dipped his gaze. A smattering of freckles covered her chest. Heat purled through his veins. He fixed his gaze on hers. "Sugar, I think we both can agree we seduced each other."

Ellen slapped at his hands. "What?"

Ignoring her outrage, he tightened his grip and smiled. "I see you have forgotten last night." He pulled her closer, enjoying the press of her body against his. "Like how you took the chair next to mine?"

Her gaze skittered sideways, and teeth nibbled her lower lip. "I didn't have a choice. The people at the other table kept bumping into me."

Yeah, he remembered. He also remembered how she had scooched over, so close he could feel the heat of her body against his. He hadn't a complaint then, and he didn't have one now. "Oh yeah, sugar?" He arched a brow. "And the dancing? Remind me, was I the one who forced you onto the dance floor?"

He remembered the slow, sensual song, of feeling her body close to his, and for just a moment, things between them seemed right, perfect. Despite his hate of dancing, last night he had never wanted the song to end.

Her face turned bright pink. "I just liked the song."

He trailed a finger along her collar bone. Goosebumps pebbled her flesh, and the vein pulsed in her throat. He smiled. "What about coming home? Remind me, did I make the offer or did you?"

She licked her lips. "Not fair. Maybelline had already left."

"You could have left with her." Holding her gaze, he traced the soft sensitive skin of her neck. "If you ask me, I think we both did a little seducing."

Her gaze locked with his. He thought he saw a look of worry and doubt in their depths. He understood the mental war she waged. Hell, hadn't he had the same conflict six years ago? An ache settled in his chest, somewhere close to where his heart rested. Grasping the back of her neck, he ran a thumb along her jawline. "Sugar, I wouldn't use you."

She dropped her gaze. "What we did was wrong."

He stiffened, and dropping his hand, he stepped back. All the heat burning inside him a moment before disappeared, replaced by a feeling of icy dread. "Excuse me?"

"Don't you get it?" Ripping up her gaze, she fanned out a hand. "We're not supposed to have sex. The first time was a mistake. The second time was wrong."

Adrenaline rushed through his veins, and blood pounded in his head. "Like hell." His words shot out, harsh and rough.

She hugged her stomach. "Dax, we're practically family. You're like a brother."

"The hell I am." He grabbed her shoulders and yanked her body against his. Despite the heavy robe, his body reacted. He wanted to thrust a hand into the opening and run a finger down the soft skin, to see if she was as turned-on as himself. He gritted his teeth and shoved aside the urge. "I'm a family friend, but I'm not family."

"You don't have to be so sensitive about it." She shrugged.

He tightened his grip, refusing to let her leave. Her damp hair brushed against his hands, licking his heated flesh. He'd only meant to give her a quick kiss, to remind her of the difference, only the minute his lips touched hers, a fire ignited inside him.

For a moment, she struggled, resisting his kiss, but seconds later, her arms drew upward. Fingers tangled in his hair, drawing his head downward. Dax obliged, wanting to consume her…to stir her the very same way she inflamed him. Only, he couldn't. But damn. He hated the fact he had to be at work.

Forcing his body to do what his mind expected, he broke free. He inhaled a deep, shuddering breath. "Listen, I meant what I said at the bar." Tucking a shaft of hair behind her ear, he reveled in the softness of her cheek against his fingertips. "I want to be your friend."

She dropped her gaze. "I won't be one of your groupies."

Did she really think that's all she meant to him? "Sugar, when have I ever asked you to be?"

She snapped up her gaze. "What happened last night… What happened before…" She licked her lips. "Can't happen again."

Laughing, he traced a thumb down her neck,

feeling her pulse leap in her throat. His blood stirred. He threaded fingers through her hair and tilted her head. "I think we can both agree we've moved past that point."

Her head jerked back seconds before she slammed a palm against his chest and stepped away.

She glared. "Do you have the very same arrangement with half the women in Aberdeen?"

Her words hit too close to the truth and too close to his past. He flinched. "Not half." He shrugged. "Some, maybe. But not since—"

Fire licked her gaze, and pink crawled up her neck. "Since when?" She arched her brows. "Since Angel?"

Angel? His stomach twisted. Had she seen Angel's arrival? "I told you, Angel means nothing."

A sharp hiss rushed from her. She burst out of his grip and marched across the room. Ripping open the door, she pointed. "Get out."

He froze. "Excuse me?"

She pointed to the door. "I...said...get...OUT."

Dax frowned. "Ellen, let me explain—"

"Do I need to call Ben?" Ellen crossed her arms over her chest. "I'm sure he'd be thrilled to know his *best* friend had sex with his sister."

Dax stilled. She was right. Ben wouldn't be happy. Especially if he heard the news from someone else. He clenched his jaw. Stepping outside, he stopped and turned. "This conversation isn't over."

"You're wrong. Not only is this conversation over, but so are we." She slammed the door.

Dax remained in place, waiting for her to see reason. When the door remained closed, he jammed his hands into his pockets and started across the lawn.

Seconds? Minutes later, the door burst open.

Hope flared inside him. He turned and stepped forward.

Ellen strode to the porch railing, carrying a large, black container. "Dax, this is what I think about you, your calendar, *and* your offer." She upended the bin.

The wind kicked up. A blizzard of rainbow flakes floated across her yard.

He let out a laugh. "I'll see you tomorrow, Ellen."

"I'll see you in hell first."

He winked. "Yup, probably there, too." He pivoted, and whistling, he walked to his house. A less-committed man would be discouraged. Not Dax, though. Ellen could deny the attraction all she wanted, but he knew the truth. Now, he just had to figure out a way to make her understand. Whatever she thought, nothing would stop him from taking what he wanted. And he wanted her.

Chapter 14

For the first time in all his years on the fire crew, Dax couldn't wait for work to end. Since yesterday's fight, Ellen had occupied his mind. She hadn't even given him an opportunity to clarify things. She just kicked him out.

Oh, he knew she thought he used her. Hell, he couldn't blame her. Six years ago, he had done the same without the intention. Now, though, things were different for him, for them, and had been for a long while. At Ben's wedding, when Ellen arrived, everything coalesced in his mind, and he just *knew*— Making her see the truth, though.

A little niggle of worry crept through him. For too many years, his friendship with Ben had warred with his desire. The thought of what could happen if she refused to listen frightened him. For too long, the Jordans had been his family. He couldn't lose them now. He scraped fingers through his damp hair. *What a mess.*

Voices floated from the station's kitchen followed by the splash of water against dishes. The leg of a chair scraped against the floor. Soon, men would crowd the locker room, packing their overnight bags before leaving.

Dax opened his locker. The metal door slammed against the next. Wiping the moisture from his brow, he dropped onto the long wooden bench. A dull ache rose from his muscles after his strenuous workout. He raised his arms, stretching them taut. The tightness eased a bit. He dropped his arms, and resting elbows on his knees, he stared at the clothing hanging from hooks, but all he saw was Ellen's fury. What the hell had he said that was so wrong? He had only spoken the truth. Slipping one foot into a boot, he laced them tight. He grabbed the second and slid his foot inside.

The door to the locker room scraped open.

Peering across the room, Dax finished tying the laces.

Jakob Newsome strolled inside. He scratched the thin strip of hair on his muscular belly just above the waistband of his blue-and-white-striped boxers. His hair stood in disarray, and his eyes still held the look of sleep.

Yawning, he strolled to the locker beside Dax's. "Just finish working out?"

Nodding, Dax dropped his foot to the floor and stood. Grabbing his duffel from the locker, he slung the bag onto the bench. "Just waking up?"

"Quiet night. I seized the opportunity."

Jakob hadn't lied. They received one call early in the evening. An unusual occurrence, to be sure. At this time of the year, though, things wouldn't remain quiet. With the holidays coming, more accidents involving drunk drivers, endless fights at bars and house parties, more sickness, and death were a guarantee. Dax looked over. "Don't get used to nights like them."

Pressing hands to his sides, Jakob arched his back. The muscles flexed in his arms and chest. He let out another yawn. "Not my first rodeo."

Shrugging, Dax unzipped his bag. Grabbing the damp towel hanging from the corner of the locker door, he tossed the cloth into his duffel. He turned and slid his gaze over his crew member.

At twenty-eight, Jakob had worked hard to maintain a muscular physique. Long, lean muscles rippled down his arms, across his back and chest, and bulged in his thighs. The slight bend in his nose, where Dax's fist had connected twelve years ago, only slightly detracted from his handsome face and sharp green eyes.

"Working out?"

Jakob yanked on a tank top. Smiling, he fisted one hand and flexed. A bicep the size of Dax's fist bulged. "Gotta impress the ladies." Relaxing his arm, he winked, nudging Dax in the side. "Right?"

The muscles bunched in Dax's neck. He dropped his gaze and dug through the locker. "Sure. Whatever." Grabbing his uniform, he dumped the clothing into the duffel.

Chuckling, Jakob stood and slipped off his boxers. "Heard the hometown heartbreaker is on the prowl again."

Dax stiffened. Once, he had embraced the term. Now, though, the connotation stung. Carefully, he zipped close the bag. "What are you talking about?"

"Heard you scored with Ellen."

Clenching his jaw, Dax slowly rotated. "Excuse me?"

Jakob scrubbed a hand across his chin and sniggered. "I remember when we dated. Didn't get so lucky then." He winked. " 'Course, we were just in high school. Still…"

Dax dropped his gaze to Jakob's nose. "Yeah, I

remember. Tell me, how did you two break up?" He snapped his fingers. "Oh right, Emily had something to do with it."

Jakob's cheeks turned bright pink. He grabbed a bar of soap from the locker. "Can't fault me." He turned back and nudged Dax in the side. "Gotta go with the ones who give it up, right?"

Slowly, Dax fisted a hand. "I'd be careful in how you talk about Ellen."

Jakob fanned a hand. "Take it easy. Just making conversation." He dug out a dirty, gray towel from the locker. "Besides, you should hardly talk. Not like you're opposed to an easy score."

Heat coursed through Dax's veins. An image of his fists slamming into Jakob's cocky grin surged through his mind. He remembered the feeling of satisfaction of the sharp pain in his knuckles and the crack of bone as his fist slammed into Jakob's nose the last time. "I never promised a woman something I wouldn't give."

Jakob snorted. "Big deal. I was a teenager. What's your excuse now?"

What was his excuse? Dax dropped the bag onto the floor. "Things are different."

"You think?" Jakob sneered. "I'm thinking the next pretty woman will change your mind."

Dax flexed his fingers. He couldn't fault Jakob for his assessment. After all, he hadn't stuck with one woman longer than he needed. Still, with Ellen...

Jakob slung a towel over his shoulder. "Though, once Ben finds out, he'll end the whole situation."

Dax's chest tightened. He knew the truth of Jakob's words. Still, he had to believe his friend would view him differently. But, if Jakob heard about him and

Ellen, it wouldn't be long before Ben did, too. No way could he let his friend find out by gossip. Gritting his teeth, he snagged the bag from the floor. "Gotta go."

"Hey, Dax?"

Straightening, Dax gripped the bag. "What?"

Jakob winked. "When you're done with Ellen, maybe you could put in a word for me?"

Fury curled through every inch of Dax's body, and bright red flashed before his eyes. He dropped the duffel. The thud of leather hitting wood sounded. "How about I put your crooked nose back into place?" He shot out his fist and connected squarely with Jakob's nose. Pain shot up his hand but didn't deflect from the satisfying crunch of bone against cartilage.

Jakob's head snapped back. The loud slam of head against metal ricocheted through the room. Deep red spurted from his nose. He yanked up his towel, pressing the cloth against the bloodied mess. "What the hell did you do that for?"

Dax shrugged. "Felt like it." He grabbed his bag from the bench. "You're gonna need ice and probably a doctor. Nothing else will help your ugly mug." Whistling softly, he strode from the room. Yeah, the second time was as satisfying as the first.

****

Flexing his sore hand, Dax stepped out of the station. With each breath he took, a misty puff of cloud floated from his lips. Pressure built in his chest. He stared across the park.

Holiday decorations filled the area. Large, colorful ornaments dripped from leafless tree branches. An array of lights draped across shrubs. Holiday figurines lined the walkways weaving through the area, and red ribbons adorned the newly built white gazebo.

He slid his gaze to the squat, gray brick building and then to the distinctive, black vehicle parked in the reserved spot. He wasn't surprised to see Ben at city hall, even on a Sunday. After all, Ben and dedication were synonymous.

Dax tightened his grip on his bag. A heavy weight settled on his shoulders. He needed to explain to Ben before word reached him. How would he take the news? Would he think like Jakob, or would he see more?

Digging the fob from his pocket, he unlocked the vehicle. He wouldn't know until they spoke, but he'd be damned if he'd let Ben ruin his plans. He slung the bag onto the passenger seat and slammed shut the door. Shoving his hands into his pockets, he dug out his cell phone. He punched in a quick text. His cell buzzed back. He glanced down and read Ben's message.

—*I'll have Ava let you in*—

Slipping the cell into his coat pocket, he glanced around.

Typically, Aberdeen took its time waking, especially on a Sunday. During the winter, most people waited until sunlight warmed the air before venturing out into the frigid air. By seven thirty, they'd give up the battle and head to town bundled in warm parkas and heavy boots. This year, though, the weather had been more temperate.

A soft drizzle rained downward.

Dax ignored the damp and headed across the street.

A few people, carrying bright umbrellas, sauntered along the paths crisscrossing through the park.

Dax darted up the solid, gray stone steps.

Ava Miller, a cute little redhead, with deep brown eyes and a sprinkling of freckles dotting her nose, held the door open and smiled. "Morning, Dax."

Her voice came out all soft and whispery.

Licking her lips, she slid her gaze over him. One hand fluttered down the front of her fitted shirt, exposing rounded breasts and a flat stomach. "I didn't expect to see you here."

Dax skimmed his gaze over her long, athletic legs encased in black leggings. Last spring and summer, she'd been on his radar. Now, he wondered why she ever held his interest. "The question you should ask is why are *you* here?"

Blushing, she took a step back. "I thought I'd help Ben for a little bit."

Stepping inside the massive, wood-paneled hallway, Dax wagged a finger. "Better watch out. He works a lot. One good deed and you'll find yourself working weekends, too."

A soft giggle rippled from her. "Oh, don't worry. He knows I'm only helping get him off on a good footing." She started down the hallway.

Dax walked beside her. Doors reaching the height of ten feet or more lined both sides of the hallway. At the far end, soft morning light shone through the glass windows. He could just make out the tall Christmas tree nestled in the front lobby.

The echo of his boots rapped against the marble tile floors. The soft caress of her arm brushed against his, and the delicate scent of vanilla and cinnamon surrounded him. He glanced down to the top of her head at the same time her gaze met his. He knew the look lurking in those brown depths—an open invitation if he wanted. He didn't, so he moved ever so slightly, putting some distance between them, and focused on the upcoming meeting with Ben—an encounter he dreaded.

A brass plaque tacked to the front of a wooden door read *Benjamin R. Jordan, Mayor*. He nudged open the door and waved Ava inside, then followed.

Deep burgundy carpet swathed the reception area, and heavy wood furniture filled the space.

He strode across the room, ready to get the meeting over.

"Dax, I was wondering—"

He didn't pause in his stride, knowing the question she wanted to ask. Not wishing to hurt her feelings, he stepped into Ben's office before she could finish and shut the door.

Ben sat behind a desk filled with stacks of papers and folders. Two computer screens rested on one side of the desk. Another sat on the other side. Steam curled from a ceramic cup positioned near the keyboard. Behind his desk ran a long, mahogany credenza. Bright light from the large window above reflected off the books and pictures lining the top.

Dax skimmed his gaze over the images—Ben and Lily at their wedding, another of them on election night, one of Claire with Robert, and a family picture from when Ben and Ellen were young children.

A picture of Robert, Ben's father, occupied a prominent spot right in the center. What would the man who had been more like a father than his own say if he knew? A heavy feeling settled in Dax's heart. He yanked away his gaze and shut the door. "So, how's running a city treating you?"

Ben sipped his coffee and studied Dax. "Just like being a police chief—a lot of minutiae wrapped in politics." He placed the cup on the desk and fanned a hand. "Have a seat."

Years had passed since the memory of being a naughty child flared through Dax, but right now, in this moment, the feeling of misbehaving overwhelmed him. He dropped into the worn, maroon leather chair and stretched out his legs.

"What's going on?" Ben tossed down his pen and stretched both arms over his head. "Didn't expect to see you until church."

Dax flexed his hand. "Came to talk."

Dropping his hands, Ben propped elbows on the desk and threaded together his fingers. "Okay. What's going on?"

Rolling one shoulder, Dax raked fingers through his hair. "Listen, I don't want you to learn about this from gossip."

Ben stilled, and the muscle flexed in his jaw. "What?"

Through the many years he'd known Ben, they never had a conflict. Now, though, tension filled the room, and unspoken words hung heavy in the air. Dax exhaled. "Your sister and I have—" He ran his gaze around the room, searching for the right way to break the news. Only once, in all their years of friendship had he lied to Ben, and that time mirrored Friday. He didn't want today to be the second time. Smoothing his palms against his pants, he met Ben's serious gaze. Only thing he could do was speak the truth. Running a hand over his face, he heaved a sigh. "Your sister and I had sex."

A heartbeat of silence filled the space separating

them.

Lifting a hand, Ben curled his fingers into his palm. "What did you say?"

A deep fury burned in the depths of Ben's gaze and a scowl as dark as night crossed his lips. Dax had seen Ben direct his anger at plenty of people, but never him. He wouldn't back down, though. Leaning forward, he pressed fists on the edge of the desk. "Do you really want me to repeat the words?"

The muscle flexed in Ben's cheek. "What the hell, Dax?" He gripped a pen. His knuckles turned white. "Are you using my sister?"

Dax watched the play of emotions on Ben's face. He couldn't blame Ben for his anger. Hell, if the situation had been reversed and Ben had messed with Darci, he'd feel the same. Only, he knew his feelings were different. He shook his head. "No."

Sighing, Ben tossed down the pen. "What are your intentions?"

What was his plan? Nothing short-term, surely. But long-term? His chest tightened. Could he make such a promise? He rubbed clammy palms against his pants. "Honestly, I don't know."

A dark frown creased Ben's mouth. "Dammit, Dax. We are talking about my sister."

"I know who she is." Dax scowled. "Do you think I would ruin everything just to use her?"

A harsh sigh ripped from Ben. "No." He scrapped a nail along the desk's surface. "*But* I won't allow you to hurt her, either."

Dax's stomach knotted. He flexed his fingers and glared. "Who said I will?"

Ben snorted. "I know your history."

The muscles in Dax's shoulders bunched. "Maybe I've changed."

Tapping fingers against the desk, Ben stared for a moment before sighing. "Yeah, I suppose." A whisper of a smile creased his lips. "I sure did."

The silence stretched.

Ben rapped the pen on the desk and glared. "I won't have you hurt Ellen."

For a moment, Dax wondered if she would hurt him. He didn't voice his concern. "I won't." Running a finger against his reddened knuckles, he met Ben's gaze. "She's worried about your reaction."

"So should you be."

Dax gritted his teeth. His fist still hurt from punching Jakob, but he wouldn't shy away from a fight with Ben, if necessary. He met Ben's glare. "But I'm not."

Leaning back in his chair, Ben crossed his arms over his chest. "So, now what?"

Damned if Dax knew. He swiveled his gaze to the image of Robert. The memories of Ben's father flashed through him. Growing up, Robert always had one adage he'd tell them. This moment felt like one of those times. "I'll do what I have to do."

Ben's brow shot up. He glanced over his shoulder before turning back. A half-smile flitted across his lips. "All right, then."

Dax relaxed his fist. "Listen, I'd rather you not discuss this with her."

Ben arched a brow. "Can I ask why?"

How could he explain he wanted Ellen to see him as more than just a person who used women, but as a man who really liked her? That he wanted her to agree, not because of her brother, but because no matter what, she'd chosen him anyway? "Things are new."

Ben stared for a moment. Finally, he nodded. "Fine. But she's not oblivious to the gossip in town. She'll wonder why I don't say anything."

He sagged in the chair and eased out a breath. This situation he could handle. "I'll take care of it."

Ben snorted. "Good luck."

Luck—the one thing he needed most. Dax shrugged. "So, we're good?"

Ben stood and grabbed his coat from the back of his chair. Slipping on the garment, he fixed his gaze on Dax while straightening his sleeves. "Tread lightly, friend. Because I promise, if you're using her, you'll live to regret your decision." He grabbed his leather portfolio and walked out of the room.

The door quietly shut.

Dax scrubbed a hand over his eyes. He had no doubt Ben meant every word. The possibility of losing more than just Ellen flitted through his head. He couldn't lose Ben, too.

Chapter 15

Ellen peered out the window. Soft rain poured from thick, dark clouds, and rivulets cascaded down the pane. Pressing a hand against the cold glass, she traced a finger through the cloudy mist and stared at Dax's house.

His truck pulled into his drive.

Catching her breath, she stepped back, fearful he'd see her watching only to realize the impossibility. With the distance separating their places, the most he'd see was light shining out the window. Her curiosity piqued. Chewing the edge of her nail, she again peeked out. Had he worked, or had he spent the night elsewhere?

The headlights flashed off. Seconds later, he hopped out and sauntered across the drive.

Fisting her hand, she stared at the familiar blue coat and dark pants. She slipped a glance at the clock. Eight a.m. He'd just finished his shift. So, not out on a date. *Surprise. Surprise.*

Renewed anger welled inside her at their conversation from yesterday. No wonder he walked with a swagger. He thought she'd seduced him. Fury roared upward from her stomach, filling her chest with a deep heat. Her head pounded, and her muscles tensed.

Ellen could name five times when she'd been so angry she wanted to punch something—or in this case someone. The first time happened when Jakob

Newsome cheated with Emily Roberts. The cheating had been painful, but nothing compared to hearing of the dastardly deed by Emily. Stupid Jakob didn't even have the courage to admit his horrid behavior.

The second time occurred when she found out Dax had broken Jakob's nose over the incident. She wholeheartedly agreed Jakob needed a whooping. She just wished Dax would have waited until after football season. He lost the right to play the last two games and to participate in the state championship.

The third time involved Dax and their first sleep-over, so to speak. She hadn't been upset by the sleepover, but rather by his easy dismissal of the whole event.

The fourth involved Grant. She still hadn't gotten over his betrayal.

And yesterday marked the fifth time. She leaned against the counter and glared. The confetti had melted, freezing into a kaleidoscope of colors splashed against a backdrop of white. The brief satisfaction of shredding the calendar and tossing the contents had morphed into a stinging outrage.

She shoved away from the counter. How dare he think she'd try to seduce him! Was his ego so large he couldn't imagine a woman who wouldn't? Well, she'd be damned if she'd sit beside him in a pew or across from him at the dinner table and watch him gloat.

Storming across the room, she grabbed her phone from the table and punched in the numbers.

The phone rang twice.

Claire answered.

"Mom, I won't be at church today." She feigned a cough. "Probably not dinner either."

"Oh dear. Are you sick?"

A smidgen of guilt welled up. She hated lying. Yet, the thought of seeing Dax made her mad enough to want to punch him. She doubted her mother or brother would appreciate the scene. She faked another cough and a soft moan. "Just a little cold. I really need to rest so I can go to work tomorrow."

Claire sighed. "Yes, I suppose." She paused for a moment. "Dax will be here. Do you want me to have him stop by with a plate?"

"No!" The words came out harsher and edgier than she intended. She gripped the phone. "I mean, I don't want to get him sick."

"Oh, aren't you so sweet."

If her mother knew the real reason, Ellen doubted Claire would consider her motives kind. She coughed again. "I'll talk to you later."

"Sure, honey. Take care."

Ellen hung up and placed the cell on the counter. Again, as if drawn by some magnet, she glanced toward his house. Why would he think she would willingly accept his offer? Had other women agreed to such a suggestion? She fisted her hand. Of course, they had, and the fact she'd fallen into his arms twice would only confirm that fact.

Shoving away, she marched into the living room. Flopping down on the couch, she drew a crocheted afghan over her body. The yarn scratched her arms. Fluffing a pillow, she rested her head against the soft satin. No matter what, she refused to face Dax and their convoluted past. She grabbed the remote and flipped through the channels. Yawning, she aimlessly watched television.

A soft knock sounded in the kitchen.

At some point, she'd fallen asleep. Cracking open one eye, she peered out the front window. Dusk had fallen and cast the trees in a golden glow.

The knock sounded again.

Raking fingers through her hair, Ellen kicked off the blankets and wandered into the kitchen. Spying a familiar figure through the door's window, she skidded to a stop. Fisting her hand, she marched across the room and flung open the door. "What are you doing here?"

Dax's eyes sparkled. "Came to pick you up for dinner."

Ellen pinched tight her lips. "Can't go." Coughing, she pressed a palm against her chest. "Sick."

Resting a forearm on the door jamb, he stared down and cocked a brow. "Came on pretty sudden, don't you think?"

"Gee, Dax." Crossing arms over her chest, she tapped a foot on the floor. "I didn't realize you were a doctor."

He chuckled. "Not a doctor." He dropped his arm and stepped inside.

She gasped. How dare he just assume he could enter her house whenever he wanted! "Why don't you just come in?"

"No problem, sugar." Reaching out, he pulled her against his chest.

His breath fanned her face, and his hands warmed her back. Little tingles raced through her. She shoved aside the sensation. "Why don't you save those names for women who are actually flattered by your insincerity?" She pressed palms against his chest and pushed. The man's body was like a brick wall, refusing to budge. "And I want you to stop touching me."

Instead of releasing her, he tightened his grip. "I missed you at church."

His thumbs rolled over her back, and his blue gaze held hers. Her stomach quivered. Secretly, she had to admit he looked quite attractive in his brown suede jacket and fresh denim. The wind ruffled his hair and pinked his cheeks. But what really caught her attention was the mischievous sparkle in his gaze. She wasn't surprised women fell at his feet. Dax Moore was more attractive than most men. "Like I said, I'm sick."

He arched a brow. "Sick? Or afraid you might seduce me?"

"Don't flatter yourself." Scowling, she lifted her chin. "And just for the record, I've had plenty of time to reflect on our conversation, and I say you were wrong."

"Oh? Want to explain how you came to such a conclusion?" Dropping hands to her waist, he leaned back. "Do you think you're above seducing me?"

She stiffened at the assurance in his voice. "As a matter of fact, I do."

He laughed. "Sugar, you've forgotten both nights then."

Ellen could feel her cheeks burning. She dug fingers into the soft fabric of his shirt. The muscles in his chest bunched. An image of their time together flashed through her thoughts. Her knees weakened, but she'd be darned if she'd give him the satisfaction of thinking she desired him. "Are you suggesting *I* hit on *you twice*?"

"Not hit on." He stroked a strand of her hair and winked. "Seduced."

Her heart fluttered at the soft, sensual tone in his

voice. She licked her lips. "Don't confuse me with your groupies." She slapped away his hand. "Why are you here anyway?"

"Like I said yesterday, I'd be by today."

Oh, how cocky he was. She gritted her teeth. "And like I *told* you yesterday, we are like siblings, and even the closest siblings don't want to see each other every day."

"Aw, sugar..." Leaning in, Dax pressed his lips close to her ears. "I think we can agree nothing about our relationship is like siblings."

His warm breath licked her flesh. Shivers raced down her spine, causing a warm glow to spread outward. Jeez, why wouldn't the man allow her to forget that little fact? She scowled. "What happened between us was just two nights involving too much drink. Nothing more." She fisted her hands against his chest. "And I promise, I won't be duped again."

Blue eyes sparkled. "You can deny the truth, if you want, but you can't fool me. Your eyes and body say otherwise."

She stiffened. Did she give off a vibe she wasn't aware of? Sure, her skin tingled, but why wouldn't it? His touch was bound to make shivers race down a woman's spine. And what about her eyes? Surely, he had mistaken her anger as attraction, right? She gritted her teeth. "The only thing my body is suggesting is disgust."

Smiling, he leaned down and brushed his lips against hers. "You're in denial." His teeth nipped her lip, tugging gently.

His soft breath caressed her flesh, making her think of things she wanted to avoid. "I am not."

His fingers wound through her hair, tugging gently and forcing back her head.

His deep gaze held hers. For just a second, a whisper of a smile creased his mouth before he captured her lips in a searing kiss. His mouth and hands wreaked havoc on her senses, and before she knew what happened, she slid her arms upward, cupping his head in her palms and drawing him downward. His kiss absorbed her every thought, bringing forward needs she'd desperately wanted to ignore.

Suddenly, he pulled back.

Ellen jolted, and pressing two fingers against her lips, she stepped back. "You're not supposed to kiss me."

He reached out and brushed a finger across her lower lips. "Sugar, I couldn't stop even if I wanted to." He pivoted and strolled to the door. "I'll see you tomorrow. Sleep well."

Watching him stride from the door, she fisted her hands. How the heck did he expect her to sleep now?

Chapter 16

Dax's proposition from two days ago still irked. Ellen stared out the kitchen window. A thin sliver of moonlight broke through the thick clouds filling the sky. From the looks of things, the town could expect another storm. However, the upcoming weather was the least of her worries.

She peered across the lawn. Darkness filled Dax's windows. A slow, rolling heat spread outward from her center. *What the heck?* She thought they had moved past what happened, and now, with his careless words, he had created an even greater wedge. She shoved away from the counter. How the heck was she to forget such a delicious, perfect, incredible night? *Freaking Dax and his sexy kisses.*

If he had just stayed away Friday night, she wouldn't have this problem. Only, she did. She grabbed her coat from the rack and, scooping keys and purse from the counter, she ripped open the door and dashed outside.

A thin coating of ice covered the back deck, and a cool breeze howled through the trees.

The hairs on her arms prickled, and a shiver sliced down her spine. Jamming her hands into her pockets, she decided to skip driving. Hopefully, a walk would clear her mind. Moving past her car, she sauntered toward the sidewalk.

Golden halos of streetlights illuminated the dark streets, and only the rustle of branches broke the early morning quiet. Dipping her chin into the coat's opening, she trudged on while debating her options.

She only had two, and neither of them was acceptable—leave and disappoint her mother or stay and be tempted. What the heck was she to do?

By the time she arrived at the café, she still didn't have an easy answer. Scowling, she yanked open the café's front door. Warm air blasted her face, and fresh brewed coffee tickled her nose.

Betty stood at the counter and placed pastries on silver trays. She glanced up. "Surprised to see you today."

Ellen peeled off her coat. "Oh?"

Picking up a sweet-filled tray, Betty slid the platter into the case. "You didn't go to church yesterday."

Great. Now she had to lie to her boss. Ellen weaved her way around the tables. "I didn't feel well."

Resting her arms on top of the case, Betty arched a brow. "This 'sickness' wouldn't have anything to do with your weekend, now would it?"

Ellen thought the air quotes were a bit unnecessary. She frowned. "How did you find out?"

Betty selected another pastry from the box. "Who else but your mother?"

Ellen's stomach tumbled. Had her mother heard the rumors through the endless grapevine that was Aberdeen? Oh, what did it matter? Her world was about to come apart. Plopping down on the stool, she closed her eyes. "Is she mad?"

"Of course not." Betty shrugged. "She knows sometimes a girl needs to let off a little steam, right?"

179

Images of Friday night flashed through Ellen's thoughts. Steamy was an understatement. She stiffened. *What the heck?* Her mother was okay with her having casual sex with Dax? She furrowed her brow. "What did she say?"

Betty placed the pastry on the tray. "She wasn't surprised."

Wait, what? Her stomach lurched. She swiveled around. "Really?"

"Sure. Why not? Although, she's a worrier." Betty finished emptying the box. "She knows how persuasive certain people can be."

Ellen thought about Dax's behavior throughout the weekend—Friday night with his easy companionship, Saturday with his taunts and promises, and Sunday with his teasing and kissing. Persuasive didn't even begin to describe his actions. "Tell me about it." Staring at her chipped nail polish, she could feel heat running up her cheeks. "I mean, I didn't go with the intention of sleeping with Dax, but he just has a way of making a girl forget the word no."

The clatter of tongs landing against metal sounded sharply in the room. Ellen whipped up her gaze.

Betty's eyes widened, and her jaw dropped. "Are you saying you slept with Dax?"

Ellen's stomach clenched. "Isn't that what you heard?"

Betty burst out laughing. "No. I *heard* you and Maybelline went to Martinis." She fanned a hand. "But your story sounds more exciting."

Uncomfortable heat crawled up Ellen's neck. Wasn't it just her luck? She blabbed the one thing she wanted kept secret? "No. And besides, it won't happen again." Jumping from the stool, she grabbed her apron and frowned. "Because the man is a pig."

Grabbing her coffee, Betty peered over the rim. Steam curled from the top of the creamy surface. "Oh, come on. You're too hard on him. Don't let one night ruin your friendship."

Stilling her hand, Ellen dropped her gaze.

"You did only have sex once, right?"

In the whole six years she had never whispered what happened. For a moment, she considering lying, but the idea of removing the burden was strong. Her stomach quivered. Stepping over to the coffee vat, Ellen selected a cup from the stack and tucked it beneath the spigot. Pulling the lever, she stared down and watched the coffee slowly rise. "We've actually had sex twice."

A low whistle sounded.

A lump formed in the back of Ellen's throat. She peered over, fearful she'd see disappointment on Betty's face.

Placing the drink on the counter, Betty arched a brow. "You mean this weekend, right?"

Ellen flipped the handle and turned. "I mean, two different times. Friday, and—" Setting the cup on the counter, she grabbed a packet of sugar. She had to make certain Betty would keep this information quiet until she could figure out a way to break the news without ruining a friendship. Ripping the corner of the packet, she glanced at Betty. "Promise me you won't say anything."

Betty let out a long, drawn-out sigh. "Fine."

Taking a deep breath, Ellen poured the sugar in the coffee, then grabbed a stir stick and plopped it into the cup. "Okay, years ago, when I lived in Albany, Dax would come down to see Ben." She stirred the drink. "But, if Ben was on the road, he'd hang out with me."

"Sure." Betty sipped her coffee. "Totally understand."

No, she didn't, but Ellen didn't argue that point. "One weekend Dax came down and—" She licked her lips. The memory held a bittersweet note. They'd had fun, going out to bars, drinking, dancing, and laughing just like Friday. "Ben was out of town, so Dax called me. We went out. Only, this time, things shifted from friends to…" She stared at the dark liquid, remembering more than just a long-term friendship. "More."

Betty heaved a sigh. "And you two had sex."

Tracing a finger around the rim of the cup, Ellen nodded. "The next morning, not wanting things to get weird, I suggested we go to brunch. We'd done it a hundred times before, so I didn't think anything about the offer." The memory of horror on Dax's face caused a shudder to rip through her. "He must have thought otherwise, because he made some lame excuse and bolted from my house."

Betty flinched. "Explains why you hardly came home."

The muscles in her neck bunched. Ellen lifted one shoulder. Just uttering the words brought back all the pain and humiliation she'd felt six years ago. "I didn't want to make things more uneasy." She stared at her hand. "And then, Friday happened."

"Okay, so you two had sex a couple of times." Betty fanned a hand. "No big deal."

The memory of Dax's proposition ripped through Ellen. Fury welled deep inside her. The fact he could so casually suggest such a thing proved he valued their relationship less than he did her. She gripped the cup. Coffee splashed over the sides, stinging her hand. Setting the cup on the counter, she grabbed a towel and wiped her hand. "You ever get propositioned by a friend?"

Betty jerked back. "Excuse me?"

Tossing down the towel, Ellen turned and leaned against the counter. "You know, like friends with benefits."

"Wait just a second." Betty reached out and caught her arm. "Are you sure Dax suggested such a thing?"

"Yup." Ellen nodded. "He told me so."

Betty scratched her chin. "I've got to be honest, that doesn't sound like Dax."

"Are you kidding me?" Ellen dropped a hand to a hip. "Look at his lineup card. The list is endless."

Betty rubbed her lip. "And he actually said he wants a casual relationship?"

Ellen lifted a shoulder. "Not those exact words, but he said some friends have sex."

Reaching inside the case, Betty selected a pastry. "Honey, some friends do." Dropping the cake onto a plate, she slid the Danish across the counter. "A successful marriage is based on friendship."

"Yeah, I suppose, but marriage never entered the discussion. Not that I expected it to." Digging two forks out of the utensil bin, Ellen handed one to Betty. "Anyway, yesterday, he stopped by on the way to Mom's."

Betty paused in taking a bite. "And?"

Stabbing a piece, Ellen popped a morsel into her mouth and chewed. The sweet cake tasted dry and bitter against her tongue. She swallowed. "We kissed."

Betty pointed. A few crumbs fell from the tines, scattering across the counter. "But no sex?"

Ellen thought back to the kiss. They hadn't had sex, but she would bet they both thought about it. Heck, she knew she had. She shrugged. "Only because he left."

Betty arched a brow. "If he hadn't, you would have?"

Remembering how she so easily capitulated flashed through Ellen's thoughts. She wanted to say no, but in truth…She licked her lower lip. "I don't know."

Betty pursed her lips. "And you're worried you might again?"

A little zing ripped through her. She immediately discarded the feeling. She lifted one shoulder. "Maybe." Picking up the cup, she sipped and considered her options again. She didn't know what answer was best. "A part of me thinks I should leave, but I know you need me, and I can't disappoint Mom again. But if I stay, well, who knows—if we slipped up and had sex again and Ben finds out—" A lump formed in her throat. She couldn't ruin another friendship.

Betty patted Ellen's arm. "Honey, you couldn't disappoint your mother even if you tried. As for me and Ben, you just can't worry about those things. Dax, though…" She squeezed Ellen's arm. "You're assuming he doesn't want more."

More? She wanted to laugh. She knew Dax—knew his M.O. Marriage, or even sticking with one woman, never entered his equation. Tapping fingers against the cup, Ellen scowled. "Dax doesn't commit."

"People change. Your brother did." Resting elbows

on the counter, Betty sighed. "All Dax has to do is find the right woman and, mark my words, he'll change."

Her stomach fluttered. *Had he?* She immediately dismissed the notion. Dax was Dax. He wouldn't change. Ellen ran a finger along the counter's edge. "Don't hold your breath."

Betty dug into the cake. More crumbs spilled onto the counter. "What will you do now?"

What would she do? She pressed the pad of her thumb onto a crumb. "I guess I just need to avoid him."

"Gonna be difficult." Betty patted Ellen's shoulder. "Dax isn't used to being ignored."

Ellen glanced at the counter. A stack of calendars rested in a spot next to the cash register. Dax's gorgeous face stared back. The butterflies in her stomach swirled. Betty was right. How the heck would she ignore him when he was only one yard away?

****

Completing her shift, Ellen pulled open the door and stepped outside. Cold air lashed her face, tossing her hair in disarray. Shoving back the strands, she skimmed the horizon. Thick, angry clouds replaced the early morning's thin wisps of white fluff. Every bitter gust caused another sliver of ice to slice through her flimsy coat, and hard droplets of frigid rain stung her face.

Jamming her hands into the side pockets, she drew in her shoulders and tucked chin to chest. With each exhale, puffs of white rose upward. Her feet hurt, her muscles ached, and her head pounded. By the time she reached the corner of Woodland and Main, the sky broke open.

Icy pellets pummeled downward. Within minutes,

a mixture of frigid water and hail drenched her coat and soaked her shoes. Thick hanks of hair, dripping wet, hung in front of her eyes, obscuring her view, and numbness settled in her toes, making walking more difficult. Her body was like one big ice cube, and all she could think of was a hot, steamy shower followed by warm, cozy pj's.

A truck pulled alongside.

A wave of water sprayed over her pants, soaking her already wet attire. Shoving limp ropes of hair from her eyes, she turned and scowled. *Freaking Dax.*

He pushed open the door and, pressing a palm against the cushion, he leaned forward. "Get in."

Wondrous warmth blasted from the cabin, tempting her. She stiffened, refusing to do Dax's bidding. Tightening one a hand on her coat, she lifted her chin. "I'll walk." She passed the truck, ignoring the slick moisture covering her face.

Suddenly, Dax stood on the sidewalk.

She gasped and, stepping back, she glared. His normally mussy hair lay pasted atop his head, and his dark-blue sweatshirt appeared plastered against his shoulders. The familiar jocularity and frivolity normally filling his gaze disappeared, replaced by a tick in his cheek and fire in his eyes. She took another step back and swallowed.

A zap of light followed by a loud crack sounded overhead.

Ellen jumped and pressed a hand to her chest.

Dax caught her arm.

She struggled, trying to break his hold. "I said I'd walk." He dropped his hand only to grip her waist. Without warning, he lifted her and deposited her onto the seat.

"I didn't ask." He slammed shut the door.

Ellen glared at the downpour. How dare he just assume he could order her around! While she wasn't thrilled with walking in the rain, the idea was certainly better than riding with him. She grabbed the door handle.

A brilliant streak of light flashed, and a loud clap of thunder shattered the silence.

"Don't do it."

More streaks of light sizzled across the sky.

His order irked, but she wasn't stupid either. Ellen released the handle.

He cranked the knob for the heater and slid a glance in Ellen's direction. "Why aren't you driving?"

She pressed hands against the vent and, ignoring the heat biting her fingers, she scowled. "I wanted to walk."

He snorted. "Bad call."

She snapped around her gaze. "Thanks, Einstein."

A smile twitched on his lips. He threw the truck into gear.

Through wipers whipping furiously back and forth, Ellen watched familiar houses fly past.

A strange silence filled the cabin.

Casting a sideways glance, she ran her gaze over Dax's stubbled chin and firm lips. She fisted her hands deep in her pockets.

Dax slowed the vehicle before pulling into her driveway and parking.

Opening the door, she sprang from the vehicle. Ducking her head, Ellen dodged puddles and rushed up the porch steps. With stiff fingers, she fished the keys from her purse. Three attempts later, she jammed the key into the lock.

She shoved open the door and stepped inside. Sighing, she reached out to shut the door, only to touch something very solid and extremely warm. She whipped around. Her chills evaporated, replaced by a low, tingly heat rolling through her veins.

Dax's soaked sweatshirt clung to his body, exposing every delicious muscle of his chest. The heady urge to caress the contours burned through her, causing her fingers to tingle and her belly to quiver. But *damn.* She licked her lips and calmed her racing heart. "You shouldn't be here."

Grabbing a dishtowel slung over the oven handle, he wiped his face. Finished, he tossed the damp cloth on the counter before closing the distance separating them.

Ellen inhaled. He smelled better than anything she could imagine—a mixture of soft rain and spicy cologne. She dug fingers into her palms. "You need to leave."

He cocked a brow. "Afraid you can't control yourself?"

Considering how close she was to forgetting her best intentions, she figured he wasn't far off the mark. Fisting her hands, she scowled. "Have you always been this annoying?"

He reached out and pulled her against him. "Probably."

Memories of past years floated through Ellen's thoughts—one of a ten-year-old Dax chasing her around the yard with dead snakes and disgusting bugs until screams ripped from her lungs and tears blurred her gaze, another of him at sixteen, challenging her to a wrestling match only to pin her soundly within seconds, of the time he had mocked her for dating Jakob, a boy in the opinion of the newly turned eighteen-year-old man. Pressing a palm against his chest, she glanced up. "Yeah, you have been."

He laughed. "Maybe you made things too easy?"

She met his gaze. A gentleness entered the depths of his eyes. Her heart fluttered. She curled fingers into his shirt. "All women make things too easy for you."

His hands clutched her waist, and his thumbs made lazy circles along her back. "Not all."

She arched a brow. "Oh? Really? Name one."

Leaning down, he brushed his lips over hers. "You."

Through his damp shirt, she could feel the beat of his heart and the heat of his flesh. "I'm just a convenience to you."

At her words, his eyes darkened, and the vein in his neck pulsed. "Ah, sugar, don't you know?" He wound fingers through her hair and lowered his head. "You've never been convenient."

His lips grazed hers, softly for just a moment, then firmer and more determined. He trailed lazy kisses down her neck, scorching her flesh with the heat of his touch. She clung as if her life depended on it, and at this moment, she wasn't so very certain it didn't. Desire swelled—a rolling burn needing to be quenched.

With each caress of his lips and stroke of his fingers, she could feel her willpower weakening. Closing her eyes, she dug deep inside for all the reasons why she couldn't let his words sway her—he only wanted sex, he'd burned her once before, and he'd do so again. Yet, her biggest fear, the very one she couldn't accept, loomed—the possibility of ruining a friendship. As she dug fingers into his shirt, a little ache settled in her heart. "Dax, we can't. We're friends."

He ran a thumb down her cheek and searched her eyes. "You'll never stop being my friend."

The words, spoken so softly, caused the wall to crumble further. She stifled a groan. "I'll hate myself for this tomorrow."

Grinning, he ran hands down her sides. "I'll make certain you don't."

Shivers coursed through her. His words fanned over her, holding promises she couldn't resist. She bit her lip. Oh, who was she kidding? Resisting Dax was futile. Weaving her fingers through his, she pulled him across the kitchen. For today, she'd forget about the ramifications and hope tomorrow things wouldn't change.

Chapter 17

Ellen woke, and turning, she glanced at the empty bed space. Gripping the edge of the sheet, she gazed around the room. The door was closed, and a deafening silence filled the space. A scowl she couldn't quite contain slipped across her lips. So, Dax had rushed away again. *Figures.* She should have expected such an action.

Hadn't he done the very same thing the first time?

Hadn't she done the same thing the second time?

What had possessed her to sleep with him a third time, knowing how the night would end? Talk about a glutton for punishment. She had no one to blame but herself. Worse though, was the fact that she had dragged him into her room.

She kicked aside the sheets and strolled toward the window. Shoving aside the curtain, she peered toward Dax's. She spied his truck in the driveway, but his house remained dark. *What time had he left?* Certainly not immediately afterward. She'd have known.

He probably waited until she had fallen asleep. The man didn't even have the courage to face her. Hadn't she expected this behavior all along, and yesterday, when she agreed, hadn't she known the outcome? Really, she had no one to blame but herself. But, dang, the fact he snuck out still stung.

She shrugged off the hurt. So, he escaped without a

goodbye. Fine by her. What did she care anyway? Dropping the curtain, she stormed into the bathroom and readied herself for work.

Twenty minutes later, still piqued by her submission and his escape, she marched into the café.

"I saw Dax's truck parked in your driveway last night." Betty chuckled. "Guess resisting him was harder than you expected."

Ripping off her coat, Ellen flung the garment on the rack. "I don't know what happened. Yesterday, I left determined to ignore him, and then he drives me home, and bam—" She slammed her palms together. "We've had sex, and he's sneaking out of my house."

Betty arched her brows. "Please tell me you remember the sexy stuff in between."

Yeah, right. Like she could ever forget. Sighing, she plopped into the chair and dropped her chin into her hand. "What's wrong with me? I know the guy. How come the minute he looks at me, I fall into his bed?"

Betty pressed a hand to Ellen's shoulder. "Honey, you're not doing anything wrong. All he needs to do is flash those baby blues, share a secretive smile, and say the right words." She snapped her fingers. "Before the woman realizes what happened, she's caught in his perfectly made trap."

Ellen tapped fingers against the counter. "He called me inconvenient. Not words a woman wants to hear."

"And yet you still slept with him." Betty arched a brow. "Seems to me he knew exactly what to say."

Ellen's stomach knotted. Had he given her another line? One she bought hook, line, and sinker? Of course, he had. Frowning, she jumped from the chair and began to pace. "I just don't understand why, though."

Pivoting, she thrust out a hand. "First, he sleeps with me, then drops me like yesterday's news. Then, he gets me drunk, *I* sleep with him, and the next day *he* propositions me. *Then,* he drives me home, accuses me of seducing him, and *I* fall into his arms a third time? Sick, right?"

Betty sipped her coffee. "If you ask me, it sounds like you dig him."

Skidding to a halt, Ellen swiveled and scowled. "What? Don't be ridiculous."

"I don't know—" Blowing away the steam rising from her cup, she eyed Ellen over the rim. "Wouldn't be out of the ordinary. You and Dax are close friends. Like I said, some friends make the best relationships."

"What kind of friend skips out without even a farewell?" She shoved one hand on her hip. "And besides, I know him. He's only in it for the moment. Our friendship, or the loss of it, means nothing to him." She shook her head. "I might be a glutton, but I'm not into that kind of punishment."

Betty strolled over to the coffeemaker and poured a cup. "Did you ever consider he didn't want to disturb you because of how early you need to wake?"

Was Betty right? Was he being kind? But the memory of six years ago, and the pain she'd endured, was lodged in her thoughts. Ellen frowned. "No."

"You need to cut Dax some slack. Find out first before you judge him."

Ellen sighed. "I suppose."

"Grumble if you want, but in my opinion, you two share an attraction." Sliding the drink toward Ellen, Betty wagged her brows. "Not really a bad thing, if you can manage it."

Dropping onto the stool, Ellen wrapped fingers around the warm cup. She considered Betty's words. For whatever reason, the stupid part of her brain was drawn to him. The logical part, though, knew nothing positive would come from having sex with Dax—especially when the gossip started. "What about Ben, though?" She sipped her drink. "Once he finds out, he'll explode."

"Oh, don't you worry about your brother." Betty fanned a hand. "He's a man. He'll understand."

She couldn't imagine how Betty could come to such a conclusion. After all, Ben wasn't the type of guy who lived in a world colored in grays, and encroaching on his friendship wasn't exactly gray. "And then, there's Mom…"

"Of all people, she'll understand."

Ellen paused in sipping her drink. "What do you mean?"

"Story is not for me to tell, but trust me, your mother won't be upset." Betty picked up a towel. "Listen, the only thing you need to do is let Ben know. Once he's in the loop, he'll accept your decision."

"Oh really? You think he'll be thrilled to know his best friend wants a casual relationship with his sister?" Ellen snorted. "I don't think so."

"So, don't tell him the proposition part." Wiping the counter, Betty looked over her shoulder. "Not really his business anyway. That's between you and Dax. Just be upfront about exploring your options."

Ellen chewed her lip for a moment. "Wouldn't that be the same as lying?"

"Oh, honey, don't complicate things." Betty sighed.

"But—"

Betty stopped wiping and frowned. "Do you think Ben tells you everything about his relationship with Lily? Their disagreements? Their promises? Of course not. And neither should you." Shoving aside the towel, she pressed hands onto the cleaned surface and stared hard at Ellen. "All you need to do is ask yourself whether you want what Dax is offering. If you do, go for it. If not, you better stay the hell away."

The café door swung open.

Pivoting, Ellen silently cursed. Of all the rotten luck, her cousin just had to show up this morning. She swept her gaze over Maybelline's outrageous outfit. "Where the heck do you find your clothing?"

Maybelline's eyes sparkled. She plucked the lapel of her furry, purple-and-pink-striped coat and waggled her brows. "I got this premium ensemble at Too Good to Be True." Stopping in front of the counter, she placed her cardinal red purse, bedazzled in an array of colorful crystals, onto the surface. "Pretty snazzy, right?"

Betty laughed. "Snazzy is one way of describing the look."

Maybelline flipped open her purse and dug out a wallet coated in black faux fur. "A mocha, please."

"Coming up." Betty walked to the stack of cups and selected one.

Maybelline loosened the lime-green-and-fuchsia tartan scarf from her neck. "So, what's up?"

Sliding the portafilter into the coffee grinder, Betty peered over her shoulder. "Ellen and I were just discussing having sex with Dax."

Ellen gasped and narrowed her eyes at Betty before

turning back to Maybelline and praying she hadn't heard the damning truth.

Flipping open the wallet, Maybelline wiggled her brows. "Oh yeah?" She handed Ellen her card. "Sign me up please."

Ellen scowled. Figures—this information she'd hear. "Oh, for heaven's sake." Rolling her eyes, she snatched the payment from Maybelline's hands and ran it through the machine. A sharp clacking sound rent the air. She tore off the receipt and slid it across the counter. "Is there a guy in town you're not interested in?"

"No need for sarcasm." Scowling, Maybelline snatched the paper and stuffed it into her purse. "I'll have you know when it comes to Dax, I like to keep my options open. You never know when he will go for a five-foot-two, fluffy-haired brunette."

Betty chuckled. "Yeah, well, you're gonna have to get in line." She poured milk into the metal canister. "Because he and Ellen are something of a couple."

Ellen glared. "You *promised!*"

Betty sighed. "Oh, come on. How long did you really think you could keep something this juicy a secret?"

She had a point. Still, for her to tell Maybelline of all people—who was perhaps the biggest gossip in Aberdeen. "You do realize Maybelline will blab this information, right?"

Maybelline gasped and, ripping her gaze to Ellen, she scowled. "*Excuse me?*"

"She's right." Betty waved a hand. "But, if it wasn't Maybelline, it would be someone else. You and Dax as a couple is definitely gossip-worthy."

Heat rushed to Ellen's cheeks. Stepping back, she raised both hands. "We are *not* a couple."

Maybelline jerked back. The tower of curls atop her head bobbled precariously. She narrowed her gaze. "So now I know why on Friday you refused to leave with me." She shook her head. "Here I thought we went out to have fun, and all you wanted was to get with Dax. Jeez, thanks a lot."

No way would she allow Maybelline to rewrite history. "In case you forgot, *you're* the one who left me so you could chase after Cooper Miller." A dreamy smile filled Maybelline's face. Ellen stilled the urge to roll her eyes. She hadn't lied about Maybelline falling for every guy in town. In Maybelline's mind, they were all worth going after.

"Oh, yeah, right." Maybelline tapped one silver-tipped nail on the counter. "He is pretty cute for a redhead."

Ellen gritted her teeth. "Which is why Dax *drove* me home."

"See, that's where Ellen and I disagree." Betty poured the steamed milk into the cup, then slid the drink across the counter. "Clearly, she must feel something for him. Otherwise, she wouldn't have slept with him three times."

"Three times?" Grabbing the cup, Maybelline glared. "Jeez, can't say no much?"

Ellen's stomach tumbled. For Betty to suggest something as ridiculous as she and Dax as a couple was one thing. After all, no one would believe he had any romantic intentions. But, to tell Maybelline—and effectively the whole town in the process—they had sex...well...jeez, who wouldn't expect such a thing?

She scowled at Betty. "Are you happy?"

Betty waggled her brows. "Can't say I'm not."

"Yeah, well, guess who won't be." Snapping a lid on top, Maybelline peered upward. "Ben."

"Which is why she was just about to tell him."

Ellen stiffened. Now? Something this big couldn't be discussed without some serious thought. Why, in her opinion, dropping a nuclear bomb would have the same effect. She whipped around to face Betty. "I thought I'd wait until later." Like never, if she had her way.

"And have him find out first?" Betty gave a low whistle. "You *are* a glutton."

Crud. Betty was right. She reached beneath the counter and dug out her purse. "But, if I don't come back, you'll know Ben didn't take the news well."

"Stop worrying, and just tell him the truth." After giving her a slight shove, Betty wagged a finger. "And remember, don't complicate things."

"Right." Ellen nodded. "Keep it simple."

Betty smiled. "See, you've got this."

Ellen drew on her coat and slung her purse over a shoulder. "Let's hope." She started for the door.

"Don't worry," Maybelline yelled. "We'll be praying for you."

Ellen glanced over her shoulder and scowled. Were there enough prayers in the world to help her?

****

Hurrying past the holiday decorations adorning the park, Ellen studied the gray building where her brother worked. In only minutes, he'd receive a shock of a lifetime. Her stomach squeezed.

How best to tell him? Should she start with the first time six years ago? She envisioned his reaction to Dax skipping out. *Nope. Won't start there.* Okay, then the second? Her stomach knotted. Shoot, she couldn't tell him about that time either, considering she had escaped—not to mention her inebriated state. Ben totally wouldn't understand either reason. Last night? The muscles bunched in her neck.

Now she looked like a sucker.

She considered Betty's suggestion. Should she say they were trying out things? Maybe if she added their years of friendship, he'd understand? Her head pounded. *Jeez.* How could a simple problem snowball into an avalanche?

Ellen marched across the street. She knew how her brother appreciated honesty, but the truth would crush him. Her stomach lurched. She closed her eyes and thanked the good Lord she hadn't eaten yet.

Stopping at the top of the gray stone steps, she stared at the large wooden doors. A million images ripped through her thoughts—all were of Ben filled with looks of anger, disappointment, and disgust. And what about her mother? Betty said she'd understand. But would she? Oh, what did it matter? Once Ben found out, she wouldn't have to worry about her mother. Rubbing damp hands against the sides of her coat, she took a deep breath and pulled on the brass handle.

A slight swoosh and a loud screech sounded.

Stepping inside the massive lobby, she tucked shaking hands into her pockets, despite the warmth of the building. Behind her, the door shut with a soft click.

A few people dressed in heavy coats and warm caps moved through the building. Damp shoes squeaked against the smooth tile.

Forcing a serene expression, she hurried down the passageway. Pictures of former mayors hung on both sides of the hall. As she neared her father's image, her heart hammered. She dipped her gaze, but not before she spied his kind eyes and his welcoming smile. A tightness filled her. If alive, how would he handle the news?

She could picture him sitting her down and listening. He'd probably discuss something about actions and consequences, but in the end, he'd wrap her in his warm, safe embrace and remind her of his love. A shaky exhale escaped her. Hopefully, Ben will be as understanding.

Stopping in front of the large, double doors, she stared at her brother's name scrawled across the brass plaque. How could she tell him? A weight, much like a boulder, rested on her shoulders. What she needed was a reason and not something about friendship either. No way would Ben buy such nonsense.

She chewed her lip. Nothing immediately came to mind. Okay, she'd do what she always did when an answer eluded her. She'd run with the moment. The method worked before, and she vowed it would work now. Feeling only slightly better, she strode into the front office.

Dark walls and maroon carpet filled the space. A black-and-white picture of Aberdeen from decades past hung on one wall. A massive bookshelf filled the other wall. Ava, his secretary, was nowhere to be found.

The shuffle of paper and the rap of fingers against keyboards sounded through the doors of Ben's office. She glanced at her watch. A few minutes before eight. She shoved open the door.

Ben snapped up his gaze. "Ellen? Everything okay?"

Was she that obvious? She forced a smile and walked inside. "Can't I come and see my brother?" She dropped into one of the leather chairs facing Ben's desk.

"Of course." Frowning, he glanced at his watch. "But aren't you supposed to be at work?"

"We had a lull. Betty suggested I..." Feeling heat burning her cheeks, she wrung together fingers and licked her lips. "I mean, I wanted to come and thank you for fixing my window."

Leaning back in his chair, he studied her. "Just don't break it again."

She squirmed in the seat.

The leather crunched.

She glanced at the credenza. Her father's proud visage stared back. Swallowing, she returned her attention to Ben and cleared her throat. "So, you like being mayor?"

He picked up his coffee mug. "Sure."

"And Lily? How is she doing?"

Ben sipped his coffee. "She's fine." Sighing, he rested his cup on top of the desk. "Ellen, why are you here?"

How the heck could she explain to Ben what she didn't understand herself? He might accept guys having noncommittal relationships, but not his sister. And he definitely wouldn't approve of his best friend and his sister having sex. Fisting hands, she let out a deep, shaky breath. "Okay, I did come for a reason. Please don't get mad."

"I can't promise anything until I've heard what you

have to say." Grabbing his cup, he took another sip.

Of course, he wouldn't. If anything, Ben was a stickler for hearing all the details before coming to any conclusion. "I came to tell you, I'm…" She licked her lips. Now would be an excellent time for something, *anything,* to come to mind. She glanced at the stack of folders on his desk. The top one read *sex offenders.* An idea arrived—not the best one, but the *only* one. "I mean to say—" She swallowed. "I think I'm a sex addict."

Ben choked. Coffee sprayed across the desk. His face turned beet-red, and a muscle worked in his cheek. Slowly, he placed the cup on a coaster. Fisting one hand, he pinched together his brows. "Excuse me?"

Oh man. Of all the things to say. Why hadn't she just kept it simple like Betty suggested? Her insides felt all twisty and confused. Bounding from the chair, she began to pace. "Well, what other reason could there be for me sleeping with Dax?" Pivoting, she faced her brother and flung out a hand. "I mean, he's *your* best friend and practically a second brother to us. Both of which I should have remembered, but well—"

"You're making me dizzy." Ben sighed. "Sit down."

Dropping into the chair, she dug fingers into the leather armrest and waited for Ben's explosion.

Instead, he rested both elbows on the desk and clasped together his hands.

The longer he stared, the more she regretted her rash actions. Why hadn't she just told the truth? Having sex with a friend wasn't the worst thing in the world. People did it all the time—which was why the whole deal had the name *friends with benefits.* Now she had dug herself a big hole, and to her brother, of all people.

Finally, he exhaled. Leaning back, he crossed arms over his chest and locked gazes. "Having sex with Dax doesn't make you an addict."

Her face heated. Jeez, of all the things she never expected to discuss with her brother, sex was probably near the top—somewhere close to when she had her menstrual cycle and who she lost her virginity to. She dropped her gaze. "Really? Then explain to me why we've—"

"Ellen, do you like Dax?"

His question might have come out soft and gentle, but that didn't stop her stomach from lurching. She ripped up her gaze. "Of course, he's a friend."

Shoving away his cup, Ben leaned in and stared hard. "I mean, do you like him for more than friendship?" He scrubbed fingers over his face before fisting his hand on the desk. "Do you *love* him?"

Ellen stared back. Whatever she expected him to say, asking whether she loved Dax never factored into the equation. Love and Dax did not correlate, and she was smart enough not to fall into such a futile fantasy. "What? No." Pressing her back into the cushions, she shook her head. "I mean, of course not. I understand Dax wouldn't want—"

"I'm not asking about what Dax wants," Ben snapped. "I'm asking about your feelings."

"What I feel doesn't matter. I just thought you should know I've slept with him." Unable to meet her brother's gaze, she jumped from the chair and paced. "A few times now, and I promise, they weren't planned." Stopping, she turned and pressed palms together as if in prayer. "Just please, don't let our mistake ruin your friendship."

One second passed, then another. Finally, he raked fingers through his hair. "Of course, I won't. You're both grown adults. You can do what you want." He stood and walked around the desk. With a sigh, he grabbed her shoulders and pulled her against his chest. "But I will *always* protect you."

His words brushed across the top of her hair, and all the tension building inside dissipated. Pressing her cheek against his chest, she curled her fingers into his shirt and eased out a sigh.

He leaned back and narrowed his eyes. "But also know, Dax is a friend. I don't want you hurting him, either. If you love him, you need to be honest with him."

Ellen pushed against his chest, breaking free. "Don't be ridiculous, Ben." She turned and headed toward the door. "Dax doesn't want love." She didn't add the words burning through her thoughts—Dax wants convenience.

Chapter 18

Crossing through the park, Ellen smiled, and a bubbly euphoria filled her. The awkward discussion had gone better than she could have imagined. Every horrible thing she figured he'd say never happened. Instead, he'd been kind, sympathetic, and understanding. His reaction had been completely the opposite to the anger and demands she expected. Slowing her pace, she frowned. Why? Hearing his friend and sister had sex had to be shocking, right? Only, instead of being surprised, he had been calm.

Her elation exploded like an overfilled balloon. An icy shiver, which had nothing to do with the frigid temperatures, sliced down her spine. She skidded to a stop and fisted her hands. Someone bumped her from behind. She turned.

"Oh, excuse me, Ellen. I guess I was too busy enjoying the holiday scene that I didn't realize you stopped." Mr. Winders shook his head. "Guess I need to pay better attention." He strolled past her.

Ellen stared at his back. Mr. Winders wasn't the only one who missed the signs. Frowning, she glanced at City Hall, then toward the fire station. *How dare he!* Her anger was irrational. After all, Dax had taken the brunt of Ben's fury, whereas she got the calm, reasonable response. Still, he had no right to discuss something so personal with her brother without first informing her. A knot formed in her stomach. Hadn't she done the same to Dax? She pushed the thought aside. Ben was *her* brother not Dax's. Pivoting, she hurried across the street and ripped open the door to the café.

Betty and Maybelline stood at the counter, chatting. They turned.

Maybelline smiled. "Looks like you survived."

Shushing Maybelline, Betty turned her attention to Ellen. "You okay?"

Nope, not even a little. Heck, she couldn't even form a coherent thought. Ellen marched toward them. "I am, but I guarantee someone who won't be."

"Uh oh." Betty frowned. "What did Dax do now?"

"He told Ben. Can you believe it?" Storming behind the counter, Ellen slammed her purse onto the counter. "And here I told Ben I was a sex addict."

Maybelline rubbed her hands and waggled her brows. "Oh, I like the sound of that."

"Would you hush." Betty glared at Maybelline before turning back to Ellen and sighed. "Okay, why a sex addict?"

Ellen fanned a hand. "Well, I couldn't use the whole friends-with-benefits thing. He'd think I lost my mind."

"So, sex addiction was your solution?" Betty shook her head. "I told you not to complicate things."

"Too late." Ellen frowned, ignoring the heat burning her face. "You know I'm terrible at this stuff."

Betty chuckled. "I'll say." She pressed a hand against the metal counter. "So now what?"

Ellen slid the purse strap on her shoulder. "Well, for starters, Dax owes me an explanation."

"Now, wait just a second." Betty caught Ellen's arm, stopping her. "What was so wrong with him telling Ben?"

"He should have told me." Ellen ripped away from Betty's grip. "I've spent years worrying about Ben's reaction for no reason."

"So, then, why are you upset?"

"Dax lied." Ellen jammed a finger into her chest. "To me."

"Did you ever consider he had a reason for not telling you?" Flicking a glance toward Maybelline, Betty arched brows. "Maybe he worried Ben or your mother would hear the gossip."

What possible reason could he have to share their secret—to her brother no less. Ellen skimmed her gaze around the café. Only one couple sat at a table, sipping coffee and conversing quietly. The rest of the morning rush had departed. Clutching the strap of her bag, she hurried around the counter. "No, but I intend to find out."

Betty pressed hands on the counter. "Don't be rash. Think about what I told you earlier. All you need to do is decide what *you* want."

Maybelline slipped her gaze from Ellen to Betty. "What did you tell her?"

"None of your business." Betty wagged a finger. "That information is between me and Ellen—and I guess Dax, too." She faced Ellen and tapped the side of her head. "Just think before you speak, 'kay?"

Ellen huffed. "I'll do my best, but I'm not making any promises." She pivoted and strode from the café. During the ride home, she considered Betty's words. Now that Ben knew and didn't appear upset, some of the pressure was off. Betty mentioned she needed to decide for herself what she wanted. So, did she want a casual relationship with Dax? How would such a relationship even work?

She mulled over the idea. Seeing as she knew him and his proclivities, she figured maybe she wouldn't be bothered. After all, Dax never asked for forever. And she did love him—as a friend, of course, nothing more, like Ben suggested. In Albany, she knew several friends who had such a relationship. When things went south, none of them were upset. A few even remained friends.

Really, when she considered things, they weren't doing anything wrong. They were just two friends enjoying a few weeks together. No big deal. Besides, by New Year's, she'd be back in Albany, which meant she wouldn't have to see his revolving door of women. *Easy peasy.*

She parked the car, and clutching the steering wheel, she stared out the window. Through the border of leafless trees, she spied his truck. At the thought of the upcoming confrontation, she froze, her stomach tumbling. What if he had changed his mind? She shoved aside the thought. The whole friends-with-benefits thing had been his idea, and the one thing she knew for certain, turning down a relationship involving casual sex was not in Dax's vernacular.

She closed her eyes and inhaled. *So, this is it...*before shoving open the door and stepping out.

Great drifts of white rolled across the ground.

Pushing aside branches, she stepped into his yard. Moving past his truck, she heard a loud clank emanating from the garage. She peered at the closed bay door. Through the panes of glass lights shone.

Hiking her purse strap higher, she walked to the side of the garage.

Another clank sounded.

She peered through the open side door. Dust swirled in the overhead light, and oil scented the air. Rock music blasted from a radio sitting atop a massive shelf filled with tools and car parts. A red, metal chest reaching the top of the hot rod's hood was positioned near the car's front end. On the top rested some wrenches and ratchets. A ton of unfamiliar paraphernalia and gizmos peeked out from open drawers.

Shifting her gaze, Ellen caught sight of Dax half buried beneath the engine's hood. A lamp dangled from the hood's rim. His golden hair shimmered in the incandescent light. A streak of black soot marred his tanned forearm, and a film of dust soiled the faded yellow shirt covering his broad shoulders. With every crank of the handle, his bicep bulged, and his forearms flexed. All moisture dried from her mouth, and a low heat warmed her stomach.

Man, oh man. She could stare at him for the rest of her life. *Wait. What? Forever?* No way—not if Dax had a say. Shaking off the ridiculous thought, she stepped inside.

After tossing the tool he held into the top drawer of the chest, he brushed his bicep against his forehead. He peered over and stilled. Dropping his arm, he flashed a brilliant smile. "Ellen."

He said her name like a soft caress, causing little bubbles to burst in her stomach. Stepping closer, she licked her lips. "Remember your proposition?"

Pressing lips into a tight line, he ran fingers

through his hair before exhaling. "Ellen, I ne—"

She put up a hand. "I agree."

He jerked back and furrowed his brow. "What?"

Her smile faltered. Had he changed his mind? "I mean, if it's still on the table."

He leaned against the side of the car and crossed his ankles. "You suddenly have a change of heart?"

She shrugged. "I talked with Ben today, and he—"

He stiffened for just a second before grabbing a stained rag off the side of the car and rubbing the grease from his hands. When he looked back, fire lit his gaze. "He told you?"

"No." Ellen jammed hands against her hips. "I figured it out when I went to tell him, and he didn't act surprised." She glared, remembering his high-handedness. "By the way, you had no right to tell him. Especially since you didn't tell me."

"Sorry, baby girl." He continued wiping his hands. "I just didn't want him to find out about us through the grapevine."

So, Betty was right. He, too, worried. At least, that was something. "I wish you would have told me." She crossed arms over her chest. "Maybe then I wouldn't have made a fool of myself by telling him I'm a sex addict."

He slowed wiping his hands and cocked a brow. "Excuse me?"

His blue eyes sparkled. Oh, didn't it just figure he'd find this situation amusing? She huffed. "That's right. I needed an excuse, and the only thing to come to mind was sex addiction."

Dropping his hands, he snapped the towel against his jeans. "So, what did he say?"

"What the heck do you think he'd say?" She scowled. "Congratulations! You're a sex addict."

Chuckling, Dax tossed down the rag and pulled her against him. "I meant about us."

"Oh." She dipped her gaze, knowing her face had turned red. She remembered Ben's suggestion of loving Dax and all that nonsense. No way could she tell him something so preposterous. Dropping her gaze, she noticed a little smudge of grease streaking across his chin. She brushed a thumb against the mark. "He just said we're adults and could do what we wanted. Of course, I assured him we're friends, just not in love." She rubbed the filth from her finger. "I mean, Ben's not stupid."

"I see." He clutched her waist and frowned. "Anything else I need to know?"

She lifted one shoulder. "I didn't mention the whole proposition thing, so you better not either, because if he finds out, he won't be happy."

He heaved a sigh. "Ellen, you worry too much."

Seriously, was he that obtuse? Had he forgotten the unstated boundaries among best friends and sisters? "I disagree." She picked at a piece of fluff on his shirt. "Besides, *I* won't be the reason you're not friends."

"Ellen, my relationship with Ben is fine."

His tone came out hard and sharp. *Why? Didn't he understand?* When things ended, everything would change. "Sure now, but later…" She fanned a hand. "I won't be the reason you're not. If Ben finds out that you propositioned me like I'm one of your groupies…" A shudder coursed down her spine. She shook her head. "This is for the best."

Tilting back his head, Dax closed his eyes.

Ellen saw the muscles work in his throat. She frowned. "You didn't think I'd actually tell him you wanted the whole friends-with-benefits thing, did you?"

He snapped open his eyes. "What? No." Raking fingers through his hair, he let out a deep exhale. "About what you think—"

Ellen put a palm over his mouth. "I've already agreed. I don't want to discuss it further. For now, we'll have a simple relationship, and if either one of us tires or wants to move on—" A choking sensation filled her chest, knowing he would be the only person moving on. She couldn't worry about what would happen later. Having made her decision, she forced a smile. "When that happens, we'll return to being just friends."

The muscles flexed in his cheek, and his gaze searched her face. "I don't want you to regret your decision."

Ellen bit her lip. Would she? She prayed not, but who knew what would happen? Besides, she couldn't stop today worrying about tomorrow. She lifted one shoulder. "Everyone has regrets."

He scrubbed a hand over his face.

She frowned. "Don't tell me you don't?"

He froze for just a moment. When his gaze reconnected with hers, a faraway look had settled inside. "I did once."

She arched a brow. "And—?"

Pulling her against him, he held her waist and rested his chin on her head. "I won't make the same mistake again."

She heard the conviction in his voice and wondered over it. Dax had always seemed so carefree and easy-going. What mistake could he have made that would make him so unyielding? "So…" She leaned back and stuck out a hand. "We agree?"

His gaze dropped to her hand. When his gaze finally met hers, his eyes had darkened, and his lips pulled downward. He curled his fingers into a fist for a moment before thrusting out his palm. "Agreed."

Ellen shook his hand. The relief she expected never appeared, and she knew, despite what she had said, in just a few weeks, she would lose her very best friend.

Chapter 19

Ellen stretched arms over her head and smiled. *Okay, maybe this friends-with-benefits thing would work out.* After all, last night certainly had been friendly—and not just the sex part either, but the *whole* evening.

Dax had gone out later and picked up a pizza. They ate the meal while sipping wine and watching some horror flick she hadn't wanted to see but knew he enjoyed. Through all the gory parts—and there were plenty—she had kept fingers over her eyes, much to Dax's amusement. But what really surprised her was how normal things seemed. The whole evening reminded her of the past—before sex changed everything. The only awkward moment came when Dax mentioned the agreement.

Ellen had refused to discuss the topic. She made her decision, and after all, she wasn't stupid. She knew how things would end. One day, he'd decide he wanted to move on. When the day arrived, she wouldn't be angry, resentful, or leave with hard feelings. A little voice rang through her head on a loop, demanding to know, *when would that day come? Tomorrow? The next? Or after the holidays?* Her throat tightened. She shrugged off the feeling. Why borrow trouble? Especially after their great time last night. Right now, she just needed to get past the people's curiosity. *Easy peasy.*

She glanced at the clock. 4:30 am. *Holy crow.* If she didn't hurry, she'd be late. Kicking off the sheets, she climbed from the bed and searched for her clothing. Her bra lay on the floor next to her stinky, coffee-stained sneakers. The rest of her clothing was M.I.A. Frowning, she tossed the bra onto the unmade bed.

No way could she traipse across the yards wearing nothing but the outfit the good Lord had blessed her in, even if the clouds hid the moon, and the sun wouldn't shine for another three hours or so. She eyed the door. The sound of the television floated upstairs. Dax was probably in the living room watching some sports show. She nibbled her lip. Should she go and ask? She could imagine his reaction seeing her naked. A slow smile split her face. Well, *that* would only cause her to be later.

Seeing as she had no other choice, she quickly put on the bra. Opening the closet door, she spied a row of shirts, from dressy to work, hanging neatly upon the rod. She selected a T-shirt and slipped the soft fabric over her head. The scent of Dax wafted upward.

Little tingles raced across her flesh, and a warm, fuzzy feeling curled through her stomach. During the years she'd dated Grant, she'd worn his shirts on a few occasions, and never had his cologne evoked the same feeling.

Hurrying to the dresser, she opened the top drawer. Inside laid neatly folded boxers and bundles of socks. She wasn't exactly thrilled wearing men's underwear, but she sure as certain hated the idea of no undies, either. Seeing no other option, she yanked out a pair of blue boxers and a roll of thick, coarse socks and tossed them onto the bed.

Next she rifled through the stacks of jeans and work pants until she felt her fingers graze upon soft fabric wadded near the back. Extracting the garment, she held it up and smiled softly.

The faded, orange sweats reminded her of high school, and for a moment, she pictured him wearing them during football practice. Back then, she had been so busy watching Jakob that she barely noticed Dax. But she remembered the crowds of silly women seeking his and Ben's attention. Another frown sliced her lips. Heck, how many times had he arrived at practice with one woman and left with another? Would the same happen to her? Just a matter of time, the logical part of her brain whispered.

Slamming shut the drawer, she looked up and stilled. Two pictures sat upon the dresser. Tossing the sweats onto the bed, she selected one. Digging fingers into the soft, velvet backing, she stared at the image of Dax at his academy graduation.

Somehow, she'd gotten wedged against his side. His arm hung loosely over her shoulders. On his left stood Claire. Directly behind the trio stood Ben and her father. His family wasn't in the picture. By then, his sister had married and moved to Florida with their mother, and his dad had been long gone from Dax's life. Her family was his family, and that realization made the reality of what they did even more complicated and nerve-racking.

She shifted her gaze to her mother. Claire stood next to Dax, clutching his forearm and smiling as if his success was hers, too. Why wouldn't she feel proud? She had been his part-time mother, guiding him through his latch-key life and helping him see his potential. Carefully, she replaced the picture.

Ben had understood. Would her mother be as tolerant, or would she be horrified by their breach of friendship? Somehow, she couldn't picture her mother's being excited, knowing anything with Dax wouldn't be long-term, and the one thing Claire wanted most for her children was marriage.

Dropping onto the bed, Ellen absently pulled on the boxers while staring at the picture. Over the years, his boyish face had thinned, becoming more chiseled, and his youthful build had disappeared, changing into the hardened form of a man. His eyes, though, still held a spark of laughter that had a way of making a girl's knees weaken. No wonder he had no problem attracting women. Her throat tightened.

Scowling, she tugged on the sweats. Of course, she knew at some point he'd settle down and find his perfect Mrs. Right. She'd be beautiful, too. Dax could have any woman he wanted. He wouldn't choose someone plain and boring. No, he'd go for the cream of the crop. Someone like Jenny Pickler or Angel Whatever-her-last-name. But when?

Grabbing the socks, Ellen rammed one foot into the tube. She had no one to blame but herself. She should have rooted for answers last night. Instead, she acted like she was perfectly content with their agreement. Why would he think otherwise? After all, she was the one who accepted the offer.

Now, she was stuck in the balance, waiting for the day to arrive. She yanked on the other sock, then slipped her feet into the shoes. Nothing she could do about it now. She'd made her decision, but dang, why hadn't she just *asked?* Hurrying down the stairs, she spied Dax sitting on the couch, sipping coffee, and watching the television. Would he know she had on his boxers? Heat burned her face. Saying a quick prayer that he didn't ask, she reached the bottom step and stopped.

With the coffee mug perched against his lips, he looked up and swept his gaze over her. Carefully placing the cup on a coaster, he stood.

A slow, sexy smile split his lips. Ellen's stomach fluttered. But damn, he looked amazing in his uniform. The shirt stretched across his broad shoulders, and every time he flexed his biceps, the fabric tightened just a bit. Her heart hammered, and her blood surged. *Oh man.* Why couldn't he be out running or doing something manly?

An urge to wrap her arms around his neck and reach up on tippy-toes and plant a kiss on his perfectly formed lips burned through her, but the memory of that morning six years ago gave her pause. Instead, she curled fingers into the hem of her shirt, and, dropping her gaze, she took the last step. "I couldn't find my clothing."

Laughing, he strolled over, and, seizing the edges of her shirt, he pulled her against him. "I'm washing them."

She snapped up her gaze just in time for him to capture her mouth in a totally hot, completely absorbing kiss. A shiver skittered down her spine, and dang if she didn't wrap her arms around his neck.

He pulled back and winked. "You look surprised."

She shrugged. "That's because I am."

Pushing aside her hair, he brushed his lips across

her neck. "I'm a thirty-year-old man. I know my way around house cleaning." Grabbing her hand, he tugged her to the kitchen. "Come on. I'll drive you to work."

"I really should go home and change."

Grabbing a coat off the rack, he held open the lapels. "Why?"

Oh, I don't know…maybe because I'm wearing your boxers. But of course, she couldn't admit that truth. No doubt Dax would feel that was too relationshippy—not that she could exactly blame him— but what the heck was she to do? Go al fresco? *No freaking way.* Dropping her gaze from him to the brown-and-tan checked coat, she lifted one shoulder. "Because these are sweats, and I can't wear your clothing to work." She slipped her arms into the sleeves, and, turning to face him, she fastened one button. "Besides, you're working, and I have to get home after my shift."

Straightening her collar, he brushed his lips across hers. "Let me take you."

She heard the urgency in his voice. Saying no would be practical. After all, she *did* have to get home later. On the other hand, she could easily walk the distance from the café to home. Plus, a teeny-tiny part of her wasn't ready to end their perfect time together. She sighed. "You're sure it's not too much trouble? You don't have to be to work for another hour."

Draping arms over her shoulders, he tilted up her chin. "Sugar, if it was, I wouldn't have offered."

A sudden thought ripped through her. "People will see us. What will we tell them?"

Grabbing another coat off the rack, he turned and slipped his arms inside. "Why do we have to explain?"

He picked up his keys. "Our relationship is none of their business."

His answer came so easy. She wished the truth was equally so.

Taking her hand, he opened the door. "Come, sugar. Don't want you to be late."

She glanced toward her mother's house. Was she out on her walk? Ellen skimmed her gaze over the dark sky and dismissed the worry. Her mother liked to rise early, but no way would she step outside before sunrise. She climbed into the truck and strapped the seatbelt over her shoulders.

Dax jammed the key into the ignition and started the engine.

She shot him a sideways glance. "So now what?"

Dax cranked on the heater, and, turning, he arched a brow. "What do you mean?"

She tapped fingers on the armrest. Didn't he understand that all the questions she had avoided last night lingered in the forefront of her thoughts? Only, if she asked and he gave her honest answers, she'd have more pain and regret and possibly ruin everything, even their friendship. She cursed herself. Why hadn't she just kept quiet?

Blessed heat filled the cabin.

Ellen pressed her hands against the blast of hot air. "Just wondered what you will do after you drop me off."

He glanced her way. A smile filled his face. "Knowing your brother, he's probably already at work, so I suppose I could go see him."

Her stomach lurched. "No way. You can't."

He burst out laughing. "Why not."

She glared. "Just because he knows doesn't mean he wants us to flaunt our deal."

He stared out the window. "Why are you worried?"

A dark look settled on his face, and he gripped the steering wheel so tight his knuckles turned white. She swallowed. "I just don't think he'd want to know about our casual relationship."

Easing his grip, he blew out a breath. "Sugar, trust me, your brother understands."

She wanted to ask what Ben understood but didn't dare. No doubt, he meant Ben knew he didn't stick with one woman long enough to form an attachment. Still, to know her brother didn't care about her feelings bothered her. So, instead of mentioning that sorry fact, she stared at the passing scenery.

"So, with this…" Dax cleared his throat. "*Deal—* Does this mean that after the holidays you still plan on returning to Albany?"

His question caught her off guard. His gruff tone, too. She glanced in his direction. His face gave nothing away, but she saw the way the cords in his neck bunched just a bit. She shrugged. Of course, she planned to, but somehow, the burning urgency that consumed her weeks ago had suddenly eased. Was it because she liked her job at Betty's and found she excelled at the role, or was it more? And if she did stay, how would she feel watching Dax find someone he truly liked?

She knew the possibility of him finding someone else was very real. But just because she understood that fact didn't make the pain any less. "Haven't decided." Nibbling the edge of her lip, she turned toward him. "What about you? With your wingman settled down, have you considered doing the same?"

Dax studied her for a moment before turning and staring straight ahead. "I know what women want." His Adam's apple bobbed, and his fingers flexed on the steering wheel. "Women believe in happily-ever-after. But love isn't like that. It's rough, and it's ugly."

Of course, he would have those thoughts. She never met his dad, but she'd heard of the man who had run from the family before Dax reached five. She ran a finger across the soft fabric of the sweats. His words bothered her. "My parents had a happy marriage for twenty years."

He pulled up alongside the curb in front of the café. Turning off the engine, he pulled out the keys and met her gaze. "Yeah, they did."

Pain and longing filled his words. Her heart ached. She didn't know how to respond. Instead, she looked toward the café. She was a few minutes past opening time and already a line of people waited. She turned. "You don't have to come in."

Just as quickly, he shrugged off the mood and winked. "I know, sugar." He shoved open his door.

Since when had he become so stubborn? The Dax of her youth had been easy-going and laid back. Now though, at every turn, he refused to see the problem of being seen together. She met him at the front of the truck.

Grabbing her hand, he walked her across the street. Pulling open the door, he glanced down. "What are you worried about now?"

She frowned. "Why are you so stubborn?"

Holding open the door, he laughed. "Sugar, the word you want is relentless."

Rolling her eyes, she walked through the door. Everyone in the café turned and stared. As if that wasn't bad enough, Dax had to go and drop his arm over her shoulders like an anchor—immovable and determined. She scowled. "This surely won't help the rumors."

Tugging her closer, he leaned down. "I never worry about rumors."

His voice came out in a whisper, but she was positive she heard a hint of laughter lurking in his words. Of course, he wouldn't care. Gossip only added to his success with women and earned him admiration from men. However, she didn't need anything to fan the flames. Walking toward the counter, Ellen forced a smile, as if being glued to Dax's waist was the most normal thing in the world, when in fact, she wanted to dig a hole in the ground.

Betty stood behind the counter, making a drink. She glanced up and cocked a brow. "Seems like you've gotten things resolved."

Ellen shot him an I-told-you-so look. He had the nerve to wink. At least, though, he dropped his arm.

He walked behind the counter and grab a cup from the stack.

Betty never said a word.

Not that Ellen expected her to. Dax could pretty much rob the Aberdeen National Bank, and no one would raise the alarm. After all, for as long as she could recall, the residents had placed Dax on a pedestal— somewhere between the heavenly father and George Aberdeen, the town's founder.

He made polite conversation with Betty.

Ellen paid no attention. Her mind spun with all the

ramifications of their decision. Surely he knew how easily word spread, and, while Ben knew—and no doubt her mother too—did he have to make it appear like they were a couple when they were anything but serious?

And what about Angel? Sure, he insisted they were just friends, but Ellen had doubts. Angel was far too attractive to be ignored. Maybe he didn't care, knowing another woman would fill the space as soon as one left. Of course, another woman was always ready to fill the spot, but still, didn't he have any worries?

Finished pouring coffee, Dax set the cup on the counter and dug out his wallet and dropped a ten on the counter.

While slipping the apron loop over her neck, Ellen silently prayed Dax would leave. Instead, he pulled her against him, and horror of all horrors, he kissed her.

Releasing her, he brushed a thumb across her lip and winked. "I'll see you tomorrow."

Watching him leave, Ellen had the insane urge to ask him why he would make such a public statement. Without a thought, she followed him out the door. A soft, cold wind blew across her face, tugging at the strands of her hair and chilling her flesh. She rubbed hands down her exposed arms. The action did nothing to ease the cold, and man, oh, man, if only he would wrap her in his warm, safe embrace. "Dax?"

He stopped, and, turning, he furrowed his brows. "What's wrong?"

She wanted to ask him about Angel, what he pictured as his future, but more importantly, she wanted to know what he thought about them. But she couldn't form the words. Instead, she sighed. "Aren't you worried?"

He ran a thumb over the key's edge. "About what?"

"About us." She licked her lips. "I don't want to ruin your life." His gaze turned all soft and warm.

He pulled her against him. "Sugar, my life is perfect. Stop worrying." He brushed his lips across hers. "I'll see you tomorrow."

Watching him leave, Ellen knew she had a bigger problem than wearing his shirt or showing up at work together or the possibility of her mother finding out. The truth was even worse. Not only was she an addict, but Dax was her drug.

Chapter 20

Twenty-four hours—the exact amount of time he'd been away from Ellen—felt like an eternity. He finished stuffing his clothing into his bag and zipped shut the duffle. His day with Ellen filled his thoughts.

Straightening, he rolled his shoulders, attempting to ease some of the stiffness. Hell, he spent yesterday and most of last night replaying their conversation. He had wanted to explain her mistaken assumption. Instead, she refused to hear him out. How could she possibly think he'd ever jeopardize their relationship with such an offer— Especially after their first time together. Why hadn't he stopped and corrected her misassumption? He raked fingers through his hair. *Cowardice*—the word ripped through his thoughts.

He clenched his jaw and tightened his hands on the tote's straps. If he told the truth, would he ruin everything? Oh, he knew she harbored plenty of doubt, and with good reason. Hell, hadn't she seen him with dozens of women? None had meant anything, and he regretted them all, but would she believe him?

Shoving open the station door, he stepped outside. A sharp breeze sent a chill across his face. He dipped his hands into the coat pockets and tucked his chin into the opening. The parking lot had a thin sheen of moisture coating the black surface.

Jakob and Ryan followed, discussing Saturday's

calendar signing. As single men, they loved all the attention.

Two years ago, Dax would have, too. Now though… He gritted his teeth, reminding himself of the hospital and their needs. One more contracted calendar signing in Albany, and then he'd be done. Six new men would replace him and the current crew. For the first time since the start of the whole charade, he looked forward to the event.

Finally, he could put Angel out of his life. She'd return to the luxury apartment in New York City she always bragged about, and he could further his relationship with Ellen without Angel working against it. He couldn't wait.

"Morning, Dax."

Dax pivoted.

Ava, Ben's secretary, rushed across the street.

Dax swept his gaze over her. She looked cute in her emerald coat and patent heels. Some guy would be lucky to have her hanging from his arm. He knew she wished that guy was him. But now? Skimming his gaze across the park, he spotted the café. Did Ellen miss him as much as he missed her? A hand, soft and gentle, touched his coat sleeve. He turned back.

Ava glanced over her shoulder, before turning back and frowning. "Everything okay?"

Knowing in a few minutes he would be, he grinned. "Yup. Fine."

"Dax, I'm wondering…" She dropped her gaze to the ground.

Her cheeks turned pink. He wondered if Ben had said something after Ellen's visit yesterday. His chest tightened. He'd be damned if he'd let anyone stop him.

"Something wrong?"

She ripped up her gaze and took a deep breath. "I'm not normally this forward, but do you want to go out sometime?"

He eased out a breath. Four months ago, he'd have seized the chance. Now though, he couldn't even fathom the idea. "Thanks, darlin', but I'm seeing someone else."

She flicked up her gaze. "Ben's sister, right?"

Of course, she knew. The word traveled fast in town. "Yeah. Something like that." He pulled open his truck door and paused. She deserved a better response than something vague and heartless. "You know, when you first moved to town, if you'd asked, I would have said yes."

She lifted her brows. "Really?"

He nodded.

She licked her lips. "Maybe, after—?"

Her words were like a sucker punch to his gut. He couldn't blame her. Hell, didn't half the town think the same? Ben had suggested something to the same effect. He understood why people believed as they did. What they refused to realize was that he had changed. He was a different person now. Maybe he had been for a while. He didn't know. Still, she deserved better than false promises and future hope. "There won't be an after."

She stared for just a moment before she gave him an almost imperceptible nod. Then, she dipped her gaze and walked away.

He climbed into his truck and watched as Ava made her way across the street. Regret and remorse nudged his conscience. Never had he turned down a date. He liked to keep things easy. Find the targets, flatter them until they caved, seal the deal, and then get out before they dreamed of impossible fantasies. Up until six years ago, things had worked perfectly.

Leaning back, he closed his eyes. The truth was things had changed a lot farther back. He had spent the last decade or so fighting the truth. He wasn't interested in fighting anymore.

Ellen had asked him if his life was perfect. Hell, three months ago, he would have thought the same as what he told her yesterday. He knew with a certainty, though, his life had been far from terrific. He'd just fooled himself into believing it to be. Now, though, he knew perfection meant a stubborn brunette who found worries in the dark.

Smiling, he glanced toward the café again. She thought his intentions were temporary and that in a day, maybe a week, or possibly a month, he'd change his mind and dump her. He wasn't surprised she didn't see that he was older, wiser, and more seasoned. He would just have to make her understand otherwise. And, tonight, he would start by treating her to a nice, home-cooked dinner, à la Dax Moore style.

Pulling out of the lot, he drove to Colorful Explosions and darted inside. Choosing the flowers was easy. He purchased Ellen's favorite—a mixture of daisies in the color of the rainbow. Carrying the green cellophane-wrapped bouquet, he stepped from the shop.

Next, he stopped at Stop 'n Shop and purchased the items for dinner. In no way would anyone consider him a chef, but he knew his way around the kitchen enough to know how to bake a potato, chop a salad, and boil a lobster. For wine, he chose an expensive white.

Afterward, he drove to Candi's Candies. Stepping

inside the cute shop, he swung his gaze around the room, enjoying the homey quality of rustic tables filled with boxes of sugary sweetness. The scent of chocolate and sugar surrounded him. The soles of his boots scraped against the hardwood floors announcing his presence.

The white, antique, barroom-style doors swung open. Candi, the owner, stepped out. She, with her husband, Mark, moved to Aberdeen just a few years earlier and opened the shop. They were an instant success.

Her smile caused her chubby cheeks to rise upward and her blue eyes to sparkle. Curly red hair swirled around her head in disarray—a normal look on most days. Wiping hands on a brown-and-pink-striped apron, she walked to the counter. She rested forearms atop the counter. "Morning, Dax. How can I help you today?"

Dax stared at the desserts lining the shelves. Every imaginable confection filled the case—cakes of every variety with decorative swirls of frosting and dustings of shimmery sugar crystals, dainty pastries and tasty cookies decorated in colorful icing and sugary sprinkles lined paper-lined trays, and dozens of pies with golden crusts and juicy fruit were sure to entice any appetite. Resting palms on the metal top, he glanced up. "I need something for dinner tonight."

Tilting her head to the side, Candi curled her lips. "The desserts depend on the meal." She waved a hand. "What are we talking—the basic run-of-the-mill dinner or something special?"

"Lobster."

A low whistle rumbled from Candi. "I see." She cocked a brow. "So, definitely special."

Shrugging, Dax shifted his gaze back to the desserts. He didn't have anything to hide, but he didn't see the point in stating what the town already knew. "Just dinner."

"I can see you don't want to discuss your date." Candi slid open the glass door and reached inside. Peering over the top, she winked. "Don't really need to, either."

Curling fingers, Dax rested his wrists on the surface and let out a soft laugh. "Yeah, I figured."

"Well, you know the town." Candi drew out a small cheesecake. Milk chocolate dripped down the sides, and fresh raspberries dotted the surface. She placed the cake into a pink-and-brown-speckled box. "The place thrives on gossip."

Even though he knew how much people loved to gossip, the fact his relationship with Ellen was the hot topic irritated him. Didn't they have anyone else to discuss? Like Ben being mayor? Or Jenny Pickler running out of the country? Or Karla Sweet and the tawdry details of her fourth divorce? Digging his wallet from his pocket, Dax glanced up. "Ain't that the truth." He placed a twenty on the counter.

Candi yanked on a spool coiled with pink twine and drew off a long strand. She snipped the end, and, with nimble fingers, she wrapped the string around the box. Securing the top with a fancy bow, she slid the package across the counter. "You're gonna break a lot of women's hearts in town, you know."

Dax grabbed the box and winked. "Won't be the first time." Stepping outside, he shielded his eyes against the bright autumn sun and glanced toward the park.

Laughter rippled around the area as excited children dashed about. Mothers, bundled up in bulky coats and heavy scarves, rested upon metal and wooden slat benches and watched the children's antics.

A red sports car pulled into the vacant spot behind his truck. He gripped the twine, ignoring the bite against his flesh. Walking toward his vehicle, he dug out his keys.

A car door slammed.

He turned to see Angel, dressed in a white wool coat and a pink-and-white-striped scarf, stroll over. She smiled, but her gaze remained frigid and harsh—like a winter storm ravaging the town. Dax gritted his teeth and beeped open his truck. A brown scarf hung from a hook near the front passenger seat. Shoving aside the fabric, he carefully placed the cake on the seat, all the while steeling himself for the confrontation sure to come.

Angel hopped the curb and stopped.

The wind whipped, tugging at the frilly scarf wrapped around her neck. She captured the fabric, tucking the wooly material inside the coat's opening. Her berry-colored lips pulled back into a frown. "I've been texting you."

Her tone held as much warmth as her gaze. If she expected him to regret not answering her messages, she was sadly mistaken. He shrugged. "Been busy."

She ran a pink nail along the cut edge of the key fob and glanced inside the truck. "Dessert?"

Dax shut the door. "Is that a problem?"

"Do you have plans tonight?"

Dax shrugged before stepping away. "Not your business."

A soft snort erupted.

He swiveled.

She strolled forward.

He stared down at her, seeing the flash of fire in her green eyes and smelling her spicy perfume wafting upward. His stomach churned at her very nearness.

"Per the calendar agreement, everything you do is my business." She traced a nail down his arm. "And don't forget, we have a signing Saturday."

He hated her perfectly practiced seductive smile. Not so long ago, that suggestive look would cause his blood to heat and his skin to tingle. Now, all he felt was disgust and indifference. Snagging her fist, he tossed aside her hand. "My last one."

"We can add days."

"But we won't." He stepped to the side. "You've got the other men."

Angel caught his arm and ran her gaze over him. "But I don't want them. I want you."

Most of the men on the calendar would revel at those words, but not him. Their time ended long ago, probably longer than she realized. Ripping his coat from her grip, he walked to the driver's side. He wrenched open the door, then glanced over the top of the truck. She stared with that seductive gaze he'd come to hate. "I told you before, we're through." He climbed inside and rammed the key into the ignition. Saturday couldn't come soon enough.

Chapter 21

For the umpteenth time this morning, Ellen glanced at the clock on her cell phone. Returning the phone to her apron's pocket, she glanced out the café's window toward the fire station. Twenty-eight hours—the exact length of time since she had seen Dax. The minutes passed like drips of water—one, two, three, and still, the hours inched by ridiculously slow. *What the heck?* Since when did she miss Dax so achingly much?

She knew when—the minute he told her his life was perfect. He never came right out and said she was the reason, but the underlying words were there. *Or were they?* She tapped a finger against the counter. Maybe she read into them. Perhaps he meant his life was perfect because she was the last bastion between him and complete dominance over the women of Aberdeen.

She stiffened. Well hell, *her* perfect day burst like a balloon punctured by a pin. Jamming the filter into the basket beneath the stand of coffee beans, she rammed a hand against the switch. The low growl of gears sounded, and fine dust puffed upward. She chewed her lip. Would he stop by with that cocky smile and that swagger that made a woman swoon?

The grinder shut off.

Ellen grabbed the handle and pulled out the filter basket. Slipping the basket into the espresso machine and swiveling the knob, she watched the thick, dark espresso drip into the cup.

The backroom opened.

Ellen peered over her shoulder.

Betty stepped into the room carrying a large, silver tray. "What's wrong?"

Turning away, Ellen shrugged. "Nothing." One final drip of espresso plopped into the cup. Kneeling, she opened the fridge and grabbed a plastic gallon of milk.

"Seems like something is bothering you."

Slamming shut the door, Ellen stood and sighed. "Just thinking."

"Oh no." Betty placed the tray on the shelf. "With you, that's never encouraged."

Ellen removed the lid on the gallon, then tossed the cap on the stainless steel surface. "I just can't help thinking maybe Dax played me."

"Oh, come on." Betty shook her head. "You know Dax as well as I do. Do you honestly think he'd play you?"

Ellen propped a hip against the counter. "He played me six years ago."

"Yeah, when he was twenty-four." Betty crossed arms over her chest. "He's grown up a lot since then."

"Maybe." Ellen poured milk into the metal container. "But what about the rest of the women he used over the years?"

"You know as well as myself, Dax would never make a promise he didn't intend to keep."

Ellen considered Betty's words. She thought back to their conversation from a few weeks ago. At the time, he'd told her he needed only two hours with a woman. She'd far exceeded his timeframe, but a large part of her still had doubts. "I don't know. I just worry about—" She licked her lips. "After."

Betty sighed. "Listen, every new relationship has some uncertainty, but Dax is your friend. He wouldn't let anything ruin your friendship." She squeezed Ellen's hand. "You have to believe that."

"Yeah, maybe." Ellen lifted the wand and slid the canister beneath. Dropping the nozzle, she swiveled the knob. Steam burst upward.

"You sound like a woman falling in love."

Ellen's stomach lurched. She ripped her attention to Betty. "What?"

The café door popped open.

Maybelline, dressed in a wild silk coat of a million swirling colors, strode to the counter. "Morning, people." She patted her mile-high, bouffant hair. "How are things going?"

Betty waved a hand. "We're just discussing falling in love with Dax."

Staring at the steam, Ellen gritted her teeth. "Not love." *Jeez, what was wrong with Betty?* Only foolish, naïve women dreamed of love with Dax. She was neither. "I just don't want to be deceived."

Maybelline flipped open her fluffy, purple purse. "The way I see it, you've been with Dax for like, what?…two weeks?"

"Going on three, but what's your point?" Ellen glanced over her shoulder.

"Well…" Maybelline dug out a wallet in the shape of an origami cat. "Other than Angel, can you name any other woman who's spent as much time with him?"

"Not a fair question." Ellen swiveled the handle.

The steam stopped. She turned. "I've only been back three weeks."

"You've just proven my point." Maybelline fanned the hand holding the wallet.

The wiggly eyes on the cat rolled around, mimicking the action Ellen desperately wanted to make. "What the hell are you talking about?" She tapped the canister on the counter.

"Think about it. Dax and you—three weeks. Obviously, something is going on between you two."

The door opened again.

Claire, with Kitty in tow, stepped into the café.

Ellen groaned. Her day just went from bad to worse. She ran her gaze over her aunt and frowned. *What the heck?* She faced Claire. "Is Kitty wearing slippers?"

Maybelline clapped hands. "Aunt Kitty, you're a hoot."

Again, the cat's eyes bobbled. Ellen totally sympathized. If her mother wasn't here, she would probably do the same.

"Please." Closing her eyes, Claire huffed. "Don't get her started."

"Not just slippers." Opening her coat, Kitty fanned a hand down the front.

A blue gown with light blue trim hung from Kitty's bony frame. A white cord ran across the front, ending with a knotted bow on the side.

Ellen narrowed her gaze. "Are you wearing a hospital gown?"

"Yup." Kitty wiggled her brow. "Pretty snazzy, right? Dr. Carlson knew how much I enjoyed them, so he gave me a half-dozen."

Shaking her head, Claire dropped her purse on the counter. "I'm taking her shopping later."

Scowling, Kitty turned to Ellen. "Don't see why I can't wear them."

"Because they're not dresses." Claire gritted her teeth. "And he didn't give them to you. *You* stole them."

Kitty huffed. "Still, I wouldn't want to hurt his feelings."

Leaning against the counter, Claire kissed the side of Ellen's face. "Morning."

The scent of her mother's perfume, all roses and lilacs, surrounded Ellen, and the sticky feeling of lipstick clung to her cheek. Pressing fingers against her skin, she tried to recall the last time her mother had shown her affection. Ben's party? College, maybe? She furrowed her brow. "What was that kiss for?"

Smiling, Claire smoothed a hand along the side of Ellen's face. "I missed you and wanted to see how things are going." She gave Ellen a wide-eyed smile. "Can't a mother kiss her daughter?"

A tingling warmth swelled inside Ellen's chest. Sure, she knew her mother loved her and wanted her to stay, but until the day she moved into Lily's parents' home, her mother never said anything even remotely close to those things. Suddenly, everything fell into place. "*Mother...*"

Claire widened her eyes. "What?"

Ellen pointed. "I know what you're thinking, and you can stop right now."

"What?" Claire gripped her purse.

Ellen snagged a cup off the stack and jammed it beneath the coffeemaker. "I know you heard about Dax and me, and now you have some crazy idea like we're in love and will get married."

"Of course, I've heard." Claire lifted her chin and sniffed. "And I have to say I'm a little disappointed you didn't feel comfortable coming to me and discussing this *very* important relationship."

Tightness settled in Ellen's chest. Flipping the lever, she stared at the dark liquid filling the cup. "I didn't tell you because I have nothing to tell."

"Oh, for goodness' sake." Claire slammed a hand on the counter. "Ellen, do you think I'm blind? I see you sneaking from Dax's house or him strolling from yours. Of course, something is going on, and frankly, I have to say, I'm thrilled."

Ellen ripped her attention to her mother. She could honestly say she expected plenty of emotions from Claire, but *thrilled?* Not once did she expect to hear that word. "You're happy?"

Reaching out, Claire fanned a hand. "Of course. You and Dax have been best friends since high school. Anyone with perfect vision could see you love each other."

Now, Ellen knew her mother had lost her mind. She glanced at the clock. Not even noon yet. "Mom, a little early to start drinking, don't you think?"

Kitty gasped. "Oh sure. You can drink, but I can't." She crossed arms over her chest. The hospital gown bunched, revealing knobby knees encased in baggy stockings. "I take one fortifying nip of whiskey in the morning, and she acts like I'm an alcoholic, but she can get drunk? If you ask me, seems a bit unfair."

"Oh, please. I'm not drunk." Claire lifted her chin and narrowed her eyes. "But I am right."

Jules Hahn

"No, you're not." Ellen placed the cup on the counter. If her mother knew of hers and Dax's history, she was certain Claire would change her mind. "You do realize we're speaking about Dax? He doesn't settle down."

Fixing her gaze on Ellen, Claire flipped open her purse and drew out her wallet. "And like I told you weeks ago, Dax is just scared."

Her mother didn't understand. Claire dreamed of her children getting married, having children, and living happily ever after. But with Dax, Ellen didn't bring her hopes up to such a level. He enjoyed his single life far too much. Hadn't he admitted as much yesterday? "We're just friends."

"With benefits," Betty interjected.

"Yeah, and they're always together," Maybelline chipped in.

Ellen swept her gaze between the two women. "Thanks."

Maybelline shrugged. "Just trying to help."

Kitty clapped her hands.

Ellen swiveled.

The pink curlers wrapped around Kitty's hair bobbed and weaved. "Woo-wee." She wiggled her gray brows. "Can I have benefits with Dax, too?"

"Don't be coarse, Kitty." Claire turned to Ellen. "So, what will you do?"

"Nothing" Ellen slid the cup across the counter. Her mother didn't understand. She wasn't a miracle worker. She couldn't be expected to change a grown man's mind who had become accustomed to living the sweet life. Besides, did she even want to? *Yes,* a little voice in her head screamed. "Dax is happy with the way everything is, and…" She licked her lips and swallowed. "So am I."

"Don't be silly. Of course, you're not." Claire shook her head. "All you need to do is make him see otherwise." She slapped down a twenty. "And don't mess it up."

The café door opened again.

Five pairs of eyes swiveled.

Ellen groaned. Okay, now her day just got officially worse.

Pinning his gaze on Ellen, Dax strolled to the counter. "Morning, ladies." He pressed a kiss to both Claire's and Kitty's cheeks.

Kitty tugged on his hand. "Hey, Dax—"

He leaned back and smiled. "What's up, Kitty?"

She ran a hand along his arm and batted her lashes. "Think we could have benefits like you and Ellen?"

Dax walked behind the counter and stopped next to Ellen. Causally, he draped his arm over her shoulders, and leaning down, he pressed a kiss to Ellen's mouth.

Ellen's cheeks burned. Right now, she vowed, if she didn't have chipped and broken fingernails, she'd dig a hole right through the concrete. Casually discussing her relationship with her mother was one thing, but for Dax to kiss her right in front of her mother—so very mortifying.

"I don't know, Kitty. Burt wouldn't be happy." Laughing, Dax squeezed Ellen's shoulder. "I'd hate to get him riled up."

Kitty curled her lips. "You might have a point. Burt's old, but he's wiry." She patted Dax's hand. "You're handsome. I wouldn't want him to ruin your face."

Dax turned to Betty. "I need to speak to Ellen." He didn't wait for permission but grabbed her hand.

Ellen tried to yank free.

Tightening his grip, Dax peered over his shoulder. "We won't be long."

Ellen swiveled her gaze to her mother.

Claire mouthed the words, *Don't blow it.*

Dax drew her into the backroom.

The door swung shut behind them.

Crossing her arms over her chest, Ellen glared. "Do you realize my mom knows?"

Dax slowly smiled. "Yeah? And look, she didn't kill you either."

Ellen narrowed her gaze. "Very funny."

Wrapping his arms around her waist, Dax pulled her close. "I missed you." He brushed his lips across hers.

Sighing, she sunk into his body, reveling in his strength. His hands clasped her waist, and his lips nipped against hers, teasing and tasting. She threaded fingers through his hair, pulling his head downward. Her breath came out in soft pants, and, for a moment, she got lost in the kiss.

A clank sounded, followed by laughter.

Ellen's breath caught. She jerked back, breaking the kiss, and glanced toward the door. On the other side stood her mother. Tiny bubbles burst in the pit of her stomach. *Great. Just freaking great.* "They know we're kissing."

Dax's lips curled into a smile. "I know." He traced a thumb down the side of her cheek. "I want to treat you to dinner tonight."

She froze. He wanted to take her out like a normal

couple who enjoyed time with each other besides sex? As far as she knew, Dax didn't take women out on dates— Too much of a commitment. She studied him, searching for a punch line, but all she saw was sincerity in his gaze. She curled fingers into his shirt. "You sure?"

He brushed his mouth against hers. "Positive."

Her mother's words ran through her thoughts— Show him, and don't blow it. Two insurmountable walls she didn't know whether she could breach. Did she love him for more than just friendship? She ran her gaze over his face. Her heart fluttered. Maybe, just a little. Sighing, she stretched upward and pressed her lips against his. "Okay."

"Great." He grabbed her hands and tugged her into the café. "I'll get you at six."

"Oh, look at the lovebirds." Betty laughed. "Looks like Ellen's day just got better."

Ellen dug fingers into Dax's hand. "Are you happy now?"

He squeezed her hand. "Yup."

She shook her head. Carefully, she extracted her hand from Dax's grip, and, dropping her gaze, she walked purposely behind the counter.

"Well, ladies, I'll let you go." Dax slid his gaze to Ellen, and, winking, he turned and left the café.

"Oh man." Maybelline fixed her gaze on Dax's back. "I think you're right, Aunt Claire. I bet they'll get married."

Ellen stiffened. "We're not getting married. We're having dinner."

Claire shrugged. "You've got to start somewhere. Dinner is as good as anything else." She grabbed her cup of coffee. "Come on, Kitty. Time to go shopping."

Kitty stomped down one foot. "But I don't want to shop."

"Too bad." Claire grabbed Kitty's hand and practically dragged her across the room.

Kitty's slippers skidded across the surface.

Claire glanced down and frowned. "We're getting you boots, too."

Kitty fisted her free hand. "You ruin everyone's fun."

They walked outside.

Maybelline rubbed together her hands. "Just wait until Jenny Pickler finds out. She will be *so* mad."

"Considering she's out of the country, she's the least of Ellen's worries." Picking up her cup, Betty pointed to the calendars stacked on the counter. "Now, Angel…she's a woman with claws."

Ellen sipped her coffee. The foam had melted, and the drink had cooled. She placed the ceramic cup into the sink. All the joy she'd experienced only moments before vanished.

Chapter 22

So, Claire knew. Smiling, Dax drove home. He wasn't surprised. When Ben and Lily began their relationship, she'd practically thrust the two together. The way he saw it, his two largest obstacles were gone. Now, he only needed to overcome the third. Ellen wouldn't make it easy. Hell, the past three weeks had been like an uphill battle. Little did she realize, he was determined.

He understood her hesitance. No one could ever mistake his track record as perfect. For too many years, he worked hard to bury the past. Only, witnessing Ben's and Lily's love stirred him in unexpected ways. He wanted the same with Ellen.

In the past, no woman held his interest longer than a few hours. When he made his bold claim to Ellen all those weeks ago, he understood, even as he pricked her temper, his words sounded cocky. Now, though, he knew without a doubt, the absolute truth. He wanted Ellen, and not just in the short term, but for longer—as long as she'd have him. A whisper of a smile filled him.

Turning onto his street, he spied Amanda and Ashley Fisher, his neighbors' four-year-old twins, playing tag out front. They darted past puddles filled with muddy water while Debbie, their mother, sat on the porch, keeping a careful gaze on them. He pulled into his driveway and parked his vehicle. Climbing out, he walked to the end of the driveway. The excited squeals of laughter filled the air. He smiled. "Girls are getting big."

"Oh, don't you know it." Beaming, Debbie stood. "They're a handful, though."

The girls bounced and jumped, heedless of the spray of mud or the splatter of water. With each hop, their brown pigtails bobbed.

Amanda shot him a smile so bright she could make any person bend to her wishes. Crouching, he gently tugged on one pigtail and winked. "Not these angels."

The little girl giggled.

Debbie snorted. "Just wait. One day, you'll have one of your own, and then you'll understand."

He always figured if he had kids, he'd be a decent dad. Hopefully better than the one who fathered him. He stood and let out a little laugh. "Yeah, maybe."

Sauntering over, Debbie dropped hands to hips. "Sounds like a man with a purpose."

Dax shrugged. "Just getting older."

"Ain't we all?" Debbie studied him for a moment. "Heard you and Ellen are a couple."

Dax pulled his gaze from Amanda. "We're friends."

Debbie laughed. "No better place to start."

Ashley ran over, and, leaning against her mother's side, she popped a thumb in her mouth.

"Meanwhile, you can watch them some time." Debbie dropped a hand on Ashley's head. "After, we'll discuss what kind of angels they are."

Amanda tugged on Dax's coat. "Yeah, and maybe we could have another snowball fight."

"Oh, you think?" Dax dropped to one knee and

gave her a stern look. "You remember the last time we had a snowball fight?"

Clapping a hand over her mouth, Amanda giggled. "Ashley got black on her eye."

Pretty brown eyes sparkled, and pudgy cheeks covered in freckles curved upward. Yup, a definite heartbreaker. Pressing a hand to her shoulders, he felt her tiny frame through the heavy coat and smiled. Would he prefer a little girl who looked up at him with such worshipful eyes or a rough-and-tumble boy seeking out trouble and scaring his parents half to death? He decided either would be just fine with him. "Oh, I remember." Softly, he brushed an errant strand of hair from her eyes. "I had to put a bag of ice on it, too."

She giggled. "She looked funny."

Debbie chuckled. "See what I mean?"

Grinning, he smoothed a thumb across Amanda's soft cheek. "Maybe we should consider something else." He snapped his fingers. "I know. How about we go skating instead?"

"Oh, please." Curling together fingers against her chest, Amanda hopped from foot to foot. *"Can we, please?"*

"You're gonna regret making such a suggestion." Eyeing him, Debbie dropped her hands on both girls' shoulders. "Okay, let's leave Mr. Moore alone. He just got home from work."

Dax straightened, and, looking down at the girls, he winked. "I never regret anything." He held out his pinky. "Promise."

Amanda hooked her tiny pinky around his. "Promise."

Ashley, not about to be left out, thrust out her finger. "Promise."

Shaking her head, Debbie chuckled. "You spoil them." She nudged the girls toward the house. "Come on. Lunch time."

Watching the girls walk toward the porch, he smiled at the excitement in their voices. He ran a thumb over the key fob. Maybe he could convince Ellen to join them. A warm feeling settled in his chest. Yeah, he'd invite her, too.

Crossing the street, he noticed an unfamiliar clunker parked along the sidewalk in front of his house. He dismissed the vehicle and focused on all the things he needed to complete—clean house, iron button-down, polish shoes, prepare the meal, arrange the flowers, and pick up Ellen. He couldn't wait to see her reaction. Oh, he knew she thought he meant to take her out, and he would the next time. But right now, he just wanted them to enjoy dinner together without having people shoot curious glances their way. Besides, he had a method to his madness. Tonight, he would explain his original intention and his future hope.

Dax grabbed the groceries from the vehicle. Looping fingers through the twine on the brown-and-pink box, he gathered the bouquet. He'd worry about his duffle later. Shifting the packages into one arm, he unlocked the door and stepped into the house.

Voices rippled from the television. Running water sounded from upstairs.

The hair on his neck prickled. Placing the groceries and flowers on the table, he swung his gaze toward the living room. How the hell had someone gotten into his house? And why the hell did they take a shower?

He recalled a news article from years past about a drug addict breaking into a house and cooking a meal. Drugs weren't unknown in Aberdeen, but compared to some small towns, the prevalence was minor. He strode into the living room.

A black-and-white comedy from years ago blared on the screen. A bottle of beer, half-filled, rested on the coffee table next to a crumpled burger wrapper and an empty French fry container. A spray of salt and a blob of ketchup marred the table surface. On the leather couch rested an empty, fast-food bag. A pair of old shoes, one flopped on its side with a pair of black stocks tossed on top, cluttered the floor.

He strode across the room, and, shoving aside the curtain, he peered out the window and studied the unfamiliar car. A massive oak blocked the passenger door. A large crack ran the length of the windshield. The front bumper, with a rusty dent in the corner, hung lower on one side. A back tire appeared bald. The paint on the hood had faded from black to a splotchy gray. Had he ever seen the vehicle before? Aberdeen held its share of nice cars, as well as clunkers, which meant the car could belong to anyone.

The shower shut off.

His heart pounded, and his muscles bunched. Dropping the curtain, he turned and stretched his gaze up the length of the stairs, searching for movement. Soft sounds filtered downward—the creak of floorboards, the slam of a drawer, and finally, the clatter of something hitting the floor.

Like hell he'd wait for the intruder to make his appearance. He charged across the room and grabbed the banister. Taking the steps two at a time, Dax darted up the steps and stopped at the landing.

A light glowed through the slight gap beneath the master bedroom door.

Who in the hell would go into his room? His mother hadn't come to town. They had just spoken a few days ago, and she had no plans of returning until Christmas. Even if she had surprised him, she wouldn't use his room. His sister, in the middle of a messy divorce, wouldn't have the time or the money to visit. Not Ellen, either. He'd just left her a few minutes ago.

He crept forward.

A creak sounded.

Pressing a hand against the wall, he lifted his back foot and maneuvered past the warped board.

His bedroom door gaped slightly.

Palming the wood, he eased open the door and surveyed the scene. On his bed lay a beat-up, hard-sided luggage. Silver duct tape seamed the edges and covered the top. A pair of pants hung over the back of a chair. Tossed on the floor was a shirt.

He stepped inside. The bathroom door remained closed, but he could hear sounds emanating from within. Reaching the bed, he searched the luggage for a tag. Nothing.

The bathroom door swung open.

Dax fisted his hands and ripped up his gaze. For a moment, time stood still. The familiar face held a few wrinkles, the lanky body appeared a bit withered, and the once deep-caramel hair had acquired streaks of silver, but the vivid blue eyes were the exact replica of the ones he saw every time he looked in the mirror.

Standing before him was Thomas Franklin Moore—womanizer, deserter, and his father. Every neuron in his body snapped like a thousand zips of electricity firing all at once. He marched across the room to face the one man he never wanted to see again. "What the hell are you doing here?"

A smile lit Thomas's face. He clapped a hand upon Dax's shoulder. "It's good to be home, son."

Shrugging free from the grip, Dax stepped back, and ignoring the bright grin on Thomas' face, he glared. He'd prefer a punch to his gut than facing the man he'd tried to forget. "When you left us, you lost the right to call me son." Crossing arms over his chest, he calmed the slow simmer threatening to burst inside. "How the hell did you get into my house?"

Thomas winked. "You forget, this was my home, too." Grabbing pants filled with holes and smudged with dirt, he dug through the pockets. Finally, he extracted an item. A silver key dangled from the clasp. "Figured I'd need it at some point."

Dax dropped his gaze. A sharp pain pierced his heart. Attached to the end dangled a tiny football—the last Christmas gift he had given his father. The next day, his father was gone. At the time, he hadn't realized what a worthless man his father had been. He remembered the frequent fights, the accusations of faithlessness, of drunken stumbling and slurred words, but at five, he'd been too young to know any different. For him, his father had been a man to look up to, the person he loved with his whole heart—his father of the year. "You figured wrong."

"Aw, come on, Dax." Thomas dropped the ring in the pocket, then tossed the pants on the chair. "You're not gonna hold a bad marriage against me, are you?"

Dax gritted his teeth. "No. Now bad parenting..."

He flexed his fingers. "That's a different story."

Thomas shifted to the dresser. "Couldn't have been too horrible of a parent. Heard you're doing well."

Dax snorted. "You had no hand in my success."

Selecting a cuff link from the top, Thomas studied the gold. "Nice." He tossed the link on the dresser and turned. "Seeing as I bred you, I have to disagree."

"And that was the last thing you contributed to my life." Dax glanced out the window. Claire's house stood proudly in the afternoon sunlight. The memories of endless days watching how a normal family lived filled him. He turned back and narrowed his gaze. "Any success I had came from others' help. Not yours."

Thomas peered out the window and grunted. "Hey, you remember how I used to take you fishing out at the lake?"

Dax refused to fall into the trap of old memories too long gone to care about. Propping fists to hips, he stared at his father's reflection in the mirror. "How did you know I lived here?"

Thomas shrugged. "Still have friends in town."

Acid burned in Dax's stomach, and every muscle in his body tensed. Figures. His dad never cut ties—unless those ties included a wife and two young kids—then he didn't have an issue. "With whom? Carole Shelby? Patsy Rimmer?" Dax could have named a hundred more—all women who'd slept with his father, despite the vows of love and fidelity.

"Amongst others." Peering into the mirror, Thomas fixed the buttons of his shirt before smoothing a hand down the front. He ran fingers over the top of the cologne bottles. Finally, he selected one and removed the cap. He sniffed and winked. "Got good taste. Just like your old man."

Dax marched across the room and slammed a fist down on the bureau. The clank of glass bottles rattling against each other echoed. "What the hell are you doing in my room?"

"Used to be my room." Spritzing the scent on his shirt, he winked. "Figured you wouldn't mind."

The words roared like a locomotive. Dax stilled the urge to bloody the man who caused so much pain. "What do you want?"

Turning, Thomas shrugged. "Thought it was time to come home and see my boy. Enjoy some father-son time together."

Dax recoiled. The morning his father left returned with vivid clarity—of the angry yells and the gut-wrenching sobs, of his father kneeling before him, clutching Dax's thin shoulders while promising to visit. For too many mornings, he'd awaken, expecting to see Thomas's smiling face and sparkling blue eyes. Each night, he'd go to bed, hoping—no, *praying*—tomorrow would be the day. Eventually, Dax let his dream fade and his hope die. And now, his father returned... He clenched his teeth, grinding them back and forth. "If you wanted father-son time, you had twenty-five years to make an effort. Why now?"

Thomas plopped on the bed. Clasping his fingers, he stared at his hands. "I just never realized—" He licked his lips. "I just wanted to see you again."

Dax felt like a fist slammed his gut. "Well, now you've seen me."

Thomas slowly drew his gaze upward. "Are you asking me to leave?"

A battle raged inside Dax. He didn't want to care

about this man he only remembered through fragmented pieces of broken memories and bitter hatred. Yet, a part of him yearned to make peace with the past. If he wanted to move forward, he needed to understand his father's choices. Closing his eyes, he raked fingers through his hair. "Fine. You can stay for a bit."

"Great." Thomas wrapped his arms around Dax. "Hey, let's go out to dinner tonight like we used to— just me and you."

How many years had he yearned to hear those words? Too many, and they came far too late. Dax knocked away his father's embrace. "I just got groceries. We can eat here." Turning, he walked to the door. The reality of his past hit him with full force. The truth of his DNA sat on the bed staring back. He scowled. "This room belongs to me. You can stay in the guest room." He stormed out and slammed shut the door. Ellen's house beckoned him from the side window. He closed his eyes and gritted his teeth. Who was he to ever imagine having a normal life? The perfect life he'd envisioned disappeared like fine mist in the summer sunshine.

Chapter 23

Pacing the kitchen, Ellen glanced at the clock and frowned. Thirty minutes past his promised arrival. *What the heck?* How many times had she peered out the window, expecting to see Dax break through the shrubs or flash his vehicle's lights? Each time, she turned away a little more disappointed. The knot in her stomach tightened.

Pivoting, she took another pass around the kitchen. Finally, she stopped, and, pressing her elbows against the edge of the counter, she searched the yards. Blurry shadows of shrubs and trees lengthened, stretching across the snow-covered ground. A thin line of white slithered across the surface. Brown twigs sticking out from clumps of white shivered in the wind. She glanced past his truck to the kitchen window. Light glowed in the darkness. So, he hadn't left.

She chewed her lip. Did he expect her to show up? She grabbed her phone. Maybe just a quick text…A picture of him receiving dozens of texts from women wanting his attention flashed through her thoughts. She dropped the phone on the counter. She refused to appear desperate. Shoving away, she paced a bit more. With each step, her ire increased. How dare he say they would go out only to ditch her!

She pivoted and made another pass. Nibbling on the corner of her thumb, she recalled his invitation. Had she misinterpreted the eagerness in his gaze, or had something happened? She stopped again to stare out the window. All sorts of horrid thoughts raced through her mind.

His mother wasn't young. What if something happened to her? Or to his sister? She didn't know Darci's husband, but she'd heard stories of control and manipulation. What if some trauma occurred, and he had to deal with horror on his own? Her heart squeezed.

Hadn't he had enough battles to fight in his past? He shouldn't have to fight another alone. She had no idea where their current relationship would go, but she knew, without a doubt, their past. Through all her tribulations in life, he'd been her anchor. When Jakob cheated, he'd championed her. When she fought the restrictions of leaving, he'd defended her. When her father died, he'd held her. She wouldn't abandon him now.

Grabbing her coat, she ripped open the door and stepped out into the night. A thin layer of frost covered the deck, and the sharp bite of wind nipped her nose and cheeks. Tucking hands into her pockets, she trotted down the steps and hurried across the lawns.

A tiny part of her felt silly. He had probably just fallen asleep. He *had* worked last night. Maybe his night was busy, and sleep wasn't possible, and he simply had forgotten? After all, he was a fireman, and if she married him...

She froze in her tracks. Her heart hammered in her chest. A branch from a shrub brushed her cheek. Ignoring the scrape, she stared straight ahead to the light shining from the kitchen window. *Whoa. Where did that thought come from?*

Dax didn't want to get married. He had proven that fact repeatedly with every woman who passed through his life like a revolving door.

Dismissing the ridiculous thought, she hurried past his truck and darted up the steps. She peered into the kitchen window.

The overhead light illuminated the empty room. A bouquet of flowers wrapped in cellophane lay on the counter right next to a pink-and-brown box. Light flickered from the living room.

She flexed her fingers for just a moment before knocking. She waited for what seemed like an eternity. He didn't answer. Ignoring the tightness in her chest, she turned and started down the steps.

The door suddenly ripped open.

"Ellen…"

The smell of potatoes baking seeped from the house. A rush of air ripped from her. She hadn't realized she held her breath until that moment. Forcing a smile, she trotted up the steps. "Is everything okay?" A look she couldn't decipher crossed his face.

He shot a glance over his shoulder before resting his body against the door jamb, effectively blocking her view. "Why do you ask?"

"I just thought—" She licked her lips and took a deep breath. In for an inch, in for a mile. "I just thought we had plans."

He opened his mouth. No words came out. Finally, his lips flattened, and his jaw clenched. "Change of plans."

She arched a brow. "Oh?"

The muscle in his cheek flexed. "Yeah. Something came up."

Jules Hahn

"Something serious?" Ellen ran hands over her arms, but nothing could still the chill covering her flesh.

His cheeks turned ruddy. He dropped his gaze. "No."

A whisper of movement sounded from the door's opening.

Ellen stiffened. "Do you have company?"

His jaw clenched. "Listen, I can't talk right now." He pushed away from the door.

"I see." She swallowed. "I'll let you—" She flicked a glance toward the slight seam exposed between the door and his body. The table was set for two. Fury burned through her. She lifted her chin. "I'll let you get back to whatever you're doing." Pivoting, she marched down the steps, furious at having been duped by Dax again.

Her heart twisted with pain, and her eyes stung with tears. She gulped in the harsh air, trying desperately to ignore the anguish tearing her apart. *Why be sad?* Hadn't she known the ending all along? Thrusting out a hand, she shoved aside branches tearing her skin and tugging her hair. She stumbled in the snow, coming close to falling. She righted herself and pushed forward.

A hand reached out and caught her. "Ellen."

Stiffening, she pulled back her hand. "Don't." Pivoting, she turned. Dax stood behind her. The glow of moonlight illuminated a face filled with pain and worry. She held up a palm. "Just don't."

He took a step back and dropped his gaze. His palms fisted, then unclenched. A shudder rolled over his shoulders. Taking a deep breath, he glanced toward his house before turning back. "It's not how it looks."

258

Anger, red-hot and blistering, roared through her. How dare he deny what was so obvious. She arched a brow. "Oh? So, you're not entertaining?"

A muscle flexed in his cheek. "Not in the way you think."

"But someone is at your house, right?"

"Yes, but—" His back straightened, and his cheeks turned bright red. "I can't explain now." He reached out and took her hand. "I just need some time."

Time? For what? To sow more wild oats. She yanked free. *So very foolish.* Hadn't she learned the first time? Wasn't his evasiveness what she expected? Pivoting, she gave what she hoped was a carefree wave. "Take all the time you need."

Grabbing her shoulders, he turned her and pulled her against him. His arms wrapped around her waist, holding her pinned against his hard frame.

She wanted to fight him and resist his grip, only his mouth swooped down, capturing her lips in a searing kiss. Dang, if she didn't start responding to the urgency in his touch. His hands ran over her, skimming her body in an almost desperate manner only to finally settle on her waist. His fingers dug into her flesh, and his hot breath fanned over her skin.

A shudder ripped through him. Pulling back, he dropped his hands and stared into her eyes. "I just need some time."

Ellen saw the need filling his gaze and heard the despair in his voice. She grabbed his hands. "Is it your mother? Your sister?" She tightened her grip, feeling the warmth of his hand clinging to hers. "Let me help."

His throat worked, and his Adam's apple bobbed. Removing his hand, he brushed a finger along her forehead, then tucked a strand of hair behind her ear. As he studied her, a whisper of a smile curled on his lips. "Sugar, you can't solve this problem. *I* have to."

Her heart hurt. She gritted her teeth. "I see."

He shook his head. "No, you don't." Leaning down, he brushed his lips across hers. "I promise. I'll explain...soon."

She glanced toward his driveway. Only his vehicle occupied the space. So, whatever he had to do, he didn't trust her enough to help, as if she was just another unimportant person in his life. She shrugged. "Sure. Whatever."

Stepping back, she turned and shoved through the shrubs, then darted across the lawn. She ran up the porch steps and into her house. Slamming her back against the door, she pressed shaking fingers to her lips and closed her eyes. Somehow, despite his plea, she knew she'd just been played for a fool.

****

Dax watched Ellen disappear into the shadows. His heart hurt. He wanted to chase after her, to explain about his father, and why everything had changed. Closing his eyes, he blew out a breath. No matter what the explanation, he knew she wouldn't understand. Turning, he walked slowly up the back steps and into the house. He shut the door behind him.

"Who was that?"

Jerking back, Dax turned to see his father walk into the kitchen. "Ellen." Frowning, he swept his gaze over the man who had ruined his life in so many ways. Dressed in fresh jeans and a crisp, black, button-down shirt, his father looked ready to head out. "Dad, I told you I had stuff for dinner."

Thomas fanned a hand. "Change of plans." He strolled across the kitchen and grabbed his keys. "Just got a call. Have to head out."

Dax gritted his teeth. "Right. A call."

Pausing in dropping the keys in his pocket, Thomas turned. "Now don't be upset, son." He clapped a hand on Dax's shoulder. "I promise we'll do something tomorrow."

Dax shrugged away his grip. "Right."

Thomas stood in the center of the kitchen and ran fingers through his silver hair. Finally, he sighed. "Listen, I can change plans. Hate to disappoint you."

Too late. Far too late. Waving a hand, Dax strolled toward the living room. "Don't bother. Not in the mood to eat anyway."

"Suit yourself."

Seconds later, the door shut.

Dropping onto the couch, Dax rested his head against the back of the cushions and ran a hand across his face. *What the hell?* His father had made a big deal out of spending time with him only to change his mind. And here he rearranged his whole night to see his father? Worse, he knew, *knew,* Ellen saw the table made and jumped to the worst possible conclusion. He closed his eyes. He needed to go over and explain what happened. *And then what?*

Tell her his father came to see him? Expose his father's horrible past which so closely mimicked his own? Oh, he knew the town was aware of his family's history, including Ellen. But somehow, he figured hearing the words from his lips made things more…real, and that truth would only put more doubts in her mind. He couldn't allow such a thing to happen.

He walked into the kitchen. Ripping open the fridge, he snagged a beer and slammed shut the door. Hell, if he could, he'd drink every damn beer chilling inside, but no amount of alcohol would assuage his pain.

The sharp click of the clock's minute hand broke the silence.

He glanced upward. *Eight. Damn.* He opened the fridge and replaced the beer. Like hell he'd stay here. Walking across the room, he grabbed his coat and keys. He pulled open the door and stepped outside.

Frigid wind ripped across the ground and howled through the trees.

He spied a light shining from Ellen's bedroom window. His thoughts badgered him to walk over and have the courage to knock on her door and plead for forgiveness. Instead, he ripped open his truck door and climbed inside.

All he wanted was a moment to escape—to get away and think through his life. He jammed the keys into the ignition and backed out of the driveway. He drove nowhere in particular, but in minutes, he found himself pulling up along the front of Martinis. He slipped the truck into Park and stared at the gray-stuccoed building.

Normally, during the week, the place was considerably slower than the weekend. But, during the holidays, things changed, and people found a reason to stop by for a drink. Tonight was no exception. Raucous music ripped from the door, surrounding the line of people waiting to enter.

Dax counted more than a dozen women dressed in their holiday best, waiting to enter. Skimming his gaze down the row, he spotted Ava. She stood with another girlfriend—one he'd never seen before. Both were cute, with similar hair styles. The breeze caught their shoulder-length curls, swirling the tendrils in the breeze and tugging at their coats. Long, trim legs showed beneath dresses far too short to ever be considered demure. They dressed for any invitation.

His stomach knotted. He knew, without a doubt, he could approach her right now, and she'd be in his bed within minutes. Hell, any of the women were his for the picking. Only, the one he wanted thought he was home doing his worst.

A tiny part of him demanded he dismiss Ellen—to give up, knowing she had her mind set against them. Another part refused to quit. Dammit, he wanted her, and no one else.

In the past whenever he needed to talk about a problem, Ben was his go-to guy. Now, more than ever he needed his friend's advice. Slamming the truck into gear, he drove around the block. A light shown from inside city hall. He wasn't surprised to see Ben still at work. The man was dedicated to a fault.

He parked next to Ben's truck. Stepping out, he tucked his hands into his pockets and strode along the sidewalk. Off into the distance, he could hear the thrum of music emanating from Martinis.

Headlights flashed along James Street. A few cars zipped past. Holiday lights glittered from the trees filling the park, and dark shadows shaped like miniature houses and tiny candy canes surrounded the area. Come next week, the park would be ablaze with lights, laughter, and festive cheer. Now, though, the place was like a sleeping village waiting to erupt into life.

Pulling open the door, Dax stepped inside the cavernous lobby. A few lights glowed overhead, but otherwise, the area was vacant. Strolling down the long corridor, he heard the soft squeak of his shoes echoing on the marble floor. A thin stream of light shown beneath the seam of the office door. He took a deep breath before nudging open the door.

The front office was empty. Of course, he expected such, considering Ava was at the bar, and it was far past normal work hours. He slipped a glance toward her desk. Not one item of paper cluttered the surface. Everything was perfectly arranged, waiting for her arrival tomorrow. Had Ellen worked here, he knew the space would look like a whirlwind of disorder. He smiled. Ellen could never be considered the most organized person. Despite that fact, she always knew where to find what she needed. A shuffle of paper drew his attention. He turned and softly knocked on the inner office door before opening it. "Working late, are you?"

Ben snapped up his head. "Dax?" Leaning back, he frowned. "Thought you had plans with Ellen."

Dax's chest tightened. Digging fingers into the door jamb, he gritted his teeth. "Dad's home."

Ben froze, then frowned. "What?"

A rush of air ripped from Dax. He stepped into the room. "Dad made a surprise visit today."

Leaning back in his chair, Ben stared at Dax. "Okay." Exhaling, he raked fingers through his hair. "And how do you feel about his appearance?"

Dax glared. "How do you think?" Dropping into a chair, he stared at his hands. All sorts of thoughts swirled through his head—the need to see his father, the desire to understand why he left, the desperation to heal his past and secure his future. Yet, his father opted to go out, with who knows what woman, and forgo the opportunity for them to reconnect. *Pathetic.* "The man disappears for twenty-four years, and suddenly, he comes back and wants to have this nice, family reunion." He snorted. "Only, he didn't want much of one, considering he left to go out."

Ben crossed arms over his chest and narrowed his gaze. "And Ellen?"

Dax ripped up his head. "What about her?"

"Mom said you two had plans."

Dax sighed. "Yeah, but—" He eased out a breath. Hell, he knew the truth. He hadn't wanted her to see his father and make a comparison. Worse, he hadn't wanted her to find him lacking. "I canceled."

Leaning in, Ben propped elbows on the desk. "Want to tell me why?"

"Imagine her reaction to seeing my father and hearing about his past." Anger and resentment welled inside Dax. He'd worked so hard to forget about Thomas as easily as his father had forgotten him. He'd succeed too, until now, and then, just like the snap of fingers, his carefully made plans exploded with a resounding bang. He slammed down a fist against the hard armrest. "Do you really think I want Ellen to see my father and make the same comparison to me?"

"What I think doesn't matter." Ben uncrossed his arms and pointed. "What matters is how you feel about each other."

"I can't take the chance."

Ben ripped out a harsh growl. "Dax, why the hell would Ellen compare you to your father?"

"Isn't it obvious? You know Dad's history. You've

heard all the dirty rumors and talk." He jammed a finger in his chest. "You know me. You know my past. Am I any different than him?"

Ben stared at Dax for just a moment before a harsh growl ripped from him. "Dax, if I thought you were anything like him, I would have told you right from the beginning to stay away from Ellen." He dropped a hand to the desk. "Listen, you're only like your father if you choose to be."

Dax opened his mouth.

Ben lifted a hand. "Yes, I know your past, and yes, you've dated lots of women. I did, too. Do you consider me like your father? Do you think I'll be unfaithful to Lily?"

"Of course not." Dax dug fingers into the armrest. "But you were raised differently."

Ben jabbed a finger. "When you were six, your dad left. My father took up the slack." Fixing his gaze on Dax, he narrowed his eyes. "You were like a son to him. He treated you like one. He *raised* you like one." He curled his hand into a fist. "Now, act like his son."

Running fingers through his hair, Dax sighed. "How do I make Ellen understand?"

"I don't have the answers, Dax." Shrugging, Ben tapped his fingers on the desk. "All I can say is, if you want her, you need to figure it out. If not, leave her and move on."

Dax stared at his hands. Ben didn't understand. His family was perfect, and Ellen deserved better than him.

Chapter 24

Scrubbing fingers through her hair, Ellen stared at the ceiling. Sleep eluded her. Through most of the night, she kept replaying her encounter with Dax. The desperation in his touch had been palpable, as if she was his lifeline. So then, why had he refused her help when she offered?

He'd assured her nothing out of the ordinary had occurred, but how come he hadn't allowed her into his house? Why, even when he chased after her, had he not told her of the issue? Did he not trust her? Or was it more? Had Angel been there, and he was afraid to tell her?

Tapping a finger on the mattress, she thought of Betty's words. Angel has claws. But, if that was the case, why had Angel stayed in the house instead of confronting her? And where had she parked her car? Or had Dax picked her up? But why when he'd made plans with her?

And then another, more worrisome thought filled her. Maybe he had seen a change in Ellen, a deepening of feelings he didn't reciprocate, and ran scared? If anyone defined the term commitment-phobe, Dax would be that person. But, if so, why not just end the relationship instead of promising an explanation? Questions, one after another, shot through her thoughts, but not one answer arrived.

Shifting, she glared at the picture. How different the man was to the boy in the picture. Grabbing the frame, she studied the image. Back then, he'd been a normal guy, clinging to friendships like he'd lose them the next day. Over the years, though, he'd changed, became like a little boy, who never could be satisfied with just enough, easily flitting from one desire to the next. Only last night, he'd held her like he never wanted to let go. Was telling her he needed time his way of letting her down?

Her heart twisted. Hadn't she always known the time would come? Somehow, though, she had convinced herself that the inevitable was farther off. Now, she was faced with the truth, and it hurt more than she ever expected. *How pathetic.* Like heck she'd sit around and participate in his self-indulgent behavior. If he was ready to move on, then so was she.

She arranged the picture on the nightstand with the face down. Kicking off the sheets, she climbed from the bed. A part of her wanted to walk across the room and peer out the window, just to see whether he was home. Instead, she forced herself to walk into the bathroom.

Twenty minutes later, she strolled out and walked to the bureau. Her curiosity got the better of her. Chewing her lip, she nudged aside the curtain and peered out. Through the glow of moonlight, she spotted Dax's truck. *Was he alone?* Something feeling very close to a knife pierced her heart. She dropped the curtain and walked to the closet and grabbed her shoes. He said he needed time. She knew what his unspoken words meant. In her mind, they were effectively done.

Plopping onto the bed, she slipped her feet inside

and tied the laces. The one thing she needed to be certain of was Ben's and her mother's relationship with Dax remained, and for that to happen, she'd need to act as if she was completely fine with Dax's decision. Could she do it? What choice did she have? She'd just have to be believable. *But how?* In high school, she'd acted in a few plays, but in no way could she be considered even remotely of the same caliber as Alexis. Still, she'd been passable.

Standing, she ran her hands down her jeans. Taking a deep breath, she lifted her chin and marched from the room and down the stairs. She strolled into the kitchen. Grabbing her coat, she stuffed her arms into the sleeves. Whether she liked it or not, she was determined she'd be the best, damn passable actress the town had ever seen. Darn if she wouldn't. Snatching her keys, she stepped from the house and put aside her relationship with Dax. *Time to move on.* Arriving at the café, Ellen pulled open the door and stepped inside.

Holding a pair of tongs with a pastry clamped between the ends, Betty arched a brow. "Didn't expect to see you arrive so early."

A lump formed in Ellen's throat. Hanging her coat on the rack, she peered over her shoulder. "Yeah? Why?"

Betty arranged the treat in the case. "Just thought you'd want extra time with Dax."

"Didn't go as planned."

Betty rested elbows on top with the tongs perched in her hand. "What happened?"

Ellen pulled her apron from beneath the counter. "Not really sure." She dropped the loop over her head. "He didn't come and get me." She pulled the ties around her waist. "I thought something happened, so I went over."

"And?"

Strolling across the narrow aisle, Ellen yanked a cup from the stack. She swallowed past the lump nestled in her throat. "He said he had a change of plans."

"What change?"

Her heart ached, and her head pounded. She licked her lips. "I think he had another date." She shoved the cup under the spigot.

"What?" Betty tossed down the tongs. "No. He wouldn't do such a despicable thing."

She shrugged. "He told me he didn't." Flipping the handle, Ellen peered over her shoulder. "But I saw the table set for two."

Betty wedged a hip against the counter. "Maybe he planned to get you, but something happened? Work, maybe?"

Ellen shook her head. "Nope. He would have told me."

"And he didn't?"

Ellen stared at the coffee filling her cup. "He said he needed time." When the dark brew reached the rim, she flipped the handle. "I think he's having second thoughts. He said he'd explain…eventually."

Betty fanned a hand. "You're overthinking things again."

Ellen grabbed a packet of sugar. She shook the packet twice before tearing the corner. "You know Dax. If anyone could run from a relationship, he's the man."

"Nope. You can't get me to buy that excuse."

Staring at the white crystals falling from the

packet, Ellen sighed. "It's reality. He's changed his mind."

"What about you?" Betty stepped closer. "How do you feel?"

Miserable. Heartbroken. Lonely. Gripping the paper cup, she stared at her hands. "I knew the inevitable would happen."

"Sounds like you're giving up?"

Dropping onto the stool, Ellen ripped up her gaze. "What choice do I have?" She grabbed a stir stick and dipped it into the dark brew. Slowly stirring, she frowned. "I've been burned before. I won't get burned again."

Betty sighed. "All I know is, you've been looking for a reason to not trust Dax, and now you have one."

Ellen frowned. "Whose side are you on, anyway?"

Betty waved her hand. "Oh no, you don't. I'm not picking sides. I'm just stating you're so ready to decide Dax is in the wrong." She nodded toward Ellen's phone on the counter. "You need to give him the chance to explain." She picked up the empty metal tray.

Tapping fingers against the side of the cup, Ellen stared out the café window. Cars zoomed past, but none belong to Dax. Of course, Betty was right. He deserved the opportunity to explain. She owed it to their friendship, but she would be damned if he'd make her look like a fool again.

****

She waited three long days for Dax to appear. Not once did he arrive on her doorstep with a reason for his behavior. He never even showed up at her work. A part of her was grateful. She didn't want to have him break up in front of a room filled with curious gazes.

Betty didn't help matters. Not only did she insist Dax would talk when he was ready, but she kept pestering her about the manager job. Had things ended differently, she would have accepted the position. Now, though, she couldn't imagine staying and watching him date other women. She might be foolish for falling in love, but she wasn't a glutton for punishment either.

By the time her shift was over on Friday, she was positive things with Dax were officially over. Tightness settled in her chest, and a lump formed in her throat. Swallowing past the pain, she stepped from the café and scanned the area. She spotted him strolling down the street, with Angel. She held his arm while speaking to a man Ellen had never seen.

Dax peered over his shoulder.

His gaze landed on her. For a split second, his eyes lit, and a smile creased his face.

The man beside him turned and narrowed his eyes.

Ellen flinched at the heat she saw in his face, but nothing compared to seeing Angel clinging to Dax. A smile, as victorious and smug as any she had seen before slipped across Angel's lips.

Dax ripped away his gaze and continued walking, becoming smaller as he moved farther away.

Ellen climbed inside her car. Her heart pounded in her chest, and her hands shook. Digging through her purse, she fumbled three times before collecting her keys. She slipped them into the ignition and started her car. Her phone buzzed. She grabbed her cell and peered at the screen. A chill skittered down her spine. Licking her lips, she picked up the call. "Hello?"

"Ellen, so good to talk to you."

Her mind spun with a million thoughts. Weeks had

passed since she'd spoken to her former employer, but the last time she had, he'd been quite definite in his decision. She couldn't imagine why he'd call now. Surely, not to get her advice about some project Grant needed help on. She gripped the steering wheel. "Mr. Jorgensen, why are you calling?"

A long pause sounded across the lines. Finally, he sighed. "Listen, I know things didn't end as you expected." He cleared his throat. "I'm not one who usually reads people wrong."

Her heart slammed in her chest. Gripping the phone, Ellen eased out a breath. "I understand."

A chuckle sounded. "No. I don't think you do." Another long pause occurred. A rough exhale sounded. "Listen, I'll just come right out and say things with Grant didn't work out. He and I differed in every decision. He doesn't have the vision or the knowledge you have. My choice was wrong. Right from the beginning, I knew you were the best candidate. Unfortunately, I went against my gut instincts. I won't do that again."

A little fluttered zipped through Ellen's stomach. "I'm sorry you two couldn't make things work."

"Hell, I'm not." Paper shuffled on the other end, followed by a long sip and a clink of glass on the table.

She glanced out the window. In the distance, she could just make out Dax. Angel and the man he walked with earlier had disappeared. She studied his bent head and stooped shoulders. As he walked along the sidewalk, a solitary figure, he tucked in hands in his pockets. He looked so lonely and sad.

"He's moved on, and I wish him the best," Dave continued.

She continued to watch Dax. *Just like him.* Her heart ached, realizing how much she missed him. She wondered if he felt the same as her, like an anvil had crushed her heart and broken her bones.

"I'm wondering if you would consider coming back, as V.P. of course."

Mr. Jorgensen's voice caught her attention. She ripped away her gaze from Dax. The words she'd wanted to hear weeks ago were there. All she had to do was accept. Only, Mr. Jorgensen's statement from earlier hung heavy in her thoughts. Should she say yes? Her stomach tightened, and her muscles tensed.

She had too much to consider before she could make such a commitment—her mother's desire, Betty's needs, but especially Dax's promise. Although could she really factor him into the equation?

She stared at the pedestrians passing by her car. Snow trickled down from the sky, dusting the heads, shoulders, and pavement in white. She skimmed her gaze across the park, to the completely decorated area, ready to flip the switch and start the holiday celebration.

Ten years ago, she couldn't wait to leave. Now, when the opportunity presented itself again, a part of her fought the idea. *Why?* Too many confusing thoughts swirled through her to make a sound decision. She tightened her grip. "Thank you for the consideration, but I need some time."

The irony of the words wasn't lost on her. They were the very same Dax used. She raked fingers through her hair and stared off in the distance. Dax had disappeared. She had agreed to give him the chance to explain. Shouldn't she wait at least through the weekend before she made her decision? If he didn't come over by Sunday, she'd know they were done. She gripped the steering wheel. "You'll have my answer before Monday."

"I look forward to hearing from you."

Disconnecting the phone, she rested her head against the seat back and closed her eyes. Now, suddenly, having the opportunity she'd dreamed of for years might very well be the last thing she wanted.

Chapter 25

Friday afternoon, Dax strolled down the sidewalk. He really wasn't interested in going into town. He certainly didn't need anything. But, staying home and listening to his father ramble on about the past, none of which included himself or his sister, sounded about as much fun as having a spike driven through a tooth. Unfortunately, his father chose to join him. The ceaseless monologue of all the wonderful things Thomas had done since leaving Aberdeen continued. Correction. Of all the wonderful women he'd done.

A gust of wind whipped at Dax's face and tugged at his coat. Fisting his hands into pockets, he stared at the ground, wondering why the hell his father didn't care that his infidelity had ripped apart a family. For three days, he'd endured his father's presence. Now, he just wanted the man to leave.

Looking up, Dax peered into the window of Johnson's Pharmacy. A whisper of a smile split his face. Inside, he could see Hope, Owen's daughter, working the register. He hadn't seen her in years. Maybe later, he'd stop by and have a nice visit.

The smell of coffee drew his attention. A heavy weight settled in Dax's stomach. He shoved his hands deeper into his pockets and casually slipped a glance into the café window.

Ellen stood behind the counter, helping Mrs. Chester with her order.

His chest tightened. But damn. He missed her. On Tuesday, he'd desperately wanted to explain his father's sudden arrival. However, discussing the man who chose freedom over family felt too raw and the memories far too painful to utter the words he knew she had a right to hear. Now, three days later, he knew his avoidance was cowardly, and the thought of seeing her, of introducing his father, tore at him. How could he ever expect Ellen to see him differently, if his father opened his mouth and spouted even just a fraction of his history? Hell, look how long it took just for Ellen to see him as a friend, let alone anything serious. One mistaken word from his father and all his hard work would implode like a building being demolished. No, he couldn't take the chance, and yet, he worried she'd thought he left her.

Maybe he should. He certainly wasn't worthy. Hell, Ellen deserved the stars and the moon, not the son of a man who couldn't settle down with one woman. And hadn't he spent most of his life proving he was just like the man strolling beside him, bragging of his conquests?

A smile, as brilliant as the morning sunlight, flashed across Ellen's face. He couldn't stop himself from grinning. Lord, the woman was beyond beautiful. She'd captured him years ago, only, he had refused to acknowledge what his heart had known all along. If he could settle with one woman, he'd choose Ellen.

"So, this woman…" Thomas let out a low whistle. "She's hot. Let me tell you, off-the-charts combustible. Of course, she's all over me, just begging for me to take her into the bathroom and have my way with her." He scratched at the gray whiskers dusting his chin. "And I'm thinking, why not? Husband out of town, and the bar is fairly empty, so I lean back and wink. 'Darlin',' I say—"

When he allowed his father to stay, he hadn't expected to hear a rolling montage of endless women. Only in the days since, those stories were the only ones Thomas chose to share. The whole thing made Dax's skin crawl and his stomach churn. "How long do you plan to remain in town?"

Jerking back, Thomas frowned. "I just arrived a few days ago, son." He nudged Dax in the side again. "Tell me you're not eager for your old man to leave so soon?"

Dax gritted his teeth. "I'd prefer if you just called me by my name and not son."

Thomas shrugged. "So, you're ready to get rid of me already?"

"Just wondering. Haven't seen much of you the last few days. Figured you were ready to go."

Thomas cleared his throat. "I've just been busy catching up with some of my friends."

But not your son? Fearful Ellen would spy him out the window, Dax increased his pace. "No need to stay at my house then."

"Got a little problem with staying elsewhere." Thomas hooked fingers into his pants pockets. "See, these ladies got some entanglements that…" He shrugged. "Well, just wouldn't look appropriate for me to stay at their house."

Turning, Dax stared at his father. A swell of emotions rolled through him—anger, incredulity, but mostly disgust. His father hadn't changed a bit. "You mean, they're married?" Thomas didn't even have the decency to look ashamed of the idea.

Instead, he winked. "Trust me, the best ones are." He pulled out a pack of cigarettes and fished out a smoke. Narrowing his eyes, he pressed the cig to his lips and lit it. A large plume of white floated up. Smiling, he tucked the pack into his coat pocket. "See, they get all these pent-up emotions that their husbands can't quell. They need a little outside entertainment to work out the kinks." Taking another long puff, he nudged Dax in the side. "If you catch my drift."

The urge to pivot and escape his father's presence burned deep within Dax. He stared at the man he hardly knew. Deep wrinkles creased his father's ashen skin. "You know, you should quit smoking. You're killing yourself."

Thomas took another long drag, then exhaled a stream of gray smoke. "Gonna die sometime. Might as well die a happy man."

Skimming his gaze across the park, Dax wondered about his father's comment. Was Thomas just blustering, or was there more to the comment? "You're not worried about lung cancer?"

"Can't worry about something out of my control." Thomas took another drag. "So, about me leaving…what's the hurry? I won't be back."

Dax shot him a quick look. Was his father hiding something? If he was, exactly how much did Dax care? The answer came fast. He had about as much concern as his father showed him over the years. Dax shrugged. "Just curious. You said you wanted to come and see me." He shifted his attention to the festive scene at the park. He always enjoyed the holidays. This year, though, he didn't know if they'd hold the same appeal. By now, Ellen had probably assumed the worse. He didn't blame her.

"We're together now."

Seeing as they were headed to the hardware store, Dax figured that didn't count as a qualifying event. "Sure."

"Is it because of a woman?"

Dax stopped and gaped at his father. "What?"

"Are you wanting me to leave because of a woman."

Lord, he felt like a sixth-grade boy being pried for secrets he didn't want to share. Dax shrugged. "Just ready to get my life back on track."

Thomas waved a hand. White smoke made a zigzag in the crisp air. "Let me tell you, you don't want to settle down with just one woman. They're too demanding." He inhaled another deep puff. Slowly, he exhaled. Gray smoke spiraled upward, circling his head, before disappearing. He took one more puff before discarding the smoke onto the ground and crushing the butt with his heel. "You heard me earlier. Married women get the itch. They don't stay straight."

Dax clenched a fist. Red-hot fury burned through him. "Mom didn't."

The muscle flexed in Thomas' cheek. "No, I don't suppose she did." He stared straight ahead and began to walk. "She would have, though."

Every muscle in Dax's body tensed. How dare his father suggest such a thing! His mother didn't have a deceptive bone in her body. She worked hard to keep her family together. Harder still to raise her head above the shame of being deserted. "Like hell."

Thomas stopped and stared. "What? You think your mother was the angel, and I was the sinner?" He coughed, deep and guttural. His face turned bright red. He caught his breath, then spat on the ground. A glob of pitch-black splashed on the concrete. Catching his breath, he wiped a hand across his mouth. "Trust me, she wasn't the angel you make her out to be. Constantly nagging, always demanding my attention, and insisting we be a family like the Jordans." He growled out the last word. "The woman was relentless."

Clenching his fists, Dax stiffened. "Yeah, terrible to be like them."

"Hey, they weren't the picture-perfect family you make them out to be." Coughing, Thomas shook his head. "They put a damn lot of pressure on them kids of theirs, always requiring high grades in school and encouraging impossible dreams." He spat on the ground again and glanced toward City Hall. "Hell, they're an uppity group, thinking they're better than me—than *us*."

Dax turned, ready to snap at his father, when a hand tugged at his arm. His heart leaped for just a moment, thinking Ellen had spotted him. He turned. Angel stood behind him with one of those heart-stopping smiles that caused heat to burn through most men. All he saw was the manipulation in her gaze. He frowned. "Angel."

She curled a hand into his arm. "I've been calling you."

"Told you before, no need to. I know what I have to do."

She flicked a glance toward Thomas and arched a

brow. "And you are?"

Thomas' chest puffed up and dang if he didn't run his gaze over Angel's trim, cream-covered figure. His eyes lit up. He thrust out a hand. "Aren't you just the prettiest gal I've seen in a long while."

Her cheeks turned pink, but her eyes glimmered, and her smile widened.

Rubbing a thumb along her leather-encased palm, Thomas winked. "Thomas Moore. Dax's father."

Shifting her gaze between the two men, Angel arched a brow. "I see where Dax gets his handsomeness." Casually, she extracted her hand from his grip and curled fingers onto Dax's bicep. "Dax and I have a special relationship."

Dax gritted his teeth. "Nothing special about work."

She laughed.

The bright tinkling sound drew men's attention, but, for Dax her laughter only made his jaw clench and his anger burn.

Tightening her grip on his arm, she leaned in so that her body seamed his. "I remember times we did plenty of stuff that had nothing to do with work."

Thomas thrust down his brows, then scratched his chin. "Don't tell me my son let you get away."

She gazed up at Dax and smiled. "Yup. Seems he's interested in some local girl."

Dax's muscles twitched, and the urge to slam his fist into something hard burned through him. He shook away her grip. "Did you need something?"

"Now, son." Thomas scowled. "No need to be so rude. This lovely lady just wants to spend some time with you."

Ignoring his father's comment, Dax stopped in front of Peterson's Hardware store and faced Angel. "What did you want?"

She smiled, but no light shone from her eyes. "Just making certain you'll pick me up tomorrow. Remember, the signing?"

As if he could forget. "Right. Seven."

She trailed a finger down his arm. "Don't be late." She leaned in and brushed her lips close to his ear. "Oh, and Jakob isn't riding with us. It will be just us two." She squeezed his arm. "Looking forward to spending some time together." She stepped back and winked. "Make sure to tell your girlfriend I said hi."

Turning, Dax watched her stroll down the sidewalk toward her hotel. Her head was raised, and her back was ramrod straight. His gut churned. How the hell had she gotten Jakob to back out of the ride? Hell, the man kept talking about her for days on end, and now, suddenly he wouldn't be with them. It didn't make sense. He narrowed his eyes. Angel was up to something.

A low whistle sounded.

Dax turned to see his father watching Angel.

"Now, there's the woman you want." Thomas didn't say anything for a minute or two. He dug into his pocket and grabbed out his smokes. Drawing out another, he studied Dax while lighting the cigarette. Dropping the pack into his pocket, he blew out a breath. "Heard from Maisy Webber, you and that Jordan girl are a couple. Is it true?"

Dax shrugged. "We're friends."

Inhaling, Thomas pointed a finger. "Mark my words, son. Those Jordans won't ever settle for the

283

likes of us. They think they're better than us lowly folks." He tucked one hand in his pocket and stared at Angel's departing back. "Besides, that one is a sight better than any Jordan girl could be."

Dax ripped open the store's door. He refused to let his father's words break him, but he couldn't help wondering if maybe his father hadn't spoken the truth. Why would Ellen settle for him when she deserved so much better?

Chapter 26

On Saturday morning, Ellen paced the kitchen. She thought she would go stir crazy if she didn't get out of the house. Every inch of her body tightened and tensed, like her muscles wanted to jump from her skin and flop on the floor.

Since Friday night, she'd cleaned every nook and cranny of the place, trying to ease some of the tension building within her. She'd lost track of how many times she stopped in front of the kitchen window, hoping and praying Dax would show. By the time darkness had fully fallen and the clock struck ten, she gave up and forced herself to bed.

Now, with the rising sun, Ellen couldn't take another minute in the house. When she peered out her window earlier in the morning and spotted Dax leaving, she gave up any pretense of seeing him today.

She glanced at her cell phone. Maybe she should just call Mr. Jorgensen and accept the offer. She ran her fingers over the keys, carefully punching in each number. Only, when she reached the last one, she stopped and dropped her hand. She didn't know why, but she just couldn't make the call. Not yet. Not until she knew for certain things were over, and if that fact didn't make her a fool, she sure didn't know what did. How ridiculous was she to keep hoping he'd show?

Placing the phone on the counter, she walked over to the table and sat. Tapping her fingers, she wondered what she should do now. She couldn't stay home. Not when she felt like a trapped animal.

A rap sounded on the door.

Her heart caught. *Dax?* Pivoting, she frowned. Not Dax, but Maybelline. She fanned a hand.

Opening the door, Maybelline stepped inside.

Ellen ran her gaze over Maybelline's crazy bouffant hair and chartreuse-colored balls dangling of her ears, past the lime-green fuzzy coat, straight down to the purple, zebra-striped leggings tucked into black biker boots. "What the heck?"

"Thought we'd go shopping." Maybelline dropped her purse with about a gazillion crystals tacked to the cherry-red leather on the counter.

"I didn't mean about you showing up." She arched brows. "I mean your outfit."

Maybelline smoothed a hand down the front of her coat. "Pretty snazzy, right?" She patted her hair. "You know, I think I could really have given Alexis a run for her money at the whole modeling thing."

Ellen stood and skimmed her gaze over Maybelline. "Can't argue. Someone sure would be running."

Maybelline scowled. "Listen, do you want to go with me or not?"

Ellen flicked a glance out the window. No sign of Dax's truck in sight. "Sure. Let me go change." She darted up the stairs and got ready. Thankfully, she and Dax had gone to Albany a few weeks earlier and grabbed some of her clothing from her apartment. At the time, he'd wanted her to clear out the place, but something held her back. Now, she wondered if perhaps intuition had warned her. Or was Betty right, and she continued to search for a reason to protect herself from Dax. She didn't have the answer. Stepping into the kitchen, she spied Maybelline sitting at the table reading a magazine.

Tossing the magazine on the table, Maybelline stood. "Okay, let's get this done."

Ellen grabbed her coat and purse. "Where to?"

"To the mall in Albany." Maybelline opened the door. "I'll drive."

Ellen eyed Maybelline's clunker. More rust than paint covered the surface, and, at the minimum, the tires seemed in desperate need of a rotation. She glanced toward her shiny car with the pristine white paint and the sparkling black rubber rimming the wheels. "You sure you wouldn't rather take, say, something a little safer?"

Smoothing a hand over the maroon-and- rusted surface, Maybelline kissed the hood. "And hurt Ruby's feelings? I don't think so."

"You've given your car a name?" Ellen pulled open the passenger door and slung her purse inside.

"Of course, she's like a trusted friend. She deserves one." Maybelline patted the hood. "Don't you, Ruby?"

Slipping into the seat, Ellen rolled her eyes. She'd never understand her cousin.

Maybelline climbed inside.

Reaching around, Ellen grasped the seat belt. "I just hope we make it to Albany and back in this clunker."

Gasping, Maybelline pressed her hands on both sides of the steering wheel and glared. "Are you trying to hurt her feelings?"

"Oh, for heaven's sake." Ellen snapped close the buckle. "So, why the mall?"

Maybelline started the car. "Thought we could get some holiday clothing." Flipping the gears, she slowly backed from the driveway.

Settling her purse on her lap, Ellen stared at Dax's house. A tightness settled in her chest. Not too long ago she expected to be here for the holidays. Now, though, she wasn't certain. If she took the job with Mr. Jorgensen, she would need a dress. The company always put on a glitzy affair for the holidays.

"I saw this emerald-colored sparkly number at Newman's." Maybelline pulled out onto Timber. "Dax would love to see you in that dress."

Ellen dug fingers into the soft leather of her purse. Yanking away her gaze, she turned to Maybelline. She might as well break the news to someone. "Mr. Jorgensen offered me a job back at the firm."

"What?" Maybelline shifted her gaze from the road and gaped.

The car swerved on the slick pavement.

Ellen yelped. "Pay attention." She jammed a hand against the dashboard. "You'll get us killed before we even leave town."

Righting the car, Maybelline scowled. "You're not going to take it, are you?"

Ellen eased out a breath. "I haven't decided."

"What does Dax think?"

Staring at the passing scenery, Ellen forced herself to remain calm, even though her stomach churned, and her head pounded. She fisted one hand. "I haven't told him, but I'm certain he won't care."

"What? Of course, he will."

If he cared, he'd have stopped by during the past week. He hadn't, which said everything she needed know. Not to mention seeing him with Angel yesterday. Ellen didn't bother to mention any of those details. She stared out the front windshield and watched the *Welcome to Aberdeen* sign fly past. Her heart squeezed. In the past, she never spared a glance toward the sign. Today, though, a little lump formed in the back of her throat. "Dax and I broke up."

Again, Maybelline whipped her attention to Ellen, causing the car to swerve again. "What? When? How?"

Ellen really didn't want to discuss the breakup, but she knew her cousin wouldn't let up until she gotten all the gory details. Slowly, she explained the events with as little as emotion as possible, knowing Maybelline would listen for even the slightest inflection of tone. A sensation of pride filled her. She made it through the whole recitation without even a hint of pain. Only when she mentioned Angel did her voice crack.

Maybelline frowned. "I don't believe he's with Angel."

"Oh?" Ellen turned. "And why not? They were together at Ben's wedding *and* his election party. They dated before I returned. Maybe he changed his mind and decided he wanted her more."

Maybelline shook her head. "Dax doesn't like Angel. She's not his type."

"Oh please." Ellen clutched the door's arm rest and stared at the snowbanks flying past in a blur of white. "The fact she's a woman makes her his type."

"I refuse to think he'd go with her." Maybelline pressed on the gas.

The car whizzed down the highway.

A wide ribbon of murky darkness with blue-white sheets of ice floating on its surface stretched along the side of the car. Ellen said a silent prayer they didn't hit a patch of ice and send them careening off the road and into the river. "Slow down. I don't want to go swimming."

Maybelline patted the dashboard. "Ruby will keep us safe."

"Yeah?" Ellen clenched her teeth. "Does she float, too?"

Maybelline tapped fingers on the steering wheel. "You know his dad is in town."

Ellen stiffened. His father had come to town, and he hadn't said a word? "When?"

"Not sure. Mrs. Webber told me yesterday." Maybelline rounded a wide curve on the highway before turning onto the road leading to the mall. "Said she saw them walking together. Surprised you hadn't heard by now."

Ellen was, too. After all, she worked at the café, which basically was a hotbed of gossip. Staring straight ahead, she shifted through this new information. "That must have been who I saw him with."

Maybelline turned. "Explain, please."

"I saw him walking with a man yesterday." Ellen clenched her hands. Up ahead, she spied the shopping center. "He introduced him to Angel."

"What?" Maybelline whipped around her gaze.

The car swerved before fishtailing.

Ellen rammed a hand against the dashboard. Her stomach wobbled. She said a quick prayer they didn't crash into an oncoming car. Thankfully, the tires caught onto a dry stretch of road. The car straightened. She turned and glared at her cousin. "Jeez, Maybelline…pay attention."

Maybelline scowled. "Are you telling me, he introduced Angel to his father, but not you?" She shook her head. "That's not good."

"What do you mean?"

Pulling into the mall parking lot, Maybelline shrugged. "Well, duh. Everyone knows when a guy is serious, they introduce the woman to his family."

Dropping her gaze, Ellen stared at her hands. Of course, Maybelline was right. Hadn't she heard that very thing dozens of times from her mother? So, Dax was comfortable enough to introduce Angel but not her? Wasn't that proof enough their relationship meant little?

Maybelline chattered on, spouting all sorts of speculation and opinions.

Ellen paid no attention. Her thoughts centered on Dax with his father and Angel. *Was he the reason Dax hadn't shown?* She chewed her lip. *But why?* Why wouldn't he want to introduce Ellen to his father? Or was there more? Her chest tightened.

Maybelline glared at the crowded lot. "What the heck is going on? I've never seen the mall this busy."

Ellen glanced out the window.

Cars moved up and down the lanes, searching for a spot.

Maybelline crept behind them, blasting her horn every minute or so.

Ellen bit her tongue, knowing any comment wouldn't be appreciated.

Finally, a parking space became available.

Maybelline slammed on her brakes.

Ellen forgot all about Dax and his father. She was too busy worrying over whether she had whiplash or not. "Jeez."

Whipping the car into the vacant spot, Maybelline smiled. "You didn't think I'd give up such a plum location, did you?" She turned off the car. "We're practically in front of the mall."

Ellen grabbed her purse and climbed out. Slipping the purse strap over a shoulder, she followed Maybelline across the lot and into the mall.

A crowd of women swarmed toward the center of the concourse.

"What the heck?" Maybelline stepped up on her tippy toes and bobbed left and right. "I can't see what's going on. Can you?"

Ellen skimmed her gaze across the group and pointed. "Something is going on over there."

"Let's go upstairs." Maybelline pivoted and stepped on the escalator.

Upstairs, Ellen gazed into shop windows, spying several cute business outfits. In the past, she'd always gotten a little happy rush at the thought of purchasing a new outfit or pair of shoes for work. Today, though, the same zing evaded her. Sighing, she moved on to the next window. Nestled on a swatch of black velvet was a bold silver watch with a large black bezel. She pictured the watch on Dax's wrist. A soft feeling filled her. She pushed aside the thought. Why did she torture herself anyway?

"I *don't* believe it."

Turning, Ellen spied Maybelline crouching between two potted palms and staring through the glass railing edging the walkway. She dismissed the watch and walked over. "What are you doing?"

Maybelline pointed. "Look."

Ellen shifted her gaze, easily spying the table filled with firefighters. A long line of women, each of them clutching calendars, waited for their turn. But what really held her attention was the woman standing behind Dax, with her hand resting possessively on his shoulder. Angel, attired in a slinky green dress, stood close enough that not a minute's worth of space separated them. Her stomach churned.

"Talk about brazen." Maybelline yanked Ellen's hand.

Ellen dropped to her knees. A burst of pain shot up her legs, matching the ache in her heart.

Scowling, Maybelline pressed both hands against the glass. "Doesn't she realize Dax is with you?"

Ellen swallowed past the lump in her throat. "We're not together, remember?"

Inching closer, Maybelline peered toward Ellen and shook her head. "He never made it official. Right now, he's just cheating on you."

Ellen's stomach knotted. "And that makes this situation better? How?"

"Not better." Maybelline shrugged. "But, at least, you'll have your weapons ready."

Ellen frowned. "What weapons?"

"You know, something to use to hurt him." Maybelline shook her head. "Weapons, duh…"

A few people stopped and stared.

Maybelline scowled. "What are you looking at? Just keep on moving." Waving them on, she turned back to Ellen. "Jeez, you spy on people, and suddenly everyone is nosy. They really need to learn to mind their own business."

Ellen didn't bother to point out the very fact they did the same thing. "What are you talking about?"

Maybelline huffed. "Listen, Dax tells you there's nothing between him and Angel, right? Now, you'll have proof." She rocked back on her heels. "How do you think I found out about John and stupid Jenny Pickler?"

Despite Maybelline's arguments, Ellen didn't feel comfortable following such a devious scheme. Besides, she wouldn't ever use the proof with Dax. She wasn't vindictive, especially since she'd anticipated this behavior all along.

"Would you look at the women?" Maybelline fisted her hands. "Come on, people. Never seen a firefighter before?"

As much as she didn't want to look, Ellen couldn't seem to stop herself. Her heart ached. She didn't want to see any more. Standing, she hiked her purse onto a shoulder. "I've seen enough."

Maybelline yanked her hand. "Wait. Don't you want to know what Dax is doing?"

Ellen flicked a glance to the table below. She watched him lean back and grabbed a water bottle.

Tilting back his head, he stilled.

For a brief second, he appeared to look upward, almost as if he spotted her. But she knew that was impossible. The mall was far too busy for her to stand out. Her heart wobbled. She desperately wanted to yank away her gaze. Only she couldn't seem to make her eyes follow her thoughts. She licked her lips and gripped her purse.

Suddenly, Angel pressed hands to his shoulders and leaned down. Whispering something in his ear, she looked up and smiled.

Ellen had a chilling feeling Angel saw her. Her body tensed, and her pulse raced.

Dax slowly placed the bottle on the table. Picking up the pen, he scribbled across the calendar before handing the packet to the young woman and then nodding toward the next in line.

Blood pounded through Ellen's veins. "I already know what he's doing." Turning, she walked away. "He's making his choice."

****

Dax stared at the cluster of women snaking around the red velvet ropes and filling the area for as far as the eye could see. He'd already signed dozens of calendars, and from the looks of things, he had hours yet to go before he'd finish. He gritted his teeth and forced a smile. His fingers hurt from clutching the pen. He'd lost track of how many times he had to remind himself of the reason for the calendar. In the beginning, he'd been thrilled to help the hospital. If he hadn't taken up Angel on her offer, maybe he still would be. Hell. She'd made a mess of his life.

The next woman stepped up.

He didn't even bother to look up. "Afternoon, darlin'."

"Mr. Moore, you're the best man I've ever seen." Her words tumbled over one another.

"Yeah? You think?" He looked up and cringed. Jeez, the young girl looked all of sixteen. *What the hell?* He couldn't believe her parents let her get a calendar filled with half-naked men. He felt lower than a snake. "You with your parents?"

Giggling, she shoved strands of long, brunette hair off her shoulders. Pink crested her freckled cheeks. "No. I came alone."

He twirled the pen between his fingers. A part of him wanted to stand and walk away. What the hell was happening in the world? Parents let their little girls ooh and ah men who were twice their age?

Dropping the pen, he picked up his water bottle, intending to take a sip and buy himself a moment to collect his thoughts. He scanned the upper level then ripped his gaze back to the potted palms. His heart slammed, and his palms moistened. He blinked twice, certain he was mistaken, but no, he wasn't. He recognized Ellen's long hair and her trim figure. The urge to run up the escalator and catch her so he could explain filled him. The smell of expensive perfume surrounded him seconds before hands pressed against his shoulder, drawing him back against the seat. He stiffened.

"Don't think about leaving."

Angel's sugary sweet voice whispered in his ear. Her fingers grazed his neck. He clutched the bottle so tight water splashed over the top.

"Keep smiling, darlin'. You don't want your girlfriend to think you're miserable, now do you?"

Carefully, he set down the bottle and picked up the pen. A quick glance upward told him all he needed. Ellen had disappeared. Forcing a smile, he winked at the young woman. "So, what do you want me to write?"

Chapter 27

As they left the mall's parking lot, Ellen stared out the window, heedless of Maybelline's reckless driving. A heaviness filled her body, and an ache pierced her heart. She curled fingers into the soft leather of her purse and considered her options.

She watched the passing scenery, but all she saw were images of Dax with Angel at her mother's house for Christmas. He'd look so handsome and sexy. A victorious smile would crease Angel's beautiful face. Her stomach tightened. No, she refused to endure such a scene.

A thin, black line shown from the top of the purse's pocket. She slipped out her phone. Six o'clock. Should she call Mr. Jorgensen and give her decision? A tightness settled in her chest. Later, when she was alone.

Maybelline slowed the car then stopped.

Ellen looked up to see a nondescript building. Written across the glass windows in big, bold script read the words *Barley and Grapes—Purveyor of Albany's Finest*. She turned. "Why are we stopping?"

"I think after today, we both could use a drink." Maybelline extracted the keys from the ignition. "You wanna come inside?"

Ellen peered at the shop. She could go in and try to put the scene of the mall behind her, *or* she could do the one thing she knew could no longer be put off. She shook her head. A heaviness filled her. No matter what she had hoped, she knew the truth. Now, she had no reason to put off the inevitable. "No. I'll wait."

Shrugging, Maybelline shoved open the door and stepped out.

With shaking fingers, Ellen searched her contacts and called the number.

Mr. Jorgensen answered the phone in seconds.

Breathing deep, Ellen blurted out the words before she could stop herself. "Mr. Jorgenson, I've given your offer some thought, and…" She closed her eyes, and refusing to let any doubt creep in, she quickly rushed on. "I accept. I'll be there on Monday." She didn't wait for his response. Dropping the phone into her purse, she blinked back the tears. Now, everything was official. She and Dax were over. At least, Dax would remain friends with her mother and brother.

A few minutes later, Maybelline strolled out from the store, hugging a large box. Opening the back door, she slid the package onto the seat.

Frowning, Ellen peered inside the carton and frowned. "Nine bottles for the two of us?"

Maybelline climbed into the driver's seat. "I figured we'd need a bunch to forget the day. Plus, I called Alexis." She started the car. "Thought we'd have a girls' night in."

Ellen hadn't seen Alexis since her return from California, and as much as she didn't want her humiliation to get out in public, she knew Alexis would understand. Heavens knows, her ex had cheated enough for her to be sympathetic to Ellen's plight. Staring out the window, she looked at the sky. Thick clouds, painted in deep purples, dusky blues, and brilliant pinks, rolled across the heavens. Any other time, she'd be in awe of the beautiful sight. Today, though, the image of Angel and Dax refused to budge. Her heart clenched.

By the time they arrived at Ellen's house, Alexis's high-end luxury car was parked in front.

The driver's side door whipped open. From the fuzzy, cashmere beret atop her shimmery blonde hair right down to the tips of her knee-high, three-inch-heeled leather boots, every inch of Alexis was painted in black. Sliding the strap of an expensive clutch to her shoulder, she strolled over to Maybelline's clunker. "What's up, ladies?"

Maybelline climbed out and opened the back passenger door. "Just a day from hell." She grabbed the box. "We're drinking away the night."

"Sounds perfect." Alexis followed Ellen up the porch steps. "So, shopping in Albany, and no one thought to call me. I'm a little hurt.'

Ellen slid the key into the lock and opened the door. "Be thankful."

Stepping inside the house, Maybelline placed the box on the counter. "Plus, we didn't do any shopping." She tossed down her purse and glared at Ellen. "We caught Dax cheating."

Ellen slung her purse and keys on the counter. "Not cheating. We broke up."

Alexis paused in grabbing a bottle and furrowed her brow. "What? When?"

Scowling, Maybelline dug through the drawers until she found a bottle opener. She grabbed the bottle from Alexis and twisted the corkscrew inside the top.

Scrunching her face, she swiveled the cap. "We saw Angel with Dax today, and she was all over him so, you do the math."

"You don't honestly believe Dax would be serious with any woman, right?" Ellen grabbed three goblets from the cupboard and set them on the counter. "I just happened to be stupid enough to believe I meant more."

Alexis grabbed her hand. "I know Dax. He wouldn't do anything to jeopardize—"

Ellen cocked a brow. "What? His relationship with Ben?" She held out her glass.

Maybelline poured deep, ruby wine all the way to the rim.

"Of course not." Leaning back against the counter, Ellen sipped her wine. During the ride home, she figured out why he hadn't showed. "This way, if I break up with him, his relationship with Ben and my mother will remain intact."

"You're crazy." Maybelline took a healthy swallow of her wine.

Alexis tapped a finger. "That's not what I intended to say." She fixed her gaze on Ellen. "What you have with Dax is different."

"No. He has the same relationship with every woman." As much as she didn't want to tell them about that night six years ago, she really didn't see how she could get out of it. Dropping onto a kitchen chair, she licked her lips. "I know you two think things just happened with me and Dax recently, but we have a past."

Maybelline rolled her eyes. "Of course, you do. You've been friends forever."

Ellen stared at her hand. "I mean—" Taking a deep

breath, she told them the story, from the very beginning of when he'd come to Albany six years right to their current pact. By the time she finished, she counted two empty bottles of wine on the counter.

No one said a word.

Maybelline placed her glass on the counter with a loud clink. "I don't believe it." She scowled. "You slept with Dax six years ago and never mentioned a word?"

Alexis snorted. "I think you're missing the bigger picture." She turned to Ellen. "So, just because he left you six years ago, you expect the same now."

Ellen arched her brow. "Have you seen him do anything different?"

"Nope." Placing her glass down on the counter, Alexis leaned back and shrugged. "But doesn't mean he won't."

"What the heck are these?"

Ellen turned to see Maybelline holding up the sweats. Her stomach lurched. Jeez, why hadn't she given them back? Of course, she hadn't seen him since the day she wore them, so that explained why. "They're Dax's."

Maybelline frowned. "No, they're not."

"Sure, they are." Ellen buried her face into her glass, remembering that morning and how he'd told her his life was perfect. He hadn't lied. He did have a perfect life. Every woman fell at his feet, including her. "I found them in his dresser."

"Maybelline's right. Those aren't Dax's."

Snapping up her gaze, Ellen turned to Alexis. "They're our high school colors."

Maybelline scoffed. "Our colors were orange and black. Not pink." She turned around the pants. "*And* we didn't have SUNY written on the back."

Ellen stared at the faded pink fabric. Her head pounded. "I thought they were a part of his high school football uniform."

Alexis snorted. "Yeah, Dax likes women, but he doesn't dress like them."

"You know what I think?" Scowling, Maybelline waved the fabric. "He kept them as a trophy."

Raking fingers through her hair, Ellen ripped her gaze to Maybelline. "His what?"

Stretching out her arm, Maybelline held the sweats between two fingers and wrinkled her nose. "You know, like he keeps souvenirs of his conquests."

Ellen's stomach lurched. The wine surged upward. She pressed fingers against her lips. "No."

Maybelline waved the pants. "I'm telling you men are pigs."

Alexis held up her glass. "No argument here." Sipping the wine, she studied the sweats. "I wonder who they belong to."

"Who cares? They belong to some woman, and he kept them." Glaring, Maybelline waved the sweats in the air. "I say we burn them."

Ellen reached for the pants. "We are not burning them."

A devilish look settled in Alexis's eyes. "I kind of like the idea."

Of all the people in this room, Ellen figured Alexis was the voice of reason. She turned and dropped a hand to her hips. "You can't be serious."

"Of course, she is." Flinging out an arm, Maybelline pointed toward Alexis. "She knows men are pigs. She was married to one long enough."

"Again, no argument." Alexis peered over the rim of her glass before taking a sip.

Frowning, Ellen waved a hand around the room. "Just exactly where did you intend to burn them to make this 'statement'?"

"Outside." Maybelline flung open the door and pointed. "This way the whole town knows our opinion."

"What?" Ellen threw up her arms. Wine splashed over the rim and landed on her sleeve. She ignored the stain marring her shirt. "You want to burn them in the yard?"

Nodding, Maybelline skimmed her gaze around the room. "We need a lighter." She turned to Ellen and waved her fingers. "Where do you keep it?"

Ellen scrubbed fingers through her hair. "This idea is terrible."

"Not terrible." Alexis raised her glass. "Brilliant."

Maybelline clanked her glass against Alexis's. "Now, about that lighter?"

"How the heck would I know?" Ellen scowled. Whatever thought rolling through Maybelline's head right now wasn't good. "I don't smoke, and this place doesn't belong to me."

"No worries." Maybelline pointed across the room. "Alexis, you search over there. I'll check out these drawers."

Seconds later, a shriek sounded.

Ellen pivoted.

With a hand in the air, Maybelline waved an orange lighter. "I'm telling you, this is fate." She marched across the room and snatched Dax's crumpled shirt off the washer. "We're burning this shirt, too."

Grabbing the freshly opened bottle of wine, Alexis

waved it upward. "We'll need more vino for this debacle."

"Good call." Maybelline stepped outside. The door slammed shut behind her.

Alexis grabbed the knob and opened the door.

A brisk wind ripped through the opening. A few patches of snow lingered on the ground.

Goosebumps pebbled Ellen's flesh, but whether from the cold or dread, she wasn't certain. She grabbed Alexis' arm. "If you think this is gonna be a debacle, why did you agree?"

Shrugging, Alexis stepped outside. "Do you honestly think either of us can stop Maybelline?"

Good point.

Maybelline stood in the yard, waving the clothing. "What the heck are you two doing? Time to light this night on fire and raise some hell."

"I like raising hell."

Peering into the darkness, Ellen spotted Kitty crouched in the grass by the shrubs separating Dax's backyard from hers. "What are you doing?"

Kitty slowly stood before shuffling over. "The neighborhood watch."

The porch light lit up Kitty's tiny frame. Dressed in another ridiculous hospital gown—this one blue—a pair of fluffy slippers with her stockings rolled down to her ankles, and gray hair that looked like she'd stuck her finger into an electrical socket, she resembled something straight out of a horror flick. Ellen frowned. "Does Mom know you're out?"

"Nope, and I'm not gonna tell her." Climbing the steps, Kitty wagged a finger at Ellen. "And you aren't, either. Now exactly what kind of hell we're gonna raise?" She skimmed her gaze around the three women. "Not the Baptist kind, I hope? I don't want to tempt the fates, if you know what I mean."

Maybelline held up the pants and Dax's shirt. "Just the good, old-fashioned kind. We're making a statement."

Kitty scratched her chin. "What kind of statement?"

"The men-are-pigs kind." Standing in the center of the gravel driveway, Maybelline peered across the lawn, then toward the road. "This spot is perfect." She pointed to an area centered between the garage, the driveway, and the house. "Dax will get to watch his piggishness going up in smoke."

Kitty nudged Alexis in the side. "What is she talking about?"

Sipping the wine, Alexis pointed to the sweats in Maybelline's hand. "We're burning Dax's trophies."

Stepping closer, Kitty grabbed an edge of the sweats and pressed her nose into the fabric. "These pants belong to Dax?"

"Yup." Maybelline tossed them on the porch rail.

"I'm telling you..." Kitty shook her head. "You just never know about men. Here he is a firefighter, and he wears women's clothing. How disappointing."

Alexis snorted. "Well, you'll be happy to know, Dax doesn't wear women's clothing."

Kitty pulled her gaze from the sweats and arched a brow. "You say?"

"Yup." Alexis walked over to stand next to Kitty. Holding the glass, she pointed toward the pants. "They belong to one of his girlfriends."

"Well, now that's different." Rubbing together her

hands, Kitty looked around and frowned. "I think we have a problem, though."

Maybelline plopped hands to hips. "What kind of problem?"

Kitty fanned a hand toward the railing. "Two tiny pieces of fabric won't start a decent bonfire." She waggled her brow. "But I know what will help. I'll be right back."

Watching Kitty disappear into the night made a sinking feeling settle in the pit of Ellen's stomach. "I really think we need—"

"More ignition." Maybelline pivoted. "I'll be right back." She disappeared toward her car.

Headlights flashed across the yard before fading into darkness.

As Maybelline drove away, the rumble of the car faded.

Ellen turned. "Where is she going?"

"To get ignition." Pouring more wine into Ellen's glass, Alexis shrugged. "Whatever that means."

"Are we really allowing those two to start a fire?"

Sipping her wine, Alexis shrugged. "Don't see how we can stop them." She squeezed Ellen's hand. "You okay?"

She wasn't, but she refused to admit that fact to Alexis. Her friend had her own heartbreak to deal with. "I'm moving back to Albany." If those words surprised Alexis, she didn't show it.

Alexis flicked a glance toward Dax's house. "Running away?"

Was she? Ellen stared at the sweats. A soft breeze ruffled the fabric. She still couldn't believe he'd keep an outfit belonging to Angel. Weaving together her fingers, she shrugged. "Grant left the firm. Mr. Jorgensen offered me the job."

Alexis tapped a nail on the edge of the glass. "And you took it."

Snapping up her gaze, Ellen frowned. "You didn't expect me to stay, did you?"

Alexis stared up at the sky. A few stars twinkled against the darkness. "I didn't expect to stay, either." She fixed her gaze on Ellen. "But funny thing is, I found I like Aberdeen." A half-smile split her face. "Even with all the faults."

"Yeah, but you didn't sleep with your best friend, either."

Headlights flashed across the yard.

Shrugging, Alexis strolled toward Maybelline's car. "What did you get?"

Maybelline hopped out of the car. "Mr. Harley has some hay bales in his yard. I borrowed some."

"You're planning on burning them." Laughing, Alexis set her glass on the hood. "That's called stealing."

Scowling, Maybelline popped the trunk. "Don't be a party pooper. Mr. Harley won't even miss them."

Ellen walked to the trunk. Tucked inside was a mound of twigs and sticks, smelling decidedly like fall and farms.

Maybelline scooped up a handful of straw and pressed it against her chest. Little clouds of hay dust surrounded her. She let out a cough. "You guys gonna help?"

Fanning a hand, Alexis peered into the trunk. "Couldn't you bring the whole bale? You had to break it into pieces?"

"Heck no." Maybelline glanced over her shoulder. "You know how much one weighs?"

"I imagine they're heavy enough." Alexis reached inside the trunk and grabbed a mound of straw. "If Ted knew I wore an outfit costing him thousands while carrying hay, he'd have a stroke." She smiled. "Which makes hauling this bale all the more satisfying."

Stomping past Ellen, Maybelline glared. "Come on. We're doing this for you."

"Gee, thanks." Sighing, Ellen reached inside the trunk and grabbed a bundle of straw. The heavy smell of dried grass surrounded her. She walked over to the spot and dropped her pile.

A half-dozen more times, they made the trek until only a few crumpled pieces of straw remained in the trunk.

Dusting off her hands, Maybelline nudged the mound of hay with her foot. "I need a drink."

"I've got you covered." Kitty burst through the shrubs, looking more like an Appalachian Santa than an elderly aunt. A large, black trash bag dangled over one of her shoulders. A bottle rested under an arm. She clasped another in her free hand. A trail of clothing littered the lawn from Claire's to Ellen's.

Alexis rushed over and grabbed the bag. "Kitty, what did you get?"

Kitty picked up a few items of clothing. "Accelerant." She wiped a hand across her forehead. "Had to sneak into the house. Thankfully, Claire was already sleeping upstairs."

Maybelline strolled over. A few twigs were stuck in her hair and clinging to her coat. "What about Burt?"

Kitty waved a bottle. "Out like the dead."

Alexis dropped the bag next to the pants and shirts.

Grabbing the bottle out from Kitty's arm, Maybelline held it up in the light. "What have you got there?"

"Why, those are the two best men a girl can have." Kitty waved the bottle. "Jack and Jim. These guys are guaranteed to never disappoint." She unscrewed the top of the half-empty bottle of whiskey and took a big swallow.

Ellen, along with Maybelline and Alexis, just stared.

"What?" Kitty wiped the back of her hand against her mouth. "Haven't you ever seen someone drink straight from a bottle? You're supposed to drink Jack this way. He's not high class." She handed the bottle to Maybelline. "At least, that's what Frank always told me."

Maybelline grabbed the bottle and took a quick sip. Sputtering, she shoved the bottle toward Alexis.

Fanning a hand, Alexis dismissed the offer and turned to Kitty. "Don't you mean Burt?"

Kitty grabbed the bottle and took another big swallow before handing it back to Maybelline. "Nope. I'm talking about Frank Sinatra."

Maybelline stared. "Are you saying you met Frank Sinatra?"

"Met him? Sweetheart, Frank and I had what you could call a little secret dalliance." Kitty waggled her brows. " 'Course that was before Burt."

Ellen rolled her eyes. *Kitty and her crazy imagination.* "You can't expect us to believe you had an affair with Frank Sinatra."

"It's true." Kitty grabbed a few more items and

tossed them onto the pile. All were men's clothing. "I'd prove it, but then it wouldn't be a secret, now, would it?

Ellen pulled a familiar brown sweater from the pile. "Isn't this Burt's favorite?"

Snatching the cardigan, Kitty tossed the garment on the mound. "It most certainly is, which is why I'm burning it." She grabbed a pair of ugly green pants. "These are Burt's, too."

Maybelline took another drink of whiskey. With tears streaming down her cheeks, she pounded her chest and glanced at Kitty. "Why would you burn his favorite sweater?"

"Because forty years ago, Eunice Beck gave it as a Christmas present." Kitty opened the other bottle of whiskey and took a long drink. "She always did want what I had."

Seeing as Ellen couldn't imagine sweet Mrs. Beck liking grumpy, old Burt she dismissed the comment. Besides, she had bigger issues—namely Dax's empty driveway. If he wasn't home to see the fire, why bother? A flash of light drew her attention. She turned in time to see Maybelline press the flame against some clothing.

A low glow started.

Within minutes, the flames consumed the pile of clothing and dried grass.

Kitty waved the bottle in the air. "Woo-wee. I knew I'd have a great time with you gals. Better than those two poopers." She tilted her head across the yard toward Claire's house.

What had only moment before been a low flame, now suddenly stretched ever upward. Intense heat blew off the flames, and orange sparks shot upward, scattering across the night sky.

Every muscle in Ellen's body tensed. What if she burned down Lily's house? Just the thought made her heart palpitate and her palms break out in sweat. Running her gaze around the area, she searched for a hose. She spotted one coiled near the fire. Rushing over, she grabbed the metal handle. The sweat from her palm evaporated, replaced by stinging heat. Tossing aside the hose, she fanned her hands. "Okay, who put the hose next to the fire?"

"I did." Maybelline downed another shot. "Why?"

"Thanks a lot." Ellen thrust out her throbbing palm. "I've burnt my hand."

"No reason to get sarcastic." Maybelline fisted hands against her hips. "A simple thank you would have sufficed."

Ellen bit back the response. Instead, she looked at the growing flames. "If I burn down Lily's house, Ben is sure to kill me."

"Ben's the least of your worries." Maybelline shifted her gaze above Ellen's shoulder. "The pig just arrived." She patted Ellen's shoulder. "And he doesn't look happy."

A second later, two heavy hands landed on Ellen's shoulders, pinning her to the ground. Any worry over the fire disappeared. Slowly, she turned. The flash of fire lit Dax's eyes, matching the fury burning in his depths. The muscle flexed in his cheek.

Just great. Now, how the heck would she explain this mess?

Chapter 28

On the ride home, as the sun slid behind the line of trees, Dax made his decision. For better or for worse, Ellen deserved an explanation about why he'd avoided her this week. He didn't know the exact words he would say. He just knew he needed to see her and to make her understand why.

Turning onto his street, he spotted the lights on at his house. He had no idea whether his father would be home or not. Since his arrival, the promised father-son reunion hadn't come to fruition. Dax didn't know whether to be upset or relieved by his father's easy dismissal. For certain, he hadn't expected miracles, and considering his father had been out of the picture for twenty-four years without one phone call or letter, he didn't expect much in the way of fatherly devotion. On the other hand, a show of fatherliness would have gone a long way in healing Dax's hurt.

Was it unrealistic to expect a man nearing sixty to change? Dax raked fingers through his hair. *Probably.* He pushed thoughts of his father from his mind and focused on his last image of Ellen. Her face had been a mirror of her feelings. Stunned surprise, followed by disbelief, then anger, and finally that stubborn look he knew so well. He'd known the minute she'd made up her mind, too. When Angel placed her hands on his shoulders, Ellen's look had changed. Her eyes had narrowed, and her back had straightened.

Damn. Why the hell didn't she trust him, and why didn't she understand she meant far more than Angel ever had? He had hoped, with enough time, she'd figure out things. He knew what he asked wasn't fair. After all, six years had to pass before he realized his feelings. Hell, would he need to wait another six years before she reciprocated?

Spotting his father's clunker parked out front, he gritted his teeth. Figures, tonight his father stayed home. Pulling into the driveway, he glanced toward Ellen's house. His heart pounded. Ramming the truck into Park, he stared at the far-too-familiar yellow glow lighting up Ellen's yard. Snatching the keys from the ignition, he shoved open the door. Without a thought of grabbing his coat, he raced across the gravel.

His breath came out in harsh pants, and his palms were slick with moisture. Digging fingers into his pockets, he searched for his cell phone to call the fire into the station. Too late, he realized he'd left his phone inside his coat.

He kept his gaze fixed on the growing orange orb. *Dang.* Was it him, or were the flames teasing the eaves of the garage? Shoving aside the shrub, he bolted into her yard, then skidded to a stop. What had looked like a massive fire was nothing more than a bonfire. An illegal one, for sure, but minor, nonetheless. He skimmed his gaze to the cluster of women circling the inferno, drinking—*whiskey? What the hell.* Fisting his hands, he strode across the clearing.

A little form moved from behind the flames. He jerked back. Kitty, too? He pulled his mouth into a frown. When Ben finds out…Skimming his gaze across the yard, he shuddered. The wind picked up, scattering fiery twigs upward toward the roof of the house. A mound of fabric combined with broken sticks and dried leaves circled the fire. What the hell were these women thinking? Didn't they realize the clutter provided a perfect source of fuel for the flames?

Laughter rippled through the group.

Frowning, he marched across the lawn, running his gaze across the women. All faced him. All, except Ellen, but not one noticed him. They were too busy sharing the bottle and giggling. Stopping directly behind Ellen, he took a deep breath. He thought he'd need a dozen more to calm the fury burning deep within.

Glances shifted his way. The laughter slowly died.

Maybelline quickly shoved the bottle toward Ellen. "You don't have to worry about Ben killing you."

Ellen hadn't noticed him yet. At least, she had the decency to shove away the bottle. When he lit into her, he wanted her to be nice and sober.

Maybelline glanced up and scowled. "Because the pig just arrived." She patted Ellen's shoulder. "And he doesn't look happy."

Dax stilled the urge to roll his eyes. He was a paramedic, obligated to save lives, not take them—no matter how provoked he might feel. He dropped his gaze. Ellen froze for a split second before shifting slightly, as if ready to bolt. He'd be damned if he'd let her. Clutching her shoulders, he stilled the urge to squeeze some sense into her. "What the hell is going on?" His voice was gruffer than he intended. But damn, he couldn't stop the fear raging through him. When she turned, her eyes were wide, and her mouth was open. He glared, silently warning her to stay.

"Now we've got ourselves a party." Kitty shuffled over. "Grab that hose and spray me, Dax, so you can judge us."

Dax looked at Kitty. "Excuse me?"

"We're gonna have a wet T-shirt contest." Kitty pulled at her blue hospital gown. "Now you get us all good and wet. I want to make certain we're doing this right." She wagged a finger. "And don't be siding with Ellen just 'cause you're dating her. You must be fair. I can't help that my goods are pointing farther south than Ellen's. You'll need a creative mind and imagine them as they were, say forty—oh heck, who am I kidding? Fifty years ago."

Ellen's nostrils flared. "We're not having any kind of contest."

Scowling, Kitty waved a thumb at Ellen. "Who invited the party pooper?"

Ignoring Kitty's outrageous question, Dax turned his attention to the flames. His ire kicked up even further. "Are you trying to burn down the house?"

"You know what we need?" Kitty waved a bottle. "We need some of my best friend. He's been known to drop the tension a bit." She took a sip before handing the bottle to Dax.

Dax eyed Kitty. From the glassy look in her eyes and the wobble in her step, he figured she had enough hooch to last the night. Grabbing the bottle, he upended the contents.

"Hey!" Kitty stared at the circle of golden-yellow snow. Her cheeks puffed up, and her eyes bulged. She fisted her gnarled hand, and tilting back her head, she glared. "I meant have a drink, and not throw out the stuff."

"I think you've had enough, Kitty." Tossing the bottle onto the muddied ground, Dax scanned the area. "You're not supposed to have bonfires in the city."

Ellen waved her arms. "This?" She circled her hands near the flames. "Why, it's just a piddly little fire."

Dax ripped his gaze around the area and spotted clumps of straw. "You used hay?"

Kitty crossed both arms over her chest. "Yeah. You gotta problem."

"Yeah, I do." Dax looked upward, saw little flaming strands flying in the brisk wind. The tension in his neck increased. He jabbed a finger in the air. "You see those red ashes? They're called tinder and can ignite the house on fire."

As if to prove his point, one twig flared a bright orange as it floated across the black sky. Only by the grace of God, the shoot drifted downward, landing into a pile of slush. Reaching down, Dax grabbed the metal nozzle. Heat singed his palm. He ignored the pain. "Who had the brilliant idea to use straw?"

Maybelline jammed pudgy fists onto her hips. "For your information, me."

"Not your best." Dax arched a brow. "Where did you steal the stuff?"

"I didn't steal." Maybelline scowled. "I borrowed."

Okay, now he knew the truth—Maybelline was nuts. "How the hell did you plan to give it back once you burned it?"

"I don't know, Dax. You're smart. You figure it out." Maybelline lifted her chin. "Besides, we needed the hay. The clothing wouldn't burn."

Dax frowned. "Why the hell were you burning clothing?"

"We're making a statement." Kitty waved a pair of Burt's polyester pants in the air. "We hate men in general."

"You in specific," Maybelline added.

"Me?" Dax glared. Had they lost their mind? How could they possibly blame him for a fire out of control? "What the hell did I do?"

"I'll tell you what…" Maybelline marched across the lawn and grabbed the sweats off the porch rail. Storming back, she flung the pants at Dax.

He nipped them out of the air. "What the hell are these?"

Ellen crossed arms over her chest and tapped a foot on the ground. "Why don't you tell us?"

He looked at them and smiled. "Oh yeah, I remember." He winked at Ellen. "You looked damn fine in them."

Ellen stiffened.

Maybelline thrust a fist into Dax's arm. "Pig."

The hose slipped from his grip. Dax rubbed his arm. "What the hell? Why the anger?" Retrieving the hose, he glared at Maybelline. "Unless you couldn't tell, I gave her a compliment."

Maybelline thrust up her arms. "You men are so stupid." She pointed toward the pants. "What? Did you think she'd never figure it out?"

Dax tossed the sweats onto the black trash bag. "I have no idea what you're talking about."

"Oh, look at you." Ellen pressed her mouth into a thin line. "You have so many girlfriends you can't even keep track of your trophies."

Jerking back, Dax scowled. Exactly how much of the booze had Ellen drunk? He studied her for a moment. She didn't appear drunk—just furious. "What?"

Ellen fanned her hands toward the mound of clothing. "Are you telling me you don't recognize these sweats?"

Running a finger across his lips, Dax studied the pants. "Sorry, baby girl." He reached out.

Ellen slapped his hand. "Don't *baby girl* me." Dropping hands to her hips, she tilted back her head. "I bet you keep dozens hidden all over the place."

He tried to recall when he'd ever seen those sweats before, but other than the time Ellen wore them, nothing came to mind. "Honestly, I don't know who they belong to." He shrugged. "I suppose someone left them at my house. Who knows? They're not important."

Ellen scowled. "Maybe you like the ego stroke."

Jeez, did she think so little of him? "I thought they were yours."

Ellen narrowed her eyes. "Why would I keep my sweats in *your* dresser?"

Fisting her hands, Maybelline glared at Dax. "They belong to Angel, don't they?"

"Angel wouldn't be caught dead in sweats." Spraying water onto the fire, Dax laughed. The sizzle of fire sounded, and the reek of smoke filled the air. He didn't stop until the last orange ember faded to black. Tossing the hose onto the ground, he turned. "Party's over. Time for everyone to go home."

Chapter 29

Personally, Ellen was relieved. The fire had grown to exponential proportions in very little time. She glanced toward the building, then back at what had been the fire but now was little more than muddy ash. Heck, what would she have done if the fire had imploded? A shudder ripped through her. If Dax hadn't arrived, she didn't know what she'd have done. Just imagining Ben finding out was enough to send chills down her spine.

Alexis sighed. "Dax's is right." She clutched Kitty's arm. "Come on, Kitty, Maybelline. I will take you home."

Maybelline stomped a foot on the ground and frowned. "But the party was just getting started."

"Yeah. You're a real party pooper." Kitty glared at Dax. "Jeez, who knew firemen could be such drags."

"I've got my car," Maybelline complained.

"Sorry, darlin', but I think you're safer riding with me." Alexis turned back to Dax and winked. "I had only a glass or two of wine."

Ellen, seeing a chance for escape, pivoted and rushed toward the porch.

"Ellen."

Her name ripped from him like a whip. She ignored his command. He might want to talk, but she'd be darned if she spent another minute with him. Oh, she certainly had plenty of grievances. His insulting behavior topped her list. If he wanted to string along a dozen women, who was she to stop him? However, when they made the agreement to sleep together, she certainly didn't intend for him to start building his future date list. But since he had made his choice, what was left to discuss? *Nothing.*

Secondly, his lame excuse about the stupid sweats really irked. Now, if he wanted to keep articles of women's clothing for his personal satisfaction, she wouldn't stop him. But he could have at least informed her before she left the house wearing them. Why, the fact he hadn't told her bordered on lying, and she just couldn't tolerate such deception. Her parents raised her better. Heck, they *raised* him better.

And lastly, for him to just assume he could waltz over and boss her around. What the heck? They had an agreement, not a marriage. This place was *her house.* Sure, she never intended to have the blasted fire, but still, he had no right to ruin *her party.* If she wasn't so upset, she'd tell him her thoughts in great length.

She reached the last step. His hand caught her wrist, jerking her to a stop. She spun about. "What?"

He matched her glare. "Going somewhere?"

"As a matter of fact, I'm going inside." She tugged.

Smiling, he dragged her up the steps and across the porch. He shoved open the door and fanned a hand. "Happy to oblige you."

She narrowed her eyes. He certainly took her dismissal better than she expected. She lifted her chin and stepped inside the kitchen, then reached for the door.

Dax stopped the action by stepping inside.

She flung both arms in the air. "I thought you said the party was over."

Laughing, he shut the door and pulled her into his arms. "The party out there ended." He brushed his lips over the top of her head. "We're just getting started inside."

She didn't want to notice how great his body felt pressed against hers, but dang, she wasn't made of steel. Every nuance of his body was seamed against hers, stealing all her resolve. Pulling back, she crossed her arms over her chest. "Don't you have plans?"

He drew her against him. "Yup."

His words ripped through her. She dropped her hands. So, she was right in her assumption. He had made plans with Angel. Refusing to allow him to see her pain, she stepped back. "Well, I don't want to keep you."

He tightened his hold. "Aw, sugar." His fingers brushed a strand of hair off her shoulders.

A shiver tickled its way down her flesh. He pressed his lips against the side of her neck. A sigh rippled from her. "But I thought—"

He brushed his lips across hers, quickly.

The kiss was over before she realized what happened.

"You came to the mall today."

His words were like a bucket of ice dropping on her head. She stared upward. "You saw me?"

Smiling, he curled fingers around her waist, drawing her even closer. "Babe, I could spot you in a crowded concert hall."

Her heart fluttered. She wanted to believe him. Oh, how she wanted to think what he said was the truth, only she'd seen him with her own eyes. "You were with Angel."

"I know you saw that, too, but trust me, I have no interest in her." His thumbs made lazy circles across the lower flesh of her back. "I don't want to be with anyone but you." He captured her lips with a kiss.

She didn't want to respond—only she couldn't stop herself. His lips moved over hers, burning her with an intensity she'd never experienced before. She wrapped arms around his shoulders and sunk into his kiss. Through his shirt, she could feel the thump of his heart, matching hers beat to beat.

He pulled back. "And I intend to prove that fact to you."

She knew the right answer. Only, knowing she'd never, ever have another moment like this with him again caused a piercing ache, sharp and debilitating, to grip her. Nodding, she let him lead her up the stairs.

****

The next morning, Ellen paced the kitchen. Overhead, the soft tread of footsteps sounded. Dax was awake. Her stomach tightened. She stared down at her cell. Mr. Jorgensen had texted her, welcoming her back to the team. Heck, all her old co-workers, ones she hadn't heard from in weeks, suddenly flooded her messages with congratulations. She should feel thrilled. Hadn't she worked long and hard for this promotion?

Only, what had seemed so important just a few weeks ago, now felt hollow and vacant. She really made a mess of things now. She couldn't call Mr. Jorgensen and tell him she'd changed her mind. She made a commitment, and no matter what, she'd follow through, even if it killed her.

Propping elbows on the counter, she glanced out the window. A thin film of white covered the ground, and soft flurries of snow fell from the gray sky. Weak sunshine broke through gunmetal-colored clouds. She skimmed her gaze across her yard to Dax's. *Was his father still in town?*

Maybelline's words rolled through her thoughts. Why had he not mentioned him? More importantly, why had Angel gotten the honor of meeting his father, but not her? An ache pierced her heart. The answer was obvious. She wasn't important enough. She blinked back the tears. All these years, she'd fought hard to avoid the truth, and now, she could no longer deny the fact. She loved Dax. She loved him in ways she never thought possible.

Raking fingers through her hair, she stared outside. *What a mess.* No way could she tell him. He'd be gone like a flash, returning to his carefree life of dating any woman whenever he wanted. He would anyway, but she didn't want to put him in a position where he had to say the words just to keep his friendship with her family intact. She'd just have to bury the feeling. Besides, what did it matter? Effective Monday, she'd be back in Albany.

She threaded together her fingers. Today, she'd tell him about the promotion. He'd probably be relieved. She wouldn't blame him. No one expected to tame a wild animal. Dax was no different. He loved his freedom. He loved the right to come and go as he pleased.

Sighing, she glanced at the message from Mr. Jorgensen. Going back to Albany was for the best for everyone, but especially for Dax and his relationship with Ben and her mother. She knew her mother would be disappointed. Ben might be surprised. Either way, she and Dax would just have to present an amicable breakup and go on as if this chapter in their lives never happened. But, oh, how could she when her heart was so entangled with his?

The door to the kitchen swung open.

She dropped her phone on the counter and turned. Her breath caught. Dax strode into the kitchen wearing a bright smile. Water clung to the tips of his hair, and blond stubble graced his chin. He held one hand behind his back. The other swung with an easy confidence only he could exude. She stifled a sigh. She could get used to seeing him every day.

She stiffened. No, she couldn't get used to seeing him daily, because he didn't want a long-term relationship, and she had made her decision. All they had was an agreement. Forever hadn't been a part of the discussion. She wouldn't force them now. Besides, they had started this endeavor as friends, and they'd end it that way, too.

Still, the idea caused her heart to ache. She wasn't supposed to fall in love with her best friend, and yet, hadn't she been stupid enough to do just that very thing? Now, she was like the rest of the women in Aberdeen. Falling for the one man who held marriage lower than anything else. "Hi." Her word came out in a soft whisper.

He strolled over, and wrapping one arm around her waist, he drew her close. "Morning, sugar."

He gave her a nice, gentle kiss, leaving her wanting for more.

Leaning back, he pulled his hand away from his

back. "Where did you get this picture?"

Ellen dropped her gaze to the frame of them fishing all those years ago. Heat burned her cheeks. "Oh, um...Mom insisted I bring it."

He dropped his gaze to the image. "You remember that day?"

Tears pricked her eyes. After today, all she'd have are memories. "Yeah. You were mad I caught a bigger fish."

"Not true." He stared down at the image. "My anger was directed at other things."

Frowning, she stared at the picture. "At what?"

"Jakob Newsome."

She jerked up her gaze. Jeez, she'd forgotten all about him. Now, with Dax's words, she remembered why he'd taken her fishing—to help her forget Jakob's horrible breakup. Later, she found out Dax had beaten the daylights out of Jakob. "You broke his nose."

Dax pulled her closer. "I wanted to break his neck."

She laughed. "Would have had a hard time getting hired by the fire department."

Dax placed the picture on the counter. "Would have been worth it." He rubbed together his hands. "So, breakfast?"

The question bothering her all morning pricked again. She glanced out the window. "Dax, when were you going to introduce me to your father?"

Silence filled the room.

She turned.

Red covered his cheeks. He opened the cupboard and drew out a mug. "So, you knew?"

"I saw you with him in town the other day." She

took a deep breath. "Angel was with you. You introduced them."

A muscle flexed in his cheek. Lifting the pot, he poured coffee into the cup. "Yeah, so?"

The casual way he replied irritated her. She folded both arms across her chest. "How come you introduced Angel?"

Taking a sip of the black stuff, he lifted one shoulder. "Does it matter?"

"To me it does." Shoving away from the counter, she walked toward the table. She fingered the ruffled edge of a placemat. Her heart thundered. "If you're not interested in Angel, why go through the trouble of having her meet your father?"

He placed the cup on the counter. Turning, he leaned back, pressing palms onto the surface, then tapped one finger against the edge. "It's called being polite."

Yes, introducing Angel was the proper thing to do. But, what about herself? Where did she rank on this scale? "So, you're polite enough to introduce her, but not me?" She jammed a finger against her chest. "Makes me wonder what my status is on your list of important people."

He crossed his arms over his chest. "You can't be serious?" His mouth pulled down, and his brows furrowed. "Are you actually jealous of Angel, even though I told you she means nothing to me?"

"I'm not jealous!" Why did he refuse to understand? If she was so important, why wouldn't he take two minutes to have his father meet her? "I just wonder why you'd introduce someone who you don't like to your father?"

He gave a half-laugh. "This discussion is ridiculous."

Ellen stiffened. Oh, so now her feelings didn't matter. She lifted her chin. "So, I'm just overreacting?"

He strode across the room and wrapped his arms around her. Pulling her close, he brushed his lips across the top of her head.

She could feel the thump of his heart against her cheek and the warmth of his fingers on her back.

Rubbing his chin across the top of her head, he sighed. "Angel is different."

Jerking back, Ellen broke free from his grip and glared. "Hey, I know how you love different."

He caught her elbow and stared. "What the hell does that mean?"

His eyes blazed with blue fire, holding hers captive. Her head pounded, and her stomach knotted. "It means you don't have to worry about this any longer." She fanned a hand between them. "I'm moving back to Albany."

He tightened his grip on her arm. "Running away, are you?"

She broke free from his grip. How dare he accuse her of doing the very same thing he'd done! "Me? Running away?" She snorted. "You should talk."

A deadly silence surrounded him. His blue gaze darkened. Slowly, he curled his fingers into a fist. "Meaning?"

She wouldn't back away from his anger. He had a right to know the pain he'd caused then and the pain he caused now. "Six years ago, you ran—that's what I mean."

The muscles worked in his throat. A coldness

settled in his gaze. "What the hell did you expect to happen? I was twenty-four and slept with my best friend's sister." He took a step closer. "Did you think I'd get down on my knees and profess love and propose marriage?"

Oh, how easy he dismissed his cold attitude. Even now, he didn't realize how much his abrupt departure hurt. Hell, from all appearances he hadn't cared then, and he sure as hell didn't care now. "I never expected a proposal, but I did expect you to remain my friend."

He cocked his head to the side and raised his brows. "Correct me if I'm wrong, but weren't you the one who refused to come home?" He crossed both arms over his chest. "You avoided me at all costs. Looks like I'm not the only one at fault."

"Does it ease your conscience to blame me?" She lifted her chin. "Fine. But know this, I'm not a silly twenty-two-year-old looking for marriage. My boss offered me the promotion I've worked hard for, and I've accepted it. So now, you can go back to your perfectly empty life, dating all the women you want, and growing old and alone all by yourself."

The air stilled.

His shoulders straightened, and his nostrils flared. "Is that what you think of me?"

His words came out gruff and forceful. She straightened her shoulders and met his glare. "Neither of us agreed to forever, but if you think I'll stay around and be your little plaything, then you're sadly mistaken."

He fisted his hands. "Because I'm Aberdeen's guaranteed heartbreaker? Isn't that what you really mean?" The muscles worked in his throat. Striding across the room, he ripped open the door. Pivoting, he ran his gaze over her. He twisted his mouth into a snarl. "Well, darlin', I'd hate to crush your opinion of me."

The door slammed shut.

Ellen stared at the door but only saw the sadness and hurt that had filled in his gaze. A weightiness settled in her chest, and a pain pierced her heart. She hadn't meant to hurt him, and oh, how could she ever face him again?

Chapter 30

Dax flung shut the door and strode across the deck. The thick snow covering the surface muffled the pound of his footsteps. He worked his shoulders, rolling them back and forth while rocking his head. Ellen, the one woman he loved more than life itself, just flat-out suggested he was no better than the rumors. Hearing the words come from her was the same as ripping his heart from his chest.

Digging keys from his pocket, he shoved through the shrubs. His father's car was parked in front of the house. Inside the kitchen window, he could see movement. He wasn't in the mood to talk to anyone, least of all his father.

Opening his truck, he climbed inside and jammed the key into the ignition. He pressed the back of his head against the seat and closed his eyes. His throat hurt. He swallowed, then blew out a soft breath.

Hometown Heartbreaker—from the moment he'd heard the name years ago, he hated the moniker. He hated the fact people assumed he went into a relationship intending to hurt someone. In his search for the right woman, he never planned on breaking hearts. Yet the one woman he wanted to keep forever just did the very thing he inadvertently done over the years. He glanced back toward his house.

His father's face lurked through the window.

She wondered why he hadn't introduced her to Thomas. How could he explain his fear she'd make the comparison of his father's behavior against his own? She wouldn't understand that despite how hard he'd tried to run from his past, he knew the truth. He was no better or worse than the man standing inside his kitchen right now—no doubt preparing for another one-night stand with some easy woman.

Dax's stomach clenched. He backed out of his driveway and drove for hours, traversing roads so familiar he could trace them by memory. Huge drifts lined the edges of the road, and patches of white spotted the black surface. Plows passed, sending curls of snow along the banks of the highway. Finally, he stopped at one place that always eased his soul.

Pulling into the narrow spot, he parked the vehicle. He slipped the key from the ignition and shoved open the door. Reaching behind the seat, he grabbed his coat. Shrugging on the garment, he tucked his hands into pockets. His fingers grazed his cell. He pulled out the phone and glanced at the screen—messages waited for reading—Angel had texted him a dozen times, and his father twice. Not one text from Ellen.

He returned the phone to his pocket without replying to any. Knee-deep snow covered the trail. He didn't care. Striding through the thick copse of leafless trees, he gazed around the area. Through a break, he spotted the tiny white cottage the Jordans had called home for years. Years ago, after Robert died, the family stop visiting the place. Instead, they chose to rent the cabin to visitors.

He weaved through the path until he reached the front door. From the cement stoop, he had a clear view of the crystallized lake. To the right ran a wooden pier leading into the water. Memories of years gone by—of him, Ben, and Ellen leaping off the edge and splashing into the cold waters flashed through his thoughts. A softness filled him. Tucking his hands into his pocket, he scanned the area. How many times had the Jordanses' house been his home-away-from-home? Too many to count. And now...

Dismissing the memories, he bent and dusted the snow off the rough doormat. Grasping the edge, he lifted the mat and extracted the small metal ring. The fob laid cold and heavy in his palm. Blowing out a breath, he slipped the key into the lock, and pushing open the door, he stepped inside.

Clouds of white breath mingled with swirls of dust dancing in the air. Dim sunlight shown through three large windows framed by white, scalloped-edged curtains. A moss-colored sofa rested against a wall covered in shiny, knotty pine. To his right was the kitchen filled with colors of summer—warm yellows and soft greens.

He walked across a woven, wool throw-rug the size of the room and stopped in front of the fieldstone fireplace. He looked at the pictures decorating the surface. Grabbing one frame, he stared at the image. Nestled beneath the glass were three perfectly pressed oak leaves. Gifts from some autumn past—no doubt, from Ellen. Replacing the frame, he walked down the narrow hallway and peeked inside each room, remembering the times he ran through this house like it was his own. When he finished, he stepped outside, and replacing the key beneath the mat, he trudged toward the dock.

In the winter, snow made its own sounds—not the soft pitter-patter of rain hitting the damp earth, nor the brisk gust of wind grinding through trees, but instead, an ethereal stillness of cold and solitude.

Flakes of snow melted against his cheeks and clung to his lashes. His feet balked at the chill, and his fingers numbed at the cold, but he continued until he reached the pier's edge. He skimmed the horizon.

Snow-cloaked spires shot upward piercing the gray-laden sky. Frozen crystals coated the water's black surface. In a few weeks, plenty of skaters would crisscross the ice. Now, though, danger lurked for the unwary who dared to chance nature's deception.

He inhaled. The sweet scent of pine hung heavy in the bitter air. He stared at the ice, but in his mind's eyes, years long gone floated through his thoughts. A warmth stole through him. He hadn't thought about that day in a decade or more—not until he spotted the picture resting on Ellen's nightstand. Now, though, he couldn't remove the image. A tension he hadn't expected burst through him. Seeing her teary eyes at the heartless breakup of teenage love had filled him with fury then.

Digging his hands deeper into his pockets, he stared across the lake. He knew what women expected. He'd never encouraged their hopes. Marriage belonged in other men's worlds, not his. His father's blood ran thick through him. He wouldn't be responsible for ruining a marriage over infidelity and betrayal.

Pulling the keys from his pocket, he tossed them in the air before snatching them just as quickly. Nothing about his childhood home life resembled Ellen's, and he'd better remember that fact. He strode back to his truck and drove home.

Dusk had descended by the time he pulled into his driveway. He glanced toward Ellen's. A light shown through her kitchen window. A gnawing burned through him. He yanked the keys from the ignition. Didn't she understand he only wanted to protect her from pain? He didn't possess the world she wanted. God and fate had other plans.

Dax rammed open the door and climbed from the vehicle.

The Fischer twins, dressed in matching pink snowsuits, built a snowman with their father, Mark.

Dax's stomach tumbled. Debbie's words came back to haunt him. He forced aside the longing. Marriage, children, and stability didn't belong in his world. He waved.

They were too busy laughing to notice.

Dax trudged up the steps, and opening the door, he stepped into his kitchen. A voice blasted from the living room. Dax chucked his keys on the table. They clattered against the hardwood surface. Opening the fridge, he snagged a beer. Cracking the seal, he walked into the living room. A football game played on the television.

Thomas came down the stairs.

Sipping his beer, Dax studied the man whose life mirrored his own. For a man who complained he had no money, he sure dressed like his wallet overflowed. Swallowing, he pointed the bottle in his father's direction. "What's up?"

Thomas smoothed a hand over his hair. "Thought I'd go out tonight."

"Oh yeah?" Dax strode into the room. Plopping

onto the couch, he skimmed his gaze over the table. Empty bottles and discarded fast-food wrappers littered the surface. He tightened his grip. "Jeez, Tom, can you at least keep my place clean?"

Dropping his gaze, Thomas straightened his cuff. "Since when did you call me Tom?"

Taking a long swallow of his beer, Dax studied the man who fathered him but had never been a dad. "Since the day you left."

Fire flashed from the blue depths of Thomas's eyes. He snatched a bag off the table and grabbed a crumpled napkin. "Didn't know you were so particular."

"Plenty you don't know about me." Dax took a swig of his beer and stared at the television.

Thomas let out a sigh. "You're right."

The sound of the commentator filled the room.

He watched Thomas stuff the paper into the bag. Grabbing a coaster, he placed the bottle on the surface. "Where are you going?"

"Martinis." Thomas straightened, still clutching the bag. "You wanna go? You know, like a father and son night out?"

Snorting, Dax turned. Did Thomas think he was a six-year-old, eager for a scrap of attention? Too little, too late. The urge to say no rested on the tip of his tongue. Ellen's words flashed through his thoughts. She made her choice. Nothing more he could do. Besides, if he was honest, weren't things better this way? Placing his beer on a coaster, he stood. "Why not? Time to move on, right?"

Dax followed his father into Martinis. The same dim lights and stale smell greeted him like a warm blanket—familiar and comforting.

A low whistle sounded.

Shifting, Dax gazed at his father.

Nudging Dax in the side, Thomas winked. "Plenty of women on the prowl. Looks like it will be a good night." He tilted his head slightly. "Let's grab a spot at the bar."

Dax wove through the crush. Flirtatious eyes, encouraging smiles, and tempting bodies slid past his gaze. For the first time in months, he had the freedom to choose—only the exhilaration of predator stalking prey eluded him.

Ignoring the seat, Thomas rested elbows against the bar and leaned back. He fixed his gaze on the dance floor, watching the women bump and grind to the music.

Scowling, Dax turned away, and grabbing a stool, he plopped down on the seat and waved two fingers to Randy, the weekend bartender.

With a slight tilt of his head, Randy deposited the cash into the register. He slammed shut the drawer, then walked over. "Surprised to see you, Dax."

"Night off." Reaching across the bar, Dax grabbed a cardboard coaster. "Two beers."

Randy arched a brow and looked around. "No Ellen?"

Dax's chest constricted. Scraping a thumb across the edge of the coaster, he shifted his gaze around the room. Never had he felt so out of pocket, which was a first for him, considering Martinis had been his go-to place for years. "Nope."

Retrieving two beers from the cooler, Randy popped the tops, depositing the bottles in front of Dax.

"You two still a couple?"

Dax grabbed his bottle and took a swig.

Thomas glanced over his shoulder and arched a brow.

A stabbing pain jabbed Dax's chest. Ignoring the questioning look in his father's gaze, he clutched the bottle and clenched his teeth. "Ellen and I are just friends."

"Really?" Pressing his palms flat on the wooden surface, Randy straightened. "You two have been best friends forever. Thought maybe—"

"Nope." The piercing pain intensified. Did a heart attack feel this way? He dismissed the notion. He was perfectly fit and healthy. So, no heart attack—just irritation. "Just friends."

"Heard she's in town for a while."

Shooting up his gaze, Dax jerked. Was Randy interested in Ellen? What the hell?

Randy stepped back and furrowed his brow. "You don't mind, do you?"

Did he? The idea of another man touching her fired a rage inside he hadn't expected. Why? He didn't get jealous. Hell, most of the time he didn't care if he ever saw the woman again. Ellen, though, wasn't just any woman. She deserved the best. His head throbbed, and his throat tightened. Lifting his beer, he took a long swallow. "You'll have to go to Albany."

"But I thought—"

Dax rolled the edge of the bottle along the counter. "Don't know what to tell you." He shrugged. "She's leaving." The words tasted bitter and hot against his tongue.

"Bummer." Randy walked away.

Turning, Thomas grabbed his drink. "You okay?"

Dax shifted his gaze across the room. Sprinkled around the area stood clusters of people, laughing and chatting, each trying to attract the eye of the opposite sex. A few couples clung to one another, holding hands and kissing. He occupied a spot somewhere in the middle—not quite desiring the attention of a woman but not interested in being alone, either. He turned back to his father. "Yup. Fine."

Thomas shifted his gaze from Randy to Dax. "This Ellen." Grabbing his beer, he took a drink, then swiped a gnarled hand against his mouth. "Anyone I know?"

Stiffening for just a moment, Dax swallowed his beer. "Ellen Jordan."

Thomas's face twisted. He stared at the mirror behind the bar. "That mousy thing?"

Dax set his beer on the counter and frowned. "You remember her?"

Slowly, Thomas turned. "Of course." He waved his bottle. "She was a little younger than you, wasn't she?"

"Darci's age."

"Right. Your mother would always come home gushing over how perfect their life appeared." Taking a swig of his beer, he glanced around the room and grunted. "She expected our life to be just like theirs."

Clenching his teeth, Dax flexed his fingers and drew in a slow, steady breath. "And that would have been horrible, right?"

Thomas shot Dax a sideways glance and lifted his beer. "You can do better than her."

The urge to slam a fist into his father's face consumed Dax. He clutched the bottle so tight his knuckles hurt. "You see, Dad, that's where you're wrong."

"Aw, now, son. Don't be angry." Clapping a hand on Dax's shoulder, Thomas held his gaze. "I only want my boy to have the best."

Dax knocked away his father's grip. He wouldn't be sucked in with false platitudes by a man who lacked concern over his children's welfare for the better part of two decades.

"Besides, plenty of hot chicks dig single men like us." Tilting back his drink, Thomas skimmed his gaze across the room. "Think I'm gonna make my way over to that little beauty over there. You mind?"

Peering across the room, Dax spied the group of young women. They all looked to be about college age. Far too young for his father. Hell, they were far *too* young for him. He turned back. "Aren't you a little too old?"

"Nah. Trust me, they like older men." Setting down his beer, Thomas winked. "Like the whole daddy thing. You know—stability and someone to take care of them."

Dax scowled. "Which, of course, is you?"

Shoving away from the counter, Thomas drew out a slow, lazy smile. "For tonight."

Dax forced the beer down his throat. Had his dad always been like this—chasing after women too young to have any common sense? Silent glares and quiet accusations filled his early childhood. A mother too humiliated to question. A father to self-serving to care. He'd denied the truth for years. By fourth grade, he couldn't ignore the facts any longer. He was the son of a cheat and a liar. Lifting his drink, he watched his father seek out the gazes of any women within feet of him.

Finally, he stopped in front of a brunette.

The young woman stood with her back to Dax.

Pressing the rim of the bottle against his lip, Dax studied her. Something seemed familiar.

She turned. Deep brow eyes widened slightly, and a slow smile slid across ruby-red lips.

Dax stiffened. His father was hitting on Ava, Ben's secretary? Taking a large gulp, he fixed his gaze on the scene. Did she know Thomas was his father?

Shifting, Ava glanced his way. One brow shot upward for just a moment before she turned and smiled at Thomas. Tilting her head to one side, she ran a finger down the front of her silky blouse.

Dropping his gaze briefly, a smile slid across Thomas' lips.

Dax's stomach knotted at the slimy look on his father's face, then watched as Ava leaned in slightly and sipped her drink. He knew that move. Hell, he had seen women play it out dozens of times for him. Ava wanted Thomas. Setting down the beer, he turned away and stared at the game airing on the television.

"I'm surprised to see you here."

Pivoting, Dax scowled. Angel stood behind him. Tonight, she wore a body-hugging, black shirt and leopard print leggings. A black wool blazer completed the outfit. She leaned in, so close he could feel the warmth of her breath caress his cheek. A moment of temptation spiked through him. His stomach clenched. Whatever place he and Ellen occupied right now, being with Angel wouldn't help matters. Besides, the idea of being with her repulsed him. "Why?"

She ran her gaze around the room. "You rushed

from the signing yesterday like you couldn't wait to get back to your girlfriend. Figured you two would be busy playing house."

Dax fisted a hand. Like hell he'd tell her anything. "I'm not twelve."

Tracing one soft-pink polished nail down his arm, she leaned in. A playful smile split her lips. "Does makes me wonder why you're alone, though."

Her warm, moist breath stroked his cheek, and the heavy scent of her perfume surrounded him. He clutched the bottle. How had he ever thought the smoky, overpowering smell of patchouli attractive? Scraping an edge of his nail across the foil label, he watched the game. "Don't see why it's any of your business."

"Oh now. Don't be grumpy."

He turned and glared. What had he ever seen in her? She was pure spite and vindictiveness.

Perfect white teeth flashed between ruby-red lips. "Miss Boring not doing anything for you?"

Her words ripped through him. "Darlin', I'd take her any day over you." Clutching his bottle, Dax focused his attention on the television. But the game on the screen held no appeal. All he could see was Ellen telling him she intended to leave. He fisted his hand. "Hell, I'd take *any* woman over you."

She leaned in. "I seem to recall you *taking* me a lot."

The brush of skin against his forearm caused the hair on the back of his neck to prickle, and the knot in his stomach tightened. He pulled back. "We all make mistakes." He swiveled and saw the fury in her gaze. He didn't care. "What? Did you think we'd pick up where we left off?"

Jerking back, she widened her eyes and crossed arms over her chest.

He set his empty bottle on the counter. "Like I've told you before, darlin', what we had was physical." Digging a twenty from his wallet, he tossed money next to the beer and ran his gaze over her. "And even then, you were more work than you were worth." He knew his words were cruel and hateful, and yet, nothing else seemed to make her understand—he didn't want her, and more than likely never had.

Draping his arm over Ava's shoulder, Thomas strutted over. "What's going on, son?"

Ava's eyes widened. "This your father, Dax?"

Dropping his gaze to the young woman, Dax snorted. "Yeah, something like that."

She ran a hand up Thomas's arm. "Wow, now I see where your son got his looks."

Ripping away his gaze, he turned to Thomas. "I'm heading out."

Ava leaned into Thomas' side.

Thomas looked down and winked. "Don't worry about me. I'll find a way home."

Dax flicked his gaze once more to Ava. Had he ever, *ever,* gone after a woman so young? Could he even imagine seeing anyone else? *No.* And, in fact, the idea of being with any other woman beside Ellen repulsed him. Suddenly, a burdensome weight lifted from his shoulders.

Thomas had made his choices but, just because he had, did not mean Dax had to follow the same path. He never chose to be the hometown heartthrob or heartbreaker, and he sure as hell didn't intend to remain that person, either.

Stepping outside, Dax smiled. He knew Ellen loved him. Oh, she might not have said the words, but he knew she did, which left him with only one option. He couldn't wait for her to make up her mind. He'd have to force her to see the truth.

Chapter 31

As soon as Dax left, Ellen regretted her words. Why had she allowed the discussion to get out of hand? Why had she let her jealousy get the better of her? Of course, she had no one to blame but herself. Heck, she couldn't even blame him if he did fall into Angel's arms. She closed her eyes. The thought was just too awful to contemplate.

She spent the rest of the morning cleaning her house. When she finished, she trudged upstairs and started packing. After pulling the two hard-sided bags from the closet, she tossed them on the bed and flipped open the tops. She opened the closet and stared. Just a few weeks ago, she and Dax had gone back to Albany to gather the clothing, expecting her to stay for weeks. Now, she realized the effort had been wasted.

She pulled out each item and dropped them on the bed. Carefully, she folded them, then placed them in the bag. The last item she picked up was a black, wrap dress. A sob caught in her throat. Dax had insisted she bring this dress, intending for her to wear it to his work's holiday party. Now, he'd go with someone else.

She tucked the slip of fabric on top the stack, before returning to the closet to gather her shoes. So many heels and she had only worn two. She fingered the leopard-print stilettos. He never got to see her in them.

When the last item was placed inside the luggage, Ellen straightened and glanced at the picture of her and Dax on the bedside table. She brushed a tear from the corner of her eyes. Grabbing the frame, she ran a finger across Dax's image. No matter what the future would bring, Dax being an integral part of her life was gone, and she would have to learn to deal with the loss. Separating a few items of clothing, she tucked the frame in between. Their relationship was over, their friendship in tatters, but she'd be darned if she'd let go of their past.

After closing the lid, she snapped shut the latches. She tugged the luggage off the bed, then rolled the bag down the stairs. She peered around the living room, remembering the night they ordered in pizza and watched movies. Dax had wanted some shoot-'em up movie. Ellen pleaded for a silly romance. They settled on an artsy movie neither liked. They had spent the whole time laughing and making jokes which had been more fun than the movie itself.

After pushing the bags into the kitchen, Ellen walked to the coat rack. She peered out the window. Huge mounds of snow covered the ground, in all the places except a large area filled with blackened mud—remnants of last night's debacle. If she hadn't gone along with Maybelline's bonfire idea, would she and Dax still be together, or was the ending decided the minute she spotted him with Angel at the mall?

She shrugged off the question and slipped her gaze toward his house. Dax's truck had returned. Her breath caught. Should she go over and apologize? Would that change things? Would he tell her he loved her?

No. She wasn't that silly, and Dax wasn't that

involved. Shoving her arms through the sleeves, she walked to the counter and grabbed her keys. Flipping open her purse, she glanced out the window in time to catch his back door opening. She stilled. Would he come over? Her heart pounded. She stared, watching as he stepped out the door. His father followed. Both climbed into Dax's truck. A second later, the truck backed out.

She didn't realize she gripped the keys until the sharp edges bit her palm. Turning away, she tossed the keys into her purse, and grabbing the handles of the luggage, she stepped from the house. She had only one job left. Taking a deep breath, she glanced at her mother's house. Betty might understand her departure, but Claire wouldn't. A tiny part of her wanted to run away and avoid her mother's hurt. She wouldn't, though. Mom deserved the truth—well, most of the truth.

After she placed the luggage in the trunk, she climbed into the driver's seat. Walking would be quicker, but she figured a quick getaway was her best option. She drove the short distance to her mother's. Just her luck, her mother was home. Why couldn't Sunday night be her mother's weekly poker game and not Friday?

Parking the car along the sidewalk, Ellen slipped the key from the ignition and inhaled. Her stomach quavered. Gripping the keys, she shoved open the door. A sharp wind ripped through the narrow space between the house and the hedge. The gust tugged at her hair. She tucked a stand behind her ears and climbed out.

Fisting her hands, she stared at the house. Her mother would be fine. She was positive of that fact. In fact, she'd probably be ecstatic once she realized how this promotion would benefit Ellen's life. Plus having two successful children was quite an accomplishment. Ellen made a point of filing away the information. When Claire pointed out all the flaws with the promotion, she would need every valid argument. Smoothing a hand down the front of her coat, she crossed the sidewalk and up the front porch steps.

Loud voices crackled through the air.

Peering into the window, she spied Burt sitting in the recliner, watching some black-and-white sitcom. Through the glass, she could hear perfectly the voices emanating from the television. Kitty was nowhere in sight. If she was lucky, Kitty was in bed for the night. Oh, who did she kid? She'd probably have to see her aunt, too. She stepped inside the living room.

Burt didn't pull his gaze from the television.

She shut the door as quietly as possible and tiptoed through the living room. Only when she reached the door to the kitchen did she pause. From behind closed doors, she heard her mother and Kitty bickering and smiled. While she hadn't looked forward to Kitty's arrival, she sure would miss her when she left. The thought surprised Ellen. Taking a deep breath, she pushed open the door.

Claire, standing in front of the stove, pivoted. "Ellen? I didn't expect to see you tonight."

Kitty bounded off the chair. "Woo-wee. Are we gonna have another party like last night?" She shuffled toward the coat rack next to the back door.

"No, Kitty." Smiling, she stepped farther into the room and licked her lips. "I came to say good-bye."

"Good-bye?" Kitty dropped her hand. "Where are

you going?"

"Yes, Ellen." Claire crossed arms over her chest. "Where?"

Ellen gazed at her mother. The worry in Claire's gaze belied her angry demeanor, which made stating her plans all the worse. Weaving fingers together, she stared at the ground. "Albany."

"Why are you going there?" Kitty shuffled over. Her little, apple-doll face stared upward. "Kind of far to go for a bonfire, don't you think?"

"Oh, for goodness' sake." Claire marched across the room and pressed a hip against the table. "There will be no more bonfires. Do you understand, Kitty?"

Kitty scowled. "Well, now there won't be." She fanned a hand. "Ellen's leaving."

Shaking her head, Claire pulled out a chair and dropped into the seat. She pointed to the opposite chair. "Sit."

Digging the key from her coat pocket, she tossed them on the table and sat. The sensation of being a naughty child filled her. She curled fingers into a fist and dropped her gaze.

Claire rested a hand atop Ellen's. "Explain why you're leaving when you said you'd stay until the holidays?"

She stared at her mother's hand, noticing the wedding ring on her finger. Her father had been gone for ten long years, and yet, Claire wore the set as if they were still married. One day, Ellen hoped she'd find someone to love as completely as her parents. At one point, she thought she'd found it with Dax. Of course, now, she knew the hope was foolish—as foolish as it had been six years ago. She pulled up her gaze. "Mr.

Jorgensen called the other day and offered me the promotion." Taking a deep breath, she exhaled, then forced a smile. "And I accepted."

"But—" Claire furrowed her brow. "I thought he gave the job to Grant."

Ellen lifted one shoulder. "Grant didn't work out."

"So, now you're taking a job from a man who could so easily dismiss your talents for someone else? Why?"

Ellen heard the censure in her mother's voice. How many times had she wondered the same thing? Not that she'd admit that fact to her mother. She shrugged. "I thought you'd be proud of me?"

The fire in Claire's gaze dimmed. She tilted her head to the side. "Why would you ever think I wasn't?"

Ellen could list a dozen reasons. She didn't, though. Instead, she tapped a finger on the table. "Mom, I can't imagine why you'd want me to be a barista. I have a college degree."

"Oh, I'm certain you're excellent in your career." Claire shrugged. "But can you say you were happy?"

Ellen thought back over the years. Had she been happy? At the time she figured she was. Now, though, all she remembered were the long hours, working nonstop to build the company into a powerhouse. And what had she gotten for all the efforts? Second place to a man who didn't have the qualifications or the commitment needed. "I was good."

Claire arched a brow. "But happy?"

She wasn't about to let her mother win the case. "Yes."

Claire's shoulders dropped. "What about Betty? She really wanted you to be her manager." She rested her elbows on the table. "And I thought you liked working at the café."

"Oh, I did." All the conversations she had with Betty over the last few weeks floated through her thoughts, followed by the many customers and friends she'd gotten reacquainted with. Yes, she had enjoyed her time at home, and if Mr. Jorgensen hadn't called, if she and Dax hadn't broken up, maybe she would have stayed. "We had fun, but I can't stay."

"What about Dax?"

Ellen snapped up her gaze. "What about him?"

"Did you tell him? Was he okay with your decision?"

Hardly. But she didn't bother to tell her mother about their breakup. "Mom, I know you hoped for something to happen between Dax and me, but neither of us went into the relationship with any intent other than renewing our friendship."

"You two had sex." Claire shook her head. "If you wanted to renew your friendship, you should have stuck with coffee."

"Nah…" Kitty fanned a hand. "Sex with Dax would be way better than coffee."

Claire shot Kitty a hard glare before turning back to Ellen. "Frankly, I think you're avoiding the truth. More is between you two than either will admit."

Ellen swallowed past the lump in her throat. Any feelings they shared were completely one-sided. "No, Mom. You're wrong."

Pursing her lips, Claire studied Ellen. "Do you remember our discussion at Ben's election party all those weeks ago?"

Ellen nodded.

"I told you before, Dax runs scared. He lives in the shadow of his father's past." She reached out and caught Ellen's hand. "Don't judge him too harshly. He needs time to see his dad for what he is."

Ellen jerked back. Was she the only person in town who hadn't known? What the heck? Why had no one clued her in? And where exactly was the gossip when one needed it? "So, you knew he was here, too?"

"Of course." Claire wrinkled her nose. "He hasn't changed a bit, but of course, Dax wouldn't know that. Right now, he needs time to see his father for who he is and realize he's nothing like him."

"If he figures out things, he knows where to find me." She stood. "Anyway, I'm heading home. I just wanted to leave you the key." Ellen shoved the key toward her mother, then hurried to the door, before Claire could spot the wetness in her eyes.

"I think you're making a mistake."

Claire didn't understand. She hadn't seen the look in Dax's eyes. Ellen had, though, and she'd seen the truth. He didn't want to get married—not to her, at least. After all, she wanted her mother to think she and Dax ended amicably. Turning, she spied her mother clutching the back of the chair. She closed her eyes and took a deep breath, then pressed a kiss against Mother's cheek before giving one to Kitty, as well. "I'll come back for—" Christmas almost slipped out, but she stopped herself. She couldn't add another lie. Instead, she squeezed her mother's shoulder. "I'll see you soon."

As she walked outside, she refused to glance toward Dax's house. That chapter in her life was closed. Time to begin a new one.

Chapter 32

On Sunday, Dax woke with conflicting feelings roaring through him. The memory of his fight with Ellen kept replaying through his mind. He accused her of running away. She accused him of doing the same. He might have been disheartened if two thoughts hadn't occurred.

The first was the fact she had been right. He had run away first. When he said he wouldn't have married her when she was twenty-two and he twenty-four, he hadn't lied. His reasons had been selfless, or so he thought. After all, she had the right to earn her degree and to make something of her life. He had no right to infringe on her passion.

But she was wrong when she thought he wanted his freedom. Oh, he used the cloak of dating multiple women to hide his attraction, all right. He had a valid reason, though. He didn't want to ruin his friendship with Ben. Unfortunately, the whole thing ended up backfiring, because no matter how hard he tried to rid Ellen from his thoughts, the more fixed she remained. Over time, he didn't know when his avoidance ended and his love began.

Hell, he couldn't even blame her for the accusation of calling him Aberdeen's Hometown Heartthrob. Since she had returned, she had been forced to deal with women flirting with him. While he hadn't encouraged their pursuit, he certainly hadn't discouraged them. At the time, he excused his behavior because more sales of calendars ultimately helped the hospital. But she wouldn't know that. She probably figured he wanted to keep one foot in the relationship and one foot out. He couldn't fault her. In a way, he had, just in case. Now, though, he knew the truth. He wanted Ellen with an aching need he'd never experienced before.

For too many years, he had lived in the shadows of his father's behavior, but not anymore. Last night had been a revelation. Just because his father chose to live a life of casual dating didn't mean he had to. Dax wanted more. He wanted what the Jordans had. More importantly, he wanted it with Ellen. Now, he just had to convince her.

He wouldn't have to force her, either, because he'd known the minute hurt entered her eyes, she loved him. Maybe as much as he loved her, although, he didn't see how that was possible.

Why had it taken him so long to realize what she meant? When they had sex six years ago, he'd known then that he loved her, only he let his fear over his relationship with Ben cloud his judgment.

As he sipped his coffee, he realized he wasn't completely truthful. Six years ago, he'd seized an opportunity to sleep with her. But if he was truly honest, he knew he loved her the minute she cried on his shoulder when Jakob broke her heart. He'd loved her for more than a decade. He guessed he could thank his father for the revelation. Without witnessing Thomas's disgusting display, Dax would have never made the connection. Now, though, he could say he was free from the bonds he'd allowed to restrain him.

Jules Hahn

Pounding feet overhead drew his attention.

He turned and saw the shadow of his father creeping down the stairs. More footsteps sounded. Dax frowned.

Thomas stepped into the kitchen.

A slippery smile sliced his face. Stubble lined his chin, and red rimmed his eyes. His silver-gray hair stood on end, and his face had a mottled look, as if he'd spent the night with too much drink.

Thomas strolled to the table and squeezed Dax's shoulder. "Missed a fun night."

Dax picked up his cup. "Please tell me you left Ava alone."

Thomas glanced toward the stairs. "Ava?" He scratched his chin. "Is that her name?"

The sharp rasp of stubble against calloused hands cut through the air. Dax gritted his teeth. Maybelline had called him a pig. He wondered what she'd think if she heard Thomas' comment. "She's a nice woman. She deserves better than you."

Shrugging, Thomas walked over to the cupboards and grabbed a mug off the shelf. "And I'm sure, someday, she'll find a nice young man to settle down with."

How could his father act so blasé? Hell, Dax had his share of one-night stands, but he sure as certain knew the woman's name when he slept with her.

After he finished pouring his coffee, Thomas turned. "How come you left last night?"

Dax shoved back and stood. "Didn't want to stay."

Thomas eyed Dax. "You missed a helluva night." He sipped his coffee. "Plenty of willing women in the bar. All asked about you."

354

"Wasn't interested in any of them." Dax strolled to the sink and dumped out the remaining coffee.

"It's that Ellen, isn't it?"

Dax turned at the derision in Thomas's voice. "What of it?"

Thomas scowled. "Hell, son. You've got the golden ticket. Why settle down with one when you could have any women you wanted?"

Grabbing his coat, Dax shoved his arms through the sleeves. "But I don't want any woman." He pulled open the door and, turning, he frowned. "Ava is Ben's secretary. I expect you to treat her kindly."

"If you think I'll break her heart, you have no worry. She understands the way the game is played."

Dax gritted his teeth. He was tired of his father's casual attitude. He had enough of him living in his house, doing nothing but reminiscing with friends and picking up women. "When I return, I want you gone, and don't come back."

Thomas arched his brow. "Are you kicking me out?"

"You can view it any way you want." Dax shut the door. He started down the steps just as Ben's vehicle pulled into the driveway. He skimmed his gaze toward the street and spotted a cute little car parked in front.

Ben shoved open the door. His dark gaze pinned Dax's, and his knuckles fisted white. "Ava?" Three long strides and he was inches from Dax's face. "Really?"

Stepping back, Dax crossed both arms over his chest. "Won't fight you, friend."

Ben's eyes narrowed, and a tic settled in his cheek. "How soon after you dumped Ellen did you take Ava to bed? Didn't even wait twenty-four hours?"

He didn't blame Ben for the anger ripping from him. Hell, his past behavior caught up. "I'll forgive that insult, because you don't know the facts."

Ben's face turned a deep red, and the vein in his neck throbbed. "I warned you not to use Ellen."

"And I didn't." Dax slid his gaze to Ellen's house, then back. "Your sister is the one who ended things. She's the one who took the job in Albany."

"So, you decided to go out and sleep with the first woman you came across?" Clenching and unclenching his fingers, Ben pulled his mouth into a thin line. "My secretary—of all people."

Dax didn't know what bothered him more—the fact Ben thought he'd sleep with Ava, or the fact his father had. "Ben, you need to know, I would never hurt your sister."

Ben snorted. "You've got a funny way of showing it by sleeping with another woman."

"I didn't have sex with Ava." The muscles in Dax's neck tensed. He eased out a breath and met Ben's hot gaze. "My father did."

All the anger emanating from Ben evaporated like heat in a summer rain shower. He unclenched his fist and stared toward Dax's house. "Your father?"

Dax nodded. "Yup." He started across the gravel. "If it makes you feel any better, I've kicked him out. I don't want, or need, him in my life."

"*What?* Why would you do that?*"

The words burst from Ben like a bullet from a gun. Stopping, Dax turned. "You know, it took me a long time to figure out things."

Ben arched a brow.

Dax sighed. "For years, I figured I was just like my father."

"You were never like your father."

Dax snorted. "Yeah? How do you figure?"

Ben shrugged and stepped closer. "Because I've watched you." He crossed his arms over his chest and swept his gaze over Dax. "In high school, I saw the way you watched Ellen, like you fought something you couldn't understand. Years later, I found out you went to Albany and spent the night with her."

Ben's words roared through Dax. He couldn't help being surprised. "You knew?"

"Not at first." Ben shrugged. "But a week later, I went to O'Connors. Jimmy mentioned you and Ellen had been there together the week before and how close you two seemed. At the time, I didn't think anything of it, but when Ellen started coming home less and less, and you refused to discuss her—" He shrugged. "I put two and two together. You were best friends in ways you and I could never be. I just didn't figure it would take either of you this long to figure out things."

Swiveling, Dax stared at Ellen's house. His heart pounded, and his stomach knotted. A hand settled on his shoulder. He turned. "Oh? And what were we supposed to figure out?"

Smiling, Ben squeezed Dax's shoulder. "That you love each other." He sighed. "If I ever thought you were like your father, I would never have agreed for you to date Ellen." He tightened his grip on Dax's shoulder. "You're not your father. You've never been your father, and you never will be."

The tightness eased in Dax's chest. Blowing out a breath, he met Ben's gaze. "Ellen plans on leaving. You should know, I'm not letting her."

Ben dropped his hand. Turning, he stared a moment toward the house Ellen had called home before turning back. "She's already left."

Dax's heart plunged. Ben's words staggered him. She left without giving him a chance to apologize. *Like hell.* He turned to Ben. "Then I'll go get her."

Laughing, Ben slapped a hand on Dax's back. "I don't think you'll have to go far."

"Oh?" Dax scratched his chin. The urge to drive to Albany burned through him. "Why?"

Ben rolled his eyes. "Mom's making plans." He shrugged. "I think you should let her."

Dax gritted his teeth. "Dammit, Ben. I don't want to wait. I want to tell Ellen now."

"It's only for a few days, and besides—" Ben sighed. "Might be better this way."

Scrubbing fingers through his hair, Dax scowled. "How so?"

"You'll give Ellen an opportunity to see what she's missing." Ben dug out his keys. "My sister is stubborn. She'll need time to come to the truth."

Dax couldn't argue with that assessment. Ellen *was* stubborn. He frowned. "I'll give her until Thanksgiving." He fisted his hands. "But, if she's not back by then, I swear to God, Ben, I'll—"

Ben arched a brow. "You'll what?"

All the arrogance fled from Dax. He shook his head and smiled. "I'll do the same as you. I'll convince her she loves me."

"Are you planning on marrying her?"

Dax's heart pounded. He licked his lips. "If she'll have me."

Ben winked. "She will, but she'll make your life a living hell. Trust me, I know my sister."

Laughing, Dax rubbed together his hands. For years, he had perfected the art of getting what he wanted. Back then, he thought the skill was just to gather as many women as he could. Now, he realized he'd need to use all the talents he'd acquired to win back the only woman he desired. "I can hardly wait."

Chapter 33

By Wednesday of her first week as a vice president, Ellen felt a heavy weight of depression sitting on her shoulders. She would never admit she made a mistake, but oh, how she hated her job. She disliked everything about it—from the endless meetings to the constant complaints from staff. What happened to fun? What happened to creativity?

Sighing, she tapped fingers on a stack of paper littering her desk and scowled. No fun or creativity here. Just endless proposals, contracts, and other important, yet mundane, tasks. Swiveling, she propped an elbow on her desk and stared out the window.

Angry, gray clouds obscured the midday sky, threatening another snowstorm.

Turning back, she stared at the clock on the computer and sighed. Five hours in. Another five, at least, to go. If she was back in Aberdeen, she would only have a little time left in her shift. She glanced at her calendar. Blue squares indicating meetings, hour after hour, filled the rest of her day. If she was fortunate, she'd be done by six. Considering how poorly her luck ran lately, she didn't hold out much hope.

She rested her head against the leather headrest, and closing her eyes, she ran through all the perks of her job. After a few minutes, she gave up. Oh, who did she kid? The job was flat-out boring. She had expected invigorating conversations with a team of people, discussing various angles to propel a company upward. Instead, her only stimulation was whether she wanted cream or sugar in her coffee, and frankly, three days in, neither appealed.

Snapping open her eyes, she stared around the area. The bland room with its beige walls, beige carpets, and beige furniture strangled any thoughts of creativity or excitement. Instead, the tiny space made her sleepy and bored.

Two months ago, she envisioned herself doing all sorts of wonderfully creative things. No one had mentioned the fact creativity wasn't required as a vice president. Tact, organization, and delegation were the order of the day, every day, hour upon hour, and man, how she hated all three of those duties.

Turning, she ran her gaze along the shelving on the opposite side of the room. A few knick knacks left by Janice, the former V.P. filled the space—a bronze elephant, apparently a symbol of luck, success, and wisdom. She just wished some of those emotions filled her. Clearly, Janice had a penchant for animals because she'd also collected a few bird statutes—currently mired in a thick layer of dust—and a wooden turtle the size of shoe box painted in a hideous mixture of colors from fuchsia to lime green. She smiled. Maybelline would love the darn things.

On one shelf sat a framed picture with a quote stating *Creativity is everything. Uniformity is nothing.* Three days later, she didn't know what the heck the saying meant. Another shelf had four books stacked one atop the other. All were on the art of managing—a welcome-to-the-new-job gift from Mr. Jorgensen. Ellen had promptly placed them on one shelf and forgot all about them.

Then, there was *the picture.* Without thinking, she smoothed a hand down the front of her perfectly pressed black suit, then pulled at the waistband. She missed the comfort of jeans. She missed her sneakers, too. The balls of her feet were swollen and achy, and her toes felt pinched and constricted. She chewed on the edge of her nail. Maybe she should keep a pair of slippers in the office. Would Mr. Jorgensen care? She sighed. *Probably.*

Strolling across the room, she picked up the frame and studied the picture. She and Dax had looked so happy and carefree. A tightness settled in her chest. She missed being home with her family and friends. More importantly, she missed Dax.

Did he miss her?

She supposed he didn't. Since she left on Saturday, he hadn't called. Knowing him, he probably found another woman to fill the spot she'd vacated. Tears threatened to fall. Brushing at the moisture, she stared at his hand, clasped on her shoulder as if he never wanted to let her go. Oh, how she missed his touch.

What about his father? Was he still in town? Had they reconnected and helped Dax figure out his past? She hoped he realized Dax was an incredible person. If she could wish anything for Dax, she wanted him to find peace and happiness. All these, he'd projected an image of a carefree, easygoing man, without a worry in the world. Now, she knew, his personality was just a foil hiding his hurt.

A knock sounded on her door.

Quickly, she replaced the frame on the shelf and turned.

Mr. Jorgensen stood in the doorway with a frown on his mouth and a cloudy look in his eyes.

Whatever had she done wrong this time? She forced a smile. "Mr. Jorgensen?"

Striding into the office, he ran a hand over thick, salt-and-pepper hair. As he walked to the chair, he scanned the area. He stopped behind one of the orange-colored, woven chairs. Leaning in, he rested elbows along the back and clasped together his fingers. He swept his gaze over her desk before turning. "Looks like you've brought your organization skills to your new position."

Shooting a quick glance at her desk, she could feel her cheeks flushing. Paper littered the surface. Janice never had a messy desk. Everything had been placed in appropriate colored folders and filed in orderly drawers.

Since her return, not one thing had been organized, and no matter how hard she tried to effect structure, within two hours of starting, her desk resembled a mess. "I know." She walked over, and grabbing a stack of manila folders, she tapped them in a neat pile. "I just seem to work better this way."

Mr. Jorgensen raised a brow. "I find that hard to believe."

Ellen dropped her gaze, only to realize she clutched the folders so tightly creases formed along the edge. She carefully placed them on her desk. Settling into her chair, she rested forearms on the stack and folded together her fingers. "Did you need to discuss a project?"

Sighing, Mr. Jorgensen walked around the chair

and dropped into the seat. He smoothed a hand over charcoal gray slacks. "I just wondered if you were still pleased with your job."

Ellen gave him a tight smile. "Never been happier."

****

After a week of work, Ellen came home tired and stressed. In just a week would be Thanksgiving. All her family and friends in Aberdeen would be enjoying the holiday, and she'd be stuck here catching up on work. Her heart twisted.

She slung her purse on the little table next to the door and dropped her overflowing briefcase on the floor. After she plopped down on the couch, she kicked off her high heels. Resting her head against the cushion, she closed her eyes and wiggled her aching, cramped toes. A soft sigh rumbled. Somehow, she'd made it through the week. A week of hell, she amended.

Why had she always glamorized the job of vice president? She wasn't suited to the position. She hated making decisions, especially when those decisions involved millions of dollars and a successful campaign. Oh sure, when she was just the creative person, she hadn't really given any thought to success or failure. Probably because she knew her ideas were topnotch. Now, though, she had to rely on other people's ideas and that fact didn't sit well, at all. Any wrong decision on her part would cost the customer and reflect poorly on Mr. Jorgensen.

How did Ben handle such pressure? He'd run the police department successfully and would probably be even better as a mayor. Why hadn't she gotten even just an ounce of his ability?

Dismissing her worry, she grabbed the television remote, and turning on the T.V., she floated through channels. Nothing on but romance, and the last thing she wanted was to see a happily ever after. Lord knows, happy endings were elusive and rare. Hadn't she learned the hard way with Dax?

Had he missed her this week? Probably not. He wasn't the kind of guy to wallow in a lost girlfriend when he had so many others just waiting to fill her spot. She thought back to the day they broke up. He'd looked genuinely hurt by the title he'd assumed all those years ago. *Why?* The man certainly earned the moniker. He'd worked darned hard to bed any and every woman who crossed his path, including his best friend's sister.

Her cell buzzed.

A zip of excitement surged through her. Jumping up, she raced to the door and grabbed her purse. Her hands shook, causing her to fumble in search for the phone. Finally, she gave up and upended the bag. Everything from pens to rumpled receipts scattered across the carpet. Shoving aside the mess, she grabbed the phone and skimmed the caller id. She dropped her shoulders and sighed. *Not Dax, but Betty.* For a moment, she considered not answering. After all, she didn't want to hear about Dax and his love life. However, a part of her couldn't do that to Betty, either. She pressed the button. "Hey."

"How's it going?"

Betty's voice sounded bright and cheerful. Ellen gripped the phone. "Okay."

"You like your job?"

Ellen stared at the overflowing briefcase with more work than she cared to consider. "I'm still learning."

Betty chuckled. "Yup. Being a big-time vice president takes some adjustment."

"Yeah. Probably." Ellen clutched the cell and dropped onto the couch. She tucked her feet beneath her and stared at the television. Some commercial played—poorly done and not the least bit enticing. "I just—"

"Just what?"

Ellen shrugged, despite knowing Betty couldn't see her. She licked her lip and sighed. "I don't know. How does Ben do his job? I mean, his is far more important than mine. He has all these decisions to make and think about how they affect everyone in town and still go ahead with his decision."

Betty sighed. "I guess you could say Ben's got a clear vision. He knows what he wants and knows how to get it." She paused. "I'm sure you are just the same."

Ellen ran a finger along the hem of her navy skirt. "Maybe, but…" She dug nails into the fabric. "I just thought this promotion would be more exciting."

"It's not?"

Surprise laced Betty's voice. Ellen gave a short laugh. "All I do is work on contracts and settle disputes with the staff. It's boring."

"Being in upper management isn't all it's cracked up to be." Betty chuckled. "Trust me. I've had a bunch of years running that rat race. Totally not worth it. At least, not for me."

Ellen shifted. She'd forgotten Betty once ran a large restaurant chain in Albany. "So, you hated your job?"

"Hardly." Betty coughed. "I just found the higher you go, the more you have to pick your battles. No matter what decision you make, someone will be

366

upset."

Oh, how true her words were. In the past week, Ellen had done her share of irritating people. She chewed her lip and stared at a green pot with a brown plant wilted inside. "I just wish I could be more like Ben."

"Heavens, why would you want that?"

"I don't know." Ellen ran fingers through her hair. "He's just so in control."

"Doesn't mean he's perfect. He makes mistakes just like the rest of us." Betty paused. "Besides, you have a lot of fine qualities."

Ellen snorted. "Yeah? You might want to tell Mom them."

"Now, honey, don't you realize your mother is proud of you? I will say this, though. She misses you."

"Yeah?" Ellen sat straighter. "You think?"

"Honey, I know." Betty sighed. "Aren't you dying to ask the question burning through you?"

Stiffening, Ellen clutched the phone. "What question?"

"I see you're still in denial." A low chuckle sounded. "But, in case you're wondering, Dax kicked out his father, and I say good riddance, too."

Betty's words stunned Ellen. She furrowed her brow. "Why would he do that?"

"Now, don't you go feeling sorry for Thomas. He never made any effort to be with Dax. Not when Dax was a little kid, not after he left, and definitely not when he returned. I will say, I think his coming back was a good thing."

Ellen scraped a nail across her thigh. "Oh?"

"Yup, made Dax realize he wasn't anything like his

father. 'Bout time, too."

The sound of Betty taking a drink filtered through the line. A clank sounded.

Betty let out a gusty breath. "He misses you."

Ellen snorted. "Really? I haven't heard from him in a week."

"Maybe because he thinks you don't want him."

Ellen stilled. Her heart pounded. "I doubt that."

"Do you?" Betty laughed. "Honey, I don't think I've ever seen two people more compatible, or two people work so hard not to be together"

Betty had it all wrong. She only saw what she wanted. No doubt, Claire had put up Betty to digging for answers. "He made his choice."

"I think you had a hand in helping him, and that's all I'll say in the matter." Betty coughed. "Actually, that's not true. I've got one more thing to say. Did you ever think he wanted the best for you? Maybe he let you go because he wanted you to be happy?" Another sip sounded. "I want you to know, I haven't filled the manager position yet, and I won't until you figure out things."

After she hung up, Ellen stared sightlessly at the television. Betty's words ran through her thoughts. A piercing ache settled in her heart. She didn't want to lose Dax, but how could she stop him from moving on?

Chapter 34

Ellen spent the whole weekend working. She hated every minute. Instead of feeling refreshed and energized on Monday morning, she felt more drained than ever. During every waking moment, while she read through proposals, requests, and ideas, she thought about the past weekends with Dax. Whenever he hadn't been at calendar signings, he'd spent them with her.

The years unfolded in her mind—from their youth with endless summer days hiking along the lake, to their high school years teasing each other, to now with them sharing dinner and so much more. She hated to admit it, but she missed having him around and spending all her free time with him.

As she scooped up the piles of manila folders, she sighed, a heaviness settling on her shoulders. A low pain radiated from her spine, over her shoulders, and up her neck. She gritted her teeth and shoved the folders into the briefcase. She thought about Betty's words and immediately dismissed them. Dax might miss her, but not enough to call her. A little voice niggled her thoughts. Had he not called because he thought she wanted to be a vice president? Sighing, she zipped shut her bag.

Nothing she could do about her decision now. She made her choice, and dang it, she would follow through. At least that was her resolve, but after fighting through traffic, she had some serious doubts. Like the strip of endless brake lights stretching as far as the eye could see along the black pavement, Ellen pictured her future. Decades of following the same road, without fail, going to a job she tolerated at best. She quickly chastised herself. Just like Betty suggested, she was new. She'd have to get used to the job before she made any decision. That idea eased her tension a bit.

A few minutes later, she pulled alongside the sidewalk and parked her car. She stared up at the four-story, red brick building. To most pedestrians passing by, the building looked like a stately historic home. Inside was a finely tuned hub of advertising and marketing. Her chest tightened. She ignored the feeling. She was new in her position, knowing with time she'd learn to enjoy her role. Yes, time was what she needed. *And desire.* The little word wormed its way into her thoughts.

Her cell phone buzzed. She dismissed the worry and grabbed her purse. She knew without a doubt who called—her mother. Since returning to Albany, her mother called every day. Ellen knew Claire worried about her happiness, but she also knew her mother had another motivation. Oh, she never came right out and said Dax's name, but she sure hinted enough, asking if Ellen had spoken to anyone in Aberdeen. Today would be no exception.

Ellen picked up the call. "Morning, Mom." She drew out the cup of coffee from the cupholder. "And no, I haven't heard from anyone in Aberdeen. Except Betty on Friday, and yes, I'm happy in my job." She took a sip. She didn't feel guilty over the fib because she really didn't want her mother to worry.

Claire sighed. "You sure? You don't sound happy."

Ellen stared out the window at the traffic passing by and categorized her day in her thoughts. Meetings upon meetings followed by a hasty lunch. Was it bizarre she looked forward to a lunch of wilted lettuce covered in disgusting goop? "I am." She forced out the words, hoping her voice sounded more cheerful than she felt. "It's—" She licked her lips. "Different."

"Different?" Claire paused. "How so?"

"I don't know, Mom." Ellen clutched her cup. "Just different."

Claire sighed. "Betty is hoping you'll come back. She's holding the position for you."

"I know." She stared at her nails. The beige nail polish remained, perfect and chip-free—an unusual change. As a barista, she couldn't keep her nails neat. Now, they were perfect. Frowning, she shifted her gaze to the window. "How's Burt and Kitty?"

A heavy sigh rumbled across the lines. "Burt's fine. Grumpy as usual. Kitty, though."

Ellen heard the sharp click-clack of fingers on a table.

"She keeps asking when you will be home for another campfire. Honestly, Ellen, she's like a five-year-old."

Ellen held back a chuckle, certain her mother wouldn't appreciate her amusement. "Kitty is unique."

"Easy for you to say. You're an hour away. I'm the one listening to those ridiculous stories," Claire snapped. "Get this, she insists she had an affair with Frank Sinatra. Have you ever heard anything so crazy?"

"Yeah, I know. She mentioned something along those lines."

"What did you tell her?"

"I'm guessing the same as you—that she's nuts." Smiling, Ellen peered at her watch. Jeez, she was late. "Listen, Mom, I've got to go."

"Oh, okay." Claire sighed. "I just wanted you to know that…"

Ellen shot another quick glance at her watch, then upward toward the fourth floor. Would Mr. Jorgensen know? She hated to rush her mother, but she really needed to get to work. "Yes, Mom?"

"Oh, all right." Claire let out a soft cough. "I just want you to know I miss you, and I'm proud of you."

Ellen tightened her grip on the phone and blinked back a tear. Of course, she knew her mother was proud. Hadn't she taken the job for that very reason? "Thanks, Mom. I miss you, too."

"Now, will you please reconsider coming home for the holiday?"

Ellen didn't want to disappoint her mother again, but in no way could she come home and chance seeing Dax. "I don't know…I've got a lot of stuff to do here, and…" She couldn't finish the lie. Instead, she ran fingers through her hair and sighed. "I'll think about it."

Disconnecting the call, she shoved open the door and stepped onto the slick pavement. Dodging puddles and mounds of dingy slush, she hurried around the back of her car and ripped open the passenger door. She yanked out her briefcase, and hopping the curb, she raced up the steps and inside the agency.

Mindy, the receptionist, looked up from her computer and smiled. "Morning, Ellen."

Ellen darted past her. "Morning." She hurried up the wide, sprawling stairs. Her heels sank into the thick, beige carpet lining the steps. Pivoting on the second landing, she continued up to the third floor where her office was located.

Mr. Jorgensen met her on the landing. "A little late today, I see?" He glanced at his watch. "It's eight."

Ellen had no idea what he meant by that remark, considering she'd come in early all last week and worked through her weekend, she figured she could arrive a few minutes past the suggested starting time. "Sorry." She tightened her grip on her briefcase. "I worked late last night on one of the proposals."

Mr. Jorgensen arched a brow. "Preston's project, I hope?"

Main Construction, the bane of her existence. She'd gotten three proposals from three different team members. Preston Main hated all of them. Mr. Jorgensen had stopped in at the end of the day Friday and insisted she have a proposal by Monday. She had one, but she wasn't certain he'd approve. The one thing she'd learned this past week with Preston Main was that he was a stickler for his ideas. She'd heard from one of the secretaries that his son was easier. Unfortunately, *he* wasn't the CEO, yet. "Yes. Of course." She hurried down the hallway toward her office. "All weekend."

Mr. Jorgensen fell into step beside her. "With your talent? All weekend? You don't expect me to believe such nonsense, do you?"

She heard the derision in his voice and turned. "Preston Main wants the impossible."

Lifting his chin, he narrowed his eyes and crossed his arms over his chest. "That's your job. You make sure to give the customer what they want."

Stopping by her office door, she turned. "His idea

isn't feasible. If we do what he wants, we'll look like amateurs and lose business."

Mr. Jorgensen narrowed his eyes. "And your job is to make certain that doesn't happen."

Of course, her job. She wondered how Grant made it through a month. Turning, she stepped inside her office and came to a stop. Skimming her gaze around the room, she noted the neat desk with perfectly, stacked papers, a leather holder filled with pens, and the whiteboard devoid of her carefully designed ideas. She walked over to a chair and placed her briefcase on the seat before moving to the credenza. She skimmed her gaze over the files. Every one was placed in alphabetical order.

"Looks good, doesn't it?"

Turning, Ellen stared. "You cleaned my office?"

Laughing, Mr. Jorgensen dropped into a chair. "Of course not. I had Ceci take care of the mess." He fanned a hand. "I figured you wouldn't have an excuse for not getting your work done. Now, let's discuss your accounts."

Ellen stiffened. She'd spent endless hours last week plus the whole weekend working. She clutched her purse so tight her knuckles turned white. "Mr. Jorgensen—"

He put up a hand. "Dave. You're a vice president now. I think we can dispense with the formalities."

Ellen took a deep breath. "Mr. Jorgensen, exactly what do you think I did all weekend?"

He shrugged. "You just told me. You worked on the Prestons' account." He ran two fingers along the crease of his jet-black trousers. "I hope you spent some time doing other things."

"I did go out to dinner on Saturday."

He snapped up his gaze. "I meant work. You have several, heavy hitting meetings this week. Those accounts will expect results." He frowned. "As a member of upper management, your dedication must focus solely on work." He fanned a hand. "You don't have a minute to waste searching for things."

Ellen jerked back. "And that's why you cleaned my desk?"

"Isn't it obvious?" He pressed palms against his legs. "You got little done last week because you weren't organized. Now, you shouldn't have a problem."

So, for the next dozen or so years of her life, he expected complete and absolute commitment. Three years ago, she would have easily welcomed the demands. Heck, a month ago, she was eager for the chance.

But then, she lost the position and had to refocus on a job she didn't think she wanted, only to discover all the things she missed. She got to visit with friends, talk with Betty, work eight hours, and leave. If wanting those things were wrong, then so be it. The only thing she knew now was that she refused to give up a life for a career she didn't love.

Flinging her purse onto the desk, she reached over and grabbed a pen neatly tucked inside the square leather pen holder. Clicking the pen tab, she snatched the legal pad on top of a metal tray. She stared at the yellow paper with the thin blue lines across the surface. Could she do this? *Should* she do this? She glanced over at Mr. Jorgensen. The frown was back, along with a look of impatience. Like heck she'd spend her life chained to her desk. That thought was enough to propel her hand. She scribbled out the words before she could change her mind.

Ripping off the sheet, she handed the paper to Mr. Jorgensen. "You know what, Dave? You ask too much."

He skimmed his gaze over the sheet before looking up. His brows furrowed and his lips pinched downward "You're kidding, right?"

Curling hands into fists, she pressed her knuckles into the wooden surface. She smoothed a tongue over her lower lip and exhaled. "Nope. Thanks for the opportunity, but I'm not the person you want."

Shoving away from the desk, she grabbed her purse and strolled across the room. As she brushed past Mr. Jorgensen, she felt the crisp fabric of his suitcoat against the hairs on her arms and smelled the overly spicy scent of his cologne. She stiffened and held her breath, fearful he'd say something that would persuade her to stay—only, he remained silent, which was all the more telling. Reaching the row of shelves, she shoved aside the books he'd given her and collected the one item she valued most—the picture of Dax and herself from that summer so long ago. Clutching the frame in one hand and her purse in the other, she held her head high and strode from the office without another word.

She hurried down the steps, and ripping open the front door, she dashed out into the bitter morning air. Beeping open her car, she slid inside. She placed the picture on the passenger seat, then started the engine. She reached for the gears, only to pause for a moment. She wiggled her toes in the tight, pointy-toed heels. A sting burned straight up her calf. Reaching down, she slipped off her shoes and dumped them down on the seat. Smiling, she let out a loud lusty sigh before shifting the car's gears.

Now, she was ready to leave.

****

Passing by the *Welcome to Aberdeen* sign, Ellen eased her foot off the gas and gripped the steering wheel. The exhilarating feeling of leaving a job she detested had faded with each mile she took. Now, skimming her gaze down the long road, she wondered if she'd acted too hasty. Maybe time in the position would make things better.

As soon as the thought arrived, her stomach tightened, and her head pounded. No, time wouldn't make things better. She didn't need another week, another month, or another year in the position to know she wasn't cut out to be an advertising executive in a high-powered company.

John Witherspoon High School slid past her window. Up ahead, the traffic light turned red. She eased out a breath. Again, she would come home to disappoint her mother. Nothing she could do about that fact. By now, Mr. Jorgensen had probably told everyone in the local area about her departure. Any job prospect in Albany evaporated the minute she quit.

But did she even want to resume that path? All those years working endless hours, focusing solely on her career, didn't appeal any longer, and if her decision disappointed her mother, then so be it. She wanted more.

She wanted a life.

With Dax.

She drove past Betty's. The earlier worry filling

her thoughts lifted. She could go right back to her job. After a fashion, she had excelled in her role and had enjoyed her position. Surprisingly, she wanted to be a barista. No, check that—she wanted to be a manager. Maybe not over creative types, but with young people who wanted to learn. She figured she had valuable information to impart. Careers were important, yes, but so was happiness. And if her job didn't fill her up and create the dreams she envisioned, then her career was pointless. Surely, her mother would understand.

Turning at Woodland, she couldn't help smiling. For ten years, she avoided this town and coming home, fearing she'd be compared to Ben and found lacking. Now, she didn't have that concern any longer. Ben excelled at his job. He loved it and deserved the position. She didn't have to compete with him. He was her brother after all. He'd only want the best for her.

And Dax…

She turned onto Timber and slid her gaze toward his house. Could she remain in a town where he lived, knowing he'd be dating others? Her chest tightened, and her heart hurt.

She thought back to their last argument. Their words had been hot and angry. Maybe, he wouldn't want her any longer. Maybe, he wouldn't understand. But dang, if she'd let their friendship go. If all they could share was friendship, then so be it. She'd accept his offer and move on.

She pulled into her mother's driveway, parking her car behind Claire's. Shoving open the door, she took a deep breath. As she strode up the steps, she stiffened, her heart pounding. She pulled open the door and stepped inside.

Claire and Kitty sat at the kitchen table. Both looked up.

"Woo-wee." Kitty jumped up from the chair. "Looks like we're gonna have a campfire, after all." She shuffled across the room and hugged Ellen. "I told your mother you'd be back."

A paper-soft kiss landed on Ellen's cheek. She smiled. "Yup. I'm back."

Frowning, Claire walked over and studied Ellen. "What happened?"

Ellen licked her lips. "I wasn't happy."

Sighing, Claire wrapped her arms around Ellen. "Oh, thank goodness." She squeezed. "I'm so glad you're home. Please tell me you're staying."

Ellen pulled back, and her stomach tumbled. "You're not disappointed?"

Claire ran a hand down Ellen's cheek. "Oh, honey, you could never disappoint me."

Ellen closed her eyes. She was glad to be home.

Chapter 35

Ellen strolled through the holiday festival that first night home. Twinkling lights shone from every tree branch and craft stand. Happy laughter and chatter filled the air. She smiled. She hadn't attended the festival in years. Since then, things had grown and gotten better. As she skimmed her gaze around the area, she realized improvements could be made. Her conversation with Dax about the festival floated through her thoughts. He'd encouraged her to open an agency in town. Did she want to?

Now, as she looked around, she realized his idea had merit. Plenty of the businesses were successful, but with the right help, they could do so much better. A vision, so sharp and clear, flashed through her thoughts. She swiveled her gaze and spotted an empty building. A squat, red brick, two-story shop with a crisp white door along one side and a large, glass window next to it. The old antique store had closed years ago. Now, though, she could envision a metal sign tacked above the window with the letters *EEJ* lasered across its surface.

She smiled. Yeah, maybe. Down the road, after she'd gotten the horror of working at the firm out of her thoughts. She liked the idea. What would Dax think? Deep inside, she knew he'd be happy. They might not have ended on the best of notes, but she knew he wanted her happiness—almost as much as she did.

Her heart ached. How had she let her jealousy and insecurities ruin what they had? She spent so much time worrying about him moving on, she never took the time to appreciate their relationship—to appreciate *him*. If she could change one thing, she would have taken the time to recognize his friendship. Despite her fears, she knew Dax wouldn't have hurt her.

She dug fingers into her jacket's pockets, and dropping back her head, she closed her eyes. The cool night breeze blew across her skin. She inhaled, noticing the sharp scent of pine mingling with the smells of hot chocolate and candy canes. In just a couple of days, she'd spend Thanksgiving with her family. She'd have to face Dax then. Maybe they could repair the damage.

Sighing, she popped open her eyes and blinked. Dax stood directly in front of her, looking damn fine dressed in a warm, brown leather coat and a woolly grey scarf. His cheeks were ruddy, his blue eyes guarded, and his lips held a straight line. The wind kicked up, disheveling his blond hair.

For a moment, she thought she'd conjured him in thin air, but nope…a warm cloud of breath eased from him. Her heart leaped. "Dax." Her word came out husky and soft.

He lifted a hand, before slowly letting it fall to his side. He curled his hands into fists, and stepping closer, he studied her. "You're back?"

The sounds of people's laughter faded, and the merry holiday tunes blasting from speakers disappeared. For Ellen, everything fell away, leaving just her and him, alone, surrounded by a sea of activity. She shrugged. "I am." She licked her lips. "I miss—" Should she tell him? Would her words frighten him?

He cocked a brow. "Missed what?"

She stepped closer, enough that their toes touched. Tilting back her head, she stared into his deep-blue eyes and let out a shaky breath. "You." She itched to reach up and touch his cheek—to feel the sharp rasp of stubble across her fingers. Instead, she clenched together her fingers. "I made some terrible decisions."

He closed his eyes and slowly shook his head. The muscle in his cheek worked.

So, he hadn't missed her. Tears pricked her eyes, and her throat closed. Of course, why would he? She had said horrible things to him—about him. Why would she expect him to forgive her? Now, he would be forced to tell her he'd moved on. She swallowed back tears. As long as they remained friends, she could handle the news.

He snapped open his eyes.

His piercing blue gaze held hers. No matter how much she wanted to flee and avoid the pain of his words, she wouldn't. He had a right to hear her apology for how she had treated him. She took a deep breath. "I know you don't want marriage, or anything like that, and I know I let my fears and insecurities control me." She dropped her gaze and stared at the snow-covered ground. "I'm sorry."

Despite all the commotion surrounding them, the only thing Ellen could hear was her heart pounding. Tears rimmed her eyes. Sniffing, she wiped gloved fingers across her nose, knowing with a certainty her heart was surely broken. Slowly, she drew up her gaze and gave him a watery smile. "Listen, I know you're busy. I'll let you go." Pivoting, she stepped aside, waiting for a young family to pass.

"Ellen?"

The way he said her name was like a cry to the angels, begging for mercy. A lump, hard and heavy, settled in her throat. She took a deep breath, and swallowing, she turned and forced a smile. "Yes?"

"A few weeks ago, when you told Ben about us—" He licked his lips and clenched his hands.

A look of uncertainty filled his gaze. She wondered how this man who had only ever exhibited confidence and assurance could suddenly look fearful. "What about it?"

He tilted back his head and stared upward into the night sky. His throat worked, and one fisted hand knocked against his thigh for a moment before he met her gaze. "Did you mean what you said?"

She searched her mind, trying to recall what he meant. "I don't know what—"

"About just loving me as a friend."

His voice caught. She had to blink back the tears. A lump formed in her throat. How much pain could she endure at his hands? "Yes, of course. It's just…" Dropping her gaze, she chewed on the corner of her lip for a moment before sighing. "You've been my best friend for more than two decades. I don't want to lose you."

"You won't." Stepping closer, he lifted her chin and stared into her eyes. "Not too long ago, you asked me if I had done anything I regretted."

Ellen searched his face, praying he didn't say the words she feared—that he regretted sleeping with her. The truth would be too painful. Every muscle in her back, from her neck straight down to her toes, tensed. She put up a hand. "It's okay. I understand."

He clasped her hand and pulled her closer. A soft smile flicked on his lips. "I regret saying good-bye." He wrapped his arms around her waist and stared down. "I regret not telling you about my father. I regret those horrible words I said. But, more importantly, I regret leaving you six years ago."

Ellen pulled back and stared. A breath she hadn't realized she held, rushed from her. "But—"

He drew her against him and brushed his lips across hers. "Ellen, I've loved you for the longest time." Clutching her coat's lapels, he held her imprisoned against his body. "You remember when you were fourteen and I was sixteen, and we wrestled? I think I loved you then. I just—" He gritted his teeth and closed his eyes.

He couldn't possibly love her, could he? Her heart pounded. "You what?"

"When you lived in Albany…" Licking his lips, he stared down, capturing her gaze. "I didn't go to see your brother. I came to see you."

"But Ben—"

He fanned a hand. "He was my excuse. You were my reason."

She jerked back and fisted her hands. "But you left me after—"

"Ellen, I was young, scared, and confused. You've always had my heart. I couldn't leave you, but—" He gritted his teeth. The muscles flexed in his neck. He closed his eyes. "I'm not your father or Ben."

"Oh, Dax." Ellen could see the pain and anguish on his face, as if he'd lived beneath a torturous shadow, trying to fill shoes he was never meant to wear. Reaching up, she pressed a hand to his cheek. "Why would you think I'd want you to be like either man?"

"I can't bring you a history of commitment, but I sure as hell want to try." He pulled her against him and brushed his mouth against hers. "I spent all those years running away from the only woman I ever truly loved. I'm not perfect, but if you let me, I promise I'll work every day to be the man you deserve." He threaded his fingers through hers. "I need you, Ellen. I've always needed you."

Ellen stared into his eyes. A lightness filled her, and little bubbles burst in her stomach. *These words*...how long had she waited to hear them? *Too long.* Without him, her life was just an empty shell of existence and probably always had been. She licked her lips, and finally, did the one thing she'd wanted to do for such a long time. Leaning up on tippy-toes, she brushed her lips across his and felt tingles straight down to her toes. "Me, too."

Epilogue

Ellen stared up into the eyes of the man she just married. Her heart swelled. From across the way, her mother's soft sobs mingled with Dax's mother's and the single women in town. She couldn't fault the women for their dismay. After all, Aberdeen's very own Hometown Heartthrob was off the market. She figured, had the shoes been reversed, she'd probably cry, too.

After he said his vows, Dax slipped the ring on her finger.

She stared down at his strong, tan fingers holding her hand. The warmth of his touch mingled with the cool, gold band circling her finger. She glanced upward to see the joy and love lighting Dax's gaze. Her breath caught, and tears pricked her eyes.

Dax wiped away the moisture before brushing his lips across hers.

Oh, the joy that filled her. She'd come home feeling like a failure only to accomplish the one thing she never realized she desired—she captured the heart of Mr. January.

A word about the author...

Jules Hahn has been passionate about writing since grade school. She wrote and illustrated her very first book in second grade called Goober the Squash. Always one to live in her head, Jules loves to create stories of love and romance, usually involving herself. WELCOME TO ABERDEEN was the first in the series to be published. Jules lives in Phoenix, Arizona, and is married to her high school sweetheart. Together, they have two wonderful boys. You can follow Jules's series on her webpage http://juleshahn.com

Other Titles by this Author
Hometown Player
Welcome to Aberdeen

Thank you for purchasing
this publication of The Wild Rose Press, Inc.

For questions or more information
contact us at
info@thewildrosepress.com.

The Wild Rose Press, Inc.
www.thewildrosepress.com

www.ingramcontent.com/pod-product-compliance
Lightning Source LLC
Chambersburg PA
CBHW070805030726
47504CB00003B/710